Praise for Eliz

"A star back in Britain, Eliz[...]
the attention she deserves her[...]

"An author who makes historical fiction come gloriously alive."
—*Times of London*

"I rank Elizabeth Chadwick with such historical novelist stars as Dorothy Dunnett and Anya Seton."
—Sharon Kay Penman, *New York Times* bestselling author of *Devil's Brood*

"The best writer of medieval fiction currently around."
—Richard Lee, founder and publisher, Historical Novel Society

"The reader is well aware on every page that this is life as it was lived eight hundred years ago, yet the characters are as fresh and natural as if they were living in present time."
—*Historical Novels Review*

"One of Elizabeth Chadwick's strengths is her stunning grasp of historical detail...her characters are beguiling, the story intriguing and very enjoyable."
—Barbara Erskine

"Elizabeth Chadwick is to medieval England what Philippa Gregory is to the Tudors and the Stuarts, and Bernard Cornwell is to the Dark Ages."
—*Books Monthly*, UK

LADY *of the* ENGLISH

LADY *of the* ENGLISH

ELIZABETH CHADWICK

sourcebooks
landmark

Published by Sourcebooks Landmark, an imprint of Sourcebooks, Inc.
P.O. Box 4410, Naperville, Illinois 60567-4410
(630) 961-3900
Fax: (630) 961-2168
www.sourcebooks.com

Originally published in the UK in June 2011 by Sphere.

Library of Congress Cataloging-in-Publication Data

Chadwick, Elizabeth.
  Lady of the English / Elizabeth Chadwick.
     p. cm.
  "Originally published in the UK in June 2011 by Sphere" — T.p. verso.
  1. Empresses—Fiction. 2. Queens—Fiction. 3. Widows—Fiction. 4. Fathers and daughters—Fiction. 5. Kings and rulers—Succession—Fiction. 6. England—History—12th century—Fiction. I. Title.
  PR6053.H245L33 2011
  823'.914—dc22
                                    2011021352

Printed and bound in the United States of America.
VP 10 9 8 7 6 5 4 3 2 1

Also by Elizabeth Chadwick

The Greatest Knight

The Scarlet Lion

For the King's Favor

To Defy a King

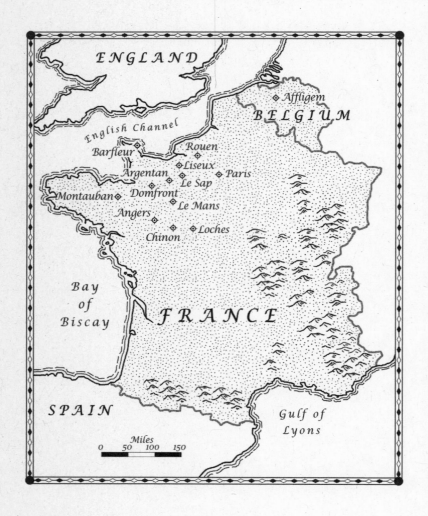

ENGLAND

English Channel

BELGIUM

◇ Affligem

◇ Rouen

Barfleur ◇
Argentan ◇ ◇ Liseux ◇ Paris
◇ Le Sap
Montauban ◇ ◇ Domfront
Angers ◇ ◇ Le Mans
Chinon ◇ ◇ Loches

FRANCE

Bay
of
Biscay

SPAIN

Gulf of
Lyons

Miles
0 50 100 150

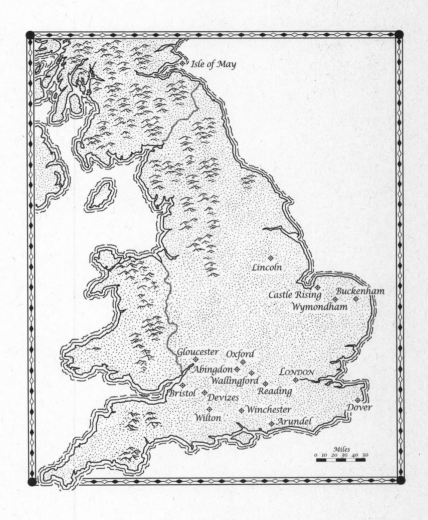

Isle of May

Lincoln

Castle Rising   Buckenham
Wymondham

Gloucester   Oxford
Abingdon
Wallingford   LONDON
Bristol   Devizes   Reading
Winchester   Dover
Wilton   Arundel

Miles
0 10 20 30 40 50

THE ENGLISH SUCCESSION

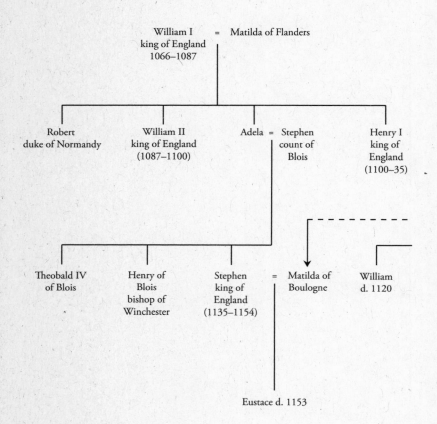

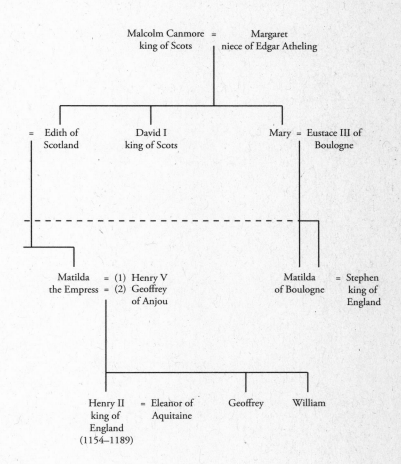

Malcolm Canmore = Margaret
king of Scots   niece of Edgar Atheling

= Edith of   David I   Mary = Eustace III of
  Scotland   king of Scots   Boulogne

Matilda   = (1) Henry V   Matilda   = Stephen
the Empress = (2) Geoffrey   of Boulogne   king of
                  of Anjou   England

Henry II   = Eleanor of   Geoffrey   William
king of   Aquitaine
England
(1154–1189)

One

*H*OLDING HER DEAD HUSBAND'S IMPERIAL CROWN, MATILDA felt the cold pressure of gemstones and hard gold against her fingertips and palms. The light from the window arch embossed the metal's soft patina with sharper glints of radiance. Heinrich had worn this crown on feast days and official occasions. She had an equivalent one of gold and sapphires, fashioned for her by the greatest goldsmiths in the empire, and in the course of their eleven-year marriage had learned to bear its weight with grace and dignity.

Her people called her "Matilda the Good." They had not always been her people, but it was how she thought of them now, and they of her, and for a moment grief squeezed her heart so tightly she caught her breath. Heinrich would never wear this diadem again, nor smile at her with that small curl of amused gravity. They would never sit together in the bedchamber companionably discussing state matters, nor share the same golden cup at banquets. No offspring born of his loins and her womb would occupy the imperial throne. The cradle was empty because God had not seen fit to let their son live beyond the hour of his birth, and now Heinrich himself lay entombed in the great red stone cathedral here and another man ruled over what had been theirs.

Matilda the Good. Matilda the Empress. Matilda the childless widow. The words crept through her mind like footfalls in a crypt. If she stayed, she would have to add Matilda the nun to her list of titles, and she had no intention of retiring to the cloister. She was twenty-three, young, vigorous, and strong, and a new life awaited in Normandy and England, the latter her birthplace, but now barely remembered.

Turning, she gave the crown to her chamberlain so that he could dismantle and pack it safely in its leather travelling case.

"Domina, if it please you, your escort is ready."

Matilda faced the white-haired knight bowing in the doorway. Like her, he was dressed for travel in a thick riding cloak and stout calf-hide boots. His left hand rested lightly on his sword pommel.

"Thank you, Drogo."

As the servants removed the last of her baggage, she paced slowly around the chamber, studying the pale walls stripped of their bright hangings, the bare benches around the hearth, the dying fire. Soon there would be nothing left to say she had ever dwelt here.

"It is difficult to bid farewell, domina," Drogo said with sympathy.

Still looking around, as if her gaze were caught in a web of invisible threads, Matilda paused at the door. She remembered being eight years old, standing in the great hall at Liège, trembling with exhaustion at the end of her long journey from England. She could still recall the fear she had felt and all the pressure of being sent out of the nest to a foreign land and a betrothal with a grown man. The match had been arranged to suit her father's political purpose and she had known she must do her duty and not incur his displeasure by failing him, because he was a great king and she was a princess of high and royal blood. It could have been a disaster but, instead, it had been the making of her: the frightened, studious little girl had been moulded into a regal woman and an able consort for the Emperor of Germany.

"I have been happy here." She touched the carved doorpost in a gesture that clung and bade farewell at the same time.

"Your lord father will be pleased to have you home."

Matilda dropped her hand and straightened her cloak. "I do not need to be cajoled like a skittish horse."

"That was not my intent, domina."

"Then what was your intent?" Drogo had been with her since that first long journey to her betrothal. He was her bodyguard and leader of her household knights: strong, dour, dependable. As a child she had thought him ancient because even then his hair had been white, although he had only been thirty years old. He looked little different now, except for a few new lines and the deepening of older ones.

"To say that an open door awaits you."

"And that I should close this one?"

"No, domina, it has made you who and what you are—and that is also why your father has summoned you."

"It is but one of his reasons and driven by necessity," she replied shortly. "I may not have seen my father in many years, but I know him well." Taking a resolute breath, she left the room, carrying herself as if she were bearing the weight and grace of her crown.

Her entourage awaited her in a semi-circle of servants, retainers, and officials. Most of her baggage had gone ahead by cart three days earlier and only the nucleus of her household remained with a handful of packhorses to carry light provisions and the items she wanted to keep with her. Her chaplain, Burchard, kept looking furtively at the gelding laden with the items from the portable chapel. Matilda followed his glance, her gaze resting but not lingering upon a certain leather casket in one of the panniers, before she turned to her mare. The salmon-red saddle was a sumptuous affair, padded and brocaded almost like her hearth chair, with a support for her spine and a rest for her feet. While not the swiftest way to travel, it was dignified and magnificent. The towns and villages through which they passed would expect nothing less than splendour from the emperor's recent widow.

Matilda mounted up, settling herself and positioning her feet precisely on the platform. Seated sideways, looking both forward and back. It was appropriate. She raised her slender right hand to Drogo, who acknowledged the signal with a salute and trotted to the head of the troop. The banners unfurled, gold and red and black, the heralds cantered out, and the cavalcade began to unwind along the road like jewels knotted on a string. The dowager empress of Germany was leaving the home of her heart to return to the home of her birth and a new set of duties.

❖❖❖

Adeliza gripped the bedclothes and stifled a gasp as Henry withdrew from her body. He was approaching sixty years old, but still hale and vigorous. The force of his thrusts had made her sore inside, and his stolid weight was crushing her into the bed. Mercifully, he gathered himself and flopped over on to his back, panting hard. Biting her lip, Adeliza placed her hand on her flat belly and strove to regain her own breath. Henry was well endowed, and the act of procreation was often awkward and uncomfortable between them but, God willing, this time she would conceive.

She had been Henry's wife and the consecrated queen of England for over four years, and still each month her flux came at the appointed time in a red cramp of disappointment and failure. Thus far no amount of prayers, gifts, penances, or potions had rectified her barrenness. Henry had a score of bastards by various mistresses, so he was potent with other women, but only had one living legitimate child, his daughter Matilda from his first marriage. His son from that union had died shortly before Henry took Adeliza to wife. He seldom spoke of the tragedy that had robbed him of his heir, drowned in a shipwreck on a bitter November night, but it had driven his policies ever since. Her part in those policies was to bear him a new male heir, but thus far she had failed in her duty.

Henry kissed her shoulder and squeezed her breast before parting the curtains and leaving the bed. She watched him scratch the curly silver hair on his broad chest. His stocky frame carried a slight paunch, but he was muscular and in proportion. Stretching, he made a sound like a contented lion. Their union, she thought, even if it brought forth no other fruit, had released his tension. His sexual appetite was prodigious and in between bedding her, he regularly sported with other women.

He poured himself wine from the flagon set on a painted coffer under the window, and on his return picked up his cloak and swept it around his shoulders. Silver and blue squirrel furs gleamed in the candlelight. Adeliza sat up and folded her hands around her knees. The soreness between her thighs diminished to a dull throb. He offered her a drink from the cup and she took a dainty sip. "Matilda will be arriving soon," he said. "Brian FitzCount is due to meet her tomorrow on the road."

Adeliza could tell from his expression that his thoughts had turned inwards to the weaving of his political web. "All is ready for her," she replied. "The servants are keeping a good fire in her chamber to make it warm and chase out the damp. I have instructed them to burn incense and put out bowls of rose petals to sweeten the air. They hung new tapestries on the walls this afternoon and the furniture is all assembled. I..."

Henry raised his hand to silence her. "I am sure her chamber will be perfect."

Adeliza flushed and looked down.

"I think you will be good company for each other, being of a similar age." Henry gave her a slightly condescending smile.

"It will be strange to call her daughter when she is older than me."

"I am sure you will both quickly grow accustomed." He was still smiling, but Adeliza could tell his attention lay elsewhere. Henry's conversations were never just idle gossip; there was always a purpose. "I want you to cultivate her. She has been a long time absent, and I need to consider her future. Some matters are rightly for the council chamber and for father and daughter, but some things are better discussed between women." He stroked the side of her face with a powerful, stubby hand. "You have a skill with people; they open themselves to you."

Adeliza frowned. "You want me to draw confidences from her?"

"I would know her mind. I have seen her once in fifteen years, and then but for a few days. Her letters give me news, but they are couched in the language of scribes and I would know her true character." A hard glint entered his eyes. "I would know if she is strong enough."

"Strong enough for what?"

"For what I have in mind for her." He turned away to pace the chamber, picking up a scroll and setting it down, fiddling with a jewelled staff, turning it end over end. Watching him, Adeliza thought that he was like one of the jugglers he employed to entertain his courtiers, keeping the balls all rotating in the air, knowing where each one was and what to do with it, adapting swiftly as a new one was tossed into the rotation, discarding another when he had no more need of it. Lacking a legitimate son, he had to look to the succession. He was grooming his nephew Stephen as a possible successor, but now Matilda was a widow and free to come home and make a new marriage, the game had changed again. To think of making Matilda heir to England and Normandy was beyond audacious. The notion of a woman ruler would make even the most liberal of his barons choke on his wine. Adeliza's brows drew together. Her husband often gambled, but he was never rash and he was accustomed to imposing his iron will on everyone.

"She is young and healthy," he said. "And she has borne a child, even if it did not survive the birthing. She will make another marriage and bear more sons if God is merciful."

A pang went through Adeliza. If God was merciful, she herself would bear sons, but she understood his need to pursue other avenues. "Do you have anyone in mind?"

"Several candidates," he replied in an offhand tone. "You need not trouble yourself on that score."

"But when the time comes, you expect me to smooth the path."

Henry climbed back into bed and pulled the covers over them both. He kissed her again, with a hard mouth. "It is a queen's duty, prerogative, and privilege to be a peacemaker," he replied. "I do not think for one moment you will fail me."

"I won't," Adeliza said. As he pinched out the bedside candle, she set her hand between her thighs and felt the slipperiness of his seed, and prayed that this time she would succeed.

Two

The Road to Rouen, Normandy, Autumn 1125

A WET UNPLEASANT MORNING HAD CLEARED TO THE EAST AS Matilda's entourage wound its way through the forests of the Beauvais towards the great city of Rouen, heart of Normandy on the banks of the Seine. Now, with barely an hour till sunset, the blue sky was welcome, but the wind had picked up and was blustering hard. Tonight they were making camp by the roadside. They should have been met at noon by a party from Rouen led by one of her father's barons, Brian FitzCount, but thus far there was no sign of it, and Matilda was growing annoyed and impatient. Her mare was lame on her offside hind leg and she was having to ride pillion on Drogo's crupper as if she were a woman of his household, rather than his liege lady. Her knights and attendants were giving her a wide berth. Drogo's placatory remark that by tomorrow night they would be in Rouen with every comfort had not improved her mood; she was accustomed to precision and smooth order.

A gust of wind struck her side-on and she had to grab Drogo's belt. "I refuse to ride into Rouen like this," she hissed.

"Domina, if it comes to the worst, I will give you this horse and saddle up my remount, but there is no point doing so for what is left of the daylight." He spoke with the pragmatic calm of one long accustomed to her demands.

She eyed the melted gold of the westering sun and knew he was right; there was no point, but it made her angry. Why couldn't people keep their promises?

Suddenly the knight drew rein and the jolt threw her against his spine. "My apologies, domina," he said. "It appears our escort is here."

Peering round him, Matilda saw a troop approaching at a steady trot. "Help me down," she commanded.

Drogo dismounted and swiftly assisted her to do the same. She shook out her gown, adjusted her cloak, and stood erect. The wind snatched at her veil, but fortunately it was well pinned to her undercap. She had to lock her legs to keep her balance.

The oncoming troop splashed to a muddy halt. Their leader flung down from the saddle of a handsome black stallion and, removing his hat, dropped to one knee before her.

"You are late," she said icily. "We have been looking for you since noon."

"Domina, I am deeply sorry. We would have been here sooner, but one of the cartwheels broke, and there was a fallen tree across our path. The wind has made everything more difficult and slowed our pace."

She was cold, tired, and in no mood for excuses. "Get up," she said with a brusque gesture.

He rose to his feet and his legs were so long that they seemed to unfold forever. They were encased in fine leather riding boots laced with red cords. His black hair swirled about his face and his eyes were a deep, peat-pool brown. His mouth had a natural upward curve that made him look as if he were smiling, even though his demeanour was serious. "Domina, I am Brian, son of Count Alan of Brittany, and lord of Wallingford Castle. I do not expect you to remember me. The last time we were in each other's presence, you were witnessing one of your father's charters in Nottingham before you went to Germany and I had not long entered your father's household as a squire."

"That was a long time ago," she said, still annoyed.

"Indeed, domina." He gestured over his shoulder at the men of his troop, who had also dismounted and were kneeling. "We have brought a fine pavilion and provisions. It will not take us long to make camp."

"It will take you even less time if you tell those men of yours to get up off their knees and start work," she said tartly. "My own will help if you have need."

His expression impassive, he bowed and went to give brisk orders. A host of workmen and serjeants began unpacking sections of a large, circular, red and blue tent from a two-wheeled cart. The outer canvas was stamped with golden lions. There was a pale silk inner lining and rich woollen hangings set on curved rods for the interior. The wind billowed the canvas like the sail of a ship in a storm. Matilda watched the men struggle with their burden and mentally shook her head. Had she not been so tired and cross, she would have burst out laughing.

One of Brian's company, a wide-shouldered young man, was examining her mare, running his hand down her lame foreleg and soothing her with soft talk. When he saw Matilda watching, he bowed and said, "She needs rest and a warm bran poultice on that knee, domina. There is nothing wrong with her beyond the strain of the road." He gently scratched the mare's neck.

He was not a groom, for his cloak was fur-lined and his tunic embroidered. His open features were raised above the average by striking hazel-gold eyes. "Were you at Nottingham with my lord FitzCount too?" she asked.

He shook his head. "No, domina, but my father would have been. He is William D'Albini, lord of Buckenham in Norfolk and one of your father's stewards."

"I do not recall him," she said, "but I know of your family."
Obviously he was a spare young blood at court, sent out with
FitzCount on escort duty. "Your own name?"

"Domina, it is William, the same as my father."

"Well then, William D'Albini, you seem to know about
horses."

He gave her a wide smile, exposing fine, strong teeth. "Well
enough, domina." He rubbed the mare's soft muzzle with a
large, gentle hand.

"I hope my lord FitzCount has a spare mount."

"I am sure he does, domina."

Matilda was not so certain. Sounds of a heated exchange
flashed across to them. Someone had mislaid the tent pegs and
everyone was blaming everyone else. "This would not have
happened at my husband's court," she said with displeasure.

D'Albini gave an equable shrug. "There are difficult days
when whatever you do, you suffer mishaps; today is one such."
Clucking his tongue to the mare, he led her away to tether her
with the other horses.

The tent pegs turned up in a different pannier to the expected
one and, following more bad-tempered oaths, were driven into
the ground and the canvas secured. Brian FitzCount directed
operations, now and then scraping his hands through his hair,
looking increasingly embarrassed and exasperated.

Gradually, however, order emerged out of chaos and Matilda
was able to enter the tent and at least be out of the wind, even
if the canvas sides flapped like wings striving to lift the structure
into the air. Her women set about making her bed, layering
several mattresses on to the strung frame and topping them with
clean sheets and soft blankets. A manservant hooked a partition
across the middle of the tent and someone else fetched a chair
with a quilted cushion. A bench and a small table arrived.
Matilda remained standing, arms folded.

Brian FitzCount entered the tent followed by servants bearing a flagon and cups, loaves of bread, and assorted cheeses and smoked meats. "The men are making a windbreak," he said. "At least it isn't raining."

"No," she agreed, thinking that rain would have been the final seasoning. She sat down on the chair. The servants spread the table with an embroidered cloth and brought food and drink. Before she could change her mind, she indicated that Brian should join her. News of the court in advance of her arrival there would be useful.

He hesitated, went to the tent entrance to bellow more instructions, then dropped the flap and returned to serve her himself. She studied his long fingers as he poured wine into silver cups. An emerald ring glinted, and another of plaited gold. His hands were clean, the nails clipped short, but they were ink-stained, as if he were a common clerk. She tried to remember him from her childhood, but found no trace. It had been too long ago and he would have been just another youth at court.

"My father is well?" She took her first sip and felt it warm its way to her stomach.

"Indeed, domina, and eager to see you, even if the circumstances are sad."

"I have seen him but once since I was a little girl," she said shortly. "I know why he is pleased to welcome me home."

Silence fell between them. She decided that the windbreak must have been successfully erected, because there were fewer flurries at the sides of the tent. She broke bread and ate it with a slice of smoked venison, gesturing him to eat too.

"Would you rather have stayed in Germany?"

The directness of his question took her by surprise; she had expected him to continue being the deferential courtier. "It was my duty to return at my father's bidding. What would have been left for me there without my husband? His successor has his own affiliations. I would either have had to marry into them, which would not suit my father's policies, or retire to a nunnery and live out my days in service to God."

"That is a worthy thing to do."

"But I am not yet ready to renounce the world." She gave him a shrewd look. "Has my father spoken to you of his plans for my future?"

He returned her stare. "He only speaks in general terms and even if I did know his heart in the matter, it would not be for me to say. You must be aware of some of his intent yourself, domina. If he did not have plans for you, then you would still be in Speyer."

"Oh, I know he has plans, but not what they are." She leaned back in the chair, beginning to relax a little. On the other side of the partition her women talked quietly among themselves.

Brian leaned back too, mirroring her posture. "When you left England, you were a serious little girl, full of learning and duty. I remember you well from that time, even if you do not remember me. You did not want to go, but you stiffened your spine and did as you were bid, because it was your duty. That part has not changed, but now you are an empress and a grown woman, accustomed to holding the reins of power and command."

She gave an acerbic smile. "It is true I do not suffer fools gladly, my lord."

"You are your father's daughter," he replied with a straight face, but there was a spark in his eyes.

Matilda almost laughed and hastily covered her mouth. It was the wine, she thought, and the tiredness. Suddenly her throat tightened with grief, because this blend of politics and near-flirting was too close to what she had had with Heinrich, and it made her ache with loss. She controlled her voice. "I am indeed my father's daughter. If you cannot tell me what my future holds, then at least tell me about the court so that I may be prepared."

He offered her more wine and she shook her head. He poured himself a half-cup. "If you were accustomed to your husband's court, then you will be accustomed to this one. They have the same denizens."

"But who is friend and who is foe? Whom can I trust, and who is competent?"

"That is for you to make your own judgement, domina, and for your father to advise you."

"So again, you will tell me nothing."

He let out a deep breath. "Your father is surrounded by men who serve him well. Your brother, the Earl of Gloucester, will be pleased indeed at your return. Your cousins Stephen and Theobald will be there also."

His expression was bland. She had a vague recollection of her Blois relations. Older youths, more concerned with male pursuits and paying her small heed except when they had to serve her and her mother at table as squires in training. "Stephen is recently married, isn't he?" There had been a letter but she had been too caught up in worry for her sick husband to pay it much heed.

"Indeed. To Maheut, heiress of Boulogne. Your father deemed it sound policy. It keeps his northern borders strong."

Matilda was thoughtful. Maheut of Boulogne was her cousin on her mother's side, even as Stephen had that kinship on her father's—and that made the family ties close indeed. What did her father intend with all this spinning of threads? He was a master loomsman and no one else could weave the cloth of politics in quite the same way. "What is Stephen like these days?"

Brian shrugged. "More settled since his marriage. He's a fine horseman and soldier. He makes friends easily and your father is fond of him."

His assessment made Matilda feel uneasy. Stephen had had the time to cultivate her father and gain his attention that she had not. "Are you?"

He looked wary. "He is good company when we ride to the hunt, and we understand each other well enough. He knows when to leave me to my books and my thoughts, and I know when to leave him to the company of other men. His wife keeps him to the mark these days. She gives him backbone, and sound advice." Brian raised his cup and drank. "Your father has imprisoned Waleran de Meulan for rebelling against him, and he is still being threatened by William le Clito."

"That is old news," she said with an impatient wave of her hand. "William le Clito will never be king because he has no ability and Waleran de Meulan was a fool to support him."

"Even so, it will still inform your father's policies and determine what he does next. Perhaps it is the reason he has raised Stephen on high—as a counterbalance."

A gust of wind flurried the side of the tent and Matilda felt invigorated by its force. She wanted everything to blow away and leave the world swept clean. Her father had kept his throne against great opposition. He had seized England and Normandy from his rash older brother Robert and cast him in prison, where he lingered even now; but Robert had left a son William le Clito, another male for Matilda to call cousin, and one who was claiming his right to rule. Powerful young hotheads like Waleran de Meulan supported his cause, and although her father had stamped down the rising, like a soldier putting out a dangerous small fire, the smoke still lingered. And where there was one fire, others would rise. Waleran had a twin brother, and their family interests straddled both England and Normandy. Weaving, she thought. It was all a matter of twisting the threads, and keeping an eye cocked for unravelling strands while dealing with others who were weaving designs of their own.

She eyed Brian thoughtfully. Her father clearly found him useful and had raised him on high. He held over a hundred knight's fees by dint of his arranged marriage to Maude of Wallingford. But what to make of him now, on this first meeting? His arrival had been less than impressive, but William D'Albini seemed to think she should give him the benefit of the doubt. She suspected he was adept at hiding his thoughts, and that they ran deep. No shallow blunderer, this one, for all the irregularity of their initial meeting.

As Brian put his cup down, her eyes were drawn again to the ink staining his elegant fingers. "Are you your own scribe, my lord?"

"Sometimes," he said with a diffident smile. "I find it easier to think with a quill in my hand, and to assemble notes, even though scribes might make the final draft. I am indebted to your father for my education."

"He obviously values you."

"As I honour and serve him." Brian cleared his throat and stood up. "I beg your leave, domina. I should go and make sure all is ready for tomorrow."

"You may go," she said formally. "I hope that one of your concerns is finding me a decent horse."

"Indeed, it is my first and most urgent business, domina." He bowed and departed the tent.

The moment he was gone, her women, Emma and Uli, bustled through the partition. She let them remove her dress and comb out her hair, then dismissed them with a flick of her fingers because she wanted to be alone to think. Fetching the coverlet from her bed, she folded it around her body, and sat cocooned in the chair, her knees drawn up and her fist pressed against her lips.

Outside, Brian stood in the wind and exhaled his tension. He had not expected the king's daughter to be so mettlesome and perceptive. She was as keen as a knife and just now he felt as if he had the cuts to prove it. When he arrived, she had looked at him as if he were an incompetent fool, and he was still smarting. He hoped he had salvaged something from the situation, but knew his reputation would be ruined if he did not have a horse for her by morning. There was nothing for it; he would have to put her up on his courser and use his squire's mount. The lad could go double with one of the serjeants.

The white-haired knight who headed her escort stepped out of his own small tent, where he had obviously been keeping a lookout for Brian. "My mistress is always vexed when things do not run as smoothly as she wishes." He spoke not to excuse Matilda, but rather to reproach Brian.

"I have apologised and done my best to mend matters," Brian replied. "Be assured the empress will enter Rouen in full dignity."

The knight gave him a strong look. "Sire, you will find that my mistress does not know how to compromise."

Brian bit his tongue on a sharp retort. "The empress will find that a fitting welcome has been prepared."

"I have served my lady since she was a child," the knight said. "I have watched her become a woman, and wield power as consort to an emperor. She has greatness within her." He glanced at the tent from which Brian had just emerged and lowered his voice. "But she is fragile too, and in need of tender care. Who will give her that, when her pride is both her shield and her sword? Who will look beyond all that and see the frightened child and the vulnerable woman?"

Something stirred within Brian that he was at a loss to identify: neither pity nor compassion, but a glimmer of something more complex and disturbing. Her eyes were the grey of lavender flowers but clear as glass and they had met his with steady challenge, and even contempt. He did not see what this ageing knight saw, but he did not know her. What he had seen was truth and integrity, and it was as if she had taken a sharpened quill and written those words indelibly across his skin.

Three

TOWER OF ROUEN, AUTUMN 1125

THE GALE HAD BLOWN ITSELF OUT, AND A CALM SUN SPARKLED on harnesses and trappings. Matilda's red silk gown gleamed in its light, as did the sleek ermines lining her cloak and the jewelled coronet securing her white silk veil. The citizens of Rouen had turned out in force to watch her arrive and she had her knights distribute alms and largesse in her name while the heralds rode ahead with their fanfares and proclamations that here was the dowager empress of Germany, the king's daughter. Her heart filled with triumph and pride as she rode through the midst of the cheering crowds, and although she carried her head high with proper dignity and pride, she also smiled as much as was appropriate.

Brian FitzCount's horse, Sable, was a spirited beast, but well schooled and mannerly. FitzCount himself rode a sturdy chestnut cob that was slightly too small for his long legs, but he was obviously pretending not to notice. Following the previous day's mishaps, there had been no further difficulties and all had run to plan. She was not yet ready to give him the benefit of the doubt, but was prepared to wait and see.

As they entered the precincts of the ducal palace on the banks of the Seine, her horse flicked its ears and pranced, responding to her tension. It was almost sixteen years since she had last stayed here shortly before her betrothal. Her memories were hazy ghosts of the past flitting among the solid stones and cobbles of now.

A groom hastened to take her bridle. Drogo dismounted to help her down, but Brian FitzCount was quicker to offer assistance. As he took her hands, she noticed that the ink stains were still there, with some fresh ones to boot; he had obviously been at work in his tent after he left hers, and she approved of him for that. It was almost comforting to think of him busy and watchful in the dark hours of the night while others slept.

A tall, broad man came striding towards her with arms outstretched. She stared at him for a moment in perplexity, and then the ground shifted under her feet and the past melded with the present as she recognised her older half-brother. "Robert?" she whispered, and then again in a full voice, "Robert!"

His dark blue eyes lit with welcome as he grasped her hands and kissed her on either cheek with hearty warmth that yet managed to preserve public decorum. "Sister! Have you journeyed well?"

"Most of the way. My mare went lame yesterday."

"I wondered when I saw you up on Brian's Sable." He glanced at Brian. "I trust he looked after you?"

"To the best of his ability," she said with a straight face.

Brian raised his brows and Robert chuckled. "That sounds ominous."

"I was late to the meet," Brian said, "and last night's gale made pitching the tents awkward to say the least. I thought we were all going to be blown to Outremer!" Bowing, he excused himself to make sure that Matilda's baggage was borne to her chamber.

Robert sobered. "You can trust Brian with your life. I'll go surety for him. He's also one of the cleverest men in our father's entourage."

"I will take your word for it," she said, smiling. Robert was her senior by twelve years and had been a young adult when she went to Germany, but the rapport between them was immediate. It was like donning a favourite garment that had been put away in a chest for years, and feeling the comfort again.

"I hope that whatever Brian has done to offend you, you won't be too harsh on him."

"He has not offended me, and he has a very fine horse. Everything is unsettled, that is all."

Her half-brother gave her a compassionate look as they walked towards the tower entrance. "I am sorry you are here in bereavement. I wish these were happier circumstances."

"Indeed, thank you, and I do deeply grieve for my husband," she said, "but I must look to the future. That is why I am here, after all. My father has summoned me for purposes beyond mourning."

Robert said nothing, but his expression was eloquent.

The doors to the great hall stood wide to receive her and a path of red cloth strewn with flowers had been laid for her to walk upon. Courtiers stood to either side and, with a great rustling of fabric and soft clink of jewellery, knelt as she passed. Matilda paced with slow dignity, looking straight ahead, every inch the empress, her soul comforted by the propriety and the ceremony.

At the far end of the hall, two ornate thrones stood upon a dais. Her father sat upon the larger one, holding a jewelled rod in his right hand. His Queen, Adeliza, sat upon the other, robed in a gown of shimmering silver silk that glittered with pearls and amethysts. Matilda processed to the foot of the dais and knelt, bowing her head. Robert knelt too, but a step behind her.

She heard the swish of her father's robe as he rose, and then his soft footfall descending the steps. "My dearest daughter."

He bent, took her hands, and, having kissed her on either cheek, raised her to her feet. "Welcome home."

Matilda looked into his face. Six years had increased and deepened the lines on his face. His hair was greyer and more sparse and the pouches beneath his eyes were more prominent, but the eyes themselves were the same hard, shrewd grey. For the moment they held warmth, and his smile was genuine.

"Sire," she said, before turning to curtsey to and be embraced by her stepmother, Adeliza, a year younger than herself, delicate and slender as a young doe.

"I am so pleased that you are here, daughter," Adeliza said.

"My lady mother." The words were incongruous and sat uncomfortably on Matilda's tongue.

Adeliza's eyes sparkled with amusement and it was plain she was thinking the same thing. "I hope I can be like a mother to you," she said, "but more than that, I hope we shall become friends and companions."

Matilda's father processed her around the gathering on his arm, and she was introduced to the great men attending the court. Not all were present; some had duties elsewhere, or had remained in England, but enough were there to make a substantial gathering. Bigod, D'Albini, Aumale, de Tosney, Martel, the archbishop of Rouen, the abbot of Bec, her cousins of Blois, Theobald and Stephen, the latter now Count of Boulogne through his young bride, the Countess Maheut.

"I am sorry for your loss, cousin," Stephen said. "I offer my sincere condolences." He spoke with grave and apparent honesty, although Matilda was wary because things were not always what they seemed. Stephen's remark was a meaningless courtesy.

"I remember you as a little girl with long braids," he added with a smile.

A vague memory surfaced. "You used to pull them," she accused.

He looked wounded. "Only in play—I never hurt you. Your brother William used to pull them too."

There was a momentary silence at Stephen's mention of Matilda's brother—almost as if his words had conjured up the young man's sea-ravaged corpse from the waters of Barfleur harbour. "God rest his soul," Stephen added swiftly. "I am glad for the memory of our play and I think of him often."

Matilda suspected that Stephen would tug her braid now if the chance arose, and he would still call it play.

"Nephew, you are a great comfort to me," Henry said, his hard grey gaze missing nothing. "I know I can always count on your strong support and I value it for my daughter too."

"Assuredly, sire." Stephen bowed, first to Henry and then to Matilda.

The talk turned briefly to matters of Boulogne and Stephen's progress there as its overlord. Matilda observed the camaraderie between her father and Stephen. The latter's gestures were sure and expansive and he knew how to engage her father's interest and make him laugh. The other men in the vicinity all laughed with him too, apart from her brother Robert, who was reserved and watchful. Stephen's small, plump wife hung on his words as if they were jewels in a diadem, but she too was constantly glancing around, assessing the men and conversations in her vicinity even while her demeanour remained becomingly modest.

Matilda thought Stephen's performance polished, but how much was lip service, and how much sincerely meant, remained to be seen.

❖❖❖

Matilda gazed round her appointed chamber. The larger furnishings and baggage, which had set out ahead, had all been arranged: her own bed with its coverings and curtains, the rich hangings from her imperial chamber, the lamps, candlesticks, chests and coffers. The lighter baggage she had brought in person was here too, waiting to be unpacked. And when that was done, she could close the door and pretend if only for a moment that she was back in Germany. A sudden wave of homesickness brought a lump to her throat.

"I hope you have all you need," Adeliza said anxiously. "I want you to feel at home."

"You are very kind."

"I remember how I felt when I arrived from Louvain and everything was strange. It was such a comfort to have familiar things around me."

Adeliza's voice was like a silvery bell. Her daintiness and innocent air gave her a childlike quality, but Matilda suspected there were more facets to her father's wife than first met the eye.

"You are right, it is." Matilda said. "I am grateful for your consideration."

Adeliza opened her arms and clasped Matilda with spontaneous warmth. "It is going to be so good to have another woman of the family to talk to."

Startled, Matilda did not return the hug, but neither did she recoil. Adeliza smelled of flowers. Her own mother had never used perfume. She had been strict and austere, dedicated to learning and to worshipping God in stern and rigorous devotion. Matilda had no memory of softness or cuddles from her. Any affection had been cerebral and this compassionate embrace almost brought tears to her eyes.

The door opened on a gust of cold air and her father strode into the room. Waving aside the curtseys of the women, he stood with his hands on his hips, looking round as if taking an inventory, although she knew he must have seen most of the furnishings when Adeliza was organising the chamber.

"You are settling well, daughter?" His brusque tone demanded a positive reply. "You have everything you need?"

"Yes, sire, thank you."

Going to the portable altar she had brought with her personal baggage, he picked up the gold cross standing at its centre and examined the gems and filigree work with a professional eye. Then the candlestick, also of gold, and the image of the Virgin and Child painted with gold leaf and lapis lazuli.

"You made a good start tonight," he said. "I was pleased with you." His attention turned to a long leather casket on a table at the side of the altar. "Is this what I think it is?" he asked with an acquisitive gleam.

Matilda curtseyed to the image of the Virgin before picking up a key lying in a small golden dish on the altar, and used it to unlock the casket. "I was married on the feast of Saint James," she said. "Heinrich and I always kept that day with special reverence. This is mine to bestow as I see fit, and I wish to give it to the foundation at Reading for the souls of my brother and my mother." She opened the box to reveal a hollow life-sized left forearm and hand wrought in solid gold, set upon a gem-studded plinth. The arm was clad in a tight-fitting sleeve with a jewel-banded cuff and the index and middle fingers raised in a gesture of blessing.

Her father expelled his breath in a long sigh. "The hand of Saint James," he said with reverence. "Indeed you have done well, my daughter." He made no attempt to unfasten the base to look inside at the relic itself, because it would have been disrespectful to do so in a secular setting, but he touched the gold with possessive fingers. "They gave you this?"

Matilda said evasively, "Before he died, my husband said I was to have it."

He gave her a sharp look. "Does the new emperor know?"

"He does by now. Would you have me return it?"

Her father quickly shook his head. "A man's dying wishes should always be honoured. Reading Abbey will be greatly exalted by this gift from an empress—and perhaps a future queen." He gave her a meaningful look.

She waited for him to say more, but he drew back with an enigmatic smile. "Such matters are not for discussion now. Settle in first and we will talk later."

She curtseyed to him and he kissed her brow and left the room, his tread assertive and buoyant.

Adeliza had curtseyed too, but remained with Matilda and went to look at the relic of Saint James herself. "Does it have healing powers?"

"So it is said."

Her stepmother bit her lip. "Do you think it would cure a barren wife?"

"I know not." Matilda had entreated the saint and her prayers on that score had been answered, but the baby had not survived his birthing and she did not know Adeliza well enough yet to open her heart on such matters.

Adeliza sighed. "I know I must accept God's will, but it is difficult, when I know it is my duty to conceive."

Matilda felt a surge of compassion for Adeliza because she had been in a similar situation herself: married to an older man and people looking at her month on month, waiting for her to quicken. When that man had already fathered children on other women, the pressure was even greater.

"He is thinking of making you his heir; you must realise that."

Matilda nodded. "I also know I am not the only one he has in mind. My father always has a plan and a contingency plan and then a plan to back up both the original and the contingency." She gave Adeliza a measuring look. "I respect him, and I know my duty, but I also know that for all my father says he loves me as a daughter, I am but another playing piece on his board. We all are."

"He is a great king," Adeliza said firmly.

"Without a doubt," Matilda agreed, and thought that whoever succeeded her father would have to be even greater in order to fill the void that the last son of William the Conqueror would leave behind.

Four

*W*ATCHING THE GAP WIDEN BETWEEN THE QUAY AT BARFLEUR and the deck on which she stood, Matilda shivered and huddled inside her cloak. Waves chopped and surged, frilled with small whitecaps, and beyond the harbour mouth, the sea was a heaving grey swell. Spume burst at the prow of the royal galley and wind bellied the square canvas sail so that the great red lion painted on it seemed to roar and flex its claws.

She had not been aboard a ship to cross the sea since she was eight years old. Inevitably she thought of her brother's last voyage from this port, ended like his life before it had properly begun as the ship struck a rock in the harbour mouth and sank in the black November night. It was daylight now and circumstances different, but although she lifted her chin and tried to look imperious, she was still afraid.

Brian FitzCount joined her. "England will be upon us before sunset," he remarked, "especially if the wind continues to blow this strongly."

"You must be accustomed to crossing the sea, my lord."

"Indeed, but I am nevertheless always glad to reach the shore. It is not so bad when there's a fair wind like this." A smile entered his voice. "And we have the extra protection of the hand of Saint James today."

"I hope you are not humouring me."

"Domina, I would not dare," he replied, his dark eyes alight.

Matilda arched her brow and said nothing. Since their first meeting, she had grown accustomed to his company and enjoyed it. He was a mainstay of her father's government and a close friend of her brother Robert. She had often sat up with them and others talking long into the night on all manner of subjects, from the best way to skin a hare to intricate aspects of papal policy and points of English common law and custom in which Brian was well versed. She loved to hear him in debate.

"This is the next stage on your voyage, domina." Brian's face was straight now, and there was an intensity in his gaze that made her look down before a spark could strike between them.

"And who knows where landfall will be."

"I am certain your father does."

"It is a pity only he knows the location and he will not share it." She glanced at her father, standing on the opposite side of the vessel with a group of courtiers. She had attended on him in Rouen when he made judgements and spun policy. He had included her in the proceedings by having her at his side, but even so, he seldom sought her opinion. Last month, without consulting her, he had rejected marriage offers for her from Lombardy and Lotharingia. She had dwelt at court now for almost a year, but time seemed to hang in suspension like a spider's web between two twigs, waiting for something beyond dust to alight on the strands. He had summoned her to join him and then done nothing about it, as if she were a valuable surety to be held in reserve.

"Matters will move apace once we reach England."

Brian's placatory tone set her teeth on edge. "You know something that I do not?"

"Domina, I do not, except that there are people there your

father needs to consult on all manner of things. Your uncle King David for one and the bishop of Salisbury for another."

Matilda shot him an exasperated look. "More talk between men. I am the king's daughter, and my father's lords have sworn allegiance to me, but it is still as if I have neither place nor voice in the world."

"But you will have one day," Brian said quietly. "Now is the time to gather your resources and prepare the soil."

The sound of retching made them both turn to regard a green-faced young nobleman heaving over the side of the ship. Brian grunted. "I doubt he's really that sick," he muttered, "unless it is with vexation."

Matilda considered Waleran de Meulan. He had been an instigator of a failed rebellion in support of her cousin William le Clito and had been held prisoner in Normandy for the past two years. That he was not currently in fetters was because he had no means of escape. Her father had deemed it unwise to leave him behind and Waleran was set to continue his captivity in England in the custody of her father's justiciar, the bishop of Salisbury. He was the son of one of her father's most trusted servants and had a twin brother, Robert, who had not been involved in the uprising. Matilda was well aware that preparing her soil would involve deciding how to deal with men such as this from powerful families, who preferred to back le Clito as rightful ruler of Normandy and England, rather than her father's line. Waleran de Meulan might look pathetic and ineffectual just now, but he was still a dangerous man.

Leaving Brian, Matilda joined Adeliza, who was sitting against the side of the ship wrapped in warm furs and buffered from the strakes by thick fleece-stuffed cushions. Against the deep colours of squirrel and sable, Adeliza's face was a wan oval and she was biting her lip. Matilda wondered if she was worried about the sea crossing, but surely she had made it often, and she was not naturally timorous. Perhaps like Waleran she was suffering from the effects of the heavy swell. Several people were ill, although none were making quite as much noise as the lord of Meulan. Then Matilda realised that her stepmother was crying.

"Madam?" Matilda looked round to call for help, but Adeliza gripped her arm.

"It is nothing," she said.

Matilda sat beside her and tucked some of the fur coverlets over the top of her own cloak. "What is wrong?"

Adeliza swallowed and wiped her eyes on her mantle. "My flux is upon me," she said in a low voice. "I thought...I thought this time I might have held on to the child. It has been forty days since last I bled...but it has come. It always comes." She rocked back and forth with her head bent. "Why can I not fulfil this duty? What have I done wrong for God to deny me?"

Matilda set a comforting arm around Adeliza's shoulders. "I am so sorry. I grieved the same when I was married to Heinrich."

"I would be a good mother," Adeliza whispered. "I know I would. If only I had one chance. Just one. Is it too much to ask?" She compressed her lips as William D'Albini picked his way over to them, his balance steady despite the freshening wind. Stooping, he handed a flask to the women.

"Honey-sweetened wine and ginger, madam," he said to Adeliza. "It is a good remedy if you are feeling unwell. My aunt Olivia swears by it. The waves are heavy today."

Matilda eyed him suspiciously, but his expression was open and he seemed to genuinely think Adeliza was suffering from *mal de mer*. She thanked him on Adeliza's behalf in a voice that encouraged him not to linger. He took the hint, his complexion flushing, and, with a bow, moved off.

Adeliza sniffed and raised her chin. "I will not feel sorry for myself," she said. "If God has other plans, then I must trust to His judgement. He will let me know what He wants of me when He is ready." Removing the stopper from the flask, she took a sip, and then passed the drink to Matilda.

"Indeed," said Matilda, and thought that sometimes God worked in very mysterious ways and she was not sure that she could wait on His will with the same patience as Adeliza.

❖❖❖

Standing in pride of place upon the high altar of Reading Abbey, the hand of Saint James pointed towards heaven in a spire of burnished gold and precious stones. The Abbey of the Virgin Mary and Saint John was in its sixth year since consecration and still under construction. Henry intended it to be the most magnificent foundation in Christendom. It would house his tomb when the time came, and it was already a shrine to the son he had lost on the *White Ship*, whose mortal remains lay at the bottom of the sea. Monks from the great abbey at Cluny performed the offices, said the prayers, and cared for the relics, which included the blood and water from the side of our Lord Jesus Christ, a piece of his shoe, and the foreskin from his circumcision. There was also a lock of the Virgin's hair. The impressive collection of intimate items from the Holy Family bestowed importance and sanctity upon the abbey, and assured a place in heaven for its founder and benefactor.

Now that the hand of Saint James had been safely delivered to the abbey custodians, Henry retired to the guest house with Matilda, Adeliza, and a few close advisers and family members, including Matilda's uncle, David, king of Scotland, Robert of Gloucester, and Brian FitzCount.

Matilda drew a lungful of the crisp autumn air before entering the lodging, then exhaled hard to release her tension. She had almost cried during the mass when the hand had been gifted to the abbey because the memories of herself and Heinrich on their wedding day had been both too close and too far away. If only she could have that time back, to relive it with the knowledge she had now as a mature woman, instead of being an overawed child.

Her father's servants arranged chairs and benches around the hearth with wine and titbits to hand. Her uncle David gave her one of his laconic smiles as an attendant took her cloak. "You did well to bring such a fine gift to the abbey, niece. Your mother would have been proud of you." He spoke the Norman French of the court with a soft Scottish burr.

"She would have seen it as my duty," Matilda replied wryly.

"And you have fulfilled it." Her uncle's expression held encouragement and a twinkle of humour. "You are her daughter, but there is more to you than that, and I would see you smile." He gave her an irreverent but avuncular chuck under the chin. "I hope you are my niece too."

Matilda managed to oblige him. She was very fond of her uncle. He had played with her when she was a child and sent letters and gifts to her in Germany more cheering than her mother's dry exhortations to duty and copies of religious works in Latin. He had sent her dolls and sweetmeats and a necklace set with Lothian garnets that she still had in her jewel casket.

"Good, then we are of a mind." He kissed her cheek and led her to sit down by the fire.

Once everyone was settled, her father called for silence. "Now we are all gathered, I wish to talk of the future." He studied each person in turn. "I had hoped in the fullness of time that the Queen and I would be blessed with a male heir, but thus far God has not seen fit to grant us that blessing."

Adeliza gazed down at her hands and toyed with her wedding ring.

"That being the case, I must consider the matter of the succession. My choices are clear. Lacking a legitimate male heir, I must look to either my nephews of Blois, or to my daughter and the eventual fruit of her womb."

Matilda raised her chin and met his stare, matching it with her own.

Her brother Robert said, "Certain factions would also have you consider William le Clito, sire."

"No." The king dismissed the suggestion with a swift chop of his hand. "Le Clito has neither the brain nor the experience to rule England and Normandy."

"But others do have experience in his stead," her uncle David said shrewdly. "The king of France supports him in order to discomfort you, and what about that young man you brought with you in chains?"

"Waleran de Meulan is a hot-headed young fool," Henry snapped.

"With some close and powerful relatives."

"Indeed, but imprisoning Waleran shows them just how far they can tread on my goodwill without suffering the consequences." He leaned forward in his chair and extended one thick, powerful hand. "I have a clear choice before me. Here is my daughter, the widow of an emperor. She has great connections by marriage and by birth. She is the fruit of my loins and through her runs the blood of the ancient English royal house. Moreover, she is the only child born to parents who were crowned sovereigns at her conception. She has experience of ruling and of being a royal consort."

Matilda's heart constricted with a mingling of pride and apprehension. She firmed her lips and strove to look as regal and dignified as his words described.

Robert said, "Few men will bow the knee to a woman, sire, no matter how competent and fitted by blood she is to the task—and I say this as someone who will gladly swear allegiance to my sister." He glanced round and received nods of approbation from the others.

"And I say to you that all men will bow to my resolve, by one means or another." Henry's hand clenched into a fist. "I am no fool. I know when a man is dead and gone, his word is no longer the law. Therefore I must make all watertight while I am still in good health. If no son is to come to me through my queen, I must look to grandsons born of my daughter."

Matilda held her father's hard grey stare. "And what man will provide those grandsons, my father? You have not said."

"Because I must still think on this business. It matters only that your husband should be of good stock and gives you sons. He will never be a king, but the advantage for him is that his son will wear England's crown. And you, my daughter, will be the vessel that brings this royal child into the world. You will be the power behind the throne until he is old enough to take that power for himself. In this you will have the backing of your kin and my committed vassals. As the mother of a future sovereign, your authority will be great, and all these men will support you." He gestured around the firelit circle and the air almost crackled with sparks of tension. "And if God is merciful, he will grant me the years to watch my grandson become a man."

And to hold on to power, Matilda thought, and knew it must be in everyone else's mind too. If her father could live that long, they might never have to deal with the threat of a woman on the throne. She said, with her hand at her slender waistline, "I am willing to do my duty, sire, and I am glad you have such trust in me, but what if you die before I bear a child? And what if I do not conceive?"

He gave her a dark look, as if he thought she was deliberately setting out to be awkward. "Those are bridges to cross in later discussions. For now I hold to the premise that my own blood in direct line shall inherit the throne, and that all of my barons shall swear allegiance to you as my heir."

There was a long, tense silence, broken by Brian FitzCount, who rose, walked round the fire and knelt at Matilda's feet. "Willingly I do so swear," he said, and bowed his head.

Her heart filled at his action and she hoped she did not look as flustered as she felt. Clasping his hands between hers, she gave him the kiss of peace on either cheek, and felt the soft burr of his stubble against her lips. His garments smelled of cedar wood and the scent took her breath.

"A noble gesture," her father said with amused tolerance, as if watching the antics of a precocious child, "but I am already certain of those gathered here. I know you will give your allegiance in public before all. It is my intent to hold an oath-taking ceremony at the Christmas court with every magnate present as a witness and participant."

Robert cupped his chin. "What of Stephen and Theobald of Blois?" His upper lip curled as he mentioned his cousin. "From his behaviour, Stephen seems to think you are grooming him for a greater part than just being the Count of Boulogne."

"I have never spoken to him in such terms," Henry said shortly. "I am fond of him; he is my nephew, and he will do very well where he is. He owes his power to me and he will obey and implement my policies."

Robert gave his father a long look. "Will you discuss this oath in council with the other lords?"

Henry tapped his fingers on the arms of his chair. "I see no need for the present."

"But men may demand to know whom my sister will wed before they swear."

"All will be done in its due time and course," Henry growled.

Matilda said, "The bishop of Salisbury is not here tonight."

"It is not a matter for him." Her father's face began to redden and Adeliza stroked his arm in a soothing gesture.

"But you assign him England's rule in your absence. Supposedly he is the most trusted man at your councils," she persisted. "What does it say for the future that he is not here now?" Matilda was aware of everyone staring at her, as if a tame hawk had turned to rend its owner with its beak. She firmed her lips and sat erect.

Her father's chest expanded. "The bishop of Salisbury is a statesman I hold in great respect," he said, his voice gritty with anger. "He will be told in due course—when I am ready to do so."

Doggedly, Matilda held her ground. "But he has been sympathetic to le Clito in the past. Might it not be prudent to give custody of the lord of Meulan to someone else—to my lord FitzCount, for example, who is indeed present tonight, and who has sworn allegiance."

Her father's eyes narrowed.

Brian cleared his throat. "It is true that Wallingford is more secure, sire. I grew up with Waleran and I know him well. Perhaps I could sit with him over a flagon of wine and talk him round."

"I agree, sire," said Robert, hastening to smooth the path. "I am not saying the bishop of Salisbury would do anything untoward and I know you trust him, but Wallingford is more secure than Devizes."

Henry continued to look irritated. "Brian, you could talk rings around Waleran de Meulan and any man you chose, but that is not the same as making him change his mind. I know and trust my justiciar, and I am not blind to the fact that he has a soft spot for Meulan and would willingly sponsor le Clito as my successor." He made a brusque gesture. "Very well, let us err on the side of caution. I will give the order to have Meulan transferred to Wallingford, but I expect every cooperation with my lord the bishop of Salisbury, is that clear?"

❖❖❖

Dismissed by her father with the evening's business completed, Matilda entered the guest chamber allotted to herself and Adeliza and breathed deeply, trying to release her tension.

Adeliza followed her quietly into the room and directed her women about their business: folding back the bedclothes; warming the sheets with hot stones wrapped in cloths; preparing a tray of wine and honey cakes.

"They call women weak reeds," Matilda said with a short laugh, "but it isn't true, because otherwise how would we bear the duties and burdens that are set upon us by men?"

Adeliza gave a small shake of her head. "I think you are courageous. I could not do this."

"If you had to, you could." Matilda fixed her young step-mother with a fierce glance.

Adeliza gestured. "But it would not suit me, whereas I can see the fire inside you."

"I do it because my father asks it of me."

"But for yourself too, I think."

Matilda wandered to the coffer that held her trinkets and picked up an ornate ivory pot of rose-scented salve. She removed the lid and inhaled the delicate scent of summer petals. She did desire to hold power in her own right, but it was so difficult when a forthright woman was considered to possess masculine tendencies and therefore suspected of being a virago and flouting the natural law. "Am I wrong about the bishop of Salisbury?" she asked

Adeliza sat down on her bed. "The bishop has long been one of your father's closest advisers," she replied with diplomacy. "He knows how to spin straw into gold."

"And how much of it does he keep for himself? How much does he take to keep his mistresses and children, his palaces and castles? How much goes to buy him a portion of every dish in the land?"

"I suspect only Roger of Salisbury knows the sums, and that they change from one moment to the next, but since he keeps your father's coffers full to the brim, he is permitted a certain leeway. Do not make him your enemy," Adeliza cautioned. "He has the power to do you great harm as well as great good."

"A bishop exists to serve God and the king, not his own interests," Matilda said. "But thank you for your advice." Taking a dab of the salve on her forefinger, she worked it into her hands. If, in the fullness of time, she were to rule England, she would need the support and goodwill of the Church, and prelates such as Roger of Salisbury needed to be either persuaded to her side, or put in their place.

❖❖❖

In the morning, the court made ready to travel from Reading to Windsor. As Matilda waited for her groom to bring her mare, she narrowed her eyes to study the bishop of Salisbury from across the courtyard. Surrounded by his entourage, he was deep in conversation with her cousin Stephen. Bishop Roger was not tall, but he was thickset and his bejewelled regalia increased his breadth and his presence. The head of his crosier glowed with Limoges work in blue enamel and his robes sparkled with so much metallic thread that he resembled a frosty morning at dawn. His white palfrey was trapped out in glittering harness, the fringed saddle cloth reaching almost to the ground. She had spoken to him on their first arrival in the courtyard, but the greeting, although courteous, had been brief and remote on both sides. The good bishop was being considerably more affable towards her cousin Stephen, she noted.

Brian FitzCount's groom brought Sable into the yard, and Brian arrived from his business and took the reins with a brief word. His dark glance flickered over the bishop and Stephen as he walked the horse over to Matilda and bowed. "Domina, I thought you would want to know that your father has transferred Waleran de Meulan into my keeping to be held at Wallingford as we discussed."

John FitzGilbert, one of the marshals, arrived with her mare. Brian took the horse and helped Matilda into the saddle before mounting Sable.

As she gathered her reins, she said, "I heard a tale that my father raised Salisbury on high because he could say mass faster than any other priest of his acquaintance, and that it was useful when shriving men before a battle."

Brian gave a mordant smile. "Roger of Salisbury is indeed a man of expedience, but that is not the whole story. He is a very clever administrator; some might say too clever for his own good, but only time will tell."

"The Queen told me he can spin straw into gold. He is certainly wearing enough on his back for that to be a possibility."

"Roger of Salisbury is not the only churchman with a taste for the finer things in life. Your cousin the abbot of Glastonbury will bear watching too."

Matilda followed his gaze to another bearded cleric, who was setting his foot to the stirrup of a magnificent dappled stallion trapped out in elaborate black leather harness studded with silver sunbursts. Stephen's brother, her cousin Henry, had recently been summoned from the abbey at Cluny to take up an appointment at Glastonbury but he was ambitious for a bishopric or even higher—Canterbury, she suspected. "Yes." She returned his knowing look. "I had noticed."

Five

A COLD AUTUMN RAIN WAS SHIVERING THE BANKS OF THE Thames and filling the wheel ruts on the road with muddy water as Brian arrived at his great fortress of Wallingford. The recently built stone keep on its high mound proclaimed the power of its lord, as did the series of ditches, palisades, and walls, slick with rainwater. Brian noted that the engineers and builders had made good progress over the summer during his absence at court. Men said that Wallingford was impregnable, and Brian could almost believe it was true.

As a groom arrived to take Sable, his wife emerged from the guest hall to greet him. "My lord." She dropped him a brief curtsey.

"Madam." He forced a smile. Untidy wisps of iron-grey hair escaped her wimple and she wore an everyday gown with the sleeves hooked back and pale dog hairs decorating her ample bosom. A pack of assorted, exuberant canines bustled around her feet, threatening to trip anyone who tried to take a step. Brian tightened his jaw. She had had plenty of notification of his arrival, but he knew from experience that changing her gown was never a priority for Maude, and that, unless prompted, it would not occur to her to do so. However, when he entered the private chamber in the domestic block, he found a jug of wine waiting on a cloth-covered trestle with fresh bread and good cheese. There was a ewer of warm water for washing, and clean raiment set out for him. Maude ran the household efficiently, but when it came to herself, saw no need to bother beyond the practical and mundane.

"I am surprised to see you," she said as he stooped to wash his hands and face. Her tone was neutral. "I suppose you are not here for long."

"A few days only," he said as he dried himself. "I've to rejoin the court by the end of the week." He looked down. One of her dogs had grabbed his shoe thong in its teeth and was worrying at it with ferocious growls. He stooped and picked up the creature, one hand under its tummy. It curled its lip at him and yapped and wriggled. Its eyes were almost hidden under a shroud of silky white fringe.

"He's still a pup." Her voice grew syrupy and fond. "He hasn't learned his manners yet, have you, Rascal?"

"Rascal?" Maude always had one dog of that name as her personal companion. If this youngster was the current "Rascal," then the old one must be dead.

"I lost his great-grandsire in the spring when you were in Normandy." Her tone held no reproach for his long absence, merely stoic resignation.

"I am sorry."

She shrugged. "He had lost his hearing and he was blind; it was for the best." She removed the pup from his arms and cuddled it to her breast.

"All has been well here?"

"Nothing that I or your constable and stewards have been unable to deal with. I would have written if there was trouble."

He nodded. They exchanged words like polite strangers. He and Maude had been wed for nineteen years and had nothing in common. They did not even have the gift and mutual upbringing of sons and daughters to bind them together and that likelihood was almost gone, for she was nearly twenty years older than he was and long into her mid-life. She was always keen to try and conceive when he came home, in the same way that she eagerly bred her dogs and her oxen and her cattle, but she led her life at Wallingford and he led his at the court and their worlds seldom collided.

"Well, only the matter of the church at Ogbourne," she said. "I would like to give it to the monks at Bec." She set the wriggling little dog on the ground.

"I think it a good idea," he said as he went to change his thick travelling tunic for a garment of finer, softer wool. "The empress will be pleased; Bec is her favourite priory." As he spoke of Matilda, warmth filled his stomach.

Maude tilted her head to one side and folded her arms. "What is she like?"

"Her father's daughter," he said. "She does not suffer fools gladly. She is regal and elegant; truly an empress." It was useless telling her of Matilda's vibrancy, of her sharp sparkle and her beauty, because Maude would not understand, and anyway, he wanted to keep such descriptions to himself—like personal treasure.

"Will the king make her his heir?" Without waiting for him to reply she continued, "He must intend to. He has enough daughters born of his concubines to bind men to him in marriage alliances. He needs her for a greater purpose—why bring her back from Germany otherwise?"

Brian nodded. His wife was astute. She might not move in the world of the court, but she was not ignorant. "It is one of his choices," he said. "But for the moment he is keeping many doors open."

"He will expect her to breed sons..." Maude's voice strengthened on the last two words and her expression grew set and forceful.

Brian excused himself before she could begin a long and tedious monologue on the matter of bloodlines: he had business to see to. His constable William Boterel brought him up to date on recent building projects. He examined the seasoned oak delivered for strengthening the castle doors and inspected the store rooms; he discussed supplies and the necessity of providing secure accommodation other than a dungeon for Waleran de Meulan, who was to be kept here as a closely guarded "guest." He visited the garrison soldiers and talked to them, then retired to his own chamber to ponder various tallies and charters until the dinner hour. Not once in that time did he think of his wife.

When they met in the great hall to dine, Maude had finally changed her gown for a clean one of plain green wool and she wore a full linen wimple in the English style that framed her wide, round face. Her cheeks, forehead, and chin were rosy as if she had given them a good scrub. As they ate roe deer with wheat frumenty and assorted fungi, she talked to him of the minutiae of her daily existence; he let her conversation flow over him and tried to think of it as soothing rather than as dull as stodge. Maude was a good woman and without their marriage, he would not have all this wealth to call upon. She ran his household well and provided a refuge from the steely sharpness of the court. Here life was predictable and grounded; he did not have to listen to and measure every single word. He told her about Waleran, and that he was to be kept at Wallingford until the king deemed him safe to release. "I have told William to see to the ordering of a suitable door with bars and locks. He's to be kept under strict house arrest until the king decrees otherwise."

She looked at him in surprise, but without trepidation. "What a shame," she said. "Why do men fight over things that do not matter? When the hens stop laying or there is murrain among the sheep that is far greater cause for concern than who sits on the throne. I remember Waleran de Meulan when he was a foolish boy too young to grow a beard."

"Now he is a foolish man," Brian said curtly. "He should not have dabbled in rebellion, and now he is reaping the consequences."

Maude tutted and, with a shake of her head, passed a scrap of meat under the table to Rascal.

As evening fell, Maude leaned towards him and laid her capable, alewife's hand on his sleeve. "Husband, will you come to bed?" There was no seduction in her voice; the request, although spoken in a low voice for privacy, was matter of fact.

"Yes, in a moment," he said with a sinking heart. "I have a few charters to look over first."

"Good, then I will expect you. I will take the dogs out while I wait." She left, calling her entourage of canines to heel and bidding a servant bring her cloak.

Brian retreated to his chamber. Sitting down in his chair he massaged his temples where a slow headache had begun to pound. It had been a long day. Eventually he picked up his quill and, drawing a sheet of parchment under his hand, wrote to the abbot of Bec, and then to the bishop of Bath. The motion of the quill across the parchment soothed him, as did the intellectual flow of his thoughts. He sometimes wondered what would have happened if his father had dedicated him to the Church instead of giving him to the king to be raised at court. Would he have found religious vows hard to keep? Perhaps, but then many clerics made a mockery of such, and lived in the lap of luxury and power with their mistresses and offspring—witness Roger of Salisbury and his castle at Devizes and his palace at Salisbury.

His work completed, he went to open the shutters and look out. He could hear Maude calling to the dogs, jollying them along in her brisk, deep voice. She would have been a fine mother to a brace of sons, he thought, and felt a surge of melancholy. Even while she irritated him, he appreciated that their marriage was not one she would have chosen for herself had the decision been in her hands, because he no more measured up to her standards than she did to his

❖❖❖

Still red-cheeked and glowing from her walk, Maude looked at Brian expectantly. The servants had made up the great bed for the night and been dismissed, taking the dog pack with them. "If we do not have an heir now, it will be too late," she said. "My fluxes barely come at all these days and you are returning to court within the week." She jutted her fleshy jaw. "I am entitled to claim the marital debt from you. I know you have no desire for me, but this is not about desire, it is about procreation."

Brian bit his lip. If the situation had not been so appalling, he would have laughed. Besides, it was no laughing matter, because if he did not pay that debt, then he was violating his oath of marriage. She removed her wimple and gown. Reluctantly he took off his tunic and his shirt, but it was she who approached him. Her chemise was plain but clean. The smell of lye soap mingled with that of fresh sweat from her recent exercise. She rubbed her hands together to warm them and, without further ado, unfastened the drawstring on his braies. Delving down, she began to fondle him. Brian closed his eyes. He wasn't a stallion in the breeding pen. He had never felt less amorous in his life and he was flaccid in her grip, which was becoming ever more desperate and vigorous. "Give me a moment," he gasped, pushing her away. "Go and get into bed."

She heaved a sigh, but did as he bade, and lay back, hitching up her nightgown and opening her legs. Brian hastily snuffed the candle and climbed in beside her. It would be better in the dark, he told himself, easier to pretend. He banished the thought of Maude's dimpled flesh from his mind; blotted out too the smell of lye and sweat. He tried to ignore the grunt she made as he mounted her and imagined instead a lithe taut body scented with royal incense and roses, eyes the blue-grey of lavender flowers and a mouth that drove him wild. Such fancies in his mind, he became hard enough to do his duty. To enter her body and give her his seed. And once inside her, it became easier to envisage that this was not Maude but Matilda, and the act not just one of procreation, but of lovemaking.

When it was over he lifted himself off her and sat up, his ribs heaving. In the aftermath of release, he felt sullied, but at least he had given her what she wanted.

"There, there," soothed Maude, patting his back as if he were a dog or a horse that had performed well. "That wasn't so difficult, was it?"

"No," he said, and thought that while he was relieved at a duty done, she was obviously satisfied that she could remove it from her own list of things to do while he was home. Her hand left him; she turned over and was soon asleep, soft snores catching at the back of her throat. Brian quietly dressed in the dark and went out. As he opened the door, he felt her dogs trotting past him into the room and he heard them leaping on to the bed, encouraged by Maude's sleepy murmur of welcome. Rousing a squire, he had the lad kindle a lantern and guide him to his own chamber. Let her have her dogs; he would seek the comfort of the written word.

Six

YOU WILL GO TO YOUR GRAVE WITH INK-STAINED FINGERS," Robert of Gloucester told Brian with deep amusement.

Brian looked at his hands and gave a self-deprecating smile before concealing them beneath his cloak. "I think you are right. The marks do come out, but by the time I get rid of one lot, more are waiting to take their place." His expression sobered. "There are worse stains in the world." He glanced round. Westminster's great hall was packed with courtiers, all robed in their furs and finery. Snow had fallen earlier that morning and there was a light dusting on the ground, fine as flour. There had been much talk concerning the oath that the king was expecting everyone to swear to Matilda, accepting her as his heir, and there was an undercurrent of deep unease, although no one had voiced their intentions of refusing to swear. Brian's gaze flickered over Stephen of Blois and Boulogne, who was talking to his brother the abbot of Glastonbury and Roger, bishop of Salisbury. Brian's mathematician's eye easily picked out patterns in the gathering. Knots of men. Factions attached to each other by strands of mutual interest and ambition. They were all so much yarn for the king's weaving—or for his undoing.

A fanfare sounded throughout the hall and, along a path cleared through the kneeling crowd by the royal marshals, the king arrived and swept to take his place on the middle throne of three set on a raised dais. He wore a hinged crown glittering with gemstones and was accompanied by Adeliza, also crowned and clad in shimmering cloth of silver. Brian watched Matilda walk to take the third throne on her father's right hand. His chest tightened as he looked at her. She wore a close-fitting gown of blood-red wool with gold embroidery at throat, hem, and cuffs, and small jewels stitched in flower patterns all over the body of the dress. Her cloak was lined with ermines. She too wore a crown, set with gold flowers and sapphires, and her hair was loose, brushed down her back and shining like a dark waterfall. Her face was set in lines of ice-like purity and Brian caught his breath at the sight of such unattainable beauty.

Robert said softly, "We have just witnessed the entrance of a future queen."

The words sent a shiver down Brian's spine. Matilda looked straight in front of her as she took her seat with regal authority, and he thought that she resembled a figure from a stained-glass window come to life, shimmering and holy. "She is already an empress," he replied.

Oaths were sworn to uphold her as her father's heir. First the archbishop of Canterbury, then York, followed by all the bishops of the land. Roger of Salisbury approached and bent an arthritic knee, gripping his crosier for support. Nevertheless, his voice was clear and steady. Brian and Robert exchanged knowing glances. Roger of Salisbury was a superlative actor and politician. Matilda responded to him with such coolness and grace that Brian thought his heart would burst. She would be a great ruler, if only given the chance.

Stephen of Blois clenched his fists and hesitated when it came to his moment. Immediately, Robert rose from his place by his father's feet and stepped forward, but Stephen recovered from his pause and the men arrived at the same time. "It is my turn to take the oath next, I believe, cousin," Stephen said, smiling but hard-eyed.

Robert raised his brows. "What makes you think that… cousin?"

Continuing to smile, Stephen said, "Is it not obvious? My mother was the daughter of a king."

Brian winced on Robert's behalf. Like his own mother, Gloucester's had been a concubine, and Stephen's remark was almost an insult. There was a sudden tightening of the atmosphere around the men, but then Robert stepped back and bowed. "Now you point it out, my lord, I see that you should indeed go first, albeit that my father is a king. All will be glad of your eagerness to make your oath of allegiance to my sister the empress."

The tension reached its zenith in an exchange of challenging stares. Stephen was the first to break eye contact and knelt to Matilda, putting his hands between hers and swearing that he would uphold her as her father's heir. He made his vow firmly, but his jaw was taut and his voice lacked power and did not carry. Robert took his own oath in ringing tones that proclaimed his loyalty and intent to all. When it came to Brian's turn, he knelt as he had done in the council room in September and pledged himself to her with every fibre of his being. He put his conviction into his voice and kept his heart out of his eyes, because too many people were watching too closely. The look she returned him was of lord to vassal, bright with approval, but cool with distance too, pointed up by the fact that she was on her feet and he was on his knees.

Following the oath-taking, the company sat to dine in formal magnificence. There was sturgeon and stuffed salmon; spicy meatballs studded with currants; swan and peacock; venison with numerous sauces. Sweetmeats of honey, rose water, and ginger. Conversations bubbled like a cauldron over a steady heat and under the influence of food and drink the atmosphere gradually became more convivial, although men were still on their guard.

Towards the end of the meal, there was a sudden bustle at the lower end of the hall and Brian watched John FitzGilbert, one of the marshals, leading a messenger along the side of the room behind the trestles. News that wouldn't wait then, Brian thought. Henry took the message from the man's hand, broke the seal, and read the contents. His face and throat began to flush and his expression grew thunderous. He bared his worn teeth at the gathered nobles. "It seems, my lords, that we have a marriage to toast this day." He glared around the trestle, striking each person with his stare before moving on to the next. "William le Clito has wed the sister-in-law of the king of France and been granted lands in the Vexin on my borders." Although he had spoken of a toast, he did not raise his cup and his words were thick with fury. "This is a ploy on the part of Louis to interfere with my policies. Well and good, he may do so, but he will not overturn my intent to see my daughter rule England."

Brian felt renewed tension running through the gathering. This news meant that William le Clito's position was now a far greater threat to the succession than before. The Vexin would make it easy for him to strike into Normandy. Many here had taken the oath only to avoid Henry's ire, and might well renege if circumstances played into le Clito's hands. They would say that if it came to a war in Normandy, who in their right mind would want to follow a woman's banner into battle? That would be a hard prejudice to shift.

Seven

MATILDA LIFTED HER HEAD AND LISTENED TO THE WIND rattling the shutters of the queen's chamber where she sat sewing with Adeliza. Now and again rain spattered too, sounding like handfuls of flung shingle striking a board. Beyond the complex of buildings the river was a turbulent grey churn, showing whitecaps on the tidal crests. Not a day to be outside unless one was forced. Spring was supposedly on the threshold, but was taking a long time to knock on the door.

Adeliza moved closer to the brazier and told her attendant, Juliana, to bring more light. "I started my flux again this morning," she said in a neutral tone as she threaded a length of silk through the eye of her needle.

"I am so sorry," Matilda said.

Adeliza shook her head. "I must accept that it is not to be and that God has other plans. I wrote to the archbishop of Tours for advice and he said I should concentrate on good works on Earth that would bear spiritual fruit. He says that God has closed up the mouth of my womb so that I may adopt immortal offspring, and he is right. Weeping and wringing my hands is foolish. Better to concentrate on the good I can do. I have already begun plans to build a leper hospital at Wilton."

Matilda murmured with understanding. Such was the work of queens. Their task was to conciliate, to make peace between warring factions, to alleviate the suffering of the sick by good works and to patronise the arts. She had done all of this in Germany for Heinrich, whilst grieving that she could not bear him a living son. Keeping busy so that there was no time to brood.

"I have also commissioned David of Galway to compose a history of your father's life."

"Who?" Matilda asked.

"The little scribe in your uncle's entourage."

"Ah." Matilda's mind filled with the image of a short, balding but still youngish man with ink-stained fingers just like Brian's. He was a favourite in the chamber after supper when tales were told. "That sounds like a fine notion. I am sure he will make an excellent work."

Adeliza secured the thread in the fabric. "It means Henry will always be remembered," she said, her words bearing a note of poignant resignation. "I want to commemorate his deeds in a work of literature that will live on when we are gone."

The women looked up as Brian FitzCount was shown into the room by Adeliza's clerk, Master Serlo. Approaching the women he bowed, his expression grim.

"What is it, my lord?" Adeliza gestured him to rise, and directed him to the opposite window seat.

He sat down, removing his rain-jewelled cap. Today his boots were laced with blue cord to match the vamp strips up the centre and they had an elegantly pointed toe. "Madam, Domina, I am sorry to tell you that the Count of Flanders is dead," he said. "Murdered by his servants while at his prayers in his private chapel."

Matilda stared at him in shocked dismay. Adeliza gasped and crossed herself. "That is wicked!" She pressed her hand over her mouth.

Brian grimaced. "Louis of France is to preside over the election of his successor, and William le Clito is his likely choice."

Matilda felt as if she had been double-punched. Charles of Flanders was a close ally of her father's and popular with his people. It was terrible to hear of his murder—wicked, as Adeliza said. Anyone who killed a man at his prayers was damned to hell. But then to be told that le Clito...She forced herself to think beyond her shock. "What's to be done?"

Brian rubbed his chin. "Your father is sending your cousin Stephen to negotiate and put forward other names for the title. Even if le Clito is elected, he will not stay in the saddle. There are already riots in Flanders over the count's death and the disturbances are not going to settle down in a minute. Your father has given the order that England is to cease supplying English wool to Flemish looms."

Matilda nodded. Such a move would cause severe unrest because without work, the weavers starved. Her father would then enrich his own candidates from England's bulging coffers, supporting their rebellions with his silver, because he could not allow William le Clito to become the entrenched lord of Flanders. Given that political decision to make, she would have done the same.

Brian bowed and excused himself to other duties while Adeliza and Matilda went from the palace to the cathedral, there to pray for the soul of Charles of Flanders. As Matilda knelt before the altar, she could not help thinking of a young man murdered at his devotions and that their own bent necks were in just such a vulnerable position, waiting for the blow to strike.

❖❖❖

Brian sat before the fire in the king's private chamber, fondling the silky ears of a sleek gazehound. Robert of Gloucester was also present, standing by the hearth, gazing into the soft yellow flames of a well-seasoned fire. They had been summoned by Henry for an unspecified reason, although Brian suspected it was concerned with the news about the young Count of Flanders, because the king now had to deal with a situation that had turned an ally into an enemy.

Henry entered the chamber with his usual vigour, his cloak an energetic swirl at his shoulders. He joined Robert at the hearth, rubbing his hands briskly, and waved aside their obeisance. Then he patted the dog and took the cup of wine that Brian poured for him.

"Curiosity is written on your faces as big as an incompetent clerk's scrawl," he said with scornful amusement before taking a hearty swallow.

"Are you not surprised, my lord father?" Robert replied. "I scarcely think you have summoned us here to talk of the weather, or hunting."

Henry grunted. "I wish that was indeed the nature of it." He sat down on a cushioned bench and stretched out his legs, crossing them at the ankle. "Let us say that the weather has changed and so has the manner of the hunting. I want to talk to you about my daughter's marriage. I have been observing her conduct over the past months and she pleases me greatly. But for her sex, she would be entirely fit to rule when I am gone."

Brian felt the heat of the flames on his face. He knew a decision had to be taken, but each time her father rejected a suitor, Brian was relieved to have a few more moments of borrowed time to enjoy her presence.

"But you had us all swear an oath to uphold her as your heir?" Robert's statement was a question. "Is she not then to rule?"

Henry raised one bushy silver eyebrow. "Indeed I did have you swear, but how many will keep their word? I am not so fond a father that I have lost my wits. It seems probable that the queen and I are not going to be blessed with heirs. Matilda bore a child to her first husband, so I know she is capable, and I hope that with a different spouse she will be fruitful. My intention is to raise my grandsons to follow in my footsteps. Should I die before they are grown, they will have their mother as a regent, and she in turn will have the backing of her close family. Robert, I am looking to you to be an adviser and protector to your sister and her children, should it be necessary, and I expect Brian to back you to the hilt."

Brian swallowed. The tension in the chamber was palpable.

"And my sister's husband?" Robert asked, his complexion red with pleasure. "Will he not desire to play his part?"

Henry shook his head. "His part will be to provide her with children and military support. He will not have a say in ruling my lands." He clenched his fist on his knee and his voice developed a harsh note as his gaze shifted between the younger men, calculating, watching narrowly for their response. "I have decided she will marry Geoffrey, heir to Anjou."

For a moment Brian forgot to breathe, then sucked a swift gulp of air over his larynx and turned his shock into a cough.

"But he is only a boy," Robert said with widening eyes. "It's scarcely a moment since he was taking suck!"

"That is the point," Henry replied. "He can be moulded and as such he can grow accustomed to the notion that he will not wear a crown."

Brian steadied himself. "What of your daughter? What will she say about marrying a raw youth, the son of a count, when she was once empress of Germany?"

"She will do as she is told," Henry said curtly. "I am her father and she will obey my will. She will not be disparaged. Geoffrey's sire is to take the throne of Jerusalem through marriage to King Baldwin's daughter, and there is no higher kingdom on earth than to rule over God's own city. When Fulke of Anjou goes to his marriage, then Geoffrey will take the title of count."

"But he will still not be of equal status with her, or her first husband."

Henry sent Brian a dark look. "Were you when you married Maude of Wallingford?"

Brian recoiled from Henry's unsubtle reminder that he had raised him from the dust and that a major part of that raising had been to wed him to Maude when he was a youngster—although he had still been several years older than Geoffrey of Anjou.

"My daughter will understand the necessity," Henry said. "This match will secure my southern border and prevent Anjou from uniting with France. Instead, it will be woven into my sphere. When Matilda bears a son, he will be heir to England, Anjou, and Normandy. This is for the greater good. It is not about Geoffrey of Anjou's status, and, as I have said, his sire is to become king of the holiest city in Christendom."

Robert tugged on his upper lip. Brian could see the advantages in terms of cold strategy, not least that Anjou would no longer be an ally of France. But serving Henry's requirements was going to be hard for Matilda with all her pride.

Robert said casually, "I thought at one time you were considering my cousin Stephen as your successor."

Henry gave him a measuring look. "A prudent man keeps more than one horse in the stable, but there is always one he prefers to ride." He extended his hand and his voice softened. "You are the son I would have chosen to wear England's crown if circumstances had been different. This is the nearest I can give to you."

Robert reddened. "I do not ask for a crown, my father."

"I know that, and it is one of the reasons I have confidence in you to hold fast for your sister and her heirs. There are very few I can trust so wholeheartedly."

Robert's flush darkened. "The Blois faction will not approve of the match. Relations between them and Anjou are unsettled.

If they have to choose between paying homage to France or to Anjou, they may well choose France."

Henry's extended hand closed into a fist and he drew it in against his body. "There is time to work on all of that, but I must lay the foundations now, and for that, I must have Anjou in my camp."

"What of the bishop of Salisbury, sire?" Brian asked. "He took the oath to the empress, but he said it was on condition that everyone be consulted on the matter of her marriage, and that she should not wed outside your lands."

Henry said frostily, "The bishop of Salisbury may be my adviser and chancellor, but he is also my servant and he will know his place. I will deal with him."

"Will you at least summon a council to debate the matter?" Robert asked.

Henry shook his head. "I will open the matter to wider debate when I deem it is time, and not before. Besides, I require a response from Anjou before I act on anything."

Eight

CHINON, ANJOU, APRIL 1127

*G*EOFFREY, SON OF FULKE, COUNT OF ANJOU, STROKED THE soft, mottled breast feathers of the young peregrine falcon on his gauntleted fist. "You summoned me, sire?" His voice was light. It had broken almost a year ago, but still grated like a cracked millstone if pressure was put upon it. He would far rather be out training his bird to the lure, but knew better than to disobey a paternal summons.

His father had been standing before the hearth contemplating the fire, but now he turned. His red hair was dusty at the temples and silver striped his beard, but he was a strong man, still in his full prime. "I have news." He gestured to the empty hawk perch near the window. Geoffrey took the peregrine and settled her there. For a moment she bated on the perch and the sound of her beating wings filled the space where no words fell. Geoffrey soothed her with a gentle forefinger until she settled and in that time he settled himself too. He knew what the news was going to be. Producing a gobbet of venison from the pouch at his belt, he fed it to her. "Are you going to accept King Baldwin's offer for the Princess Melisande?"

His father clasped his hands behind his back. "That depends on whether I can leave Anjou in safe hands."

Geoffrey sauntered over to the sideboard to pour himself a goblet of wine, then adopted a manly pose, one foot thrust out.

His father gave him a frosty look. "It is not the clothes or the stance that make the man, but his words and deeds. I need to know that you are capable of ruling Anjou as an adult when I am gone."

Geoffrey's resentment was tempered by pleasure at the notion of having power, and of being a count. He stood taller and jutted his chin, where the first coppery beard hairs had begun to sprout. "I am a man," he said proudly.

"In word and deed, my son?"

"Yes, sire. You can trust me."

His father's expression did not lighten. He left the fire to pace the room, his tread heavy and deliberate. "I am pleased to hear it, because I have a task for you beyond the wisdom of ruling Anjou." He stopped at the hawk perch, watched the bird preen, then went to Geoffrey and tilted his son's face towards the window to study his features in full light. The youth's hair was a rich, ruddy gold with a healthy gleam like layered feathers. His eyes were sea-blue with a flash of green in their depths and Fulke could see the intelligence in them as well as the arrogance and fire. He was slim with youth and his skin was fine-grained and clear, without the rash of adolescent spots that frequently bedevilled the passage into manhood. A son to be proud of. Whether he was a son to bear the weight of leadership only time would tell. "Can you do this task for me? I wonder..." Fulke stepped back and considered him further. "I have had an offer from the king of England."

"What kind of offer?" Geoffrey eyed him warily and drank his wine.

"A former empress and future queen to wife, and the opportunity to sire on her the next king of England, Duke of Normandy, and Count of Anjou."

Geoffrey stared. The words glittered on the surface of his mind before sinking into it, like small, sharp shards.

"Yes," said his father. "And that is why I asked if you were a man, because it will take one to deal with this."

Geoffrey's stomach lurched and he thought he might be sick. He drank again, forcing himself to swallow rather than retch, and walked away from his father to Pertelot on her perch. He stroked the bird's feathers, soft as the breasts of the village dairy maids. "She is old," he said, his throat working. "She has been the wife of an old man." His nostrils filled with the imagined sour, musty smell of the elderly as he spoke. Of the crypt and the tomb.

"Her husband was younger than me when he died," his father growled. "Are you saying that I am old?"

Geoffrey looked round, a flush mounting his cheeks. "No, sire."

"When you are a grown man, she will yet still be a young woman."

"But she has been used," Geoffrey said, feeling sick disappointment, and still the musty smell was in his nostrils. "She is not a virgin."

"So much the better. She will know what to expect. Henry of England wants to secure his boundaries by allying with us, but he also wants a swift young stag in his daughter's bed. If she is older than you, then time is on your side, and there are always other women. She bore a child to the emperor, so she is not barren, but the infant died. Her husband's seed was not strong enough, but I have faith in yours, and so, it seems, does the king of England."

Geoffrey said nothing because he was still clenched up inside with disappointment. Even if there was prestige at wedding a woman of so great a rank, her age and the fact that she was not a virgin and a shy young girl made him recoil. Frowning, he went to the window and leaned against the embrasure wall. He was not fourteen until August but he had had his first woman last year at harvest time in a barn, under a great, golden moon, and he had repeated the experience many times since then. He had discovered wonderful pleasure in matters of the flesh and already considered himself a skilled practitioner. His father did not know the half of it. He pursed his lips and considered. Perhaps if he used the woman well and got her with child regularly, sooner or later she would die and he could take a second wife more to his taste. And there was nothing to stop him having mistresses alongside a wife. "Will I be a king as you will be a king?" he turned to ask.

"Not while Henry sits upon the throne because he would not countenance such a notion, but he will not be there forever. It is preposterous that a woman should rule on her own. If your sons are under age when Henry goes to his grave, then who can say?" Fulke lifted a warning forefinger. "I hope I have raised you well in the matter of politics. Never let your heart or your loins rule your head. It may be that you will never be a king, but your children will be royal and Normandy will be yours for the taking. Think of our family. You will be grafted into the house of England and Normandy. I will sit on the throne of Jerusalem. Any children borne of my match will be your half-brothers and -sisters. Anjou will be mighty indeed."

Geoffrey felt a frisson. He might not desire the marriage, but the notion of such power filled him up as if he were drinking the sun. What it would be to have an empress at his beck and call. What it would be like to fill her belly with his child.

"So I ask you again," his father said. "Are you man enough in mind and body to do this thing?"

Geoffrey glinted him a look. "Yes, sire," he said. "I am."

Fulke nodded approval. "Good. Then we will go forward with this. I will have my scribe write a reply now."

❖❖❖

Matilda sat in the garden of Winchester Castle, watching a small flock of sparrows flutter and splash in a stone bird bath. Droplets sparkled and flashed to a bustling accompaniment of chirrups and tweets. She remembered walking in the gardens at Speyer with Heinrich. Arm in arm they had planned the beds and talked of nurturing the trees so that they would bear fruit for years to come. Little had either of them known.

She had come outside to enjoy the spring freshness, to finish a piece of sewing in clear daylight, and to think. There had been a strange atmosphere in the castle of late. Something was afoot. Her father was snappy and on edge while Adeliza was full of attentive kindness. Robert was always too busy with other matters to talk to her and she had barely seen Brian at all. It did not take much wit to guess the reason why.

A movement at the garden gate caught her attention and she saw her father dismissing her attendants with his usual air of authority. Putting his head down like a small, charging bull, he made his way towards her bench. He was swinging a staff of polished oak and his expression was benign but purposeful. Matilda straightened up and her heart began to pound.

"Daughter, a fine spring day to be enjoying the garden," he said, joining her. He chuckled at the sight of the bathing sparrows. "They remind me of certain courtiers."

Matilda smiled. "I was thinking of Heinrich just now, and the gardens we planned at Speyer. He always loved this time of year."

He rested the staff across his knees. "Time now, though, to plan a new garden, and turn your thoughts to the future. I have some great news for you and I hope you will be well pleased when I tell you."

"I think I know what this is about." Her voice was steady, concealing her apprehension.

"Do you indeed?" His eyes twinkled, but they were hard too—like bright chips of stone.

"You would not dismiss the servants for a trifling matter."

He gave an amused grunt. "I suppose the planning has been obvious, although few know the details. Time enough to broach it to all once I have told the most important person in this." He took her nearest hand between his and patted it.

"So whom am I to marry?"

He smiled and chose to draw out the moment further. "You will have a fine income and a splendid home; you will not want for anything. You will go to your new husband with all the glory to which a future queen is entitled. You will have a train of wealth and luxury. No one will say I have stinted my daughter."

So the treaty was already drawn up; it had gone that far. Her stomach curdled at this information so casually given. "Where am I going?" she demanded with a bite in her voice. "And who am I to wed—tell me!"

Her father beamed, and she shivered. "You are to marry the son of a man who is about to become the greatest king in Christendom."

She stared at him, blinking, trying to think whom he could mean.

"Fulke of Anjou is to marry Princess Melisande and become king of Jerusalem. When he leaves for Outremer, his son Geoffrey will become Count of Anjou in his place. He is a fine young man and he will make you strong heirs while securing our boundaries and curtailing the ambitions of the French."

The greenery and the flowers blurred around Matilda. "Geoffrey of Anjou," she said in disbelief. "You want me to wed Geoffrey of Anjou?" Nausea surged.

Now the twinkle was gone from his eyes and only the bright hardness remained. "I expect your obedience and your acceptance in good grace."

She swallowed, unable to believe he was demanding this of her. "He is a child." Her lip curled. "You want me to marry a boy, the son of a common count? You would disparage your own daughter?"

His complexion darkened. "Mind your tongue. Angevin support is vital to the security of our lands. Geoffrey of Anjou's youth is an advantage. He will very soon be a man."

"But he is not a man now; he is an untried youth of what—thirteen?"

"Almost fourteen. He will be of an age to consent when you meet to be betrothed."

She pushed herself to her feet. "Do not do this to me."

"It is your duty, daughter." He too stood up; she was tall and they were eye to eye. "You will do as I say. What use are you to me otherwise? I might as well have left you in a German nunnery. There is no better match for you than this. The boy matters little save that he fills your womb and you bear sons to inherit. As soon as that is accomplished, you may live your own life."

Matilda almost gagged. She could not go beyond the notion that she was being told to wed a boy the same age as the spotty youth who emptied the latrine pots; she felt as if her own father had smeared her with ordure. "I was an empress and you bring me down to this," she spat. "I refuse to consent." Stubborn fury surged through her as it always did when she was frightened or cornered. "Small wonder you did not bring it before all the barons!"

"My closest advisers agree it is sound policy," he said through clenched teeth.

"But your closest advisers are expected to think like you and agree with all you say," she spat. "Surely there are better men than a boy like Geoffrey of Anjou if all you want is a stallion? It is foolish to send me away to Anjou and leave the way open for others to make their play for your crown, and I had never marked you for a fool—until now."

"By God, I will not tolerate this insubordination from you," he choked, and lifting the polished staff, he shook it in her face. "I will honour you with this rod across your back unless you obey me, do you hear? I order you to get down on your knees and pray for forgiveness for defying your father and your own liege lord. I brook no such behaviour from my subjects and I will certainly not brook it from my own child, who should be an example to all!"

Tears of shock stung Matilda's eyes, but she refused to cry and continued to face him. "And how will the state be served by marrying me to an Angevin whelp?"

He struck her across the face with the back of his hand, the sound making a loud crack. The sparrows flew off chirping in alarm. "Go!" he snarled. "Get out of my sight and seek God's mercy. We will speak again tomorrow, and by all that is holy you will give me a different answer or suffer the consequences."

Matilda turned without a curtsey, and walked away, her head high. Her cheek was numb from the blow, but she could taste blood where the inside of her mouth had met her teeth. Her mind was in turmoil. As a little girl she had not wanted to go to her marriage in Germany, but she had been too small and powerless to object. Now, she *was* old enough to object, but still powerless, because what sort of power did a woman have except that which was filtered through men?

Entering the cathedral, she felt as if she were a walking effigy of herself because she had turned to stone. How could he? How could he! How was she supposed to bear this? Prostrating herself before the altar, she tried to compose herself, and consider her father's will as a dutiful daughter should, but there was no submission in her, only grief and rage. She was to be married to a boy almost half her age. Anyone with any reason could see that it was ridiculous. Her father said that his inner circle had agreed with him and that must mean her brother Robert and Brian FitzCount at the least. She had been betrayed. She had thought better of them, but plainly they too saw her as a woman to be put in her place. A breeding vessel for the next generation. And this…this boy! His head must be swollen with the power and the prestige such a match would make for him.

Her thoughts turned again to Heinrich as she stared at the candle flames wavering on the altar. If only he were still alive. She would be valued and protected. Heinrich would never have treated her like this. But she had no one. She would have to protect herself, but how? She had nowhere to turn. There was only God left and He seemed to have abandoned her too. If He had been merciful and allowed her baby son to live, she would have had a purpose and a place in life. She could have been the power behind her former husband's throne, instead of a storm-tossed pawn.

On returning to the castle, she retired to her chamber and ordered her ladies to make up her bed, saying she intended to sleep and was not going to dine in the hall.

"Madam, are you unwell?" asked Uli.

"Yes," Matilda snapped. "I am sick to the soul. Leave me, all of you. I will call for you if I have need."

"Madam—"

"Go!" she screamed. She listened to the click of the door latch, and then climbed on to the bed to lie with her back to the wall.

Matilda was roused by the sound of Adeliza talking to her maids, and the waft of savoury food smells. Moments later, the bed curtains parted and Adeliza stood in the space between them with a tray bearing a bowl of broth, steam curling on its surface, a small crusty loaf, and a portion of saffron-glazed chicken. The maids bustled about, lighting candles and closing the shutters against a lavender spring dusk. As Matilda sat up, Adeliza set down the tray on the coffer. She had brought a folded napkin and a small fingerbowl of scented water.

"I am sorry to hear you are unwell," Adeliza said softly.

"Did my father send you?" Matilda snapped.

Adeliza gave her a reproachful look. "Of course not. When I told him I was coming to speak with you and bring you food, he was exasperated with me." She gave Matilda a woman-to-woman look. "He said you didn't deserve to eat and that a spot of starvation would help put your mind in order, but he did not gainsay me when I insisted."

Matilda glared at the beautifully arranged tray. "Indeed, I would rather starve," she hissed. "And I'm not hungry."

"I do not believe that!" Adeliza remonstrated. "You have a good appetite and you will need your strength."

Matilda continued to scowl. She truly did not feel like eating, but it was another way of defying her father since he had not wanted Adeliza to bring her food. "You are right, I suppose I will," she said and reached for the bread.

Adeliza poured wine for both of them and sat down at the bedside. "Ask yourself what good this is doing you. Where will you go from here if you defy your father?"

Matilda tore the bread into small pieces. "You agree with him then." She gave Adeliza a bitter look. "You are taking his part like everyone else?"

Adeliza shook her head. "I am concerned for both of you. I know how difficult this is for you. You have lost a good husband and your position at the heart of the imperial court. But you must look to the future and think about the long term. Here, drink and be consoled."

Matilda thrust away the wine, making it slop over the edge of the cup. "You think I will find consolation in wine? Is that what I should do?" She laughed scornfully. "Drink myself into oblivion?"

Adeliza mopped up the spillage with her napkin and gazed sorrowfully at the red stain. "I think you will find consolation in the Church, and in your children in the fullness of time."

"I may find strength in God, but no comfort, and certainly no consolation from men of God," Matilda spat and felt both triumphant and guilty as her young stepmother recoiled. "As to children—I had no such consolation from my marriage with Heinrich, and neither have you with my father. Why should I put my faith in the solace of being a mother?" Her voice strained and almost cracked. "I bore Heinrich a child, and buried him on the same day."

"I'm sorry." Distress filled Adeliza's gaze. She reached out to Matilda in sympathy, but Matilda drew back. Adeliza lowered her arm and smoothed the bedclothes instead until there was no sign of a crease. She said hesitantly, "Perhaps a man only has so much good seed in his body. A younger one…" Her cheeks reddened. "I am not being disloyal to your first husband or your father, but I say to you as one woman to another that your womb may more easily quicken this time."

Matilda gave Adeliza a long look. "Would you change places with me?"

Adeliza's blush brightened her entire face. "I would think on my duty to those who desired me to make the match. I would think on the good things that might come of it. That I might bear children and grow to love a young husband as he became a man. The difference in age between us would soon close up and matter less." She set her lips. "You learn to live with what you cannot alter and find ways to thank God for what you do have. In truth, what are your alternatives? Your father will not change his mind once it is set. If you refuse, he will make one of his Blois nephews his heir and consign you to a convent.

You came home from Germany rather than become a nun. Would you choose the cloister now?"

Matilda blinked tears from her eyes, furious that she was crying. "Just for once..." she said hoarsely, "just for once, I want him to see *me*, but he never will except as a tool."

"Ah no, never think that!" Adeliza looked shocked. "He is proud of you—very proud, and that is why he is unyielding. He knows your potential and he wants the best for you."

"The best," Matilda gave a caustic laugh. "Geoffrey of Anjou is the best? God save me from the worst!"

"Look," Adeliza said patiently. "I know this betrothal has come as a shock, but it will work out, you will see." She leaned over and kissed Matilda's cheek. "I will leave you to think on it."

"You mean my father will be wondering why you have been gone for so long?"

"The king has other matters to attend to, tonight." Adeliza's voice was careful and her body taut, so that Matilda knew her father must be engaged with one of the many court concubines—probably riding her as viciously as he did his hunting horse when he was in a temper. "There is no more I can say to you. Now you must think on this for yourself."

When Adeliza had gone, Matilda resisted the urge to close the bed curtains again and retreat into her shell. Adeliza's actions had reminded her that she had a position in the world to uphold, and responsibilities. As she ate her supper, she pondered the matter. She was backed into a corner and her only recourse was to agree to the marriage as her father desired. He said it was an honourable thing, and, viewed with a super-ficial eye it was, but deep down, at the core of the matter, she knew it was shameful.

❖❖❖

Brian looked up from the letter he had been writing to his constable at Wallingford and saw Roger, bishop of Salisbury, striding towards him, his jewelled staff cleaving the air. His dark eyes were narrow and his mouth tightly pursed. Brian rose and then knelt to kiss the sapphire episcopal ring on the clenched fist. "Will you take some wine, my lord?" he asked politely.

The bishop gestured and Brian poured him a goblet from the flagon standing on the trestle. He could almost feel Salisbury breathing fire down his neck.

"What do you know of these rumours flying about?" Salisbury snapped, taking the cup from Brian's hand.

Brian's nape prickled. "There are always rumours flying at court, my lord."

"About this proposed marriage of the empress to Geoffrey of Anjou. You are deep in the king's confidence, you must have heard. You are neither a fool nor deaf, and neither am I, even if I am getting on in years." His mouth twisted.

Brian said nothing, but took time refilling his own cup.

"I know he has discussed it with you, and with Gloucester," Salisbury growled. "When is he going to bring it before the rest of us, my lord, or does he think to leave us in ignorance?"

"I am sure I can tell you nothing you do not already know, sire," Brian said woodenly.

"No, but I should not have to find out through back doors and keyholes. If he sends her to this marriage, he will rue the day. There will be unrest and men will rise up against him, mark my words."

Brian arched his brows. "You know this for a fact, my lord bishop? Shall I make a list of which men you think are a threat?" He gestured towards his writing equipment. "Should I put a double guard on Waleran de Meulan?"

Salisbury flushed. "You are insolent. I remember when you were a snivelling squire, wiping better men's backsides. You might think you are clever, but any fool can twist thread into a rope to hang himself. You cannot think this is good policy, surely?"

"You must talk to the king on the matter, sire."

"I expected him to talk to us; that is the entire point." The bishop took a swallow of wine and put his cup on the table. "Since he has not, and since I swore that I would only give my oath to his daughter if we were consulted on her marriage, I will have to consider most carefully." He twitched the sparkling edges of his cloak together. "He is leading us into a quagmire this time. Perhaps I am not the only foolish old man in this palace tonight."

"Sire, I believe that the quagmire already exists and the king is creating paths across it. If we fall in, then is it not our own fault?"

Salisbury gripped his crosier. "I have no intention of falling anywhere!"

Brian wondered if the bishop knew that the water was already over his boots.

"This marriage will shake the foundations of everything that the king has built up, you mark my words. Men will not be ruled by an Angevin stripling, and the match is a slap in the face for his nephews and the house of Blois. I do not know what he is thinking of!" His fist clenched around his staff, the bishop left at the same brisk stride that he had entered.

Heaving a sigh, Brian returned to his work, but his heart was not in it. In part he agreed with the bishop, even while he knew Salisbury was playing to his own agenda. The king was manipulating the situation to keep as many options open as possible, but in so doing, he was creating the potential for great instability. It did not help that Henry's personal attitude was one of invincibility. He had no intention of dying and giving up his power to anyone. He might plan for the future, but he was not envisaging a time when he would not be there to oversee his strategy.

Of Matilda Brian tried not to think at all, except in terms of his duty to her as his liege lady. Anything else would have been unbearable.

❖❖❖

Brian ran the curry comb down Sable's withers a final time and stood back, blotting his forearm on his brow to admire the stallion's coat, which shone in the spring sunlight like a glossy morel cherry. He enjoyed grooming the horse himself on occasion and it was a way of checking that the stable hands had been attending to their duties in the proper manner. Like writing, it also gave him a sense of calm, of setting affairs in order and making good. It was a way of escaping the furore over the matter of Matilda's marriage. She had kept to her chambers ever since being told about the proposed match with Anjou, while her father stamped about in a rage. Today he had ordered the baggage made ready for the betrothal journey. There had been strong protests at court because the wider circle of advisory prelates and barons had not been consulted over the marriage plans, but Henry had overridden all objections in a strident voice, his face like thunder, and no one had been brave enough to stand their ground and challenge him.

Brian ordered a groom to fetch Sable's tack. Several new horses were expected in the stables and lackeys were mucking out the stalls and laying fresh straw. Gilbert, the king's senior marshal, was directing operations and his eldest son had joined in with the grooms to get the job done. Brian had to leap out of the way as a large lump of dung shot out of the stable door, narrowly missing him. "Have a care," he snapped.

The son looked over his shoulder and gave an ironic salute. Brian compressed his lips and thought that John FitzGilbert would bear watching. Too sharp for his own good, that one.

The groom returned with Sable's harness, and the empress walked into the stable yard, accompanied by her ladies and her knight, Drogo. She was dressed for riding and her own groom had gone to fetch her palfrey. "Domina," Brian said, and swept her a deep bow.

She replied with an almost impatient gesture. "If you are going riding too, you might as well escort me."

Brian opened his mouth to say that he had other business, but the words stuck in his throat, and instead, he found himself bowing again and saying, "As you wish, domina."

"As I wish?" She gave him a bitter look. "I should thank God for small mercies that I am so indulged."

They left the castle and the town behind them, and took a track that led through fields and woods carpeted with celandines and violets. Brian felt the beauty of the day twist like a knife inside him. He rode and said nothing, because there was too much to say and he did not trust himself to speak.

At length, it was Matilda who broke the taut silence. "When I return from this ride, I am going to tell my father that I will accept this marriage with Anjou."

He looked straight ahead and said stiffly, "That is a wise decision, domina."

She shook her head. "I make it because I have no choice. I make it because if I refuse, the House of Anjou will become our enemy and unite with France and Flanders. I know why my father considers it a wise and prudent move." She nudged her mare closer to Sable and fixed Brian with a steady look. "But tell me, my lord, did you think of all the consequences when you discussed the matter with him in private council?"

Shadows like delicate bruises were smudged beneath her eyes and Brian had to glance away. "Yes, domina, I did…but your father would not be gainsaid, and in truth, his reasons are sound."

"And you cannot look at me, my lord."

"What would you have me do?" Now he did meet her stare and forced himself not to flinch from her scrutiny. "I am your father's liege man first, even while I honour his daughter."

"Honour." She exhaled down her nose. "I wonder at the substance with which we gild that word."

"When the time comes, I will not fail you; I swear on my own life."

"And who will call that time, my lord—you, or I? And who will decide if you have or have not failed?"

They rode in silence again, and Brian kept his distance because he knew that if he let her in, he would fall apart under the truth of her stare and he could not allow that to happen. She was right. Honour was both a gilded fancy and a stinking corpse, and she had not been the one to murder it in the name of strategy.

Nine

ROUEN, SUMMER 1127

MATILDA DROPPED A CURTSEY TO HER FUTURE HUSBAND while rebellion surged through every fibre of her being, warring with her duty to her father, to Normandy, and to England.

Geoffrey of Anjou was a truly beautiful youth, with smooth alabaster skin, hair of warm apricot-gold, and eyes the colour of clear sea shallows. He had a prominent Adam's apple, a voice that had scarcely broken, and a supercilious curl to his top lip that made her loathe him. Although he bowed to her deferentially, she could tell he did not mean it. This betrothal was a travesty, a golden cloak laid over a corpse. How in the name of Saint James was she going to lie in a marriage bed with him? As he slipped a great sapphire ring on to her finger, she was aware of her father smiling with satisfaction, and felt sick. Beside him, Adeliza smiled too, her face bright with the pleasure that Matilda was obeying her father's wishes.

The marriage was not to take place until Geoffrey was made Count of Anjou. First, today came the vow of consent, pinning her down while the bars of her cage were constructed around her.

Geoffrey escorted her to the formal feast that had been prepared in the great hall of the palace of Rouen. He extended his arm for her to set her palm to his sleeve and performed the formal bows and flourishes under the watchful gaze of her father and his. His swagger as he walked and the conceit in his eyes made her want to swipe him round the ear as she would a disrespectful page boy. She could think of nothing to say to him because they had nothing in common. She neither knew nor cared about his likes and dislikes, for whatever they were, none would match hers. The way he puffed out his chest and smiled with bravado at his cronies reminded her of a young cockerel that hadn't developed its full plumage, yet still wanted to strut on the dung heap. Was she supposed to be impressed by this?

She had to share dishes with him as they dined. He did not ask what she wanted to eat, but, showing off, displayed that he could deal with the food neatly and precisely. He carved meat from a bone with an arrogant flourish of his jewelled sleeve. He dissected a pigeon with a delicacy that was intimate and almost erotic and made Matilda feel ill as she saw the smirk on his lips. This posturing, supercilious boy was to be her consort and the father of her children?

Between courses, as Geoffrey went off with a comrade to empty his bladder, Adeliza took the opportunity to squeeze Matilda's hand. "It's not so bad," she whispered with an encouraging smile. "He is truly handsome and much older than his years, do you not think?"

Matilda could feel Adeliza willing her to return the smile and agree, wanting everything to be right. But how could it be, when she had known such a different world of power, dignity, and cherished deference where her opinions and goodwill were actively sought? She could already tell she would receive no such consideration from Geoffrey of Anjou. "I do not know," she said, "but he makes me feel much older than mine."

❖ ❖ ❖

Henry of Blois, abbot of Glastonbury, folded his robes neatly over his lap and sat down on the hearth bench to regard his brothers Stephen and Theobald. Most of Rouen slept under a clear, dark sky salted with stars, but here at Stephen's lodging, candles still burned in the sconces and a recently replenished jug of wine stood on the table. Henry poured himself a cup and drank, careful not to soil his full moustache and beard. "The deed is done," he said. "Against all advice our uncle has betrothed his daughter to the Angevin whelp."

Stephen refreshed his own cup. "That is up to him." He shifted in his chair to ease his broad frame and powerful thighs.

"You do not really believe that, do you?" Henry looked Stephen up and down. Sometimes his brother irritated him beyond belief. "Do you really want to see a woman on the throne? Are we all to become petticoat-followers?"

Stephen flushed. "It won't come to that. Matilda is just another pawn for him to move around on his chessboard. You know what he's like."

"But if it does happen, the last thing we want is Angevin influence spinning the policies. We would be finished. Better that one of us rules than a woman who has lived in Germany all of her life and is about to take a puppy for a husband."

"There is le Clito too," Theobald spoke up.

Henry faced his eldest brother, who was Count of Blois and head of the family in name, although Henry's policies and opinions were usually the ones that held sway. "He is our common enemy for the moment, I agree." He leaned forwards, the light shining on his silk sleeve. "But both of you have a claim to England and Normandy as the king's nephews. Stephen is married into the English royal house and we know one of our uncle's schemes is to bring him close to the throne. We must make sure that it stays the foremost plan despite the vows everyone has been forced to make." He fixed his gaze on Stephen. "We have to be ready with a strategy should the king die."

A look of alarm crossed Stephen's face and he signed his breast with the cross. "I wish him continued longevity."

Theobald cleared his throat. "I will not be a party to anything that threatens our uncle's well-being."

Henry mentally rolled his eyes. Sometimes he thought their wits were made of fleece. "Was I advocating any such thing? I too wish him continued long life, but even if our cousin Matilda bears a son nine months from her marriage, the king will have to stay alive and in sound mind until that son is fit to rule, and she is not even wed yet. It does not take a fool to tally up the years. The same goes for a son of his blood born of the queen." He spread his hands in an open gesture. "I am not asking you to contemplate treason, but we must plan ahead, just like a farmer husbanding his supplies for the winter. If we want to see our family prosper, we must work to ensure it happens. Do you really want to see Robert of Gloucester rule by proxy when one of you could wear a crown? Because that is what will happen if Matilda becomes queen. Robert will be the true power behind the throne."

As Henry had known he would, Stephen recoiled. There was little love lost between himself and Gloucester. Since boyhood they had been rivals over everything, from games of chess, to swordplay, to contesting for the king's attention and approval. The king had always shown them both favour and affection, but had played one off against the other. Stephen was malleable, Henry thought; furthermore he was his brother and his own best chance to become the power behind the throne—because every ruler needed a chief minister and every reign could be manipulated.

"What shall we do?" Stephen asked.

Henry touched the jewels on his sleeve, exploring with his fingertips the cold gemstones. "Find men who are reliable, utterly discreet, and who see matters the same way that we do, and make of them allies so that they will support us when the time comes. You have charm, brother, and prowess. Men like you. Use it to win them to your side."

"And those who won't be won over?"

Henry shrugged. "If we are sufficiently thorough, they will be too few to matter." He raised a warning forefinger. "But let us not act rashly in this. We must prepare the ground, and that will take time and consideration."

Ten

ROUEN, JUNE 1128

*M*ATILDA CLOSED HER EYES AND TOOK A DEEP BREATH, drawing in the smell of incense. Usually its holy scent and association with ritual, ceremony, and royalty would have soothed her, but not today. She had been at her prayers all morning, but it made no difference to her feelings. Her gown of deep blue silk was beaded with gold jetons and jewelled with sapphires, garnets, and pearls. A veil of cloth of gold, bound in place by a coronet from her German treasure, covered her hair.

"You are the most beautiful bride I have ever seen," Adeliza said as she helped Matilda to don her cloak, gleaming with the pelts of a hundred ermine.

"What does it matter, save that I fulfil my obligation and do as my father bids?" Matilda said tonelessly.

Adeliza frowned. "I thought you were reconciled to the marriage?"

"I know my duty, if that is what you mean, but I will never be reconciled, and that is the truth of it."

Adeliza's brow remained furrowed. "Everyone is proud of you. I know you have the strength to make a success of this match." Her tone was bright with reassurance. "Geoffrey looked so handsome at his knighting. Your father says he is mature for his years and he is pleased with him."

Matilda said nothing. Her betrothed and his entourage had been in Rouen all week for the marriage celebrations. Geoffrey and several of his companions had received the accolade of knighthood from her father in a grand formal ceremony. Geoffrey had been presented with a sword and a shield with a lapis-blue background, decorated with lioncels in gold leaf. He had acquitted himself well in displays of horsemanship and feats of arms, and had spent time closeted with her father. With her, Geoffrey had spent no time at all beyond formal public requirement, which had filled her with a combination of resentment and relief.

Her father had heaped upon her jewels and clothes, horses, hawks, and chests full of silver and treasure. She could have anything material from him for the asking, but all the wealth in the world could not compensate for what he was making her do. She knew he was not assuaging his guilt by such largesse, because as far as he was concerned he had nothing to be guilty about. The gifts were rather to reward her for her compliance and to express his pleasure in the match, whilst displaying his munificence to the world.

Over the next four days, the wedding party would travel the 120 miles to Le Mans, where the wedding itself was to take place in the great cathedral there before the entire nobility of Anjou.

"Would you take my place?" she asked Adeliza.

"If it were my destiny, yes," Adeliza said. "You must give this match a chance. Set a smile on your face and your heart will lighten."

Matilda curled her lip. "It would be a lie."

"It would be your duty." Adeliza's voice sharpened. "Do you think my sweetness is all there is to me? Do you know how hard it is sometimes? But I smile and go forward because I am a queen and it is my God-given role to help and support your father. When I see my life thus, it becomes a reward to serve and not something onerous."

Matilda swallowed and did not answer, because she knew she would never be able to reconcile herself to being married to this preening boy when she had once been wed to a real man of dignity and standing. Adeliza did not understand. Matilda so missed the life she had had in Germany. Here, everyone seemed to be against her, or else to think that this marriage was a fine thing and her reluctance but the contrariness of a silly, fickle woman who should better know her place. Those who frowned on the match were her father's enemies, or had their own reasons and agendas. The only person she could rely on was herself, and that made her feel terribly lonely.

Adeliza kissed her. "I must go and put on my own cloak," she said, "and see that all is in order. But for your own good, consider what I have said."

❖❖❖

"I am worried about Matilda," Adeliza said as she knelt to remove Henry's shoes and set them to one side on the sheepskin rug beside the bed. It was late and they had retired to their chamber within the fortress at Brionne where the wedding party was spending the night on its journey to Le Mans.

Henry dismissed her concern with a brusque gesture. "She is my daughter and she knows what is expected of her, and so does the young Angevin sprig." He gave an amused grunt. "He is already experienced. Not that he told me himself, and I don't listen to the bragging of those boys around him, but my sources tell me he's no virgin. He knows what to do and, God willing, he will get her with child on their wedding night."

Adeliza slowly began to rub his feet. "I cannot help but be concerned. It is a great step for her and I love her dearly." She gave him a tight little smile. "I will miss her, not only as a daughter, but as a friend."

"Matilda will return for visits, and you can write to each other," he said gruffly. "I know what gossips you women are, but you have the other ladies of the court for company, and your duties and business as my queen. There is more than enough to keep you occupied."

Adeliza smiled up at him, but she had to work hard to keep the sadness from her eyes. Books and leper hospitals, charities and little charters. She had no wish to rule and dominate the world of men, but she did desperately want to fulfil her role as a queen and a woman. Each time he lay with her, each month when she bled, served to point up her feeling of failure and inadequacy. "And I have you, my lord, also."

Henry drew her up to him and kissed her. "I admit here, if nowhere else, that I will miss her too, but I need her to make this match for me. Come, console me. It has been a while."

Adeliza yielded to him with wifely obedience. These days they seldom bedded together. Henry was still vigorous with the court concubines, but as she had continued to have her flux each month, he had ceased to visit her, as if he saw no point. She knew he preferred his women blowsy and buxom, whereas she was slender and fine-boned with barely a curve. Although she was always welcoming and compliant when he did come to her, the act itself was painful, if seldom prolonged. Henry was always swift to business like a ram in the field.

When he had finished and rolled off her, Adeliza wondered if this was what it would be like for Matilda and Geoffrey. As she straightened her garments, she remembered what she had said to Matilda about the difference between a reward and an onerous duty, and for a moment tears sparkled dangerously close to the surface.

❖ ❖ ❖

Matilda looked down at her left hand, bare except for the thin circle of gold Geoffrey had placed on her finger that morning in the cathedral of Saint-Julien at Le Mans. The magnificence of the church had penetrated the wall she had built around herself, and opened her up to feelings of wonder as she heard mass before the altar with her boy-husband at her side. Here was the majesty and essence of God. She had been awed by the greatness, and sickened too that she should be worshipping Him here, having taken vows to obey and cherish her husband. It was bearing false witness before one's maker. Contrasting it with her wedding in Speyer, she felt soiled.

Throughout the day, she had been unable to look at Geoffrey, but had felt his eyes constantly on her. How she was going to bear his hands on her body tonight, she did not know. Her only hope was in not conceiving, because then the marriage could be annulled. Her laundry maid, Osa, had told her the necessary steps to take to avoid conception.

The women had brought her to the great chamber where the marriage was to be consummated. Matilda gazed at the fine, big bed with its clean linen sheets and embroidered covers, and at the painted chests and rich brocade hangings. Her women had earlier set out her ivory combs, her pots of unguents, and her jewel and trinket boxes. Perfumed smoke twirled from a small brazier burning frankincense and bark, but she only felt nause-ated. Holy and magnificent surroundings only served to point up the ugliness of what was happening to her.

Adeliza was nodding with approval as she looked round. "You can make yourself a very pleasant chamber here," she said. "All will be well."

"So you keep saying," Matilda said shortly. "Are you trying to convince yourself too?"

Adeliza recoiled for an instant but swiftly rallied. "You must give your husband a chance at least. Come now. Drink some of this hot wine and let me help you disrobe."

Matilda suffered Adeliza's ministrations with a clenched jaw. She wanted to strike her away but knew it would be unfair to vent her anger on her stepmother, who was as powerless as she was. Neither of them had a choice, but Adeliza was the better at adapting.

Matilda stared at the wall as the women removed her red silk wedding gown and gold belt; the gilded slippers and golden hose with brocaded garter ties edged with pearls; her crown of golden flowers; her veil; the ribbons wound through her braids. All of it was carefully hung up or put away, leaving her standing barefoot in a plain chemise with simple ties at the throat. Like a virgin, she thought as the women combed down her hair until it lay like a dark-brown waterfall to her hips. A woman stripped of her power, no longer an empress, but a sacrifice. "I need to visit the latrine," she told the assembled women and crossed the room to the small dark chamber set in the thickness of the wall. Hidden in there by Osa, under the piles of moss and squares of rag for wiping purposes, was a small vial of vinegar. Biting her lip, Matilda took a piece of moss, tipped the vinegar over it, and, having pulled up her chemise, squatted and inserted the swab as high up into her female passage as she could, just as Osa had told her to do. It would prevent conception, the laundress said. There was always a danger that the man might find out, but it had a reasonable degree of success if a woman wanted to avoid pregnancy—and was certainly better than putting parsley leaves under his pillow or wearing a charm of weasel's testicles around one's neck.

Task accomplished, Matilda returned to the women. She could smell vinegar on her fingers and went to splash her hands in the laver, and then anointed her wrists with rose-scented unguent.

"Are you all right?" Adeliza eyed her with concern.

"Yes." Matilda nodded stiffly. Behind her, the women fussed with the bed, freeing the hangings from their hooks and turning down the covers. Matilda climbed between the sheets, pulled her chemise straight, and accepted a cup of wine from Adeliza. Was it better to be drunk or sober? she wondered.

The groom arrived in a rowdy jostle of companions and Matilda began to feel queasy. Geoffrey wore a plain white shirt, the equivalent of her chemise, and was still dressed in his hose and braies with a fur-lined cloak clasped across his breast. Matilda prayed for him not to remove his clothes because she didn't want to see his narrow white boy's body.

Geoffrey's companions were laughing uproariously and unsteady on their feet. Two of them swung each other around in an impromptu dance, legs flicking, heel and toe. Matilda clenched her jaw, determined to be regal in the face of this adolescent buffoonery. One young man removed the crown of flowers from his head and, dancing over to the bed, set it slantwise on her dark hair. She hesitated, torn between adjusting it to stay, or dragging it off and hurling it across the room. Adeliza leaned to take it from her, the smile on her face now set like stone.

"This is a circus!" Matilda hissed at her. "Are you still going to tell me that it will be all right?"

"All weddings have moments like this," Adeliza said, a catch in her voice. "You must trust in God. Your husband is sober and that is a good thing."

Matilda would rather he were dead drunk on the floor.

Her father arrived, his steps unsteady because, unlike his son-in-law, he had imbibed liberally. Geoffrey's father swayed with him, and the bishop of Le Mans, all three cloaked in an air of well-fed and smug bonhomie. Geoffrey was manhandled to the bed by his cronies and bundled in beside Matilda. He pushed away the more inebriated of his knights with irritation. The guests gathered in a circle round the bed to watch the bishop bless the couple and wish them fruitfulness. Matilda thought of the moss sponge blocking the opening to her womb and felt triumph tinged with nausea. It was a sin, a terrible sin, but if it won her an annulment, it was a price worth paying.

The blessing performed, the guests left the room, her father and Fulke of Anjou clasping shoulders and laughing like old friends. Adeliza went out with a parting glance of encouragement for Matilda, the smile still patched on to her face. Some of Geoffrey's friends lingered, too drunk to be aware of etiquette. Geoffrey left the bed, manhandled them out, and then slammed and bolted the door, ramming home the bar with force. He returned and stood at the foot of the bed and gazed at Matilda. She took a swallow of wine and for the first time that day, studied him properly.

His hair fell over his brow in a red-gold tumble; a slender youth whose beard was little more than fluff, and whose smooth skin had yet to coarsen with stubble. Yet he had a shine about him and the looks of a fallen angel. A shiver ran through her. She wondered how much of his foolishness just now was bravado in the face of danger, and she did indeed have it within her to be as dangerous as a lioness stalking her prey.

His fine red brows drew together in a scowl. Squaring his shoulders, he came to her side of the bed. He took the cup from her and set it decisively to one side. Then he threw back the covers and pulled her to her feet. "Now," he said, breathing swiftly, "let me see what I have given my oath for." He had grown since their betrothal and was taller than her, and his grip was hard and confident. Through her revulsion, Matilda felt a frisson of desire. That he had taken the lead and pulled her out of the bed had surprised and unbalanced her; she had expected him to fumble when the moment came, and be gauche and indecisive. These were not the actions of a boy, but of a man accustomed to getting his own way.

Geoffrey unfastened the ties of her chemise and pulled the garment over her head. He looked her up and down with leisurely thoroughness before reaching out to fondle her breasts. Her nipples had stiffened in the cold and his hand was soft-skinned but firm with intent. "Your father wants a young stallion to prove his worth at stud," he said huskily. "I thought you'd be a hag, but you're not. It's going to be a pleasure to do my duty." His hand trailed down her body to her pubic hair. "I am adept at hunting through forests and finding hidden streams."

Matilda swallowed. She wanted to strike him aside, and at the same time she was aroused. Whatever he was or was not, this boy-husband of hers had a powerful physical charisma.

"I am going to get you with child. That's what you want, isn't it? That's what you and your father need?"

She gave him an icy stare. "Do what you must and let us be finished."

He pushed her back against the wall and began kissing her, and she felt his hardness through the fine linen of his braies, and in that too he was most definitely a man. Plainly he was already experienced, because he was not awkward. She had thought to be able to disconnect from the event, but found herself responding and becoming involved, and while it was distasteful, there was pleasure too. She closed her eyes and made her mind a blank. She would think about it all later. His body was sinuous and smooth, but it was masculine too. The youth. The man. Desire wound through her veins like a drug. He pressed her against the wall, his hips grinding, and then he swung her round and pushed her on to the bed. His mouth covered hers and his lips and tongue were fierce. He dragged off his shirt and pulled down his hose and braies, impatient now. Matilda kept her eyes shut because she did not want to see that part of him.

Geoffrey was swiftly inside her, but there was no pain because her body was moist and ready. He had indeed found the hidden stream. He held himself over her and Matilda clenched her fists as he thrust back and forth. He took her parted legs and rested them on his shoulders and heaved into her, and she felt a growing pressure deep within her loins. She wanted him to finish and let her escape, and at the same time she needed him to continue and throw her off the edge of the precipice into oblivion. But Geoffrey ceased moving and lifted his chest and shoulders off the bed and suspended her there for a long, long moment. Their eyes met and held and it was like enemies facing each other on a battlefield. And then he let go with a curse of pleasure and a final thrust while Matilda stiffened as a tide of sensation rippled over her, wave upon wave of surge and release.

Geoffrey withdrew from her and rolled over on to his back. "For all that you look at me as if you hate me, you didn't hate me then, did you?" he smirked, pillowing his arms behind his head, revealing tufts of ruddy-gold hair. "In fact I think you liked it a lot."

Matilda said nothing. There was a bitter taste at the back of her throat.

"He was an older man, your first husband," Geoffrey continued. "I intend to be more vigorous in your bed than he was."

"You know nothing of my first husband," she said, feeling sick. "He was a great man." She puts emphasis on the final two words.

"I do know that he is dead." He gave her a sidelong glance from his beautiful eyes. "You are mine now. I know you think of me as a nothing and I know your father thinks of me as little more than a strutting Angevin cockerel to tread his hen, but I am Count of Anjou and my father is to be the king of Jerusalem—and I have time to build my own empires."

"But you will never be a king, even when I become Queen," Matilda retorted. "And you will never be an emperor either."

Geoffrey rolled on to his stomach and faced her. "It matters little in the scheme of things whether I have gold at my brow or not, although I see the store you set by it, madam. What matters is power. You may call yourself an empress and one day you may be a queen, but here, in this household, I am your lord and master, and I command your obedience. If I order you to kneel at my feet, then you kneel."

Revulsion surged through her. "And you would think yourself all powerful for such a petty ability...my lord?"

He clenched his fist and then grazed it gently against her jaw in a caress that nevertheless threatened violence. "Yes," he said. "I would."

Eleven

ROUEN, AUGUST 1128

WILL D'ALBINI WAS ENJOYING HIMSELF. A SELECT NUMBER OF courtiers had joined the king in his private chamber for a few hours of socialising and mirth. Will always enjoyed these occasions and took a childlike delight in the singing and stories. He had a good ear for a tune and as well as possessing a rich singing voice, he could play most instruments, both the stringed and the woodwind, and his talents were always in demand.

The king was nodding his head and tapping his feet as Adeliza told a story to the gathered audience, including several children from the royal household. "Far across the sea there was a lady who lived in a tall tower and many knights sought her hand in marriage…" Adeliza made the motion of the waves with undulations of her hands and forearms, and then stretched up to describe a tall tower. Will avidly watched her graceful movements. Her gauzy veil was neatly held in place with small gold pins, and two of ivory shape like little mice. Her eyes shone like a silky sea on an autumn morning. A small pain tugged at Will's heart, but it was a good pain. The queen was so far above him that he could dream from a distance and not be in danger. The night sky was beautiful, but you couldn't touch it.

Since the empress had gone to her marriage, everything had settled into its normal routine. There were still some rough edges as folk waited for news that she was with child, but it was only two months since the wedding, and too soon to know. Will had never been comfortable in the empress's presence. She gave him the impression of being as cold and hard as a beautiful gemstone—and a little mannish in her attitudes. He admired her, but he did not particularly like her.

"All of the knights brought the lady rich and costly gifts, silk and fur, perfumes and jewels and gold." Adeliza's fingers wove the story, and as she raised her arms, the gold thread in her sleeves twinkled. William smiled to see the children's rapt faces. Innocence was a fine thing to possess and so easily lost. Adeliza still had that air of untouched purity despite having being wed to a political merchant and cynic like Henry for seven years.

Henry chuckled as Adeliza pirouetted, waved her arms, and pretended to be a storm at sea as the hero of the tale battled his way towards his destiny with the lady. Adeliza made all the children sit in a row and pretend to be oarsmen on the ship. "You too, Will," she said, beckoning briskly, laughter in her face. "Come out of your corner and take the steerboard!"

There was no escape. Grinning, flushed with embarrassment, Will joined the youngsters and took up his appointed role. It would have been awkward to refuse and, anyway, he liked children and once he began performing, he forgot himself in the drama. Taking the part of steersman to heart, he shouted orders to the rest of the "crew," improvising as they battled storms and sea monsters, until the audience was helpless with laughter.

Once the boat had been rowed safely to shore, Adeliza led the applause and allowed William to stand and flourish a bow, his dark curls tumbling over his face. Adeliza paused to refresh her voice with a cup of wine, and one of Henry's bastard sons, Reginald, took up the tale.

Adeliza set her arm lightly on Will's. "Who would have thought what a fine and trusty sailor you are!" she said with a gentle laugh.

He cleared his throat. "Madam, I do my best on stormy seas," he answered gruffly.

"I knew you would win through." She squeezed his arm to end the moment. An instant later, her smile faded as a mud-spattered messenger was ushered into Henry's presence by Gilbert the marshal. As he drew closer, the stink of sweaty man and hot horse filled the air with a pungent note of urgency. The story stopped in its tracks, and everyone stared as the messenger knelt by the king's chair. The hair rose on the back of Will's neck.

The man knelt and extended a sealed letter to Henry. "Sire, I bring tidings from Flanders. William le Clito is dead."

Henry took the letter and stared at it. "Speak on," he said.

"Sire, he was injured in the hand during a skirmish with a foot soldier while besieging Aalst. The wound festered and he died of a fever; there is nothing more to say."

Adeliza bowed her head. "God rest his soul."

Henry slit the seal on the letter, his expression sombre, despite the fact that William le Clito had been such a thorn in his side. "He was my nephew," he said. "This grieves me deeply. I will have masses said for his soul."

Adeliza held out her hand to Henry. "Sire, his father should be told."

Will admired her courage in speaking out. She was treading dangerous ground by mentioning Henry's older brother Robert, who had been a prisoner for more than twenty years at Henry's behest and was currently locked up in Cardiff Castle.

"I commend your gentle heart." Henry sent Adeliza a flat look. "I will write to him." He flicked his hand at the messenger. "Find a fresh horse and be ready to ride."

"Sire." The messenger bowed from the chamber.

Henry's eyes narrowed thoughtfully. "A new count of Flanders will have to be chosen now."

"What happens next in the story?" an impatient little boy piped up from among the group of children, and was hastily shushed by his nurse.

Henry turned to look at him. "I have not decided yet," he said. "That is a tale for another day."

Twelve

*G*EOFFREY WAS DRUNK AGAIN. MATILDA CLENCHED HER FISTS as she listened to him roistering with his companions in the antechamber. She tried to ignore him and to keep her life separate from his, but he refused to leave her in peace. He was always swaggering about, showing her up, belittling her in front of his cronies. Recently his behaviour had deteriorated as she remained barren despite his taking her every day that she wasn't menstruating or that wasn't banned by the Church. He would hit her and bellow when she tried to discuss the business of ruling with him. With his father now king of Jerusalem, Geoffrey was count of Anjou and had no intention of sharing his power with a wife, especially one who saw fit to argue with him and contradict him.

He staggered into the chamber, a wine cup sloshing in his hand, his cheeks flushed, and his eyes glazed. He had grown again in the year since their marriage and broadened out. The bones of his face were more prominent and masculine, but the expression cladding them was still that of a petulant adolescent. "You will curtsey to me because I am your lord and husband," he slurred at her when she did not rise from her seat in the window embrasure.

Rage and defiance welled up within her. "You are a foolish

boy," she retorted with contempt, "and I do not bow my head to infants."

"And you, madam, are a hag too old for child-bearing," he sneered. "Or perhaps you do not quicken because your mannish attitudes prevent you from being a full woman. And I am saddled with this travesty!"

"No more of an abomination than me being made to wed an idiot who is as far beneath me as a pile of dung under the sky," she flashed back.

Geoffrey lurched over to her and struck her back-handed across the face. Matilda welcomed the sting of the blow as it spread across her cheek, because it confirmed her feelings about him. "You unman yourself," she scorned him. "You may be my husband, but you will never be my lord and master and you will never amount to anything more than a scrawny cockerel on top of your little midden heap! I shall never yield to you, never!"

"By Christ, you bitch, you will!" He struck her again and she leaped to her feet and struck him back with the full force of all her misery and frustration. The sound of the blow was a sharp crack. The edge of one of her rings caught the corner of his eye. He gasped and recoiled, cupping his face, and then lowered his hand and looked at the blood on his fingers.

"By God, you have gone too far!" He seized her arm and began to beat her with his fists, pummelling into her with all of his own young man's rage, made the more potent for his being drunk. At first she fought back, kicking him, raking him with her nails, drawing blood, but he was stronger and faster. He knew where to land his blows to make them count and he felled her, and then kicked her in the ribs as she lay on the floor until she could barely breathe and the world closed into red darkness around her. She was barely aware of him dragging her to the bed. The awful thought blossomed that he was going to rape her in front of his cronies. His wine-sodden breath sobbed in and out of his lungs as he unfastened his belt and proceeded to tie her hands around the foot of the bed. "You will learn to do as you are told!" he panted. With a final kick to her ribs, he strode to the door and flung it wide so that all the court could see her. "No one is to help her or touch her or talk to her!" he snarled. "Do you hear? No one, or they shall be dealt the same treatment!" He shoved his way through them, cuffing at the blood trickling down his face. People made way for him, some with expressions of deep shock on their faces, but many nodding with approval. An unruly wife ought to be put in her place, no matter her rank.

Matilda lay amid the rushes. She could feel blood dribbling from her cut lip. One eye was swelling shut and each breath she drew was agony. She did not weep. It would have hurt too much to cry and she was too shocked to do so even had she wanted.

Lying on the floor, listening to the babble of noise beyond the open door, a part of her wished to die from the shame and humiliation, but anger kept her afloat. She could hear the sniggers from some of Geoffrey's cronies, but knew there would be others looking upon this moment with disgust. A man was entitled to beat his wife if she transgressed, but, in the end, one who went too far only succeeded in emasculating himself.

Matilda concentrated on drawing one short breath after another. She didn't know which part of her hurt the most: her face, her ribs, or her arms. The belt with which he had tied her chafed her wrists and her hands tingled and then grew numb. She vowed that she would survive. No matter what Geoffrey did to her, he would not win. The voices in the antechamber faded and silence descended. One of the castle mousers padded into the room and, sitting down near the hearth, began to wash itself thoroughly with a rough pink tongue. She watched its sinuous contortions and wondered if she would ever be able to move her own body so much as an inch again.

❖❖❖

Geoffrey returned several hours later, by which time she had stiffened and to move at all was agony. He swaggered over to the trestle, poured himself more wine, and, coming to the foot of the bed, crouched down and touched the swollen side of her face. "Now," he said softly, "yield to me and be a good wife and we will say no more of this." He propped her up against the edge of the bed and she could not prevent herself from crying out. Geoffrey studied her and bit his lip. "What am I going to do with you?" he asked, his tone reasonable, full of sorrow. "All I want is a little deference and respect, and you turn on me like a madwoman."

She said nothing. She was not the one who was mad, and she was not the one who was disrespectful.

Without untying her he offered her a drink from the cup to show that he was in control. Matilda took a mouthful, rinsed it round her cut, swollen gums, and then, drawing in a breath that tore through her chest like a knife, spat the wine full into his face. "I would rather die first!" she gasped.

Geoffrey wiped wine from his dripping, nail-striped face, and his eyes flashed green in their depths. "Be careful what you wish for, wife, because I might just grant it!"

"Do it!" she croaked. "Do it and may your soul be damned!"

Abruptly he threw the cup aside and drawing his knife from its sheath, thumbed the blade and looked for the fear in her eyes, but found only defiant rage, and beyond that, a strange blankness that froze his marrow. "You are not a proper wife," he said hoarsely. "You have reneged on all of your wedding vows and I will stand no more. Go from here back to your father. I repudiate you. You sicken me." Stooping again, he slit the belt binding her wrists. Matilda gave an involuntary moan.

"I will see to it that your baggage is packed." His voice was cold. "I want you gone when I return from hunting."

He turned on his heel and strode out. In the antechamber she heard him whistling to his favourite dog and speaking to it with cheerful affection as if he were the kindest person on earth.

Matilda swallowed her nausea, knowing that if she did vomit her diaphragm would shatter. Using the edge of the bed, she levered herself to her feet, hardly able to stand because of the pain in her ribs. "I will never give in to him," she choked. "Never." The word came from a distance and meant everything and nothing.

Her women entered the room, casting frightened glances over their shoulders. When Uli took her arm, Matilda suppressed a cry.

"Come, madam, we'll put you to bed and send for a physician." Uli waved frantically at another maid to close the door

Matilda shook her head. "No," she said in a laboured voice. "He says he wants me gone, and I will do as he bids me. I will not stay here."

"But, madam, you are in no state to go anywhere!" Uli's soft brown gaze widened in concern.

"Even so, that is my order." Matilda struggled to talk and breathe. "Pack my chests. Do it now. My husband has ordained that I leave him and for once I am inclined to obey."

Uli looked aghast. "But, my lady, you are in no fit state to ride!"

"Saddle up the white ambler," Matilda gasped. "His pace is smooth..." She paused to gather herself. "Set fleeces upon and around the saddle. Tell the grooms..." Each breath was agony. She curled her spine and hunched herself protectively. Uli coaxed her to sit on the bed and sent a page running to find Drogo.

He was absent in the town and by the time he arrived, Matilda's women had already packed half of her chests.

"Dear Christ!" His expression filled with horror.

"I am leaving," Matilda told him weakly. "See that the

horses are saddled and an escort prepared. I will need a cart for my ladies and my belongings."

"What has he done to you?" Drogo's mouth curled with revulsion.

"He has set me free," Matilda replied, and a feeling of relief juxtaposed her despair. As if she had grown wings through her wounds.

"Where is he?" Drogo set his hand to the place where his sword would have been, except that he had come from prayer in the cathedral and was unarmed. "He has gone too far."

"Let it be," Matilda warned. "It matters only that he is out of the way. You would just get yourself killed or flung into a dungeon. Do as I say and see that all is made ready."

Drogo bowed and strode out to make arrangements, snarling at the servants to do as they were bidden and laying about him in his anger and guilt. A page received a sharp cuff for being tardy. Matilda closed her eyes and bowed her head. Her entire world seemed to consist of hitting and blows and miserable lashing out.

In the courtyard, the strong grey cob had been made ready for her. The horse regarded her out of placid dark eyes, its tail swishing rhythmically to deflect flies. A groom's little girl was winding a daisy chain around his breast-band and singing to herself. Matilda had given the child sweetmeats in the past and now received a curtsey and a beaming smile, revealing gaps where the little girl's baby teeth had recently fallen out. "God speed you on your journey, madam," she lisped.

Tears filled Matilda's eyes at such sweetness. "And God bless you," she whispered and had to look away. She was aware of people staring as Drogo helped her on to the horse. Some faces were shocked, others held contempt. One of her Angevin chamber ladies, Aelis, looked almost smug. Matilda averted her gaze from the young woman's sharp vixen features and lithe body. She was welcome to Geoffrey if she wanted to climb into his bed.

Drogo tucked fleeces around Matilda for support. "I should have stayed," he muttered. "I should not have gone to church."

"It would have made no difference," she replied wearily. "It was always going to happen." Grasping the reins, she summoned her will and, as the cob clopped out of the courtyard, she lifted her head to depart with pride unbowed. She did not know how she was going to manage this journey, but the taste of freedom encouraged her as she rode out under the archway. No more would Geoffrey beat and belittle her. No more would she be treated without respect. Her father might need this marriage for the security of his borders and the weaving of his policies, but there had to be a way round, and she would think upon it later. For now her goal was enduring to the next bend in the road, the next tree, the next house, each one a marker that took her further away from the hell of her marriage to Geoffrey of Anjou.

❖ ❖ ❖

Adeliza sat in the queen's chamber at Windsor, listening to Herman her chaplain reading from a bestiary while she worked on a section of altar cloth for the abbey at Reading.

"'Hear of the hedgehog,'" he said. "'What we understand by it. It is made like a little pig, prickly in its skin. In the time of the wine harvest, it mounts the vine where the clusters of grapes are growing. It knows which are the ripest and knocks them down, then it descends from the tree and spreads itself out on the grapes, then folds itself up on them, round like a ball. When it is well charged and has stuck its prickles into all the grapes, it carries them home to its children.'"

Adeliza first laughed at the charming picture the words created in her head, but then sobered. That was a tale to tell to infants, and she could imagine the actions to the story, but it had religious significance too, the hedgehog being a symbol of the Devil carrying off men's souls.

As Herman paused for breath, Henry blew into the room like a storm. He had been hunting and the scent of horse and sweat surrounded him in a pungent miasma. His grey hair stood on end where he had pulled off his hat and he was clutching a half-crumpled piece of parchment in his clenched fist. Adeliza could almost feel the anger steaming off him like hot vapour. "My dear lord, what is it?" Swiftly dismissing Herman, she went to him.

"Read for yourself," he snarled, thrusting the parchment at her. "My daughter is in Rouen and the Angevin whelp has repudiated their marriage."

Adeliza gasped in shock. "But why?" As she read the words, she covered her mouth with her hand. "Dear Jesu, why would he do that?" She raised her eyes to him in bewilderment.

"Now read this." He handed her another letter. "The messengers almost clashed on the road. It's from Angers. Geoffrey says he has sent her away because she is wilful and disobeys and insults him at every turn."

Adeliza made a small sound in her throat.

"He says he will not stand for any more and until she learns the error of her ways and is willing to yield to his authority, he will not take her back."

Adeliza bit her lip. "She did not want this match. I think she still grieves for the position she had before."

"But it was her duty to see her new marriage succeed. I will have my children fulfil their obligations, because they owe me the very breath in their bodies." His lips were so thin and tight with displeasure that they had almost disappeared. "I will have my son-in-law know his duty too. If he is not man enough to control his wife, then in what other ways is he not a man?" Breathing hard, Henry snatched the letters out of her hand. "I want you to go to Normandy."

"Me?" Adeliza stared at him in trepidation.

"I cannot leave England to deal with this stupidity. I have too much business. I will send envoys to Geoffrey while you deal with my daughter. I want you to find out what has happened, and then do your best to effect a reconciliation."

Inwardly she quailed. "What if I cannot? What if it has gone too far for that?"

He gave her a sharp look. "I trust to your skills, my dear. It is the task of a queen to be a peacemaker. Indeed, smoothing the path is one of the most important duties she can perform. If you cannot give me a son, the least you can do is bring my daughter back into the fold."

Adeliza tried not to flinch but felt as if he had struck her. "As you wish, sire," she said feeling lightheaded. "I will have my baggage packed immediately." She darted him a look. "Will you write to her too?"

"Indeed, this very minute." He stumped from the chamber, his tread hard with temper and assertion. Adeliza shivered and pressed her hands to her temples, then pulled herself together and ordered her women to begin packing. If she kept her thoughts on practical matters such as what she needed to bring and how long the journey would take; if she stayed on the surface, she could cope.

❖ ❖ ❖

When she arrived in the courtyard, cloaked for her journey, Will D'Albini was standing at her palfrey's head. The horse had been groomed until its hide shone like silk and he was talking softly to the beast and stroking its nose. He wore a sword at his hip and his fur-lined travelling cloak was pinned at his shoulder by a round gold brooch. As one of several young knights at court and a deputy to his father's office, the task of escorting Adeliza had fallen to him because he was competent and avail-able. A flush crept over his broad cheekbones as he bowed to her and assisted her into the saddle. Adeliza thanked him graciously but with preoccupation, paying him little notice.

As Will turned to his stallion, Brian FitzCount emerged from one of the buildings and hurried over to them, his expression concerned and grim. He bowed to Adeliza and straightened. "Madam, I have just heard the news from the king about the empress. I am sorry to hear it."

The sight of his agitation jolted Adeliza. "Indeed, it is sad news," she said. "Is there something you wanted to say, my lord, that you come out to me?" Her tone was gentle but firm with warning. Before Matilda's marriage, she had sometimes noticed a subtle undercurrent running between Brian and Matilda at court. Nothing that could be pinned down, and never the slightest hint of impropriety, but nevertheless an awareness, like a passing soft breath of air. Brian took a step backwards and nodded. "Of your kindness, I ask you to wish the empress well and tell her that she is in my prayers."

"She is in all our prayers," Adeliza replied, "but I will give her your message." She gathered the reins. "Messire D'Albini, I am ready."

William gestured the cavalcade to move off and Adeliza attended to her mare, giving Brian FitzCount no further opportunity for words or looks. The situation was fraught enough without adding complications.

Thirteen

ROUEN, SEPTEMBER 1129

ADELIZA WAS HORRIFIED WHEN SHE SET EYES ON MATILDA. Her face was a patchwork of fading yellow and purple bruises and she moved with the hunched care and slowness of an old woman. Her eyes, though, were fierce with challenge and reminded Adeliza of a wounded wildcat she had once seen, backed into a corner, but still spitting defiance through her terror and pain.

"Oh, my love!" Still wearing her cloak and riding boots, Adeliza crossed the chamber and took Matilda in her arms. "What has happened to you?" When Matilda stiffened in her embrace and gasped, Adeliza stepped back. "What's wrong?"

"My ribs..." Matilda grimaced. "They are still healing."

"Your ribs?" Adeliza stared at her in growing dismay.

Matilda shrugged. "They are no worse than any other part of me."

Adeliza was lost for words. She could not believe that Geoffrey of Anjou had done this to her, yet the evidence was before her eyes, and she was aware of a terrible feeling of guilt for pushing Henry's wishes on to Matilda. "Oh, my love!" she said again, and tears welled in her eyes.

Matilda's eyes remained dry. "I suppose my father has sent you to talk to me." She gestured Adeliza to a seat and eased herself down on to a padded bench against which leaned a walking stick with a knob of polished jet.

Servants brought Adeliza perfumed water to wash her hands. Someone removed her boots and slipped delicate embroidered slippers on to her feet. She was offered wine and small cakes. "Indeed he has, but that is only part of it." Leaving her chair, she came and sat beside Matilda, curving towards her so that their knees touched. "I am here because I am worried about you—the more so now." She held Matilda's hands. "You are not wearing your wedding ring."

Matilda raised her chin. "I am not going back to him."

Adeliza turned and dismissed the servants with a graceful but peremptory gesture.

"I mean it," Matilda said as the door closed behind the last one.

The fire ticked in the hearth as the logs settled. Externally the scene was one of two women sitting together in companionable harmony, but Adeliza felt as if she were being blown about in a wild storm. What was she going to do? Henry had ordered her to persuade Matilda to reconcile with her husband, but she had no idea how to begin, or even if she should.

Adeliza noticed how rough and dry Matilda's hands were— uncared for and untended, which was so unlike the Matilda she knew, who was always well groomed and used her appearance to commanding effect. She fetched a small ivory pot of salve from her baggage and removed the lid. A faint herbal scent drifted up from the surface. Taking Matilda's hands in hers again, she began rubbing the unguent into her skin, concentrating on the cracked, dry webbing between the fingers. "Tell me," she coaxed softly. "I cannot help you if you will not speak to me."

Matilda did not answer. Adeliza looked up from her task and saw that her stepdaughter's chin was trembling. "You will feel better if you cry."

Matilda shook her head. "It hurts to cry." Her voice was a tight whisper, but the dam had broken and a sob was drawn from her, then another and another, in reluctant painful heaves that gave little respite, and she had to clutch her rib cage, certain it would shatter.

Adeliza folded her in a compassionate embrace and tears swelled her own throat, yet she had to swallow them and not think about her personal situation, knowing if she did, she would find it unbearable. "Tell me," she said again, fetching a napkin from the food table to dry Matilda's eyes. "Otherwise, I will have to ask others, and they will not give me the truth, either because it does not suit them, or because they do not know."

Matilda swallowed and with an effort controlled her breathing. It was difficult to speak at first. She had told no one beyond Uli and Emma, although she was certain that the gossip had spread far and wide and Adeliza must have heard a version of the story already. She did not know how Adeliza would take the tale, because although she was loving and kind, she was also her father's wife. Matilda spoke in a low voice, and it was as if her words were about someone else, or of a vivid nightmare that wasn't real. Her bruises were proof that it had happened, but how could it be true when she was an empress and the daughter of England's king?

Adeliza held her hand, listened in shocked silence to the litany of abuse, and grew pale.

"I care not," Matilda said when she had finished. "It is no longer of concern to me."

"But it is of concern to everyone else, especially your father," Adeliza said. "Nor do I think it true that you do not care. That is not the woman I came to know when you dwelt at court."

"Perhaps I am no longer that woman," Matilda replied, tight-lipped. She looked down at their joined hands and when she spoke again her voice was more conciliatory, but still determined. "I cannot make peace. I know it is what you want from me, but it is impossible."

"You need to heal; I understand that," Adeliza soothed, "and you need time. There are many wrongs here that must be set right." Her voice strengthened with emphasis. "Your father will do all he can, but I tell you now, he will not allow you to annul this marriage."

Matilda withdrew her hand from Adeliza's. "I will not go back to that...that preening boy," she said flatly.

"Perhaps if you treated him like a man, he would act like a man."

Matilda rose and walked away to the window. "You do not know," she said, her back turned and her arms folded. "You cannot begin to imagine...My father has never beaten you, or fondled you in public before his barons, or left the bedchamber door ajar while he enjoys your body. Am I supposed to submit to this?" She swung round and pointed to her fading bruises. "To curtsey and smile and say, 'You were right to beat me, my lord.' When I was married to Heinrich, I was treated with deference and respect and decency. Now look at me. Would you walk in my shoes? Would you?"

Adeliza rubbed her temples. "In truth I would not," she said wearily. "We should not speak of it any more tonight. I want to talk to you of ordinary things and I do not want to lose your friendship...please." She made an imploring gesture, tears filling her eyes.

Matilda's expression softened. "Do not," she said in a trembling voice, "or I will cry again and drown us both." She returned to the bench and embraced Adeliza. "I am truly glad to see you, and I want to talk of ordinary things—you do not know how much."

"I have brought you something from England," Adeliza said as they parted from the embrace. "Something that belongs to you and that you need." Once more she went to her baggage, returning this time with a painted leather case. Inside was Matilda's crown of sapphires and gold flowers. "I sent to Reading for it," she said as she gave it to Matilda. "It has lain on the altar under the protection of the monks, but I felt…no, I knew I had to bring it here for you."

Matilda swallowed. "Thank you," she whispered and wiped her overflowing eyes. This time the tears came more easily and gave more relief.

"This is what you are," Adeliza said. "And no one can take that away from you—ever."

❖ ❖ ❖

It was a late November afternoon, the sky red and cold and the trees bare, the last of their leaves strewn in a crisp golden tapestry under the hooves of the horses as Matilda and Adeliza rode along the forest paths of Henry's manor at Le Petit-Quevilly on the outskirts of Rouen.

Drawing the frozen air into her lungs, Matilda felt invigorated and alive. Her bruises had faded and her body had healed in the days of busy tranquillity spent in Rouen. She had begun to find her sense of worth again and to think about her future— a future her younger brother had not had. Tomorrow was the anniversary of his drowning in the seas off Barfleur, and tonight she would attend a vigil in the cathedral to pray for his soul.

"I must soon think of returning to England," Adeliza said. "I must be there for the Christmas feast. Your father expects it of me and I have duties, much as I wish I could stay longer." She glanced at Matilda. "You are sure you will not come with me? I would welcome your company."

Matilda had expected Adeliza to return to England sooner than this, perhaps to be with her father for the anniversary of William's death, but her stepmother had chosen to stay in Rouen and be her companion and support, for which Matilda was deeply indebted. She and Adeliza were very different, but there was friendship, even affection between them, and the bond of kinship. Matilda knew Adeliza was not only here to support her, but to glean information for her father and act as peacemaker, but since each woman knew where the other stood, there was mutual understanding.

"My father will keep Christmas at Westminster with you," Matilda said. "I will do the same in Rouen, thus both England and Normandy will be served by our family. The Church and the barons will grow further accustomed to my authority as my father's deputy here." She spoke fiercely because she knew many would take persuading.

"As you wish," Adeliza said, "but I will miss you." Suddenly she exclaimed and drew rein because her gelding had started to limp on its offside hind foot.

"Madam." Will D'Albini, who had been heading their escort of serjeants, dismounted and hastened to look. He ran a competent hand down the horse's leg and picked it up. "Stone in the frog," he said and, drawing his knife, proficiently winkled out the offending piece of flint. A sharp edge had bruised the inside of the hoof. "He'll need to be led." D'Albini looked at Adeliza. "Madam, you will need to ride pillion."

Adeliza looked startled for a moment, but then nodded. "Help me down."

D'Albini did so, his face and throat suffusing with colour. Eyes lowered, he put her horse on a lead rein attached to his mount's crupper and returned to boost her on to the handsome grey. Adeliza remained gracious and proper, thanking him with detached courtesy, and expressing concern for the injured horse. Having made sure she was secure, he mounted in front of her, his face still red.

They returned to Le Petit-Quevilly with the winter dusk gathering around them like a grey woollen cloak and their breath clouding the air. Matilda's thoughts strayed to Brian FitzCount doing the same for her on the road to Rouen and her own complexion grew warm. Remembering Brian was like the winter ache in a wound. Time and distance had removed them from each other's proximity, which was perhaps a prudent thing, but there remained a quiet pain. She missed him. He had written letters offering his help should she need it and she had replied in formal words thanking him, not daring to let anything of self find its way from her mind to the vellum.

On their return, William D'Albini helped Adeliza to dismount, bowed, and went to deal with the lame horse himself.

Adeliza glanced in his wake, appreciating his kindness, and then she dismissed him from her thoughts to focus on the messenger who was standing at the manor door, drinking from a pottery cup, his satchel slung at his shoulder while he talked to an usher. Seeing the women approach, he hastily knelt. Matilda recognised him. Absalom of Winchester was one of her father's busiest couriers.

"What news?" Adeliza gestured him to rise.

Absalom looked uncomfortable. "Madam, I am on my way to England with letters under seal from the Count of Anjou. I will rest here the night and be on my way tomorrow."

"And do you know what these letters say?" Matilda demanded.

Absalom cleared his throat. "Only the gist, domina."

"Which is?" The frosty air was chilling Matilda's bones, but she would not enter the hall until she knew. "Tell me."

"The Count of Anjou says that he is considering his posi-tion…and that he is content for you to make an extended visit to Rouen."

Matilda snorted. Considering his position indeed! "As I am content not to be in Anjou," she snapped. "I will have letters of my own to send with you to my father on the morrow. Come to me before you leave."

"Yes, domina."

She eyed him. "How did the Angevin court seem to you?"

Absalom shuffled his feet. "I saw no difference to any other court ruled by a young lord, domina. There is much sport and hunting and boisterous play of an evening..."

Matilda winced at the memory.

He hesitated, and then said, "I will tell you because you are bound to find out anyway. The count's mistress is with child and flaunts herself at court as if she is his countess."

"His mistress?" Matilda stared.

"Her name is Aelis of Angers, domina. She parades around court with her hand on her belly and the count lavishes her with silks and jewels."

"It did not take her long to usurp me," Matilda said with contempt. "Let her make her bed and lie in it. They deserve each other."

Dismissed, Absalom bowed and went to find food and a place to sleep. The women continued to their chambers to prepare for their vigil in memory of the drowned young prince.

"Something must be done," Adeliza said angrily. "This is a disgraceful state of affairs. Your father has mistresses; he is a man of strong appetite in that part of his life; but none have ever been allowed to behave like that at court, even if they have borne him children." Her voice wobbled on the last word and she raised an index finger to silence Matilda as she started to speak. "Do not say you care not, because it is a lie. You do care and you should, because of the slight to your honour and your standing."

"Truly it does not matter," Matilda replied shortly. "I have told you; I am not going back to him. Let him kennel with whores as much as he likes."

❖ ❖ ❖

In the cathedral at Rouen, the women attended a mass for the soul of Matilda's brother, dead nine years now, his bones fathoms deep under the seas off Barfleur harbour. Matilda pressed her lips to the filigree cross that the archbishop presented for her to kiss. She was struggling to keep her own head above the waves as she struck out for the shore, but she did not know where the shore was. Her own boat had been wrecked when Heinrich died, and when she thought of getting into the one crewed by Geoffrey, she knew she would rather drown, because it wasn't rescue he was offering.

Her prayer beads slipped through her fingers like smooth, cold pebbles. Beside her, she could hear Adeliza murmuring under her breath and the soft click of her own beads. Was Adeliza in the water too? Counting through her hands the months and years that she had failed to conceive? Moisture glistened on her stepmother's cheeks, illuminated like clear pearls in the candle glow. Drowned sorrows. Matilda put her head down and closed her eyes.

Fourteen

ANGERS, JUNE 1131

$\mathcal{G}$EOFFREY WINCED AS HIS ONE-YEAR-OLD DAUGHTER HOWLED in her nurse's arms. Her hair was like his, a sun-gold mass of coppery ringlets. Her eyes were hazel-green like her mother's and tightly squeezed shut as she screamed to be put down. She had been named Emma for Aelis's mother and was an engaging little thing when she was not raising the rafters. She would be useful when it came to cementing a marriage alliance. King Henry of England had more illegitimate daughters than fingers and had married them all to good political advantage. There was something to be said for a quiver full of bastards.

Aelis, who was breeding again, had been mortified to bear him a daughter and was insisting that the baby swelling her womb was a boy this time. She would soon go into confinement for the birth and Geoffrey was glad because it would give him respite from her querulous demands. His patience was wearing thin, but at least her fecundity was proof that his seed was potent.

She stood before him now, one hand on her gravid belly. Every finger glittered with gold rings and her gown trailed behind her in a mute display of extravagance.

"You cannot go to Compostela," she pouted.

Geoffrey had been toying with the idea of a pilgrimage. The shrine of Saint James at Compostela was one of the holiest places in Christendom and petitioning the saint for guidance appealed to his sense of irony since Saint James held particular meaning for his wife and his father-in-law. Matilda had misappropriated the hand from the imperial treasury and her father had presented it to Reading Abbey. Geoffrey doubted Saint James would ever lie intact, but then for a saint who had performed a miraculous translation from Jerusalem to Spain, he supposed a few scattered bones did not matter. "Why not?" he replied impatiently. "You will be in confinement, so you will not see me anyway. My soul will benefit from the prayer and my body from the exercise."

"Sire, you should not go," said Engelger de Bohun, one of his knights. "Not while you do not have a legitimate heir and the matter of your wife is still in debate."

"I will not be told my business," Geoffrey snarled. His "wife," he thought bitterly. To his consternation he found he missed her. He needed to be the winner but she had bettered him. He wanted to dominate her and wear her on his arm like a tamed goshawk. He wanted to see the envy in other men's eyes that he had an empress at his beck and call. Aelis bored him because she was no more than a silly, twittery garden bird with false gaudy feathers, while Matilda was the genuine article. He was caught in a cleft stick. He could not afford to alienate Henry of England by seeking an annulment because when Henry died, a kingdom and a duchy would be his for the taking. He had to accept the bitch back if he wanted power.

Aelis said in a wheedling voice, "At least wait until after your son is born, my lord, or send someone with prayers in your stead."

Geoffrey shot her an irritated glance and compressed his lips. His daughter continued to roar and, losing patience, Geoffrey gestured the nurse to take her away. As the woman left the room with her wriggling, red-faced charge, an usher made his way over to Geoffrey and bowed. "Sire, a messenger is here from England bearing letters from King Henry."

"Bring him to my solar," Geoffrey said. "I will see him alone."

"Sire."

Clicking his fingers to his favourite hound, Bruin, Geoffrey left his courtiers and his sulking mistress and climbed the stairs to his chamber on the floor above, where he conducted his business. Rolls of parchment and ledgers lined the open shelves. A book box stood on the tiled floor filled with various volumes both secular and religious. A lectern was placed conveniently in front of a cushioned bench. This was Geoffrey's sanctuary and reminded him of his father because they had so often worked here together on the business of the domain. Geoffrey had even hung one of his father's cloaks on a peg near the door, and took comfort from its presence. The messenger carried letters but no verbal communication beyond a formal greeting. Geoffrey dismissed him and gazed at the square of parchment, the seal of England, rendered in brown wax and attached with strips of red and green braid. Eventually he picked up the penknife from the side of the lectern and cut it open. The dog flopped at his side and, with a sigh, rested its nose on its paws.

The usual salute met his scrutiny. *Henry by the Grace of God, King of England and Duke of Normandy, greetings.* The body of the letter, written by a scribe, was a list of the terms Geoffrey was required to fulfil before Matilda would agree to return to him and they made Geoffrey suck in his stomach. Henry did not know what he was asking even though he ought to. An old man, he thought, doting on his daughter, and thus made foolish. He read the lines again, still more than half disbelieving.

Stand her always in good stead in her own household, with servants of her own choosing around her. Aelis of Angers is not to be present at court or in any place that the empress may inhabit. Geoffrey clenched his fists either side of the parchment. "I will do as I see fit in my own domain!" he snarled. *That her household be in her own governance and that she be entitled to all her own correspondence both to and from the said household.* That gave him a burning sensation in his chest, because how could he trust her if he did not know what she was writing? *That she be treated with due respect in public and on state occasions. That she be given her own space and escorted everywhere by ladies of her own choosing. That you be frankly forbidden to harm her in any way whatsoever, unless it be by the will of full Church attorney.* Geoffrey's jaw was so tight that his whole face began to ache. And still it continued. *That Geoffrey was answerable to Henry for Matilda's safekeeping and she was to be treated in every respect as the daughter of a king.* In return, Henry would see that the oath of allegiance to Matilda was retaken by his barons and reinforce to his daughter that she must know her place as a wife and be obedient to her husband. *And in holding you to these terms, I applaud you as my son-in-marriage.*

Geoffrey crumpled the parchment in his fist and threw it at the wall. He certainly did not applaud what he had just read as the wisdom of a king. They were the words of a fool. And yet a fool who expected to be obeyed.

Geoffrey strode from the chamber because he needed space to expel his anger. Bruin followed him, tongue lolling. He was a dog; his faith and obedience were unconditional. "Rather a dog than a wife," Geoffrey said, and bellowed for someone to go and order his horse saddled up because he needed the speed of a fast, hard gallop to give him the illusion of freedom.

❖❖❖

"It is settled," Henry said. "You will return to your husband. He has agreed to all the terms I put to him on your behalf." He handed her the sheets of parchment he had been holding in his mottled fist.

Matilda's heart sank as she took the pages. Here in Rouen she was the happiest she had been since leaving Germany. Her chambers were comfortable and she had the spiritual sustenance of the abbey at Bec. People respected her and her life was sailing on an even keel. She had prayed for an annulment, but it was unlikely to happen now that Geoffrey had proven with a bastard daughter that his seed was not barren. She had hoped too that Geoffrey might make the repudiation official and seek to end the marriage, but plainly he felt there was more advantage to him in keeping their union intact. She read the words written in a scribe's formal script. Geoffrey's seal hung from the bottom, the image punched forcefully into the wax. At least she would have the buffer of her own household and they would be people of her choosing, but it was not her choice.

"But not immediately yet," her father said. "Certain bishops and barons have complained that the oaths of allegiance they took to you at Westminster were invalid because your marriage was not debated in council as it should have been. I want everyone to swear again before you return to Anjou. You will come with me to England and all will be done according to the law."

"Who has objected?" She was well able to guess. "Salisbury?"

Her father nodded. "As you would expect. And where he goes, so too does the bishop of Ely. Waleran de Meulan must swear too, now that he has been released from prison."

Matilda watched her father's fists clench. He was always one step ahead of the game. He would use diplomacy first, but back it up with threat and force. "And what of the house of Blois?" she asked. "I hear you have promoted my cousin Henry to the see of Winchester."

He shrugged. "He is an able administrator and will serve you well when the time comes. Stephen and Theo are your cousins, as is Stephen's wife. It is a good thing to encourage their support by nurturing them. I foresee no difficulty in having them retake the oath."

"And in having all keep it? If you are making everyone swear again, is it only for legality's sake, or are you trying to double-bind people because you fear they will break their bonds?"

His face darkened. "No one will gainsay me," he said. "No one will break their bonds." The clenched fist tightened and the force of his stare made it clear that he included her in the equation. "You will give me strong grandsons to follow in my stead and they will rule with guidance from me, and then from you and their kin should that be necessary."

Matilda did not ask what would happen if God chose otherwise because she knew it would only provoke his temper. She would go to England and a second time men would kneel to her and bestow their oaths for whatever their owners felt they were worth. Kings and bishops and magnates. And then she would return to Geoffrey and the petty Angevin court, more than 350 miles from England and 120 miles from Rouen. If God did choose otherwise, what chance did she have?

❖❖❖

Her cloak flapping around her body, Matilda stood beside Brian FitzCount on the wall walk of Northampton Castle and gazed at the town laid out to the west below the hill on which the keep stood. The first autumn winds were shredding the leaves from the trees and the river Nene ruffled under the walls in quenched shades of grey and blue. If the wind continued like this, her sea crossing would be brisk and unpleasant, but probably short. In her chamber her women were packing her chests ready for her journey. Feeling hemmed in, she had left them to their task.

Once more the barons had knelt to her in homage and vowed to accept her as her father's heir and once more she had doubted their sincerity. Feeling their reluctance, she had faced it with a set jaw and unbending gaze. If they wanted her to be as stern as a king, she would not disappoint them.

Brian leaned against the palisade. "The oath is retaken, domina," he said. "You will be a queen one day."

Matilda said nothing. They had spoken little since her return to England; two people skirting round each other because of all the traps lying in wait if they did begin to talk on a level beyond that of servant and vassal. Brian had not spoken of her marriage, but then what could he say? He did not know the full extent of what Geoffrey had done to her. Rumours were rife, but in England no one had seen the bruises. No one had watched her crawl because she could not stand up. And, when all was said and done, Brian was a man.

She was aware of how close to her he stood. Separate but within touching distance. Their cloaks billowed against each other, performing a wild mating dance. She risked a glance at him. His dark eyes were fixed on the river where a fisherman was busy pulling his boat to shore and sorting his catch. She observed the curve of his collar bones above the line of his shirt and the strong, masculine swell of his Adam's apple.

"Do you know how many times I have wished I had stayed in Germany?" she asked.

"I am glad you did not," he said without looking round.

Matilda gave a slight shake of her head and felt sad. How could she expect him to understand or go beyond his own desires? He said he was glad, but she had been talking of her feelings, not his. She looked at his hands: the gold rings; the long, elegant fingers; the smudges. "You still wear your ink stains," she said.

He took his gaze off the river and turned a little to give her a half-smile. "Robert and I have been working on an audit of the exchequer for your father, and I have been writing some thoughts on the vows that men swear."

"Indeed?" She raised her brows.

"All in your support," he qualified. "Some may say their oaths are not valid because they were made to a woman, but that is an excuse. Any oath taken before God, to whomsoever it may be, is binding. Nor was the allegiance sworn under duress. There were enough here today to have banded together and refused had they so desired, but no one did."

"You sound as if you expect some men to renege if the chance arises."

Brian grimaced. "There are many opportunists amongst us—and we both know who they are without speaking names."

"Yes." She narrowed her eyes in thought. "One day I will have to choose the men who serve me from among those gathered here. But their strengths and weaknesses will be difficult to judge when I am so far away in Anjou."

"Surely your husband will not object to correspondence that keeps you aware, because it will be in his interests too. Your father and the queen will write to you often, and the Earl of Gloucester. So shall I."

She said impatiently, "Reading the written word of another is not the same as judging for oneself. My stepmother acts her part so well that it has become the truth for her. She moves among people with a smile and a kind word. She is solicitous of my father and sweet to everyone, but how much of that is a façade she has been forced to adopt? How much will my father conceal or change to suit his own interests? I want my truth as it is, all unvarnished."

"You don't have to approach every difficulty as if it has to be bludgeoned into submission. Ice melts in sunlight when it does not do so in the frozen dark. Your stepmother knows this and it is what makes her so fine a peacemaker."

Matilda drew a steadying breath. "If men serve me as they should, then I will deal honestly with them, but I would have everyone tell the truth and not creep around it as if it is something we fear to awaken."

Brian gave her a long look, and the expression in his eyes sent a shiver down her spine. Just one move from either of them, and their hands would touch and their fingers mesh. She made a tight fist, resisting the urge to reach out. "Would you follow me if I were queen?" she asked. "Would you think England a laughing stock if a woman sat on the throne? Would you consider it an affront to the natural order?"

He shook his head. "I would rejoice."

"Then you are either the bravest man I have ever encountered, or you are lying to me."

"I am neither brave, nor a liar," he replied, the yearning look still in his eyes. "I am merely your servant and your father's servant."

"My father's first though."

"Because he is the king and he has raised me, but if you were queen, it would mean he was no longer here."

Matilda walked several paces along the battlements, putting distance between them. The sun was a splash of gold melting into the horizon. "Indeed, my father did raise you on high—by marrying you to Maude of Wallingford."

Brian nodded, wary now.

"How old were you?"

He looked down. "I do not remember; it was long ago. Perhaps sixteen."

"And how old was your wife?"

His voice roughened. "Twice my age, as you know, and a widow."

A colder evening wind blew across the battlements, making Matilda shiver. "And what did you think when you married her?"

"As I said, it was a long time ago."

"But not something you would forget, and I know your memory is keen."

He made a face, plainly uncomfortable. "I was grateful to your father. I was born without a patrimony and he raised me at court and gave me one. I have always tried to do right by Maude, but it was a match made for convenience—as most are."

"And what did your wife think of being married to such a youth?"

Brian flushed. "I never asked her. What would be the point? We are yoked to each other for better or worse and it is our duty to pull the plough in the same direction. We do as we are bidden."

"'As we are bidden,'" Matilda repeated and shivered. Tomorrow it was her duty to return to her plough and her mismatched companion.

"You will be a queen," he said softly. "A great one."

She read the longing in his eyes and was glad she had put distance between them. "But once I was an empress. My father does not want me to be queen. He wants my sons to be kings. So does Geoffrey, and that is one of the reasons he has asked for my return. It is always about the power of men."

His voice dropped lower still. "You do not know what power you wield."

She drew a deep breath to steady herself. "Brian, I do," she said and walked towards the entrance that led down to the safety of the rooms below, knowing that she should probably not have used his name because in some ways it was even more intimate than a touch.

"I will serve you to the last drop of my blood." His words curled after her on the wind, and felt like a portent of harder days to come.

Fifteen

FOREST OF LOCHES, ANJOU, SEPTEMBER 1131

BREATHING HARD, GEOFFREY REINED IN HIS SWEATING mount and patted its hot chestnut neck. He gazed round, trying to get his bearings, but they were deep in the forest and far off beaten tracks. The trees rose around him like stately cathedral columns and arched to form barrel-vault canopies above his head. The first leaves of autumn fell in a slow confetti of rust and green-gold. He had outridden the rest of the hunt while in hot pursuit of a ten-point stag and now had lost both. Only Bruin remained with him, and the hound had obviously lost the scent because he was snuffling in circles. Geoffrey tilted his head and listened, but there was no sound beyond the rustle of leaves and, somewhere, the harsh call of a jay. He reached to blow on his hunting horn, but cursed to find it missing from the hangers on his baldric, for it meant he could not summon aid, and the item was carved from elephant ivory and valuable.

He turned the horse in the direction from which he had come and sought the path, all the time listening for the horns of the other hunters, but heard nothing. A promising path turned out to be a deer trail that only led him deeper into the forest. Once, his straining ears caught the sound of a distant horn, but he was unsure of the direction, and it did not come again.

Geoffrey was pragmatic. He knew eventually he would find his way out, but still felt a glimmer of anxiety at being lost in the forest, away from the safety of his companions. The night would be cold, and he had neither provisions with him, nor the wherewithal to make a fire. He turned the chestnut towards the setting sun, because at least it was a known direction.

After a while, he began to smell woodsmoke and his hope rose, mingled with caution. The scent strengthened and moments later, Geoffrey rode into a clearing where a charcoal burner was tending one of his clamps. The smoke was mostly the product of the louver over the cooking fire in his hut, but white tendrils also swirled gently from the covered charcoal mound itself.

The man bowed in deference to Geoffrey's obvious rank, but did not kneel. His eyes were as bright as speedwells in his soot-smudged face, and he kept his fist clenched tightly around the rake in his hand.

"How do I find my way out of this place?" Geoffrey asked. "Do you know which way leads to Loches?"

The man leaned on his staff. "If I did not know, I couldn't sell my charcoal there, could I?" he said, and began issuing a string of directions by way of various trees: the big oak, the twisted lime, the hazel coppice with the rabbit warren in its roots.

Geoffrey's nostrils flared with impatience. "Take me yourself," he snapped. "These are not directions for a man unused to these woods."

"Messire, I dare not leave the clamp lest it flares up again." The burner gestured to the smoking mound. "This is my livelihood."

"Christ, I'll pay you for it; I'll pay you what you earn in a month; just show me the way. You can ride pillion."

The man pondered for a moment and then, with a curt nod, laid down his rake and brought a stool so that he could mount up behind Geoffrey. "It's that way," he said, pointing a grimy hand.

The path twisted and meandered like a hungry snake, but the charcoal burner navigated with confidence, using various obscure landmarks that were obvious only to himself. Geoffrey realised uncomfortably that he was a stranger in his own land. Here, in these woods, this man had the authority of knowledge while he possessed none. "What do ordinary men say of the Count of Anjou?" he asked curiously as they rode along.

His companion shrugged. "It is not my place to speak, messire, but were I to do so, I would say that men do not yet know what to think of him. He is a young man and still to come into his full flowering. It is said he should watch those who serve him lest they are serving their own ends. When the count visits his castles, his bailiffs take goods to provision the place from the local people, promising to pay them, but they never do. It has happened to me with my charcoal before now, but if folk complain they are beaten or imprisoned. Perhaps these men think that they can gain advantage because their lord is inexperienced, but it was an abuse of his father's day also."

Geoffrey contained his instinct to kick the filthy creature off his horse and have him clapped in fetters for his insolence. It was in his own interests to keep his subjects sweet and see justice done. He knew his father-in-law had put a stop to such abuses among the officials of his own court, and that he had received praise from the people because of it. Over and above that, Henry had taken control of the situation and stopped men from lining their own pockets At the expense of himself and his subjects. This charcoal burner might be crude and soot-smirched, but he spoke a refreshing truth.

"What else do they say?" he asked.

By the time they reached the castle at Loches, Geoffrey had a very clear view of how he and his court were viewed by his people, and it was mostly uncomplimentary. He had been given much food for thought. He had also been highly entertained by his guide, whose name was Thomas Charbonnier. The charcoal burner's expression when he finally realised he had been riding pillion behind the Count of Anjou himself was priceless and Geoffrey was deeply amused to witness the shock from both peasant and castle attendants alike; the latter horrified that their lord had been sharing his horse with a man of such dubious credentials. Charcoal burners were always viewed with suspicion. Living their itinerant lives in the forest, they were only one step away from being poachers, and outlaws. Charbonnier knelt, with bowed head, but Geoffrey raised him to his feet and, laughing, ordered the servants to give the man food and drink and a horse to carry him home.

"A donkey would be better, sire," Charbonnier said. "A horse would take too much caring for and cost too much to feed. Men would envy me. If it did not die, it would be stolen. But a donkey will bear a burden of charcoal and be coveted by few."

"So all you desire is a donkey?"

"Yes, sire."

Geoffrey chuckled. "Therein lies wisdom," he said. "Perhaps I should make you my fool."

Charbonnier gave him a shrewd blue look. "I am no man's fool, sire."

"Indeed not. But would you not like to give up the life of a charcoal burner for one at court? Wear fine clothes and sleep on a feather mattress and know that your wife and children were well fed? That to me seems the deed of a wise man."

Charbonnier puckered his face in thought. "Indeed, I would enjoy such things," he acknowledged, "but I would be changed. I would be more than a simple charcoal burner and that would not be so wise, sire."

In the end Geoffrey sent him on his way with the requested donkey laden with provisions and a promise to buy whatever charcoal he produced. Watching the peasant go on his way, happy with his donkey and his lot, Geoffrey felt a momentary pang that was almost envy.

"Sire," said his chamberlain, bowing. "Your lady wife arrived while you were gone. She is settling in the wall chamber of the west tower."

Geoffrey's heart sank. He'd known her return was imminent; it was part of the reason he had gone hunting, because he had felt it was his last opportunity to taste true freedom. He dismissed the man with a curt wave and, pinching his upper lip, turned to look down the road that the charcoal burner had taken with his new donkey. Losing his way today might have been a portent, and his conversation with the forest dweller as they journeyed to Loches had made him very thoughtful indeed.

Matilda paced the chambers she had been allotted by Geoffrey's tense attendants. Preparations had been made to receive her, but the fine details of laying a fire and providing warm washing water and refreshments had led to a last-minute flurry. Now everyone had gone, apart from the members of her own household. Geoffrey was out hunting, for which she was glad because it gave her time to assemble her defences. She still did not know what she was doing here. Although safeguards had been put around her by letter and strict agreement, she was uneasy. In her absence, her rivals in England could work upon the matter of the succession to their own advantage, and although she had an increased household, she was still isolated. Drogo had not returned with her, but had taken the cowl and become a monk at the abbey of Prémontré. Others had replaced him, but they were her father's men, not knights of her choosing.

At least there had been neither sign of Aelis nor evidence of her occupation here, although Matilda had not asked about her. Geoffrey's servants had shown her to her quarters, seen to her hospitality, but otherwise kept their distance. She felt as if she were standing inside a gilded cage, but was unsure whether it offered her protection from what was to come, or was a place to imprison her until the time came for her to be disposed of.

Her chamber door suddenly flung open, making her start, and Geoffrey strode in, vibrant as a young lion. His red-gold hair was a mass of wind-ruffled curls and his eyes were as vivid as clear green-blue glass. He had grown and broadened during the time they had been apart; the soft angles of adolescence had hardened into the chiselled bones of young manhood. He was breathtaking. And she hated him and she feared him.

"Lady wife, welcome home." He flourished a mocking bow.

She felt a horrible mingling of arousal and trepidation. Already she was preparing to fight him to the death. If he beat her again, one of them would die.

"I trust your chamber is to your liking." He looked round, hands on his hips.

"Thank you, my lord, it is—or it will be when my people have finished making it so." Her attendants had knelt as Geoffrey entered the room. She gestured them to stand and continue with their tasks.

His jaw tightened, but there was bleak amusement in his eyes. "Strange to say, but I have missed your presence," he said. "The challenge and the icy looks have been wanting. No one else can send such a chill down my spine with a single glance."

She eyed him with contempt. "I would have had an annulment were it possible."

"My sweet wife, I considered giving you one." He glanced at the servants again. "But since it is not to be and we must both bear our crosses as best we may, shall we discuss matters?"

"Now?" She fought her fear.

"Why not? Better sooner than later." He raised his hand, then paused in mid-gesture and turned his palm over towards her. "Will you dismiss your people?" There was an edge to his voice, but obviously he was abiding by the letter of their reunion, if not the spirit.

She wondered what he would do if she refused him "Leave us," she commanded with a brusque gesture, "but do not go far. I will call if I have need." She ignored her husband's snort of amused contempt.

As the servants filed out, she and Geoffrey locked stares like two opponents circling behind their shields. The latch fell and there was silence apart from the snapping of the logs in the hearth as the fire licked over the seasoned bark. Then Geoffrey crossed the space between them and slipped his arm around her waist and drew her against him. "I meant it when I said I had missed you. I also meant it when I said I considered an annulment. Why should I keep a wife who fills my cup with vinegar?"

"Because there are compensations?" she mocked. "Because it raises your rank to be married to a dowager empress and future queen? It gives you power and standing you would not otherwise have. Because you want Normandy and you will never get it without me..."

Geoffrey's grip tightened. They were both breathing hard with lust and anger. Her loins were moist with need. It had been so long, and however much she disliked, perhaps even hated him, however little she would ever forgive him for what he had done to her, the physical attraction between them was still a powerful drug.

"Oh, I admit it, wife," he said. "I would not have thought to say so, but I do, and whether you like or not, you feel the same way." He pushed himself against her and made very sure she could feel how aroused he was. Between kisses, he drew her to the freshly made bed and there took her with leisurely thoroughness, drawing off her garters, kissing her legs all the way up from instep to inner thigh, trailing his hand over her pubic mound until she moaned. He covered her with his body and entered her, fitting his hipbones inside hers, thrusting slowly, thrusting harder, taking his time until she was thrashing with need. And then he forced her over the edge and watched her shudder in climax before he surrendered to his own.

Matilda closed her eyes as the flickers of pleasure died to twinges. She ought to have felt deliciously relaxed but she was on edge. She had not had time to insert the moss, but it was near the time of her flux and he probably would not get her with child. Pushing out from beneath him, she left the bed and began to dress.

Geoffrey watched her with heavy eyes. He had dined but he was unsatisfied because she still eluded him. He studied her body as she sat down on a stool to tidy and rebraid her hair.

"Do you have anything else to 'discuss' before I summon the servants back in?" she asked.

He sat up, his gaze sharpening. "No, because your father made all very clear in his letter, as I did in mine to him. As you can see, I have complied."

Matilda vigorously wove her hair under and over. "So far yes, but the rest remains to be seen."

"On both sides, wife," he said. "I will have obedience from you."

"What of Aelis? What have you done with her?" she demanded.

There was silence from the bed. Matilda looked round and caught a look of pain on Geoffrey's face. Then it was gone as he schooled his expression to neutrality and began fastening his braies to his hose. "You need not trouble yourself about Aelis," he said curtly. "She is dead."

Matilda's stomach jolted. She wanted to say she was glad, but it was not the emotion that flowed through her. What arrived beyond the initial spark of shock, was alarm. She wondered just what this husband of hers was capable of. "How?" She made an effort to keep her voice level.

"Of the milk fever a week after giving birth to my son. She at least had an easy womb to fill. I have a daughter of her too and both shall be reared in this household. As I recall your father said nothing on that score, and the matter is not open to negotiation."

Matilda crossed herself. "God rest her soul," she muttered, thinking that Geoffrey had killed her indirectly after all.

He stood up. "I think it fair to say I have learned from my mistakes, but have you learned from yours, wife? Will you show me respect in public?"

"As you do so to me—and as you have promised to my father."

"So be it, and may our marriage be blessed and fruitful," he said grimly and left the room.

Matilda shuddered and breathed a deep sigh of relief as he closed the door. After a moment, she went to her devotional and, prostrating herself, prayed for the strength to endure and the grace to accept her lot, and, at least in public, play the role that was her duty.

When she had finished praying, she composed herself before summoning her servants back into the room, to finish their tasks. In silence the maids changed the sheet and remade the rumpled bed. Matilda took her cloak, beckoned to Uli, and climbed to the battlements to look out over the town and the wooded countryside. In the distance she could see people on the road, including a peasant leading a laden donkey. The last time she had stood on a wall walk had been at Northampton with Brian FitzCount. She felt a welling of sadness for what might have been if the road had been different, but immediately shook herself. What was the point in thinking upon roads not taken and pathways that had never existed in the first place? She had to concentrate on the one she was travelling now.

The sky was darkening towards dusk and small drops of rain spattered her face as an isolated shower blustered in from the west. She left the battlements but by a different door that led her along a corridor and past a small chamber set into the thickness of the wall. Two women sat within. One was suckling an infant, her ample white breast poking through a slit in her gown. The other knelt beside a tiny little girl who was made in Geoffrey's image, with his coppery curls and the same stubborn chin. She was stacking wooden bowls one inside the other and chattering away to herself.

On seeing Matilda, both women hastened to rise and curtsey, the wet nurse clutching the baby awkwardly to her bosom. "These are the count's children?" Matilda asked as a formality.

"Yes, madam." The wet nurse lowered her gaze to the suckling baby.

"What are their names?"

"The babe is Hamelin, madam, and this is Emma, his sister." The woman's voice was tinged with anxiety.

"Have no fear," Matilda said. "I do not persecute innocents."

She left the chamber deep in thought. With these children Geoffrey had proven that he could beget bastards with ease. They would serve his bloodline as they grew up in the same way that her father's numerous illegitimate offspring served him. Had she not been taking precautions, and given different circumstances, they could have been hers. She had almost died birthing her stillborn son in Germany and the pain and grief of that time would scar her for the rest of her life, as would the fear that she might die in the bloody struggle to deliver a child. For Heinrich, she would have laid down her life in the effort to provide him with an heir. She had no such loyalty to Geoffrey, but the sight of the babies had filled her with a bittersweet pang of longing.

Sixteen

LE MANS, ANJOU, JUNE 1132

STANDING IN GEOFFREY'S CHAMBER, MATILDA COMPRESSED her lips as she read the letter that had arrived from her father in England.

"Well?" Geoffrey arched his brow.

"He says he is considering," she replied with angry disappointment. She felt betrayed. She had sent to her father asking him to hand over the castles of Argenten, Montauban, Exemes, and Domfront in southern Normandy, which were pledged as part of her dowry, but he had declined to do so and it was a slap in the face.

"There is nothing to consider," Geoffrey snapped. "All the old spider wants to do is keep everything in his own hands and yield not one iota of power or control to anyone. It was the same when my sister was your brother's widow. He refused to return her dowry. He swallowed everything into his stout belly and there it sits. When he dies, everyone will be tearing him open with knives to get at their share."

Matilda shuddered at the image. "He has ever been thus. My stepmother says we should be patient a little longer. She will do what she can on our behalf." She did not add that Adeliza said her father was disinclined to hand over anything while she and Geoffrey had no heirs.

"He will not heed her," Geoffrey said curtly. "She does not have that kind of power over him. She is thistledown. Your father ignores people unless they sing his tune—and very few know what his tune is because he changes it at his whim, and tells no one what the notes are. He has had his barons swear to uphold you as queen one day, but be assured he will not have abandoned other plans."

Matilda said nothing because Geoffrey was right. She did not trust her father, especially when he refused to hand over her dower castles, but where else was she to turn? To Geoffrey? Their interests were mutual in many ways, but she did not trust him either. Her brother Robert might speak for her—he often knew her father's tunes. And Brian might if he deemed it right, although he was strongly committed as her father's man. But Robert and Brian were far away and her only influence was the written word, which would have as much impact as spitting in the ocean.

She made to leave and return to her own chamber, but Geoffrey caught her by the waist. "Perhaps he would be more amenable if we provided him with an heir?"

Matilda pushed against him. "Not now," she said impatiently. "I have things to do."

"But surely none more important that begetting offspring to inherit," he said. "If I ask you to render the marriage debt, you must obey."

Matilda remained rigid in his hold for a moment, but as he began to kiss her, she set her irritation aside and gave in to him. Geoffrey knew how to arouse her and the pleasure was often more intense when she was irritated or angry—like scratching an itch. He drew her to his bed, kissing her, awakening her desire. She felt his hand on her inner thigh, and then between her legs, stroking, rubbing, questing. Then he hissed through his teeth, but not with lust.

"What's this?" he demanded and, pulling back, held up the piece of moss she had inserted as a matter of routine that morning at her ablutions.

She stared, sick, horrified, and angry that she had been found out, but strangely relieved too. "Nothing," she said. "It is a woman's matter."

"A woman's matter?" he repeated. "I will know what it is, by God."

"It's a protection when the womb is delicate."

"I know what this is," Geoffrey snarled. "It's a whore's trick to prevent conception, isn't it? I have heard of such things, but I did not think to find you engaged in such foul subterfuge!" He hurled the moss across the room.

Matilda swallowed and said nothing, waiting for him to hit her. He would beat her for this. Perhaps he would kill her, and that might not be such a bad thing. Or perhaps he really would seek annulment this time.

"Why?" he snarled, setting his hand around her throat and rolling over on top of her. "Why do you do this? To spite me? Do you really hate me so much that you would deny me an heir? Do you think that God will forgive you for this? Who taught you these things? Your stepmother? Is that why she is barren? Is she a lying bitch too?"

"No!" Matilda gasped, choking at the constriction of his hand. "Adeliza knows nothing of this! It is of my own doing!" And yes it was in part to spite him and in the hopes of annulment, but she was not going to say so with his hand around her neck and his body shuddering over hers with incandescent rage. There was another reason too; one that made her eyes flood with tears. "I...my first son...He was..." She swallowed against his hand. "He was born deformed and I almost died in his bearing...I could not endure that again..."

He removed his hand and bowed his head into the space

between her shoulder and throat. She felt his body heaving against hers, and the slam of his heart against her ribs. "Your first husband was an old man," he said after a moment. "I am not and my seed is potent, although you have been denying it ground to grow. If it is God's will that you die in childbirth, then it is God's will, but I will have sons of you. You will not deny me the right."

He pushed her skirts out of the way and entered her in a swift, hard thrust. "You will bear my son," he said.

When he had finished, Matilda lay on the bed and stared at the canopy while he panted beside her. She wasn't sore because she had been ready, but she had taken no pleasure from the encounter. Did that mean she was safe this time? Did it mean her seed would not descend and mingle with his? Now he had found out, she was open and vulnerable. She had lost this particular battle and must prepare for the next one. If she did get with child, then she might die in the bearing, but at least it would be an honourable death, and while she was carrying, Geoffrey would not dare to touch her. The latter, at least, was an advantage.

He rolled over and sat up. "Take off your clothes," he said, his eyes bright and predatory.

"What?" She looked at him in dismayed surprise.

He gestured to the open shutters. "It's pouring down," he said. "What better way for you and me to spend a wet afternoon than on the business of governance and making future policy?"

❖ ❖ ❖

Outside the lazar hospital at Fugglestone, built in close proximity to the nunnery of Wilton, Adeliza stooped to the final leper in the line and placed a loaf of bread in his bandaged hand. The man bowed and thanked her with a crooked smile. A cloak of strong brown twill embraced his shoulders, fastened with a handsome bronze clasp. He had a new tunic, hose, and shoes, all of the queen's bounty, and now bread to eat, and a jug of good ale awaiting him on a trestle outside the door.

Adeliza was the patron of the leper hospital attached to the nunnery at Wilton, and she had paid out of her own funds from her rents at Shrewsbury for the provision of more beds, care, and clothing for the patients suffering from the debilitating affliction. Her predecessor, King Henry's first wife, had been wont to wash the feet of the lepers, kissing their sores and drying them with her unbound hair. Adeliza had never quite reached that level of piety. She believed it better to gift these poor souls with practical items such as clothes and food and a roof over their heads, and to pray for them to be healed.

Duty accomplished, she dined with the abbess at Wilton before retiring to the guest house. The nunnery was a peaceful spiritual retreat from the cares of the world. Henry was in the throes of an affair with a new mistress, the buxom flaxen-haired sister of Waleran de Meulan and his brother Robert, and Adeliza had chosen to look the other way and visit Fugglestone with her women while the affair ran its course. Henry would bed Isabelle de Beaumont, grow bored, and move on. He always did.

She sat down on the padded window seat and looked out at the abbey buildings. Sometimes she dreamed about wearing the veil and habit of a nun, a crucifix on her breast and an open prayer book in her hands, and at those times she felt immensely sad, but peaceful too.

As usual, William D'Albini had headed her escort on her journey to Fugglestone. She had heard him outside talking to the soldiers, and now he entered the guest hall, followed closely by his small black and white terrier dog, Serjeant. He glanced in her direction and bowed, but did not join her, and she was grateful because for the moment she was content to be solitary and she had a letter to read.

A messenger had arrived with a missive from Matilda while

Adeliza was at the leper hospital. Adeliza had set the news aside until her duties were finished, because letters from Matilda were always a treat. Savouring the moment now, she broke the seal, opened the parchment, and began to read. A few moments later, she gasped softly and sat upright on the window seat, pressing one hand to her flat belly. Matilda wrote that she was with child and that it was due in the early spring. Tears filled Adeliza's eyes. She was joyful for her stepdaughter, but felt grief for herself and even a touch of resentment that Matilda had quickened while she remained barren. Her envy made her feel guilty and sinful. "I am so pleased you have been blessed," she said aloud, to try and banish the negative emotions washing over her.

"Madam, are you unwell?" asked Juliana, one of her chamber ladies. "Do you want something?"

Adeliza shook her head. "No," she said, waving her away. "I will call if I have need." Juliana retreated, looking concerned, but Adeliza was too preoccupied to notice. Henry would be delighted, she thought. Finally his plans would begin to move forward. She knew he was considering other candidates to succeed to the throne as month on month there had been no news from Anjou. He had made men swear to Matilda, but he had put his eggs in numerous baskets just in case his daughter proved as barren as his wife. Adeliza pressed her lips together. She had come to Wilton to do her duty to the leper hospital and seek spiritual refreshment. Matilda's news was joyful; she would fix on that and she would write a reply filled with love and congratulation. But still Adeliza felt sadness settle upon her, like a layer of fine, grey gauze.

❖ ❖ ❖

Matilda closed her eyes, gripped the hands of the birth attendants, and pushed as the next contraction surged through her body. She knew the sensations because she had experienced them before in Speyer when she had laboured for two days to birth her deformed and stillborn son. She was terrified now, but not showing that fear to anyone. During her pregnancy and confinement she had read as many books and treatises concerning matters of childbirth as she could persuade physicians and churchmen to part with. She had studied the *Tractatus de egritudinibus mulierum*, the *Liber de sinthomatibus mulierum* and the *De curis mulierum*. She was determined to know as much detail as her physicians did, because such knowledge might aid her survival. An experienced soldier did not go into battle without armour. If she was going to bear this child and survive, she had to be as prepared as possible. On the day Geoffrey had discovered the piece of moss in the passage to her womb, she had had to adapt and change her focus. This child, if it lived, would be heir to Anjou, Normandy, and England and she had to do her best.

During the last three months, she had eaten a diet of light, digestible foods: eggs, chicken and partridge, plenty of fish. She had taken constant baths in sweet-scented water and anointed her skin with oil of violets to keep it supple. Having accepted the inevitability of her pregnancy, she had done everything within her own power to ensure that the carrying and bearing of this child went to plan. The rest was in God's hands. She had been labouring since the early hours of the morning, and it was now a little past noon. Outside she knew Geoffrey was pacing. He kept sending a servant to find out how the birth was progressing. She knew it was not concern for her that drove his anxiety, but for the safe delivery of his heir.

Her entire lower body felt as if it were being wrung inside a giant fist. She wondered how the baby felt, being squeezed and pushed towards the moment of birth.

Geoffrey's servant knocked again. Matilda closed her eyes and endured the contraction, pushing down with all her might, grunting and straining. Vaguely she heard the midwife's attendant telling the man that the babe was almost born. Within the hour, if all continued well.

Matilda gave a humourless laugh. "He is afraid I will birth a girl child," she gasped. "Before I entered my confinement he was constantly worrying at the possibility like a dog with fleas. He says I would do such a thing just to spite him and my father because I am contrary. It would serve them both right if I bore a daughter." She bit back a cry as the next contraction started to build. "The books say that a woman is a vessel in which the man plants his seed, so how can a woman be to blame for the sex of a child?"

"Sometimes a woman's seed is stronger than the man's, and then the baby is a girl," said the senior midwife. "That is the lore."

"In that case, all my children will be daughters!" Matilda panted.

On the next contraction the baby's head crowned at the entrance to the birth passage and emerged, followed by slippery little shoulders and crossed arms. Matilda closed her eyes, pushed again, and felt a warm, wet slither between her parted thighs.

"A boy!" The midwife beamed from ear to ear. "Madam, you have a son, and he's perfect."

An infant's thready wail filled the chamber as the woman lifted up the bawling, mucus-streaked baby for his mother to see. Matilda felt no immediate burst of maternal love, but there was satisfaction at a task accomplished and enormous relief that she had borne a living baby this time, whole of limb and wailing with lusty lungs. That was what brought a sob to her throat.

Two women cut the cord and took the infant aside to bathe him in a bowl of warm water, while two more stayed with Matilda to attend to the delivery of the afterbirth. She was so tired that it was difficult to raise the strength to expel the dark, liverish mass, but she managed. The women made her comfortable, removing the soiled bedstraw on which she had laboured, binding soft linen rags between her thighs to absorb the bleeding, and making up the bed with clean linen sheets. Matilda drank a small cup of hot wine infused with fortifying herbs and closed her eyes. She heard the soft splash of water as the women bathed the newborn in a large brass bowl, and the senior midwife cooing to him as she wrapped him in swaddling bands.

The peace of the moment was broken by a commotion at the door and Geoffrey burst into the room like a storm. "Where is the child?" he demanded. "Let me see him. Where is my son?"

The midwives gasped and clucked at the unseemly intrusion, but Geoffrey ignored them and strode over to the freshly swaddled baby lying on his fire-warmed blanket. "Unwrap him," he commanded. "Let me see that he is a boy with my own eyes."

Through her exhaustion, Matilda was filled with amused scorn and indignation. "Where would be the advantage in lying to you?" she said. "Do you really think we would say you have a son if it was a daughter?"

"I would put nothing past you," he growled, his complexion high.

"I have laboured long to bring him into the world," she said. "And before that, I carried him inside my body. I am glad to have borne a boy because he will have an immediate advantage in this world. Why should I bear a girl to spite you, when I would be spiting her too because of her very sex?"

Geoffrey looked at the unwrapped baby, taking in the evidence with his own eyes. He reached out a forefinger and touched his son's soft cheek. The infant turned his head in a rooting motion that made him smile. "I own him as mine," he said. "He is indeed a fine boy. Now we can begin to make real plans for the future. Name him Henry." With a brief nod in Matilda's direction, he left the room as briskly as he had arrived.

Matilda slumped against the pillows and fought not to cry as a maid closed the door behind him. "Bring my son to me," she said. "Let me see him."

The midwife rewrapped the baby in his swaddling and carried him gently to Matilda. She rested him in the crook of her arm and gazed down at this child whom she had not wanted to conceive because of fear, because of anger, because her life was a battleground over which she had so little control. Now the field had changed. Her fight was for him now, and she felt as if a part of her that had been hollow and hungry for a long, long time was full and warm and satisfied. "You have done well, little one," she whispered to him. "Henry." Although Geoffrey had spoken as if the naming were his sole prerogative, their son could have been called nothing else, and she was content. "You will be a great king one day," she said. "Greater even than your grandsire."

Seventeen

ROUEN, CHRISTMAS 1133

ADELIZA KNELT ON THE SHEEPSKIN RUG AND GENTLY ROLLED a ball of coloured felt strips towards the delightful red-haired baby sitting in front of her. He laughed at her, showing four teeth in each gum, and his eyes sparkled. With deliberation he leaned forward, picked up the ball, and bounced it back to her. She laughed in return and praised him, feeling joy and an underlying sadness and sense of failure. By marriage she was his grandmother, when, given God's grace, this could have been her own son. She was glad for Matilda and for Henry, who doted on his grandson, but she ached to know the kick of a baby's feet against the walls of her own womb. Henry's recent mistress, Isabelle de Beaumont, had borne him a daughter a month ago and Adeliza tried not to think about it.

Hearing a sound from the curtained-off bed behind her, she looked round as Matilda parted the hangings. Despite having slept for several hours, her stepdaughter's eyes were dark-circled and she still looked exhausted. She had removed her headdress in order to sleep and her long dark hair fell in two loosely plaited ropes to her waist. Adeliza sent a maid to fetch a hot tisane. "You still look tired out," she said with concern.

Matilda had travelled from Le Mans to join her father and the court for the Christmas feast in Rouen, bringing baby Henry with her. Geoffrey had remained in Anjou to see to his affairs. Adeliza suspected that the separation was a relief to both parties. Having arrived that morning, Matilda had pleaded weariness from long days on the road, and had gone to lie down, which was very unlike her.

The baby held out his arms to his mother and squealed for her attention. She picked him up and kissed his fluffy copper curls. "I am with child again," she said.

Now that she had spoken, the slight swell of her belly was plain to see. Adeliza swallowed a sick feeling of envy. "I am so pleased for you." She forced herself to smile. "You see I was right about marrying a younger man."

Matilda shifted Henry on to her hip and, grimacing, said nothing.

"When is the new babe due?"

"Somewhere around the feast of Pentecost."

"In the full spring then. That is always a good time to birth a child. Will you return to Anjou?"

"Not if I can remain in Rouen." Matilda put Henry down to play with his ball. "Geoffrey and I..." She heaved a sigh. "Let us say we will not miss each other. I have borne one son in Anjou. It will be a good thing to birth this one in Normandy."

Adeliza continued to smile, although she could feel the strain at her mouth corners. By the time Pentecost came she would be used to this, she thought, and to the fact that, in all likelihood, she was looking at the future king of England. "You know your father intends the Norman barons to swear to you again at the Christmas feast—and to this little one."

"Yes, he wrote to say so. That was one of the reasons Geoffrey wanted me to come to Normandy. We may not agree on many things, but in matters of policy we are as one, especially where our son is concerned." She rolled the ball towards

Henry and he picked it up in his chubby little hand, and held it like a coronation orb.

The servant returned with the tisane and Adeliza made Matilda sit down and put her feet up on a cushioned stool. "You will be well cared for," Adeliza said firmly. "I want to see those shadows banished from your eyes, and roses blooming in your cheeks."

"Yes, Mother." Matilda's face warmed with a smile as it always did when she addressed Adeliza thus. Adeliza merely looked pained.

❖❖❖

Henry sat at a trestle table in his chamber, eating small sweet cakes off a linen napkin. He had broken a piece off the one in his hand and given it to his grandson, who was mumbling it between his recently acquired front teeth.

"He's a fine boy," he said to Matilda and gave her a shrewd look. "And I hear you are with child again."

"Yes, sire." The news did not take long to travel, she thought. Her father had been eager to meet his grandson, and proud, but she had sensed a strange reserve in him too. As if his infant namesake were almost a threat because he was a reminder of the march of time.

"I also hear you are going to stay in Rouen for your confinement."

She nodded. "It will give me time to renew my connections with the court and to study matters of government at your side. It will be sensible also if I stay for a while after the birth, and return to Anjou in full summer when the roads are good." She hesitated. "I need to talk to you about my dower castles too."

Her father's expression hardened. "This is not the time for business," he said. "We can talk another day. For now I want to enjoy the pleasure of ordinary company and conversation."

Matilda narrowed her eyes. It was different when he wanted to discuss serious matters and others were at their leisure. She knew he was trying to slip out of a discussion on the subject, and it did not bode well. "As do I, my father," she said, "but I cannot do so until this matter is settled. I am asking you to turn over the castles that were due to me when I married Geoffrey. Exemes, Argentan, Domfront, and Montauban."

He fed his grandson another morsel of cake. "I know full well their names and what they are." He gave her a warning look. "You do not need to enumerate them to me as if I am some witless old man."

She fixed him with a steady gaze and refused to be browbeaten. "I am glad of that, sire, but anxious too, because it makes me wonder why you are withholding them from me and my husband."

"I withhold nothing," he snapped. "The Angevin had good English silver for your dower and riches beyond measure in the items you brought with you to your marriage. Those castles were indeed vowed to you, but you will receive them at a time of my choosing, not yours."

Matilda lifted her chin. "You manage to give crumbs of cake to your grandson; can you not see fit to do the same for me? If you do not honour my marriage agreement, then what else will you not honour? How can you expect men to keep their vows to me if you do not stand by your word?"

His complexion darkened. "Have a care what you say to me, daughter. I will not stand for your haughty words and high-handed behaviour. You shall have those castles when I see fit and not before. You have no notion what you are asking of me. It will mean displacing people. It will mean having to make new arrangements and deal with consequences."

"But there will be consequences too if you do not hand them over." She scooped her son into her lap. He laughed and reached to the platter of honey cakes. Laboriously he grasped one, took a bite, and then offered his mother the rest.

Her father wiped his hands on the napkin at his side and threw it down on the table in a screwed-up heap. "I told you, this is not the time to speak of such things," he growled as he stood up. "We will debate on a more appropriate occasion."

"In other words you are refusing to turn over those castles to me and Geoffrey. You are reneging on your promise."

"Daughter, I am telling you I will do so in my own time, not when you and that meddlesome husband of yours dictate." He stalked off, shoulders back and expression pugilistic. Matilda sighed heavily. She had not expected him to agree; this was only the first bout and she had months in which to keep at him, like water wearing down rock. He had to be made to see that the situation would only degenerate if he did not deal with it. He could not rein back time for ever.

❖❖❖

A third time the barons knelt and swore fealty to Matilda and on this occasion to her baby son too, perched upon her knee, his coppery hair gleaming on his soft round head almost like a halo or a crown. The Madonna and child was a potent image that Matilda exploited for all it was worth. The gathering was smaller than the previous two and consisted mostly of Norman barons, although Robert of Gloucester and Brian FitzCount had arrived from England on the morning of the ceremony and had added their vows and their voices to the other oath-takers gathered in Rouen Cathedral.

"So this is England's future king," her brother said, chucking Henry under the chin. "You and I should become better acquainted, young man."

"Indeed he is," Matilda replied firmly. "He will receive a full education as befits his destiny, and learn from the men who will guide and support him. He will know the law and all he needs to protect himself and his lands. He will learn to know friend from foe, and good counsel from bad."

"You speak fiercely, sister." Robert said, smiling.

"Because I must," she answered, and looked at Brian, who was gazing at Henry with a pained look in his dark eyes. "I am hoping he will learn judicious matters of exchequer from you, my lord FitzCount," she said, adding playfully, "but I will have others teach him how to raise a tent."

Brian's expression lightened. "I thought I succeeded rather well, given the circumstances, and I learn from my mistakes. I could give him the benefit of my experience."

Matilda's face grew warm. "I am sure there is much of value he can learn from you," she said.

Brian inclined his head. "Whatever you deem he needs from me, I will be honoured." He bowed and moved away to speak with some barons he had not seen in a long time.

Robert gazed after him. "It is a pity he has no heirs of his own. His wife is too old now to bear him sons or daughters." He gave her a cautionary look. "Be on your guard with him, Matilda."

She stiffened. "In what way? I hope you are not suggesting…"

"No, no, of course not." He raised his hand to stay her indignation. "He is a good friend and a powerful ally. He cares for you deeply, anyone can see that, but he is loyal to his position and he has great personal integrity—you both do. Keep within those bounds and all will be well. Give no one cause to talk of scandal—because they will if they get the opportunity."

Matilda drew herself up, prepared to be furious with him, but her thoughts were swift and by the time she exhaled she was more pensive than annoyed. "When you say 'no one,' do you mean anyone in particular?"

Robert moved closer and dipped his head towards her ear. "You know I do, and they will bear watching because they will do their best to discredit your suitability to rule England.

You must be above reproach." He glanced at a group of nobles talking behind her. Matilda did not follow his gaze but knew he was referring to Waleran, lord of Meulan, who had supported le Clito and been Brian's prisoner at Wallingford until after le Clito's death. She also knew that the bishops of Salisbury and Winchester would have their spies here, watching her every move, whom she spoke to and for how long, and reporting back to their masters. It made her skin crawl. Brian must know this too. "They will find nothing," she said, "because there is nothing to find, and I will not let them make filth out of service and friendship."

Robert nodded. "Good, but I had to warn you."

"And I thank you." She touched his sleeve. "While you are here, I need to ask a favour. I want you to talk to our father about my dower castles. He is still refusing to hand them over. If he does not, Geoffrey is within his rights to enter Normandy and seize them. If that happens, it will start a war, and that will jeopardise my claim to England and Normandy."

Robert looked dubious. "You know how stubborn he is."

"I am stubborn too when I know I am in the right. I have to press him now, because it will go beyond words if he does not yield, and if that happens, whatever the consequences, I will have to support Geoffrey."

He shook his head. "I will see what I can do, but I make no promises."

Eighteen

MATILDA COULD HEAR A CHURCH BELL TOLLING. A KNELL? A call to prayer? The sound rang and rang inside her head until it filled all the space and there was no room left for her. She felt as if she were drawing breath through a stifling cloth. A shroud, perhaps, of closely woven linen. There was a deep ache in her pelvis and the tender space between her legs. The birth of her second son had been rough. Her flesh had torn as she pushed him out, and she had lost a great deal of blood while delivering the afterbirth.

The bells ceased and she felt the blessed coolness of a moist cloth across her brow. A baby's wail filled the space where the bells had tolled, the sound fractious and insistent. Then a woman's comforting murmur, and moments later the sound of snuffling and sucking. Matilda forced her lids apart. She was cocooned and supported by a mass of pillows and piled feather mattresses. Beyond the bed curtains cool spring air flowed into the room from an open window and the sky was an arch of sunlit blue. A bowl of frankincense burned on the coffer at the foot of the bed. Near the hearth a woman was suckling a swaddled baby and another nurse was tending to one-year-old Henry, keeping him busy with some wooden animals.

"Matilda?" Adeliza leaned over her. "Are you awake, my love? Do you know me?"

What a strange question to ask. Matilda licked her lips. They felt as rough and coarse as old hide. "Of course I do," she said and coughed. Adeliza held a cup to her lips and Matilda took a drink of a bitter-tasting herbal liquid and almost gagged. "Why should I not know you?"

"You have been rambling out of your wits. You did not know me this morning. You have a fever. Drink this, it will help."

Matilda did as she was bidden and shuddered at the vile taste. "Am I dying?" she asked. "Give me the truth."

Adeliza set the cup aside, wrung out the cloth in the cold water, and replaced it on Matilda's brow. "The truth is I do not know. You are very sick. Everyone is praying for you. You know me now, when you did not before, and that is surely a good sign."

Matilda stared at the bed hangings. The twists of gold embroidery seemed to writhe like snakes. She could almost see the eyes and the scales. Coiling, winding, glowing with fire. She squeezed her lids shut to blot out the sight. "Even so," she whispered, "I must make my confession. If I should die, I wish to be buried at Bec. My father will try and insist on the cathedral, but do not let him have his way—not in this. Promise me."

Adeliza pressed her hand. "Do not speak so. God willing, you will recover."

"Promise me," Matilda repeated fiercely.

"Yes, I promise," Adeliza said with obvious reluctance.

"I want to make my confession and my bequests while I am in my senses. Will you bring Father Herbert to me, and a scribe?"

Adeliza kissed her and left the bedside to give instructions. Was she dying? Matilda sought inside herself and could not tell beyond the sapping heat of the fever and the strange, vivid flashes of colour behind her lids. Was it all for nothing? Did it end here? She felt a spark of resentment. She was not ready to die, even if she had to make preparations in case.

Adeliza returned and tenderly wiped Matilda's face and hands. "Father Herbert and his scribe are coming," she murmured.

"I want you to care for Geoffrey and Henry should the worst happen," Matilda whispered. "You will love them, and make sure they become fine princes and good men."

"Of course I will do whatever I can," Adeliza said in a choked voice.

"Do not go all foolish and cry on me," Matilda snapped. "What good will that do?" She closed her eyes once more because the embroidery on the bed curtains had started to writhe and glow again.

Father Herbert arrived to hear Matilda's confession and Adeliza chivvied everyone into the antechamber. Taking the replete baby from his wet nurse, she sat down and cradled him against her heart, feeling a great well of grief and longing.

Henry arrived from his business, stamping into the room with his usual vigour. He glanced at Adeliza cradling little Geoffrey. "I see that the infant thrives," he remarked. "How is my daughter?"

Adeliza's chin wobbled. It was all very well for folk to tell her not to weep, but she could not help it. It did not mean she was a milksop just because tears came more easily to her than they did to others. "The priest is with her, giving her comfort and confessing her," she said.

"Confessing her?" Henry's gaze filled with outrage. "She cannot be as sick as all that! She has the best physicians and care. I refuse to believe it!"

"She says she desires to be buried before the altar at Bec-Hellouin," Adeliza said in a constricted voice. "She asked me to take care of the children."

"Did she indeed?" Henry stood very still for a moment, and then he started to pace, tapping his hands behind his back.

"She said you would want her buried in the cathedral."

"Of course I want her buried there. It's where all the dukes of Normandy have their tombs, and it befits her status. I'll have none of this ridiculous Bec nonsense!"

"But if it is her dying wish…" Adeliza protested.

Henry swung round to her, his eyes glittering. "Are you truly so much of a fool, wife? Do you not know my daughter better than that?"

Adeliza flushed at the reproof.

"She is stubborn," he said. "She will fight me all the way for the right to be buried at Bec. While I refuse her, she has a reason to live. If I give her what she wants now, she might succumb. Once she is on the mend, I may yield to her wishes, but by then, it will not be necessary."

"And if she does succumb?"

His expression hardened again. "Then she will go to Rouen, because my will prevails. Do what you are best at, wife. Pray and petition God that she survives."

Adeliza bowed her head and thought that God did not always hear her prayers. She tried to obey His will and be a good wife to her husband, but sometimes it was so hard.

She decided, as she returned the baby to his nurse, that she would indeed make her petition and offer up gifts—but she would make that offering at Bec, not the cathedral, and she would ask for mercy from the Virgin Mary, a woman who knew the pain of labour and childbirth.

❖❖❖

Matilda sat enjoying the sunshine in the garden at her father's manor of Le Petit-Quevilly. It was two months since she had almost died giving birth to little Geoffrey and her recuperation was steady, but slow. This past week was the first time she had felt more like herself than a shadow. She had her sewing basket at her side, and had brought her penknife, quills, and parchments so that she could write some personal letters. Earlier she had been out riding for the first time in five months. Her husband had written asking when she would be returning to Anjou, the words couched as a polite, political enquiry, rather than eagerness to have her back. He had asked after his sons and her health and sent her a box of books to read and a beautiful cross on a gold chain enamelled in blue and gold. She had replied that she intended staying in Normandy for the time being to consolidate her position at the heart of the court.

Her father continued to be obdurate about her dower castles, repeating that he would yield them when he deemed the time was right and not before. He had given the custody of Dover Castle to her brother Robert, who was her loyal supporter and kin, but Matilda knew it was as much for Robert's aggrandisement and power as it was for building her a strong bastion of support in England.

Her women were playing a game of hoops and skittles on the path between the beds, taking turns to throw rings made of braided straw over the necks of the wooden posts. Two little girls belonging to the women had joined in too and their giggles filled the air. Henry, a little past one year old, was watching the activity keenly. Wriggling free of his nurse, he toddled forward on his chubby little legs. The woman started after him, but Matilda called her back, because she wanted to see what Henry would do. He picked up several of the withy rings, stooping with laborious determination, and then tottered over to the skittles and carefully dropped a hoop over the top of each one, before turning round to his audience with a beaming smile. Laughing, Matilda applauded him and went to pick him up and hold him on high. "Bravo!" she cried. "See, here is the winner of the game!" And then she kissed his cheek and said softly into his neck, "That's right, that's how you win. You go directly to the centre of what you must do and let others strive as they may."

Nineteen

Rouen, July 1135

*T*HAT HELLSPAWN HUSBAND OF YOURS HAS BURNED BEAUMONT to the ground and given succour at his court to barons in rebellion against me!" Henry snarled at Matilda. He shook the piece of parchment he had been reading under her nose. His voice was thick with rage. "Talvas and de Tosney. I will not have it!"

It was a hot summer evening and the shutters were open to a pale twilight woven with birdsong. Matilda had been summoned to her father's presence shortly after a messenger had arrived bearing news that Geoffrey had been aiding and abetting Normandy's rebellious barons. The chamber was sparse because Adeliza had been packing ready for a return to England. There were threats of a Welsh uprising that her father needed to deal with. The fact that Normandy and Anjou were suddenly bucking under him like a pair of untamed horses had turned his impatient bad temper to rage.

"I told you this would happen if you did not give me my dower castles." She watched him pace the chamber like an angry bear. "Even now, if you handed them over, you could prevent this."

"No man threatens me!" Henry whirled on her. "And no woman tells me how to conduct my affairs!"

Adeliza glanced up from supervising what was going into the travelling coffers, and bit her lip.

"I have no intention of giving up my castles to a man who plays host to my enemies in an effort to extort concessions from me," Henry growled.

"Every other avenue appears to have failed so far," Matilda said.

"Keep that tongue of yours behind your teeth, or by God I will lock you in a scold's bridle, my daughter or not. Do you hear me?"

"Better than you hear me, my father," she retorted because her blood was up. "You call my husband 'hellspawn' now, but when you forced me to marry him, he was a gift from God and could do no wrong. You rage as if it is my fault that this thing has happened, when surely it is all of your own doing."

"By God, you go too far!" He seized his jewelled staff from the side of his chair and advanced on her.

Adeliza was suddenly between them. "No!" she cried. "Please!" She dropped to her knees in front of Henry, head bowed and one hand extended in supplication. "I beg you, sire, do not!"

Matilda swallowed, feeling ashamed and sick and furious. Her father stood with heaving shoulders, glaring at her, and then he lowered the rod. "Be thankful that your stepmother has invoked her right as a peacemaker," he said. "She at least knows her place and her duty."

Matilda refused to drop her gaze. "Do I have your leave to retire and think on this news?"

"You have my leave to retire and consider your position," he said. "As my daughter, I expect you to know where your loyalties lie."

Matilda made an abrupt curtsey and swept from the room. Adeliza was still kneeling at Henry's feet and Matilda was mortified. Adeliza had deflected the blow meant for her and that was something she had never intended. She wanted to shout at Adeliza and embrace her at the same time. And she wanted to take her father's jewelled rod and break it over his head again and again.

❖❖❖

Adeliza bounced little Henry in her lap, watching as Matilda locked her jewel casket and placed it in a larger wooden chest.

"You should not have put yourself in his path," Matilda said crossly. "There was no need."

Adeliza kissed Henry's ruddy curls and, as he started to squirm, set him down. He trotted over to look in a coffer that a maid was packing. "There was every need. Things had gone far enough. Who knows where it might have ended."

"But it was for me to deal with, not for you to intervene."

"It is the prerogative of a queen to intervene," Adeliza said with gentle assertion. "Would you rather he had struck you?"

Matilda tightened her lips and added her cosmetic pots to the chest. Adeliza sighed. "I wish you would not part on a quarrel."

"That is up to my father. I have stayed here for too long. It is time I returned to Anjou. If it eases your path, tell him I am leaving to be a peacemaker with my own husband."

"And are you?"

Matilda said nothing but continued with her packing. After a moment, Adeliza rose and kissed her and left the room.

❖❖❖

Geoffrey eyed his namesake. "He looks like you," he said as he chucked the infant under the chin. His second son eyed him out of solemn grey eyes. His bonnet had been removed so that his father could see his hair, which was soft dark brown, sticking up in comical tufts. "Perhaps a daughter would be useful next, or even two, and then a further pair of sons to secure the inheritance." There was a sardonic gleam in his eyes. "What do you think?"

Matilda refused to be drawn. "I think you would be a fool to plan ahead in such a fashion."

"Oh, but I do need to plan ahead, because otherwise I will not be ready when the time comes."

"I said 'in such a fashion,' not that you should not plan at all."

He conceded her the point with a look of irritated amusement. "You are going to tell me now that you almost died bearing this one and it would be too dangerous for you to have more."

She arched her brow. "If I died, it would make your situation with regard to your power beyond Anjou more awkward than it already is. You need me whole and well for the time being."

"Indeed, and I am flattered you chose to return to me rather than stay with your father—or did he send you to make peace?"

"You do not know my father."

"To the contrary, I know the old spider very well indeed." His attention diverted to the nurse who was bringing Henry forward. "Last I saw he was a babe in arms, now look at him!" His expression bright with pride, Geoffrey squatted to be at eye level with his son. He was used to very small children— Aelis's two were in the nursery and there was not so great an age difference—but even so, this was his heir, the future Count of Anjou, and there was something about Henry that sent a pang of uncharacteristic tenderness through Geoffrey. Matilda had carried him in her womb, but he had set the life spark inside her body and it had been against the odds that he did so, some of them stacked by her. He stood up and lifted Henry in his arms. Holding an infant was not a suitable role for a grown man of great estate, but in this instance, it showed the world that here was his acknowledged flesh and blood, destined to rule.

Henry laughed, showing his pearly milk teeth, and pointed to the design on his father's blue tunic. "Lion," he said loudly. "My lion."

Geoffrey looked quizzically at Matilda. "'My lion'? Who has been teaching him that?"

Matilda flushed. "I tell him he is my little lion. He has a wooden one for a toy and a cushion with a big golden one embroidered on it. One day he will be a king. Why should he not acknowledge the symbols of kingship?"

"Oh, I agree," Geoffrey said. "We must foster that in him. Next teach him 'crown.'"

"He already knows that one."

"Crown," Henry said in validation of her remark, and pointed at Geoffrey's cap with its band of gold braid. "Lion. Crown. Mama."

Geoffrey chuckled and shook his head. "Indeed, I can see you have been teaching him well, but I must train him further. I suppose you have not taught him to say 'Papa' in any of this."

"I am sure he will learn swiftly enough," she replied, concealing a pang of jealousy because Geoffrey was so at ease holding their son.

"Papa." Henry bounced in Geoffrey's arms, and stared round with alert, bright eyes.

Geoffrey laughed. "You are right again," he said to her. "Usually I would hold that against you, but not today."

❖❖❖

"Well then," Geoffrey said later when the children had been taken away to the nursery and Matilda was settling into her chamber while the servants unpacked her baggage. "It seems no matter what we do, your father has no intention of handing over your dower castles." He sat down near the hearth and stretched his legs towards the fire. "Neither war nor diplomacy will shift his stance."

"He will not relinquish one iota of his power while he lives. He will play factions off against each other and keep us all like flies trapped on his web. I tried all ways to persuade him and he would have none of it. Every time I raised the discussion he said it wasn't the time, or he found other business." She frowned at him. "And then you went and burned Beaumont to the ground and aided Talvas and de Tosney to rebel."

"I was reminding him how much trouble I could give him. Normandy is not the stable ground your father would have us believe and we are not the only ones chafing under his hand. I refuse to be played for a fool. Your father may be a spider, but he cannot spin webs from beyond the grave. What if your barons renege when he dies? He is hoping he will live long enough to see his grandsons into manhood, but is that likely? We need those castles. We need that foothold."

Matilda made an impatient gesture. "So what are we to do? It is a dangerous game to stir up a wasp's nest. My father was going to sail for England, but he has deferred that business now to deal with Normandy."

"I know what I am doing," Geoffrey said with irritation. "This strife will act as a warning to your father and perturb him sufficiently to capitulate and give us our castles."

"I doubt you will win," she replied, thinking that he did not know her father very well at all.

He sent her a calculating glance. "I pity your lack of faith. Your father has spent a lifetime building up his kingdom, but buildings crumble and new ones have to be erected in their stead. I may not match him yet in terms of experience and guile, but I am younger and stronger, and I have the time that is running out for him. I know he does not intend me to wear a crown—in truth, I do not much care to wear one either. You are welcome to it. But Normandy is a different matter and, sooner or later, I always get what I want."

"Normandy is as much mine by right of inheritance as England," Matilda said, tensing her body. She hated his arrogance.

"Yes, but when you are queen and duchess and countess, how can you be everywhere at once? It stands to sense that I should be your deputy in this—and surely you do not want me in England."

"No." She almost shuddered.

He came to her and began to remove her garments, his touch as delicate as a woman's. "Give me free rein in Normandy until our sons are of age," he said, his voice persuasive and smoky with desire. "And I will gain our castles and deal with your father and prove my worth to you."

"And what worth would that be?" She felt the familiar coils of reluctance and craving snake through her body. "First you ask for castles, and now you seek a duchy."

"Is it wrong to be ambitious? Do you not desire a kingdom?" He cupped her breast and rubbed it through her chemise, stroking his thumb across her nipple until her flesh stiffened and she gasped.

"It is my duty," she said.

"Ah yes, duty." He drew her to the bed. "But duty and desire can sometimes be bedmates, no? I will show you what I am worth."

Twenty

HENRY OF BLOIS, ABBOT OF GLASTONBURY, BISHOP OF Winchester, picked up the large ruby sitting on the trestle and held it up to the light for a moment, before handing it to his visitor, Roger, bishop of Salisbury. Outside a chill autumn rain was steadily falling, but here in Henry's private chamber, a warm fire and hot spiced wine were keeping the cold and damp nicely at bay.

Salisbury examined the gem with an acquisitive eye. "How much is this worth?"

Henry shrugged. "It depends on the value the owner sets upon it, and what its function is going to be. Perhaps it might decorate a cup, or embellish a reliquary." He studied his folded hands for a moment. "Perhaps it might be used as the centrepiece for a new crown." He fixed Salisbury with a knowing stare. "I leave you to do as you will with it. I need not know the fine details."

Salisbury drew his purse from beneath his robes and dropped the jewel inside. "Of course not, my lord," he said, returning the look. "But you will want to be told the outcome in due course."

Henry took to fiddling with the small bust of a Roman emperor he had picked up in Italy a few years ago while visiting the pope. "Of course," he said. "I will be waiting in Winchester to hear."

"And your brother?"

"Stephen is close by Wissant. He knows to ride the moment he receives a messenger from the court. Martel will make sure to inform him. Everyone of consequence knows their place and what to do."

Salisbury nodded. "But Stephen has no notion?"

Henry snorted. "Stephen's conscience is tender. He wants the meat without seeing the blood, so I have spared him that. Do not worry. I can deal with him—and Theo."

Salisbury pursed his lips. "It still never does to underestimate anyone."

"I don't," Henry replied.

He saw his visitor on his way. Walking past the rain-drenched gardens, Salisbury paused to study the marble statue of a man clad in sweeping layers of fabric and a muscled breastplate. He was posed with one arm raised in mid oratory and his bare gaze was fixed on the horizon.

"Julius Caesar," Henry said.

"Some might cavil at your pleasure in decorating your home with pagan images," Salisbury remarked, brows drawn together.

Henry thought that the old man was probably secretly admiring his statues and plotting how he could obtain a few himself for either the palace at Salisbury, or his castle at Devizes. Certainly if his mistress knew, she would want one, the acquisitive bitch. "Indeed, some might, but I pay them no heed. There are always those who complain at the slightest opportunity, as well you know. I bought these in Rome, the city of the pope, where people have them in their homes and gardens as a matter of course. Rome once had a great and powerful culture and these statues spur me on to the service of England. Julius Caesar might not have been a Christian, but he was an emperor."

Salisbury grimaced. "So you gain inspiration from him?"

"I do, my lord, but of course never as much as the Church. My greatest duty is to God on high."

"Indeed," Salisbury said and walked ponderously into the courtyard, where an attendant had brought his horse. "Who knows, perhaps one day we will see you installed at Canterbury." He heaved himself into the saddle with the aid of a mounting block and a boost up from an attendant. "I will set this business in motion immediately." He placed his hand lightly over his belt area where the ruby nestled in its pouch.

Henry nodded and felt a churning sensation in his own belt area that was part excitement and part tension. The deed was set in motion. There was no going back now. He retraced his steps and considered his prized statue of Caesar. Its purchase and transportation had cost him the best part of a hundred marks, but it had been worth it because in England it was a rarity, often remarked upon by envious visitors, and to him a symbol of ruling power.

Henry continued back to his chamber and knelt at his small, personal devotional. Gazing upon the crucified Christ he lit a candle and prostrated himself. Sometimes for the greater good, a king had to die.

❖❖❖

"Here," said Adeliza. "I made this for you." She held out to Henry the hood she had been sewing for him to wear when next he went hunting. "Will you try it and see how it fits?"

She saw his impatient expression and felt cold. Of late it was so difficult to reach him. He was preoccupied with the business of government. His visits to her chamber had grown even less frequent and when they dined together with the court, he was brusque and distant. He seemed to have decided that since he could not beget a child on her, there was no point in bothering.

Something must have shown in her face because he checked

himself and grimaced. "It is finely made," he said, "and sure to keep my head warm if there's a cold frost." He tugged the hood on and allowed her to arrange the lower part around his shoulders, but she could feel his tension. He was eager to be away to his hunting and political meetings at his lodge at Lyons-la-Forêt. Women, other than court concubines and laundry maids, were not part of the arrangement.

In the antechamber a squire dropped a couple of boar spears with a loud clatter and was reprimanded by a chamberlain. Henry removed the hood and directed another servant to pack it in his baggage.

"You should begin preparing your own things," he said. "I want to be in England by Christmas if the weather holds fair and I can finish sorting out the difficulties that wretched daughter of mine and her husband are causing me." His expression soured for a moment.

"I hope you can," Adeliza said in a heartfelt voice. "I wish you good hunting, and good resolutions." She curtseyed to him.

"If there is not good hunting at Lyons, then I will replace my gamekeepers," he growled. "And as to the resolutions... one way or another, I will determine the matter." He kissed her and patted her cheek. "Put on your ermine and come and speed us on our way."

As he strode from the room shouting to his attendants, Adeliza bade her women fetch her cloak. She was in a pensive mood. The continuing rebellion in south Normandy was a serious thorn in Henry's plans and his temper was vile. Matilda and Geoffrey showed no sign of backing down, nor did Adeliza believe they would. Those four castles had become a solid barrier across the road to progress.

Wrapped in sleek, soft ermine, she left the warmth of her hearth for the bleak chill of the November morning. This was always a difficult time for Henry, marking as it did the anniversary when his legitimate son and heir and many of his other offspring by various mistresses had died on the crossing from Normandy to England. Henry had said little in public, but she knew how long he had spent on his knees in prayer and how much he was fretting about not being at Reading for the anniversary mass. His chaplain had told her that the king had been suffering from bad dreams too, in which he was murdered by a conspiracy of knights, bishops, and ordinary servants.

The yard teemed with men, horses, and dogs. Slender gaze-hounds with broad leather collars, snappy terriers stiff-bodied and belligerent, loose-jowelled slot hounds with floppy ears, eager bratchets straining at their leashes, and all the dogs making a terrible din. Henry reached for his bridle, set his foot in the stirrup, and gained the saddle with ease. Seeing him laughing and joking with his courtiers, still hard, still tough, it was difficult to believe he was almost seventy years old.

Walking around the periphery of the throng to avoid muddying her shoes, she noticed a group of men talking together as they waited for their grooms. Something about the way they were hunched towards each other set her on edge, but she did not know why. There was Hugh Bigod, lord of Framlingham: a short man as snappy and belligerent as the terrier dogs causing fights in the yard. She did not trust him and she knew Henry kept a close watch on his doings. With him were William Martel, one of Henry's stewards, and also Waleran de Meulan. The latter was cocking his head to listen to what they had to say, which was unusual, because although he was of their affinity, his tastes were generally more refined and intellectual. She caught Martel's eye. He bowed to her and as she inclined her head in return, the others turned, made their obeisance, and dispersed across the yard. Her feeling of unease increased, although it was nothing she could name.

❖❖❖

Adeliza spent the next few days packing her baggage for a sea crossing to England and hoped it would come about this time. She had suggested to Henry before he set out for his week's hunting that perhaps he should hand over just one of the disputed dower castles as a token, and he had grumbled that he required no advice from her about how to rule his dominions. However, later, she had heard him voicing the same thing to his eldest son, Robert, and of course, by then, it was Henry's idea. Naturally he expected concessions in return and peace from Geoffrey, but at least it was a step forward. Now, if only Matilda and Geoffrey would accept the olive branch and cease pressing Henry so hard, perhaps they might have peace to celebrate Christ's mass, in England.

She sat down in the window embrasure to compose a letter to Matilda, counselling her to be tactful and conciliatory with her father. She enquired after little Henry and Geoffrey too. She had embroidered smocks for both infants, picking away at the tiny stitches when the light was good enough at midday. But sewing gowns for another woman's children was a labour of love that left her hollow with yearning.

She was dipping her quill in the ink when she happened to glance up and, through the open window, saw a horseman galloping through the gateway and dismounting almost before his horse had stopped. She recognised his broad figure as he strode towards the manor and wondered what brought William D'Albini to her in such haste. Her heart began to thump and, calling to Juliana, she abandoned her letters and hurried to the hall.

He stood by the fire, clutching his hat in his hands and rotating it by its brim as he might count prayer beads in church. His tangled dark curls had obviously not seen a comb in a while and his garments were heavily mud-spattered. The expression in his large hazel eyes filled her with alarm.

"Madam," he said as he saw her, and fell to his knees.

She gestured him to rise and bade a servant bring him wine. "Your news can wait until you have wet your throat," she said, and was proud of her control. Whatever it was, she knew her life was about to change.

She watched him take the proffered cup in his large right hand, raise it to his lips, and drink thirstily.

"Thank you, madam." He returned the cup to the servant and hesitated, glancing around. "Perhaps this is for your ears alone for the moment."

She waved the man out of earshot; Juliana too. "What is it?"

"Madam, you should prepare yourself for grave news. The king was stricken with sickness and fever five nights since. We thought it was but the result of dining too heavily, but he worsened, and this morning he joined his Holy Father in heaven. I offered to bear the tidings here, although I regret with all my heart that I should cause you grief."

Adeliza stared at him, disbelieving. His words seemed to have stopped her own breath. She opened her mouth to question and deny, but no sound emerged. The edges of her vision darkened and she swayed.

"Madam!" She heard his exclamation and felt the strength of his arms as he caught her. He shouted for help and supported her to the bench by the fire while Juliana hastened to attend her. Adeliza knew she was breathing again, for the vile taint of burning feathers assaulted her nose. She tried to sip from a cup of hot, honey-sweetened wine that someone placed in her hands, but her jaw was chattering too much. This would not do, she told herself. This just would not do.

"I have sent for your chaplain, madam," Will said.

She nodded, feeling nauseated. "Tell me again. I cannot believe it is true. He was taken sick, you say."

"Yes, madam. Late at night after a day's hunting. He had

dined well...we all had, especially my lord. It was lampreys, his favourite dish. He must have eaten a bad one, because he sickened in the night with purging and a fever. His physician said that lampreys had never agreed with him..."

"They used to make him belch," Adeliza said in a distant voice. "But he was never ill beyond indigestion."

"His condition worsened and it became clear that his life was in the hands of God, who chose to take him to His bosom. There was nothing anyone could do."

Adeliza's gorge rose. Clapping her hand to her mouth, she excused herself and was violently sick down the waste shaft of the latrine chute built into the thickness of the wall.

"Madam, are you all right?" She felt Juliana's arm slip around her waist.

Adeliza nodded. "No more feathers," she said, swallowing hard. Henry was dead and it was as if something had been ripped out of her. "I wasn't there to comfort him. He died and I wasn't there."

"Madam..."

She shook her head at Juliana and, having smoothed her dress and rinsed her mouth with wine, returned to the hall. William D'Albini was sitting on the hearth bench with his back to her and she saw him rake one of his hands distractedly through his tousled curls. There was more she needed to know, but not here. "Bring him to my chamber," she said to Juliana. "I will speak with him privately."

❖❖❖

Adeliza sat down in the window embrasure where the daylight was still bleak and clear, and folded her hands in her lap beneath the thick fur covering of the ermine cloak. Will D'Albini was ushered into the room and hesitated near the door. Then he cleared his throat, squared his shoulders, and came to kneel to her, his manner one of dogged resolution.

She bade him rise and take the seat on the other side of the embrasure.

"I am sorry for your distress, madam."

"I should have been there," she said.

"There is nothing you could have done, and he had the best of care. He expressed his wish to be buried at Reading, and the earls present swore to escort his body there and remain together until they had discharged their duty to him. They are bringing him to Rouen first."

"Has a messenger been sent to the Countess of Anjou?"

"As far as I know, madam." He looked towards the window, his shoulders tense, then turned back to her. "Madam...the king did not name his daughter the Countess of Anjou as his successor."

Adeliza stared at him in astonished dismay. "Then whom did he name?"

"I do not know, madam. All Hugh Bigod said was that he heard the king absolve his lords of the oaths they had taken to uphold the countess and her son."

"Hugh Bigod?" Adeliza quivered. "Why would the king say such a thing to him? He is just a courtier, not a close confidant. If my husband was going to make such a change, even in extremity, he would do it through a priest and with witnesses such as the Earl of Gloucester to hear him."

Will's colour heightened. "Different people took it in turns to keep watch over the king. He said openly in council that the Count and Countess of Anjou had vexed him greatly and he was rethinking his plans for the future."

"But he did not say what these plans were?"

Will shook his head. "Many desired assurances that the Count of Anjou would have no part in ruling Normandy and England, and I believe he was trying to placate them. I do not know what his will was in this."

Adeliza gnawed her lower lip. She was not sure that anyone had known Henry's mind except Henry himself. She felt as if she were falling down a deep, black hole. "So what is to happen now? Who is to take the reins?"

"I do not know, madam. When I rode out, a council was gathering to discuss what to do and how much store to set by the word of Hugh Bigod."

Adeliza swallowed. Hugh Bigod would sell his own mother; everyone knew that. The decision for men would be whether to go with his word and be absolved of the oaths sworn to Matilda and little Henry, or stay true to what they had vowed. But if her husband had not named a successor on his deathbed, then the aftermath would be like a host of kites circling and descending to feed on a kill. "You heard and saw nothing?"

He looked uneasy, but held her gaze. "Madam, I did not… but as I was leaving, I saw William Martel preparing to ride, and I do not think he was going to Anjou. More than that, I cannot tell you."

In her mind's eye, Adeliza could see William Martel on a galloping horse. He would go to Boulogne, she thought. To his great friend and lord, Stephen of Blois, Count of Mortain. Where else would he ride in such haste? She must write to Matilda and warn her. But what if Henry truly had cut his daughter out of his plans and Hugh Bigod was telling the truth? Dear God, already they were a rudderless ship.

Her stomach was churning. She would never hold Henry's child in her lap. She would never sit in state beside him again. She was a widow, a queen without a king, bereft of her throne. In one fell swoop that part of her life was over. She wanted to hide in a dark corner and nurse her grief, and knew she could not. There were things that needed to be done for Henry. A fitting funeral. Prayers for his soul. And surely her role of peace-weaver was more necessary than ever, even if other functions had abruptly ceased. She must take this one step at a time. "I thank you for bringing this news to me so swiftly," she said. "Please, take your ease and ask my stewards for anything you need, but you will excuse me. I have matters to attend to and letters to write, and my mourning to consider."

"Of course." He rose and bowed. "If I can help, you have only to say…"

"Thank you," she said, knowing that there was nothing anyone could do.

Twenty-one

LE MANS, DECEMBER 1135

MATILDA CLOSED HER EYES AND ENJOYED THE SENSATION OF warm, scented water lapping around her feet and ankles as she took a footbath. She was briefly relaxing in her chamber after a long day working on various religious grants and charters but there was more still to do. Geoffrey wanted to talk to her about Normandy, where he continued to support the rebellion against her father, although of late he had distanced himself. They had heard a rumour last week that her father might hand over one of the dower castles, but Matilda would only believe it when the keys of the keep were actually in her hand.

Emma combed Matilda's long, dark hair, intermittently dipping the tines in a solution of nutmeg and rose water, filling the air with a marvellous perfume. In the background, Henry was chattering to his nurse. His vocabulary was prodigious for his years and already he had a fierce intelligence and a temper to match. The screaming tantrums when he was not allowed his own way were devastating. There was no placating him; he just had to be allowed to thrash them out, and then he would sleep, exhausted. The physicians opined that it might be caused by his beacon-red hair, which was a sign of an imbalance of his humours, but there was nothing to be done about that. He was what he was. In between tantrums, he had a vast, sunny nature and an enquiring mind that absorbed information at a gargantuan rate. He was sturdy and robust with his royal grandfather's build and stamina, and copious amounts of energy. Matilda foresaw that when the time came for his lessons it would take stern use of the rod to keep him in his seat. His baby brother was somewhat more placid, although since learning to walk had to be constantly watched. Her monthly time was overdue, but it was too soon to be certain of a third pregnancy. She hoped not, but suspected that hope was going to be thwarted. Her breasts were sore and the taste of mead made her feel nauseous.

There was a sudden commotion at the chamber door, and her young half-brother Reynald burst into the room.

Matilda sat up so rapidly in alarm that she sent the perfume bowl flying off the maid's knees, splattering the aromatic contents far and wide.

Reynald was mired from travelling the winter roads and red-cheeked from the abrasion of the wind. She rose to face him, her hair unbound and tumbling down her back. She was only wearing a chemise and swiftly picked up her cloak to cover herself. "What is it?" she demanded. The last time she had seen him had been in Rouen, living in comfort as a hearth knight in her brother Robert's retinue, and for him to be here now meant something terrible must have happened.

Beneath the windburn, Reginald's complexion was grey with exhaustion as he knelt to her. "Sister, I am sorry to bear grave news, but our father is dead of a sudden sickness while at his hunting lodge." He twisted a ring from the middle finger of his left hand and held it out to her.

Matilda stared at the great blue sapphire that was one of her father's favourite jewels. She felt her breath stop and then start again, stop and start. Her legs buckled and her women reached for her, but she forced herself upright again, shaking them off; refusing wine; refusing to sit down. "Tell me," she said.

Reynald relayed what he knew, which was not a great deal because, although he was Henry's son, he had been on the periphery of what was happening, but it was enough for her to know that her father was dead and traitors were claiming he had absolved them of their oaths to her and her son as he died. Yet more damning was the fact that it was Reynald who brought the news and not an entourage intent on offering her the crown of England and the duchy of Normandy. While it might yet happen, the omens did not bode well. All she had was her father's ring, and that was a frippery.

"Why did no one send to me when he first fell sick?" she demanded.

Reynald shook his head. "At first we thought he might rally...and then—well, I do not know." He lowered his gaze and looked shame-faced.

"I do," she said with angry contempt. Amid a gathering of men all fighting for position, the rights of a woman in Anjou and an infant prince must seem small and distant—a godsend when other agendas were at work. Turning away from Reynald, she paced the room, trying to think, but her mind was a labyrinth leading to dead ends.

"There is more," Reynald said unhappily. "William Martel left the court on a fast horse within an hour of our father's dying."

Matilda stopped pacing. For a moment her mind went blank as even the labyrinth ceased to exist. She felt the hard gold pressure of the ring inside her palm.

"Sister?" Reynald cleared his throat.

Awareness returned like the sun bursting out from behind a cloud, flooding everything with harsh clarity. "Where is Stephen?" she demanded, and knew the answer already. From the port of Wissant in Boulogne, it was only a short sea crossing to England.

Reynald said diffidently, "Martel might have been taking the news to Count Theobald."

Matilda threw him an exasperated look. "Is it likely? Let me ask you another question. Where is the bishop of Winchester? Where is the bishop of Salisbury? Where is our father's treasury?"

Her half-brother swallowed. "Surely not."

"'Surely'?" Matilda scoffed. "I can think of nothing more likely." Her first impulse was to pack her baggage and ride straight for Rouen, but she knew it was important to think matters through. If Stephen had preempted everyone and made a grab for England, then she had to work from a firm foundation. She had to organise and prepare. She had to know who her allies were and what support she had. "First I must find out what has happened," she said. "And secure what I can. If Stephen has made a bid for England, then it leaves Normandy open, does it not?" Turning, she went to Henry and picked him up. "My son is the true heir to England and Normandy, sworn three times before God, and his right comes through me. My father would not disinherit his own grandson. I will let no one take my son's right away—no one." She sent Reynald a fierce look.

"No one!" Henry repeated in a loud shout.

Reynald took a step forward and knelt at her feet. "You have my allegiance," he said.

She set her free hand on his shoulder. "I will make you an earl when I am queen. This I swear to you, but I have a boon to ask of you now."

"Name it and it is yours," he replied, his expression fierce with eagerness, chagrin, and youth.

"I need you to go back to Rouen," she said, and then she told him why.

❖❖❖

Geoffrey sat Henry on his knee and bounced him up and down. "Ride!" Henry yelled. "Ride a horse!"

"We have to take Domfront, Montauban, Exemes, and Argentan now, and swiftly," Geoffrey said. "We dare not delay."

Matilda felt light-headed with exhaustion, but she couldn't lie down or rest. There were still letters to write, allies to muster, lists to tally, strategies to devise, and baggage to pack. Reynald had already left on his errand, taking the swiftest courser in the stables. "I agree," she said, "but what if they refuse to open their gates?"

Geoffrey paused to bounce Henry again and make him laugh, then he said, "They will acknowledge you because they are too close to the borders of Anjou and they do not want a hostile army under their walls. You have your father's ring, and if we move swiftly, there will be no time for our enemies to send a countermand to the constables. Warrin Algason has overall responsibility for those castles and he is predisposed towards us anyway."

She made herself concentrate. Geoffrey was speaking sense. There were times when she hated him with every fibre of her being, but he had become an astute battle commander and skilful strategist. He had been as dismayed as she was about what had happened at her father's deathbed, but he had not been surprised. "The house of Blois was always going to have plans," he said. "And so will others. There will be more schemes abounding just now than lumps of gristle in siege-time soup."

"My father would not absolve men of an oath he had made them swear three times," she said, her eyes dark with anger.

"It does not alter the fact that the lords of Normandy and England are prepared to go along with the lie for the moment."

"Henry and I have to go to Argentan alone."

He arched one tawny eyebrow.

"I am their liege lady. If I arrive at their gates with an Angevin army led by you, what does it say? You must follow on with the troops but only after they have given their allegiance to me. That is the best policy." She steeled herself to argue, but Geoffrey merely looked thoughtful.

"You are right," he said. "And there is no point us being together when split up we can do more. You take the homage of Argentan, Montauban, Domfront, and Exemes. I will ride as far as Alençon with you, then go on to Mayenne and enlist the support of the lord Juhel, and join you later." He fixed her with a clear blue-green stare. "Our differences often run deep and wide, but we have a common purpose in this that binds us beyond our quarrels. If our son is to have Normandy and England when he is a grown man, it is up to us to obtain it for him."

She gave him a hard look. "They will be mine, first."

Geoffrey's expression filled with exasperated amusement. "As you will, but you have to win them, and you cannot do that without my help. If you are to rule England and Normandy, you will need an able deputy and, whether you like it or not, you will have to delegate. Normandy does not come with a crown, but it is the key to unlock everything else." He gestured to the bench at his side. "Christ, sit down before you fall down, woman. There is nothing more you can do until the morning."

She remained upright. "Yes there is," she said. "I must pray for my father's soul."

Geoffrey curled his lip. "Your father's soul may need all the prayers it can garner, but you will be no use to yourself or anyone else if you do not take some respite."

She did not answer him, but left the room and made her way to the chapel. Geoffrey was right, but she was stubborn and this was her duty. The December night was cold and she shivered as she prostrated herself before the altar. The only source of heat in the chapel was from the candles burning on the altar and in the devotional sconces and her breath rose in white vapour. Gold shimmered in the reflection of the flames from the jewelled cross on the altar and the enamelled triptych depicting the Virgin and Child enthroned. The tiles of the chapel floor were cold under her knees. Her stomach was queasy because she had not eaten all day. "Why?" she asked. "Why, my father? Did you truly absolve men of their oaths? Did you ever intend me to be queen, or was it all just another game to keep us on a leash?" She remembered him dandling Henry on his knee, smiling fondly, calling him a fine little king, but with that look in his eyes that said no one was a king but himself. Now he was no longer a king in the living world, just a naked soul in the afterlife. The grip had left the reins, and those who would ride would have to fight tooth and nail to mount the horse and stay in the saddle. Her heart ached, her chest was tight, but she did not give in to tears, because tears were a sign of weakness and she had to put aside all such chinks in her armour. She had a kingdom and a duchy to claim. Arms outspread, body prostrate, she prayed to God and His Holy Mother to give her the strength to carry this thing forward and see it through to the end.

❖ ❖ ❖

By the time the walls of Argentan came into view, Matilda was wilting in the saddle. Ten days ago, she had thought she might be with child again. Now she was certain, because the sickness was fully upon her and a deep, weary exhaustion. She could not afford to be ill with this pregnancy. She had to secure southern Normandy and show she was a force to be reckoned with, because if they dismissed her, they dismissed Henry too, and all her future lineage.

Geoffrey had escorted her as far as Alençon, and then ridden eastwards to secure the support of Juhel de Mayenne, first giving her a strong escort of heavily armed knights and serjeants. However, she had met with neither resistance nor hostility. Travellers she had encountered were wary and deferential. The peasants had kept their distance. Lords of estates and small castles had come to pay their respects and homage, which was encouraging.

As she approached the town walls, she banished a thread of trepidation and straightened her spine. Argentan was hers by right. She came not as a supplicant, but as its sovereign lady.

Word must have gone ahead, for the gates stood wide and an entourage of knights bearing banners came trotting out to greet her two by two. At their head rode the marshal, Warrin Algason, a dour-faced man of middle years as solid as his strong dappled horse. "Domina, I bid you welcome." Dismounting, Algason knelt to her, his knights following in a jingle of mail and weaponry. Held out across the palms of his hands were the castle keys.

Matilda bade him rise and come to her, and then stooped to give him the kiss of peace and accept the keys from him. "What news?"

Algason shook his head. "There is no word from Rouen, domina, beyond that of your lord father's death."

She said nothing, preferring to wait until she had been escorted to the fortress and shown to a well-appointed private chamber. Her women fetched warm water so that she could wash her hands and face and Algason had wine and pastries brought. "You should know, domina, that your lord father left instructions that in the event of his death, I was to hand over your dower castles."

"A pity that he set such terms when he could have done it in life," she replied tartly, but felt vindicated that her father had given his border marshal such an instruction, because it meant he had still intended the crown to be hers.

Algason looked uncomfortable. "It was my duty to obey him, as now I obey you."

"And if he had ordered you to close the gates against me, would you have done so?"

"I am a simple man, domina. I follow my orders and I remain loyal to my liege. My life is yours now."

She reassessed him with a tactical eye. He said he was simple, and perhaps in certain ways he was, but that did not mean unintelligent. He was a marshal and that meant he was an astute and accomplished soldier, well able to cover many tasks at once. She believed him when he said he would remain loyal.

The weariness she had been holding at bay seeped over her now that she was safe and her dower castles claimed. She could do nothing else until she knew more. Just watch and wait, prepare and rest, so that when the moment did arrive, she was ready.

❖❖❖

Two days later her brother Reynald arrived at Argentan, his horse stumbling with exhaustion. Concealed under a blanket on the crupper were two decorated leather cases, and although his face was smudged with weariness, he was triumphant.

"I thought I was too late," he told her as he brought the items to her chamber. "They were gone from the abbey treasury when I arrived in Rouen, but Queen Adeliza had them safe in her keeping and she was glad to give them to me. She said you and your son were the rightful owners, no matter what was decided, and that no one else should have them." He made a face. "She gave them to me in her private chamber and bade me leave straight away. I had to hasten from the city as the gates were closing for the night, but the queen gave me a letter of safe conduct with the old king's counterseal and the guards accepted it. I rode all night, changed horses, and rode again all day to get myself clear."

Matilda ran her hands over the polished, embossed leather of the casings. "You have done well," she said. "I was unsure if you would succeed." She swallowed a knot of emotion. "I am grateful to Adeliza. It can have been no easy task to obtain these from the treasury in the first place, and there will be repercussions..."

"She has sent you letters," Reynald said. "I have them in my satchel." He gave her an eloquent look. "They are going to offer England and Normandy to Theobald of Blois. They were talking about it in Rouen as if they had already decided."

"They?" Matilda raised her brows.

Reynald dropped his gaze. "The archbishop of Rouen, the Earl of Leicester, Waleran de Meulan, and...our brother Robert."

The words were like a blow to her solar plexus. "Not Robert," she said.

"I do not believe he had much choice," Reynald looked miserable. Matilda felt sick. Not for the first time she wished she could crush to dust these men who thought her a lesser being. Even her own brother, her supposed backbone, was prepared to turn away from her.

She unfastened the straps on the nearest leather casing. Inside lay the hinged panels of the imperial crown she had brought back from Germany. As Matilda touched the great ruby set in the front section, Warrin Algason arrived, his chest heaving from his run up the turret stairs. "Domina, sire!" He sketched a swift bow. "I have news. Stephen, Count of Mortain, has claimed the throne of England and been handed the treasury by the bishop of Winchester."

Matilda felt the initial jolt of the words, but the impact was not colossal because she had braced herself to receive just such tidings. Ever since the death of le Clito, Stephen had been her closest rival for the throne, and the faction that gathered around him had long been ready to pounce. While she had been playing a waiting game and arguing over these castles, they too had been biding their time, but closer to the hub of the wheel, and so secretively organised that even Theobald, head of the Blois family, had been kept in ignorance. Having assembled the crown, she held it between her hands as she had done in Germany. "So," she said, "I am brought a diadem, but no country."

"If we muster swiftly and ride north, we can nip this thing in the bud." Reynald's young voice cracked with eagerness.

Matilda shook her head. "It is too late for that. If Stephen has indeed claimed the throne and has access to the treasury, he is already too strong." Distaste entered her expression. "He will buy men and goodwill with my father's wealth, but when it is all squandered, they will abandon him." She stood the crown on top of the case. "What we must do is bide our time and make ready."

When Reynald had gone, she summoned her scribe and while he prepared his inks and parchment she showed Henry the imperial crown and the one from the second case of filigree and gold flowers. "One day these will be yours as king of England and Duke of Normandy. This I swear to you, my son."

The vow was a lifeline to hope, but it was one thing to swear an oath, another to bring it to fruition. She had found the first strand of grey in her hair last night as she combed it and wondered how many more there would be before she was an anointed queen.

❖❖❖

It was very late when Matilda eventually retired. Her new pregnancy was making her nauseous, and her eyes were sore because she had been awake for too long, and had held back too many tears. She was exhausted but too keyed up to sleep. She had drafted letters to allies and vassals, to the pope, to her uncle King David...to Brian. The wording would need to be considered and altered, but they were begun. Now, propped against a pile of pillows and bolsters, she opened the letter Adeliza had enclosed with the crowns.

The message was in Adeliza's own hand, and although she used the formal language of the queen of England, there were clear indications of the suffering woman beneath. Matilda had been unable to cry for herself or for her father, but now the dry burning of her eyes became a flood of scalding tears and she had to set the letter aside as drops fell upon the ink and smudged the words.

By the grace of God and because it was the right thing to do, Adeliza was sending her these crowns. She wrote of her grief at Henry's death and wished she could have been a better wife in the time allotted. She wrote that for the sake of Henry's soul and her own, she intended to go to Wilton and live there in retirement, perhaps eventually to take vows.

"He did not deserve you," Matilda said, wiping her eyes on the heel of her hand. "Why do you not see your own worth?" She was angry with Adeliza for choosing the path of retreat and contemplation, because it was not an option open to herself, even had she desired it, and she was furious with her father. And grieving, too, because now she would never be able to tell him what she thought, or show him that she was more capable of ruling than any son he had begotten.

She picked the letter up again and looked at the smeared writing that moments ago had been so delicate and clear. Adeliza would hate to see it in this state. Matilda folded the parchment and set it on her bedside coffer. Her stepmother might retire to a nunnery, but she was still a dowager queen. She was still young, and grief was not everything. Grief was just the moment before you tied off the thread and began the next one. That was when you made your choice about what you were going to sew next.

Twenty-two

STANDING UPRIGHT, SWATHED IN HIS FUR-LINED CLOAK, Brian breathed shallowly through his open mouth. The cold weather and the heavy perfume of incense did not mask the aroma of decay emanating from the coffin shrouded in purple silk standing before the altar of Reading Abbey. The lead seals confining the liquefying body of the former king were not secure and foulsome black ooze seeped from one edge. A bowl had been placed under the damaged corner and now and again a drip plinked into the basin. Henry had been dead for over a month. In Rouen he had been eviscerated and his bowels interred in the cathedral. His body had been packed with salt and wrapped in a bull's hide, then sealed in the coffin and brought to England when the wind eventually turned fair for a crossing. Two months in which the salt had drawn fluids from the body and now the dreadful brine solution was dripping into a bowl on the floor of Reading Abbey while the archbishop of Canterbury conducted the funeral mass.

Stephen wore the crown that had been set upon his head a fortnight ago at Westminster, and bore himself with regal dignity. He had set his shoulder to the bier and helped to carry the coffin into the abbey church. Henry, bishop of Winchester, and Roger, bishop of Salisbury, each wore embellished robes worth a small barony. Their faces were solemn too, but, as with many gathered here, aglow with an underlying smugness that was almost as distasteful as the stench emanating from the coffin.

There was no doubt in Brian's mind that Stephen had stolen the crown of England and the duchy of Normandy, although like everyone else he had bent his knee and sworn his fealty despite feeling sickened. Henry's corpse had still been warm when Stephen had taken ship from Wissant and made his bid for the throne, and if it had not been pre-planned, Brian would eat his red leather boots, silver laces and all.

Stephen's speed had been such that his acquisition of England had become a fact before anyone had had a chance to think. The Londoners had supported him to the hilt, as had the citizens of Winchester. Canterbury and Dover had closed their gates, but only until they realised that Stephen had gained access to the treasury at Winchester. Hugh Bigod had sworn on his soul that he had heard Henry absolve his barons of their oaths to Matilda on his deathbed, but Brian did not believe it because that was not Henry's way. He suspected Henry had not said anything, because he was still clinging to power with his final breath.

Henry's sudden death had caused the ground to heave up beneath Brian. He had had no choice but to give his fealty to Stephen because everyone else had done so and there was no one with whom to ally. The king of Scots was too far removed to be of immediate help, and Matilda herself was far away in Anjou. What use was rebelling for a cause that had no head, and no direction? He could not talk matters over with Robert of Gloucester because he was still in Normandy. Robert was not in open rebellion, but neither had he come to court to bend the knee at Stephen's throne.

Once the former king had been lowered into his tomb before the altar, the mourners and attendees processed solemnly out of the abbey into the raw January day.

Waleran de Meulan paused at Brian's side and gave him a calculating look. "Well," he said in a quiet voice, his breath making swift, short clouds in the air, "the business is finished now and we can move on with a new reign. I for one am glad to be out of there. The embalmers did a poor job of hiding the corruption of the world."

"He deserved better," Brian said.

De Meulan shrugged. "It hardly matters now, does it?"

"It always matters, my lord. We owe respect and the correct duty to a man whether he be living or dead." De Meulan annoyed Brian. There was friction between them going back to de Meulan's house arrest at Wallingford, and in the years since then, their antipathy had continued apace. Waleran and his twin brother were keen to monopolise the king's ear and anyone not of their faction was already being forced out to the edges and isolated.

Waleran wrapped his hands around his belt and thrust out one foreleg in a dominant pose. "It must be difficult for you," he said. "You have no kin in England to rely on, beyond those belonging to your wife, and none of them are worth the time and trouble." He shot Brian a malicious look. "You have no heirs and the lands King Henry bestowed on you were in right of your marriage. They were in the king's gift, and what was given might be taken away again should a vassal prove disloyal to his sovereign lord."

"Your meaning?" Brian said icily. "Let us have it out in the open, my lord."

Waleran shrugged. "My meaning is obvious, FitzCount. You may be a scion of the house of Brittany, but, like my lord of Gloucester, you are bastard born and you, even more than he, depended on the largesse of the king for your power. He raised you up from the dust and to the dust you could return."

Brian was sickened. "So could any man."

"Some more than others." With a nod of his head, Waleran

joined his twin brother, Robert de Beaumont, and Hugh Bigod, who was swaggering like a plump cockerel. Brian stood alone for a moment, and thus Waleran's point about isolation was emphasised. However, moments later, he was joined by Miles FitzWalter, the castellan of Hereford, a tough, pragmatic border warlord.

"De Meulan should watch his step," Miles said amiably. "Those who walk with their heads in the air usually don't see the shit on the ground until they tread in it."

Brian grunted with reluctant amusement. "You noticed it too, my lord?"

"One always has to be wary of factions at court," Miles replied. "If I were you, I would put in appearances when necessary and find reasons to spend time on your lands."

Brian nodded. "I have thought for a while that I should attend more to my affairs at Wallingford. The buildings need supervision and repair and my wife complains that she never sees me." He had to swallow a grimace at that. "What of your own affairs, my lord?"

Miles rumpled his thinning sandy hair and gave a taut smile. "Being a soldier, I like to know all is in order. Sometimes you have to strike swiftly, as our new king has admirably demonstrated, and sometimes it is wise to be cautious. My lord of Gloucester is doing the latter just now." He glanced in the direction of Stephen, who was flanked by the Beaumont brothers, Bigod, and the bishops of Salisbury and Winchester. "But he will have to come to terms one way or the other. For myself, I will wait and see what kind of king has been bought for us while I mourn the passing of a truly great sovereign. I doubt you or I will see his like again in our lifetime."

❖ ❖ ❖

"Madam," the nun said, and gestured through the open door into the chamber that had been prepared.

Adeliza gazed round as she stepped over the threshold. The room was sparse, but sufficient to her needs, and it was clean. A smell of fresh limewash filled the air and when she touched the wall, the paint came away on her fingertips in a moist white smudge. Braziers had been lit to warm the room and aromatic smoke curled gently towards the rafters. The bed had a rope frame and a down mattress covered with a close-woven linen sheet, a bolster and two large, soft pillows. This was all she needed. Somewhere tranquil to retreat and pray and come to terms with the vast changes in her life.

For fifteen years she had been queen of England, the consort of one of the greatest kings in Christendom. Now all that was stripped away. She had her dower estates and her lineage, but no longer was she the hub of the domestic court. She had been little more than a child when she married Henry. Now she had to discover the woman within the girl, and if that involved becoming a nun, so be it. There were so many things in the world that made her want to turn her face from it and look inwards to a life of contemplation. She would write to Matilda; she would do what she could to support and comfort her, because she still had a stepmother's responsibilities, but beyond that, she would embrace the life at Wilton and see that the adjoining lazar house at Fugglestone flourished. She would put away her sleek silk gowns and be humble before God, and in the fullness of time, God would show her what He wanted of her.

❖❖❖

Matilda squeezed her eyes tightly shut, and pushed for all she was worth in a final effort to expel the baby from her womb. Beyond the walls of the great keep at Argentan, the July heat was stultifying, and although the thick stone kept the worst of the heat at bay, her hair was plastered to her skull with sweat and her body shone as if she had been anointed. As always, the labour had been difficult and she had sent numerous prayers and exhortations to the Blessed Mary, asking her to help her safely deliver this third child. Geoffrey had spent most of the last few months on the battlefield in a campaign tent; now it was her turn to fight.

The senior midwife told her not to push, but instead to pant. She did so and felt a stretching soreness between her legs, and then a sudden gushing release. An instant later the woman held up a wailing, slime-covered infant. "A fine boy," the midwife said with a beaming smile. "Madam, you and your lord have another son."

Matilda lay back against the bolsters, spent. "Geoffrey wanted a daughter this time for his marriage policies," she panted, smiling at the same time. "He will call me contrary, but I doubt he will complain further than that." Indeed, she suspected the boastful cockerel side of him would be crowing from every dung heap in the vicinity that three times he had sired a son on her, proof of the outstanding virility of his seed. "How is he to be named, madam?"

"William," she said straight away. "For his grandfather, who conquered England and Normandy."

"Not Fulke then, for the count's father?"

Matilda gave the midwife a sharp look, but decided not to reprimand her for questioning the decision. "That I have a middle son named for his Angevin heritage is sufficient," she said curtly. "My father-in-law may be king of Jerusalem, but Jerusalem is far away and England and Normandy are not."

"Yes, madam." Chastened, the woman cut the cord and gave the baby to her assistants to wash while she delivered the afterbirth. Matilda glanced towards the window. The sun was past its zenith now, but the world outside continued to bake. There would be storms soon, she thought, of all kinds.

Eventually, the bathed and swaddled newborn was handed to her. Matilda cradled him in the crook of her left arm. His minute lashes were dusted with gold and his little mouth made pursed sucking motions. She praised God that he had come safely into the world. Now she had to pray for her own recovery. Childbirth was so debilitating. Three sons in four years. Whether Geoffrey wanted daughters or not, Matilda was determined that this was the last time she risked herself in the birthing straw. She would not lie with him again because she had a country and a duchy to win and, if not for this baby, her efforts would have begun much earlier.

"Bring my other sons," she ordered her women. "Let them see their new brother."

Henry and Geoffrey were duly escorted into the confinement chamber. Henry was eager to see the baby, but, having looked, soon lost interest. He was a big boy, and felt no strong affinity for the infant in his mother's arms. There was a slight squirm of jealousy in his stomach because her arm was curved around the baby and not him, but he wasn't overwhelmed by the feeling, because he knew he was still the best. He pressed a dutiful kiss to the infant's forehead and then ran off to explore the chamber, clambering up on to the window seat and peering through the arrow-slit. Geoffrey stayed on the bed with Matilda and did his best to say the word "William."

Matilda looked at her three sons. Future kings, dukes, and counts, but only if she and Geoffrey could secure that future for them, and there were so many setbacks to overcome.

In April the pope had ruled that Stephen was justified in taking the crown and had issued letters of sanction. The king of France had acknowledged Stephen's claim. She intended contesting the papal decision, but it would take time and while the diplomatic battle was being fought out, Stephen was becoming ever more entrenched. Not long after the pope's ruling, her brother Robert had capitulated and sworn his oath to him. She hoped it was a temporary measure born of expedience, and that while at court he would talk to others and bring his influence to bear, but it still felt like betrayal and desertion, especially after he had been willing, with others, to offer the crown to Stephen's brother Theobald.

Her third son had fallen asleep in her arms, making little crowing sounds as he breathed. She handed him gently to a midwife to be settled in his cradle where he at least could slumber for the moment in peace and innocence.

Twenty-three

*M*AMA, LOOK—LOOK AT ME!"

Matilda turned from talking to the saddler and watched Henry sit upright in the saddle of a small bay pony. He struck a pose and lifted his chin. The September breeze ruffled his red-gold hair and turned his irises the hue of sea-coloured glass. He had begun riding lessons two weeks ago and was enjoying every moment. For now, the tuition consisted of having one of the grooms lead him round the courtyard at a sedate walk. A saddle had been especially made to fit his size so that he would not slop about between pommel and cantle. He would not be allowed to take the reins on his own for a while to come, nor would he have the strength and stature, but he was already confident around horses, and was developing balance, knowledge, and maturity.

"Indeed you look very fine," she replied proudly. "Every inch a king."

"I want to gallop!"

"And so you shall, but not quite yet. You have to learn a few more things first and grow a little more."

"But I'm a big boy now!"

Her lips twitched at the indignation in his voice. "Indeed, but you need to grow bigger yet."

The groom led the pony off at a sedate walk. "Faster," Henry cried. "I want to go faster."

She glanced towards the battlements as she heard a shout. Moments later, a soldier came running towards her from that direction. "Domina, there is an English lord at the gate begging entrance. Sir Baldwin de Redvers and his company."

Matilda drew a swift breath. Baldwin de Redvers was the sole English baron to have refused to swear to Stephen. He said he had given his oath to support her and would keep it until his dying breath. Stephen had besieged him in his castle at Exeter and de Redvers had been forced to surrender when the wells ran dry in the blistering summer heat. When last heard of, he had been holding out at Carisbrooke Castle on the Isle of Wight and interfering with Stephen's shipping between England and Normandy.

"Admit him," she commanded, "and bid him welcome."

The gates opened upon a troop of horsemen on jaded horses. The men themselves were dusty from their journey and their equipment showed hard wear, but their armour was cared for and the men themselves, although obviously weary, had made an effort to look spruce and proud.

"My queen." De Redvers dismounted and knelt at her feet with bowed head. His men followed his lead and the women too, for they had brought their wives and children into exile with them.

"Get up," she said. "All of you." She raised de Redvers herself and gave him the kiss of peace on his sunburned cheeks. A swift command sent servants running to prepare food and drink. More orders set others to finding stables and lodgings for the newcomers. She welcomed the rest of the entourage briefly, and beckoned to Henry's groom to lead over boy and pony.

"This is my son and heir," she said. "The future Duke of Normandy and king of England. Henry, these are our loyal men. What do you say?"

"God's greeting," Henry piped. "Be welcome." He bowed in the saddle.

De Redvers knelt again, and his entourage followed suit. Matilda tapped his shoulder in a wordless command to rise.

The knight's hard mouth wore the trace of a curve. "My lord is already a fine little knight," he said.

"Every day he grows nearer to the crown that is his birth-right," Matilda replied. "One day he will be a well-grown king, and we will not forget the service you do us. Come within, and give me your news."

❖ ❖ ❖

De Redvers washed the dust of the road from his hands and face and drank deeply from his goblet. "I have come to offer you and the Count of Anjou my sword and my services," he said. "I cannot sustain my position in England. I have lost my lands. All I have is what I have brought with me on the back of my packhorses. But while I have breath in my body, I will fight for you, and for your son."

"I thank you for your loyalty," Matilda replied. "As soon as I am in a position to reward you and your men, I will do so. For the moment, you are welcome to food and lodgings for yourself, and your dependents. I have a skilled armourer in the castle. Your equipment will all be refurbished and replaced."

De Redvers bowed his thanks. "I have heard of the skills of Robert of Argentan," he said. "And seen his work. The Earl of Gloucester wears hauberks of his fashioning."

"He has no access to them while he is at court," Matilda said curtly.

"I think it is only a matter of time before he leaves Stephen, domina. When I was besieged at Exeter, I heard and saw many things. The king is pushed this way and that by those who would be the power behind his rule. He treats the Earl of Gloucester with courtesy, but he shuts him out of his councils. The Beaumont brothers are the stars in the firmament—and the bishop of Winchester, although there is antagonism between him and the Beaumonts because both want to be Stephen's right hand."

Matilda sat down and gestured Baldwin to do so too. This was the kind of news she needed—direct and from a man who was fiercely loyal to her. "Enough to split the court asunder?"

"Not as yet, domina, but there are cracks that can be worked upon. The Beaumonts and the bishop of Winchester are vying for control of the king and the bishop of Salisbury is busy with his own agenda because he fears losing his grip on the treasury. Winchester has his eye on the see of Canterbury when William de Corbeis dies—and it won't be long now. Corbeis is very frail—but the Beaumonts have their own candidate in mind. The Earl of Gloucester and William of Ypres do not see eye to eye. Some who have bent the knee out of expediency are only waiting their moment to change allegiance."

"And Brian of Wallingford?" She felt an ache deep within her, because he too had sworn and he had betrayed her.

"He has been little in the king's company, domina. I have heard say he is busy on his estates attending to his own concerns, but I would say he too has been displaced at court."

So there were conflicts to be exploited. Matilda stowed away the information to consider later. Divide and conquer. She hoped Robert was doing that at Stephen's court and had not deserted her. She needed to go to England herself, but first she had to be certain of her footing. To strike from this small corner of southern Normandy was impossible. "The Count of Anjou is preparing a campaign," she said. "Stay here and refurbish your arms, then join him when he crosses the border. He will appreciate seasoned troops."

"Domina, it is you I serve," Baldwin said with a frown.

She gave him a tight smile. "Which I acknowledge and you have my sincere gratitude. But for now you will best serve me by liaising with my husband. When I come to England, I will make you an earl and you will have all restored to you and more, I promise."

He looked fierce. "I do not do this for wealth and prestige. I do it because I took an oath on my honour that only my death will break."

"Bless you," Matilda said, and had to swallow the lump in her throat. So many had sworn, but so few had kept their word, even those she loved and trusted. Everyone was out for gain, so to have de Redvers give her everything for loyalty stirred her deeply.

❖ ❖ ❖

Matilda placed her foot in Baldwin's cupped hand and accepted his boost into the saddle. Around them the men of Argentan were mounted up and ready to ride. The morning sun flashed on hauberk rings and lances, turning the gathering into a silver shoal. Horses pawed and whinnied. Banners snapped in the stiff autumn breeze.

In the background the nursemaids held up Henry and little Geoffrey to watch the entourage ride out. Even the baby was there, cocooned in his nurse's arms. Matilda looked over her shoulder at her sons, and then faced the front, her jaw set with determination. A scout had arrived from Geoffrey the previous evening, asking for her to bring reinforcements to Lisieux as swiftly as she could. King Stephen had sent an army under Waleran de Meulan to defend the town and there was a danger that Waleran might turn and threaten Argentan itself. Matilda did not believe he would because she was strong in the regions she did control, but even so, she dared not ignore the possibility.

Geoffrey's campaign thus far had met with mixed fortunes. He had taken Carrouges and Asnabec with ease. Montreuil had resisted, but Les Moutiers had surrendered. Geoffrey had been on the point of seizing Lisieux, when de Meulan had arrived with a strong contingent and barred his way.

As the dawn brightened in the east, Matilda's reinforcements rode at a trot towards Lisieux, twenty-five miles away. She quelled the urge to increase the pace. They had to conserve the horses' energy in case they had to fight when they arrived. She was praying that the sight of the troops, well equipped and led by seasoned captains, would make Waleran withdraw.

Her captain, Alexander de Bohun, had sent scouts ahead on faster horses and as her army approached Lisieux, one of them returned at a sweated gallop. "Madam, the town is burning! My lord of Meulan has fired the suburbs and the flames have spread!"

Matilda lifted her head. Distantly she could indeed smell smoke on the wind.

The scout patted his trembling horse. "The Count of Anjou has turned to Le Sap instead."

Matilda's eyes darkened. "What?"

De Bohun said, "Neither side will risk a pitched battle, domina. If de Meulan has fired Lisieux, either it is to destroy the means by which our army can supply itself, or because he cannot control his men. We do not have enough soldiers to ride into Lisieux ourselves and face de Meulan."

"Le Sap. How far is that?"

"About nineteen miles to the south," said de Bohun. "If we push the horses harder, we can be there in a little over two hours."

"Then push them," she said grimly. If they could take Le Sap, then at least it would be a base from which to renew assault on Lisieux once Geoffrey's troops were bolstered by her reinforcements.

De Bohun gave the order and Matilda had her remount brought up: the strong white gelding she had ridden on the day she fled her marriage from Geoffrey. That smooth pace and stamina would stand her in good stead now. Around her the soldiers who had spare horses took the opportunity to change them and those who did not retired to the back of the column. De Redvers bowed as he handed her a costrel of wine and a drinking horn inlaid with silver. "To your health, domina," he said.

She took a few fortifying swallows. "If we had arrived half a day earlier, we could have made a difference," she said in frustration as she returned the horn.

"Perhaps," de Redvers said with a shrug, "but you cannot look back. With good fortune, the Count of Anjou will have succeeded at Le Sap, and if Meulan has burned Lisieux, it benefits us, because it will not endear him to the people."

By the time they arrived at Le Sap, the sun was westering at their backs, and once again there was smoke in the air, powerful and pungent. Bodies of men and animals littered the road. Many houses in the small town were ablaze and the church was writhing in flames while the priest stood outside with his deacons, wringing his hands and weeping to God. On the castle walls, Geoffrey's lioncel banner flew with those of his allies: Talvas, Aquitaine, Vendôme, and Nevers. Knights and serjeants were busy making billets. A miserable crowd of prisoners huddled against the castle walls, their wrists and ankles clamped by fetters.

A makeshift gallows had been erected and several corpses dangled from it, their necks tilting to touch their shoulders. One man had been mutilated too, his entrails hanging out in slick bluish ropes. The smell of the butcher's shambles, bloody and rich, joined the raw stink of smoke and Matilda covered her face with her wimple and gagged.

"Domina, thank Christ you are here."

She turned at the touch on her arm and faced Geoffrey's close friend and ally, William Talvas. His face was smirched with grease from his hauberk and there was a superficial nick under one cheekbone that had dried in a beaded black line.

She eyed him askance. "It seems I did not arrive in time for Lisieux, but you appear to have taken Le Sap—if rather messily," she added with a pointed glance over her shoulder at the burning church.

"We sent for aid because there is sickness in the camp. Many of the soldiers have the bloody flux and cannot fight and there are wounded from our other battles. We badly need the replacements."

"Where is the Count of Anjou?" She had expected to see Geoffrey before now, striding about, directing operations in his usual high-handed manner.

Talvas rubbed the back of his neck. "That is another reason I am glad you are here. He has been wounded. That man we hanged—he hurled a javelin from a whip sling and it struck Geoffrey in the foot. He's in the solar chamber having the injury seen to by a chirurgeon."

Matilda fought down panic. She could not afford to lose Geoffrey now with so much at stake and their sons so small. "How bad?"

Talvas shrugged. "He'll only be wearing one boot for a while."

Matilda hurried off in search of her husband and found him lying in the solar as Talvas had said. He had drunk the best part of a flagon of wine and was still drinking. Red stars flushed his cheekbones and his eyes were opaque with pain. His hair was plastered to his head with dirt and sweat, its colour closer to dingy brown than bright gold. He lay on bloodstained sheets, clad in his battle-soiled shirt and braies. The chirurgeon was washing his hands in a bowl of red water. On a table at his side was an unfolded bundle of the tools of his trade, including several fearsome-looking needles. Geoffrey's leg, heavily bandaged, was propped up on several pillows. "Dear God!" she gasped.

He turned his bloodshot gaze towards her. "Ah, my sweet

wife. I was wondering when you would arrive. I am afraid you are too late to do anything save gloat over my condition."

"Why would I want to do that when you are fighting for my interests?" she snapped. She was more shaken than she wanted to admit. "How bad is it?"

He made a face. "My foot has a slit in it like a gutted herring. I cannot walk; I cannot ride. Christ, I'll have to use a forked branch for a crutch like one of those beggars at a monastery gate—probably for weeks."

"Is this true?" Matilda turned to the chirurgeon who gave a doleful nod.

"I have done my best, domina, but the count will be unable to sit a horse for several days and certainly not set his foot on the ground."

She folded her lips together and turned back to her husband. Anxiety made her waspish. She did not want to think about William le Clito, who had died from a minor wound in the hand that had festered and poisoned his blood. "Then what is to happen? You cannot stay here in this burned-out shell, and Waleran de Meulan is in the vicinity with seasoned troops."

"I have injured my foot, not lost my wits," he spat. "I am perfectly aware of the whereabouts of de Meulan. Since when have you acquired the knowledge to command in the field?"

"Since you asked me to bring you reinforcements from Argentan," she retorted.

"Which did not arrive soon enough. If you had pushed faster, I could have taken Lisieux."

Matilda's eyes flashed. "We came with all the haste we could muster. If you had wanted us sooner, you should have sent for us in better time. That is your lack, not mine, my lord."

He pushed himself upright. "Christ, hold your tongue, you sour bitch. Do you know how hellish this campaign has been? Do you know how much sweat and blood it has taken to push this far while you have been sitting safe behind your high walls at Argentan, and then, after one day's ride and no fighting, have the bile to tell me I have failed?" His voice ended on a ragged note and tears of fury shone in his eyes.

She made an impatient throwing gesture. "The fact remains that you did not take Lisieux and this place is not secure. Someone needs to plan what happens next. I have brought you reinforcements and supplies, but not enough to feed all of your men and mine. We will have to send out foragers, but how far afield will they have to go?"

Geoffrey looked away into the shadows of the bed. "I will talk to you no more," he said hoarsely.

The chirurgeon came to the bed and felt Geoffrey's brow. "He has a fever, domina," he said. "Better to return in a while when he is rested."

"Very well," she said. "But decisions have to be made."

❖ ❖ ❖

That night, Matilda barely slept. There was constant toing and froing in the camp. Scouts arrived by lantern-light and departed again. The men played music round their fires, drank, told tales, and grew loud. Brawls broke out and were mostly settled with the whips and fists of the commanders. The wounded groaned on their pallets. Some died. The fire from the burned church subdued to glowing embers, but the stink of smoke hung on the air. Matilda checked on Geoffrey a couple of times, but the chirurgeon had dosed him with syrup of the white poppy to give him ease, and he was deep in a drugged sleep. Many of the troops were sick with bloody bowel motions. William Talvas had fallen victim in the night, and had retired to groan in his tent. Towards dawn, Matilda gave up on sleep and, gritty-eyed with tiredness, went to mass. The morning light did not make the situation look any better and more men were falling sick. Without Geoffrey to lead the campaign it was going to founder.

Matilda went to him following her prayers and found him sitting up, awake and aware, in great pain and full of bad temper.

"The campaign will have to cease until the spring," he growled. "I cannot lead the troops. Talvas has the flux, and William of Aquitaine does not have the authority. If we press on now, it will be a disaster. We have made some gains; let us consolidate those."

She was tempted to beat him about his bad foot with the fire poker. "So you give up after two weeks? Will your allies still be willing to campaign with you in the spring after this? We have planned this for so long, and now you turn tail and run like a whipped cur!"

"I am not running anywhere," he snarled. "I will not have you impugn my courage. We have no choice but to withdraw. Do you not see? Pah! Of course you don't, because it is ever your way to be blind and stubborn if something does not suit you. If we advance as we are, we face disaster, even with the reinforcements from Argentan. Christ, you foolish bitch, we will be destroyed in the field and there will be no spring campaign at all, no duchy and no England. Is that what you want, because that is what you will get!"

Matilda stared at him. She knew he was right, but she was still furious and sick with disappointment. If there was dysentery in the camp, there was the danger that Geoffrey might succumb to its ravages, and while she had no love for him, she needed him, and so did their boys. But not like this. She turned to leave, pausing at the door. "Pray, what message shall I bring to our sons at Argentan from their illustrious father?"

He narrowed his eyes. "I do not need you to bear my messages. I shall visit as soon as I am able and speak to them myself." His voice softened slightly. "Tell Henry I will take him riding when I come. And tell the little ones that I hold them in my prayers—even if they are too young to understand. The baby...does he look like me?"

Her instinct was to lash out and say no, but it wasn't true and she believed in the truth above all things. "He has my hair and your eyes," she said, "and he thrives." She left then, and for a moment had to hide in a corner and compose herself. It took an effort, like lacing up a garment with frozen hands, but she succeeded in pulling everything taut, and when she arrived in the great hall, she was filled with regal vigour and purpose, and no one would have guessed how close to weeping she was. She could not afford the softness of a woman. In a man's world, she had to have the heart and stomach of a man.

Twenty-four

Normandy, May 1137

WILL D'ALBINI HANDED THE WOMAN A COIN IN EXCHANGE for the small pile of laundered shirts and braies she had placed on his coffer. He was no fop, but he liked clean underwear, and finding a decent laundress was always one of his first priorities once he had dealt with his tent and his horses.

"Rushed off my feet, I am," she said as she tucked the silver penny in the pouch at her belt. "Those Flemings think a shirt gets washed and dried faster than you can toast bread on a stick." With a shrug of her ample shoulders and a belated curtsey, she stumped from his tent.

Will's lips twitched. Leaving his squire to place the fresh shirts in his travelling coffer, he followed the woman out into the bright summer morning and gazed at the bustle of the camp. The king had crossed from England to Normandy in March in order to secure the province and treat with King Louis of France. A campaign was being organised to march on the castles held by the empress and force her out, but it had been hampered because Geoffrey of Anjou had crossed the border with a large army and was ravaging the Hiémois. He had destroyed Bazoches-au-Houlme, razing the church, which had been full of folk taking shelter. William D'Ypres, Stephen's chief mercenary captain, had attempted to bring Geoffrey to battle, but many of Stephen's Norman lords were reluctant to obey the command of a bastard Flemish mercenary with a shady past. There was tension in the camp and frayed tempers. Will was keeping his head down and staying clear of trouble as much as he could. He admired D'Ypres as a soldier, but he was wary of the large Flemish contingent Stephen maintained as the backbone of his army. Not that D'Ypres was in camp just now. He had been out on a patrol since yesterday afternoon.

Stephen was preparing to advance on Lisieux and force Geoffrey to commit himself. At the same time he was negotiating with various Norman lords and trying to gain their support. Yesterday, Will had served wine to Rotrou of Mortagne, who had agreed to Stephen's terms. Today, Stephen was conducting talks with the lords of Tancarville and Laigle.

Going to the camp fire, Will helped himself to a small loaf of bread, breaking it open and tucking into it a thick slice of bacon from the rashers his cook was frying in a huge skillet, then, chewing with enjoyment, he went to look at his horses. Forcilez, his pied destrier, swung his head and blew a gust of hay-scented breath over him. Will fed him a piece of crust and ran his hand down the solid black and white shoulder. Thus far the stallion was holding his condition despite three months in the field and Will was pleased with his stamina.

Turning at a sudden rumble of hooves, he was in time to see William D'Ypres ride past with his entourage. The mercenary captain's expression was thunderous. Something bad had happened, that was for certain. Swallowing the last of his breakfast, Will hastened over to Stephen's pavilion, where he was expected anyway.

❖ ❖ ❖

D'Ypres spoke to Stephen with his rage controlled, and all the more powerful for it.

"He knew," he growled. "Robert of Gloucester knew about the trap I set for him. How many Normans here in camp are working on his behalf and not ours?" He shot a glare at Will who was decanting the wine for the imminent meeting with Laigle and de Tancarville.

Will turned to Stephen. "Do you want me to leave, sire?"

Stephen shook his head. "I trust your discretion, Will. I hardly think you have been sneaking information out of the camp to the Earl of Gloucester or the Count of Anjou."

"Well, someone has," D'Ypres spat, "because the whoreson suddenly turned back from the place where I know he had arranged to meet Geoffrey of Anjou's man. My informants are men I can rely on."

Will said, "I did not realise my lord of Gloucester was a sworn enemy."

D'Ypres curled his lip. "He may have made his oath to our lord king, but he is just biding his moment to turn to the other side."

"What of the count's man?" Stephen asked. "Was he there?"

"No trace beyond a few hoofprints, sire. The Angevins sneak around like smoke and shadows, and when Gloucester saw my troop, he fled."

Will busied himself with the wine. From what he could glean, D'Ypres was convinced Robert of Gloucester was passing information to the Angevins and planning to defect to their company. That could well be the case, but if D'Ypres had failed to trap Robert in the act, there was nothing to be done. Indeed, there were likely to be serious repercussions from this failed attempt, and both Stephen and D'Ypres must be aware that they were treading on precarious ground.

❖❖❖

The consequences arrived two days later as Stephen was striking camp for his march on Lisieux. Robert of Gloucester had been absent from the court ever since D'Ypres's failed attempt to trap him in treacherous dealings, but now he arrived at the head of his knights, and was cheered by the Normans and English in the camp because he was popular and the eldest surviving son of the old king. Will was attending Stephen with some others, including D'Ypres, when Robert flung into the tent, his eyes hard with anger.

Stephen immediately rose to his feet.

Robert knelt in obeisance. "Sire," he said curtly.

Stephen kissed him and raised him to his feet. "I am pleased you are here," he said. "There is a matter we must set to rights between us."

"Indeed there is," Robert said. "I will not be spied upon by your Flemish cur and have my name dragged through the slime. I will not be subjected to attacks on the road when I am about my legitimate business."

"How is meeting up with Angevin spies legitimate business?" D'Ypres demanded, stepping forward.

"You cross the line!" Robert bared his teeth. "But then why should I expect you to know what honour is when you were banished from your own family for dishonour!"

D'Ypres flushed. "Do not speak to me of crossing lines, my lord. You are so far over your own, you will never find the way back!"

"Peace!" Stephen raised his hand. "I will not have this wrangling between my lords. I have said this matter must be set to rights, not inflamed!"

"Then leash your dog and whip him to order," Robert said. "I do not deny I was going to meet with the Angevins, but not to commit treason. I was garnering intelligence as any commander does—intelligence that I would have brought to you, except I was unable to complete the rendezvous because of this lackwit's blundering. So now I have no intelligence. If he was acting alone, I have to ask if the dog sits in place of the master, and if he was not, then what does it say of your motives, sire?"

Stephen's face was scarlet. "It says I am a prudent man. What does it say of you that you did not come to me openly and tell me you were meeting with a spy from the enemy camp? What am I to glean from that in my turn?"

Gloucester stood tall. "These arrangements are delicate. I deemed it safer to hold back until I had information. But of course now I have none. My hands are empty, and it is not my fault."

"You were going to defect," D'Ypres growled.

Gloucester arched his brow at the mercenary. "You have proof? Doubtless had your ambush succeeded, you would have brought my corpse before the king and sworn your lies over the wound between my shoulder blades." He glared at Stephen. "I swore my oath to you on the proviso that you would rule in justice and honour. Where is that justice and honour now?"

"You swore your loyalty too," Stephen replied.

"Have I violated that loyalty in any way?"

Stephen lifted both hands, palm facing outwards. "Indeed no, but you did not signal your intentions clearly. Let us treat this as what it is: an unfortunate misunderstanding. I swear to you it will not happen again, but in your turn, come to me with your plans next time, rather than hoarding them to yourself. On that understanding, let us have peace, because we have an army to set on the road."

Gloucester gave a curt nod. "So be it," he said, "but I will not stand for more."

Stephen leaned forward and gave him the kiss of peace. "Good," he said. "And now you and William will make your peace too."

D'Ypres's throat swelled until the veins bulged and he looked as if he were harbouring a craw full of unspoken words.

Gloucester hesitated and then gripped the Fleming's shoulders and the men exchanged an embrace that expressed violence rather than resolution, even if form was observed. Both dogs might have been leashed, but neither was muzzled.

Will decided to remain clear of the pair of them and do his best to avoid being bitten. He was certain it would come to bloodshed, even if for the moment it had been postponed. What he was less certain of was the truth, because it seemed to him that everyone was dancing around their own versions of it and feeding the flames, while the fire that mattered dwindled and went out.

Will's vow to avoid trouble lasted little more than a week. The king had camped at Livarot, intending to retake Lisieux and bring Geoffrey of Anjou to battle. He saw to it that his own men erected their tents and tended their mounts, then retired to his own pavilion.

Having dropped the tent flap behind him, he went to the small devotional at his bedside and knelt to thank God for being with him through another day. He asked His protection from evil and begged forgiveness for his sins. Standing on the devotional was a small, exquisite incense box that Queen Adeliza had given him as a gift in the days when he had sometimes ridden as her escort. He cupped the dainty thing in his large hand, running his thumb over the inlaid silver and the intricate cerulean-blue enamelling. Inside were several pieces of precious frankincense and a small silver spoon, the end of which bore an image of the Virgin. He was frugal with the frankincense and only burned it on special occasions, because he wanted to preserve her original gift for as long as he could, and because frankincense, given to the baby Jesus in the stable at Bethlehem, was a very precious commodity, not to be squandered on the mundane. In its smoke was the breath of God and kings.

He often thought of Adeliza when he prayed. His vision of "Heaven's Queen" was inextricably bound up with his image of her at a crown-wearing, robed in cloth of silver and a cloak of blue. It was how he always thought of her, although he knew she was living quietly in retirement at Wilton and devoting herself to good works. She would always be a queen to him. He thought that when he returned to England, should his road pass by Wilton, he would go there and pay his respects.

His wistful ruminations were rudely curtailed by loud shouts from outside the tent. He put down the little incense box and hurried out just in time to have a Norman soldier crash into him, blood pouring from his broken nose and cut lip. A Fleming pounced upon the man with a snarl and smashed his bunched fist into his victim's face again. Will had staggered at the first assault, but righted himself, seized the Fleming by the shoulders and flung him to one side. A dagger flashed and pain streaked along Will's ribs. He avoided the second slash of the knife and managed to grab the Fleming's wrist and with a hard twist disarm him. Several Albini knights who had been frozen with astonishment now leaped into the fray. The Fleming was caught and pinned, but more of his comrades appeared out of the night, intent on his rescue, and they brought in pursuit more Normans, in a rapid chain of violent brawls. Will ducked back inside his tent, grabbed his sword and shield, and jammed on his helm. His side throbbed like a drum in time to the swift beat of his heart. He did not know how hard he was bleeding, but there was as yet no stain on the outside of his gambeson. Plunging back out of the tent, he rallied his men around him and drove Flemings and Normans alike away from his ground. Shouts, screams, and the clash of weapons rent the night. Two loose packhorses galloped past. Across from Will's camp, the great round pavilion belonging to the Norman lord Hugh de Gournay was on fire. Will seized a water jug from outside his cook tent and ran to help beat out the flames, shouting over his shoulder for his men to bring the barrels of sand that they had been using to clean their hauberks. Mounted men pounded through the camp, brandishing spears and swords: the personal knights of the king's household riding through to restore order and round up the instigators.

"Whoreson Flemings!" spat a Norman knight who was beating at the flames of de Gournay's tent with a leather cape.

"They started this?" Will panted.

The man nodded. "Over provisions!" he said between thuds of the cape. "Caught one of the bastards stealing a tun of wine from our supplies...Said he had the right to take it because we were hoarding stocks and their lot had none. Next moment all of his cronies arrived and we weren't going to stand by and let them steal what's ours."

Will's knights started shovelling sand on the fire, but it was plain that Hugh de Gournay's tent was a lost cause and all they could do was clear the ground and prevent the flames from spreading. De Gournay was in a seething fury as he regarded the destruction of his camp, his face black and a horse blanket clutched in his grip from his efforts to put out the flames. "I will have no more of this behaviour from the king's Flemings," he said through clenched teeth. "Enough is enough." He gestured to the knight standing beside Will. "Pack up what's left of this mess. We're leaving." He started to turn away.

"But what of the march upon Lisieux?" Will pressed his hand to his side where blood had now begun to soak through his gambeson.

"What of it?" de Gournay said with a large shrug. "Let the king use his Flemings since he loves them so much. Robert of Gloucester is right. He lets them do as they please. The Flemings are a law unto themselves. If the king will not heed complaints in council, then let us see if he heeds this! If I were you, I'd do the same: take your men and go." He strode off shouting orders.

Will wove his way back to his own camp and ordered one of his knights to fetch a chirurgeon. The night's brawl had created a high demand for such services and by the time one arrived, Will had peeled off his garments and packed his wound with linen bandages. He had several nasty burns and singed brows as result of the fight with de Gournay's now incinerated tent. The chirurgeon clucked his tongue as he threaded his needle with the hair from a destrier tail. "You are fortunate the blade filleted along your ribs and not under them," he said, "or else you'd be a corpse, and I've seen too many of them tonight. Plenty of men will be stitched in their shrouds following this foolish brawl, never mind put back in their skins."

Will clenched his fists on his knees and squeezed his eyes shut as the chirurgeon began his work.

"More than just de Gournay have left the camp," the man said between stitches. "I counted at least a dozen Norman lords riding out. The king's numbers will be much weakened."

Will grimaced. He supposed Stephen might persuade some to return, but whatever happened, there would be no advance on Lisieux now. The rift was too great and the divided could not conquer.

Will's wound made him feverish, and after an attempt to ride Forcilez split some of the stitches and renewed the bleeding, he was confined to the camp while he healed and could only watch as Stephen's force fractured and shattered like a wave destroyed on a rock. The assault on Lisieux was postponed and then abandoned.

On the first day that Will was properly able to leave his bed, Geoffrey of Anjou, the devil himself, rode into camp under a banner of truce and the game took a new turn.

Twenty-five

BRIMMING WITH RESTLESS ENERGY, GEOFFREY PACED Matilda's chamber at Argentan, a cup of wine in his hand. Matilda eyed him warily because he seemed very pleased with himself, and she did not trust him. He had but recently arrived and thus far had said nothing, preferring to greet his sons and busy himself with the domestic trivia of returning home.

"What have you done?" she demanded.

He paused and turned. He still walked with a slight limp, courtesy of the spear injury to his foot at Le Sap. "I suppose I should anticipate no other form of greeting from my loving wife."

"Perhaps because I expect you still to be in the field. Unless you are here to tell me you have won a great victory over Stephen and driven him all the way back to Wissant?"

Geoffrey shrugged. "In a manner of speaking I have."

A servant arrived bearing soft white towels and a bowl filled with steaming water and rose petals. Having set them down, he bowed from the room at a flick from Matilda's fingers. Geoffrey sat on a padded stool near the fire and extended his boots to her.

"Meaning?" Kneeling, she eased the boots from his feet. The supple calfhide was well waxed and the stitches so close-fitting that they were invisible. It was the duty of a wife to wash her husband's feet when he returned from battle campaign or came to her chamber after a day in the field, but she hated having to perform the task for Geoffrey, who was plainly enjoying her discomfort. "I would have thought you would send messengers had you accomplished such a thing."

"Why, when I can come to Argentan, visit you and my sons, and tell you myself? That is killing three birds with one stone, which is what I have done with Stephen." His voice sharpened as she removed the boot from the foot that had suffered the spear injury. "Careful."

"Don't fuss." She gave him a look that was cold on the surface and fire beneath. It was a long time since they had shared a bed, and he still held that attraction for her. She wanted to claw his back and see the red beads well upon his shoulder blades like rubies. His expression mirrored hers. Hastily she concentrated on the task of removing his stockings and leg bindings and soaking his feet in the water. The sole of his left foot bore a livid scar and was slightly swollen because he had had his foot in the stirrup for most of the day. His right one, high-arched and pale as alabaster, might have belonged to an angel.

"Stephen has gone," he said. "Sent the troops to their homes and headed back to England. His campaign is over, perhaps even finished."

Matilda ceased her task and looked up at him, frowning. "Why are you not in pursuit?"

He gave a satisfied smile. "Because he has paid me not to do so to the tune of two thousand marks a year for the next three years."

Anger flashed through her like a sheet of fire. "You have arranged a truce for three years without my say-so?"

Geoffrey shot her a look. "Do not take that tone with me, wife. I know what I am about."

"That is not the point. The point is that you did not seek my counsel!"

He rolled his eyes with exasperation. "There was not time, and you are as stubborn as a mule and have no idea how to negotiate, even when negotiation would be to your own advantage."

She thrust the towel into his hands, indicating that she was done with serving him, duty or not. "But still it is mine to do," she snapped. "So what are you about, my lord husband? Grant me the fount of your deep wisdom."

"God on the Cross, woman, you could curdle fresh milk with your looks. If you will cease your haughtiness and unstopper your ears, I will tell you."

She made no move to pick up the towel and he had to lean over to dry his own feet.

"I am listening," she said.

"But will you hear?" He threw the towel aside. "Stephen cannot control his troops. The Normans might hate me, but they do not like him either, and he has done nothing to appease them. Instead he has ridden over them roughshod with his Flemings. He has allowed the quarrels between his troops to become wide rifts and he can no longer trust the Normans to serve him in the field. Since the attack on your brother by D'Ypres's men, the Normans do not trust Stephen. I have spoken to Robert, and I have letters from him to you in my baggage that you will find interesting. Your brother's flirtation with Stephen has run its course. By next campaigning season, Caen will be ours." He raised one golden eyebrow at her. "Stephen thinks he can buy his way out of trouble, but we can use that money to buy equipment, and men." A scornful smile crossed his face. "He has financed his own downfall."

It was all very clever, like a garment cut and stitched from perfectly fitting geometric pieces. She could not fault Geoffrey's reasoning, even if it galled her to see him so smug. "My father built up his wealth carefully for the good of all," she said, "and now Stephen squanders it, as if it is a never-ending resource. He just lets it trickle away through his fingers."

"Well, at least he is pouring it in our direction. We have two thousand marks. Your brother is on the verge of changing his allegiance and Stephen's army has broken up and turned for home. By next year, he will have even less money in his coffers to pay the hangers on, while we will be more prepared and stronger still. A truce is only a truce while both parties keep to it." He stood up, barefoot, and stroked his forefinger down her cheek. "The day is coming. Stephen doesn't know it yet, but then the only time he was swift on the uptake was when he stole your inheritance, and even that was the doing of others." He circled his arm around her waist and drew her against his body. "I have been a long time in the field," he said. "Have you missed me?"

She followed him to the bed, step by step. She was eager to read what Robert had written, but if the truce was a fait accompli, there was no immediate hurry. "Like a pulled tooth."

He laughed darkly. "My love, you are a constant joy."

She flashed him a look full of challenge and desire. "Liar," she said. Physical appetite was something she could control and ignore unless he was with her. When they were together, it was like a firesteel striking sparks on dry tinder, but without that proximity, there was nothing. It wasn't love, but it was need, and it was mutual.

"No more than you," he answered, and pulled her down with him.

Twenty-six

ADELIZA WATCHED THE GRAVEDIGGERS SHOVEL EARTH OVER the coffin of the young woman who had died in the leper hospital the previous evening. Her name was Godif and her father had been one of Henry's minor chamber servants. Adeliza had prayed, given alms, and paid for masses to be said. Standing now by the grave with the nuns and others of Godif's community, she shivered despite her fur-lined cloak. Life was so short, and filled with suffering. Godif had been a gentle, sweet creature, never complaining about her pain and the vile indignities that the disease visited upon her body. She was in a better place now; she had to be. Adeliza rubbed her arms and tears pricked her eyes. For poor Godif; for herself.

When the grave had been filled in, Adeliza returned to the nunnery. Since arriving more than two years ago, she had moved into a purpose-built small lodge. The nuns called it "the queen's hall" and she had not discouraged them. Part of her pain at losing Henry had been the loss of her rank and influence as Stephen's queen took over her role. Stephen had removed the patronage of Waltham Abbey from her and given it to his wife, and Adeliza was deeply hurt because Waltham, like Wilton, was personal to her, but Stephen had claimed it, saying it was the prerogative of a reigning queen.

Adeliza still had the wealth of Arundel and the income from Shrewsbury, but no longer was it her task and privilege to sit in state at official crown-wearings, and she was not encouraged to visit the court. Not that she had any desire to do so because everything had changed since Henry died. All that formidable power was gone and without a controlling hand on the reins the different factions were free to foment suspicion and unrest. All Henry had worked for was being torn down and replaced by something less robust and true. Wealth poured out of the treasury like blood from an opened vein and no one was doing anything to stanch it. Instead they were queuing to drink their fill. Waleran de Meulan strutted the corridors of the court like a beady-eyed cockerel. Henry of Winchester paraded as if he were already the archbishop of Canterbury. Hugh Bigod was swollen with false importance, waiting for Stephen to pour out yet more largesse and grant him an earldom, always dropping unsubtle reminders that he had been the recipient of the old king's last words, where he absolved everyone of their oaths to Matilda.

A cheerful fire burned in the hearth of her hall and Melisande, her kinswoman and attendant, had arranged a jug of spring flowers on the bench near the window. A pleasant background smell of incense filled the air, mingling with the aroma of warm bread from a basket of small loaves. Adeliza gave her cloak to her other lady, Juliana, and smoothed her dress. She felt relieved to be back in her quarters and, at the same time, a little guilty and unsettled. Here, life was safe and comfortable and enclosed, but it felt like an indulgent bolt hole sometimes. She turned to the jug of flowers and lightly touched the petals.

"Madam, you have a visitor," Rothard her chamberlain announced from the doorway. "Messire William D'Albini is in the guest chamber."

The name filled her with surprise and sent a small jolt through her composed of pleasure and apprehension. She had not seen him since Henry's funeral and could not imagine what he was doing here. "Did he say what he wanted?"

"No, madam, save to pay his respects."

"Then by all means admit him."

Rothard departed. Feeling flustered and curious, Adeliza directed Juliana to fetch the silver goblets from the small sideboard. Melisande plumped the cushions on the hearth bench and put a new log on the fire.

When Will D'Albini entered the room, his vigour seemed to fill it with such robust masculine virility that it took Adeliza's breath, because she had grown accustomed to a life among nuns.

"Madam, my Queen." Removing his hat, he knelt at her feet and bowed his head. His hair was as she remembered: a tumble of dark, glossy curls, thick and strong.

"That is no longer my title," she said, gesturing him to rise, "but I thank you for it nevertheless; it was gallantly spoken."

He rose to his feet. "Madam, you will always be a queen to me."

Adeliza stepped back a little so that she would not have to crane her neck. The light streaming through the window emphasised the tawny colour of his eyes, and picked up the green flecking around the pupils. It also revealed that he was red to the tips of his ears. "Please, sit," she said, and gestured to the bench. "Will you take wine?"

He gave an awkward smile as he sat down. "I should be pouring yours."

"Not at all. You and your father might have been the king's wine stewards, but you are my guest and it is kind of you to visit." She gave him the larger of the two silver cups, but his broad hand still dwarfed it. "What brings you to Wilton?"

His flush intensified. "I was in Winchester with the king, and Wilton was not far. One of my family's serjeants recently died a leper, and I wanted to give alms to a lazar house. I intend founding a leper hospital of my own and I wanted to ask your advice."

"Indeed?" She was warmed and flattered by his attention. "I would need to know the size of the foundation you were thinking of building and whether you want to house men and women both."

They spoke for a while on the specifics of what he wanted to do, and Adeliza found herself enjoying the conversation. It was a subject she could discuss with expertise and authority and she was flattered he had thought to come to her rather than seek the wisdom of clerics and priests. On their second cup of wine, she told him as much.

He fidgeted with his cup. "I wanted a gentle opinion," he said, "one I could trust, and I wanted to see how you were faring."

"That is kind of you," she replied. "As you can see, I am well. I have everything I need, and I am content to do my duty to God."

He looked at her sidelong. "But you do not take the vows of a nun?"

"I am not worthy." She looked down. "I am waiting for a sign from God to show me what He wants." She put her cup to one side, aware that in a moment she would be in tears and that she had drunk too much and said more than she should. "Will you stay to dine?"

He shook his head and eased to his feet. "I will not trouble you further today. I can see I have tired you."

"Not at all," she said quickly. "I am just a little saddened, that is all."

He hesitated. "I am sorry if I have brought you to that sadness."

Adeliza touched his arm lightly. "No," she said, "I have enjoyed your company." She found a smile to ease the troubled look in his eyes.

He cleared his throat. "You will not mind if I visit on another occasion?"

"You are welcome," she said graciously, feeling a little torn between pleasure and caution at his request.

She accompanied him to take his leave. A small boy was playing in a noxious puddle of rainwater and dung near the stable wall, leaping in and out of it, shouting loudly each time he made a splash. He was perhaps five or six years old, and clad in a woollen tunic of bright blue and a brown hood. He had removed his shoes and placed them neatly to one side of the water, but there was no redeeming his garments. Will gave a broad chuckle and folded his arms. "He's in trouble when his mother catches him," he said.

"We buried his mother just before you arrived," Adeliza replied. "She was a leper at the hostel. I daresay he's given his nurse the slip. He's as swift as an elver." She clapped her hands. "Adam!" Her voice was peremptory.

He jumped at her shout and anxiety furrowed his smooth, pale brow. "I was only breaking up the sky in the picture," he said in a high-pitched treble.

"Look at the state of you! Where's Hella?"

The child thrust out his lower lip. "Don't know."

"Why were you breaking up the sky?" Will asked.

"Because I thought I might look through it to heaven and see my mama again," he said. "I can't break the sky with my hands because I can't reach it."

Adeliza made a small sound and turned away, her fist clenched against her lips. Will crouched to the child's level, his great hands resting on his long, powerful thigh bones. "You cannot part the reflected sky with your feet either, child," he said gently. "You know that really, don't you?"

The boy sucked his lower lip and nodded.

"She would want you to grieve for her like a good son, but wouldn't she also want you to go on with your life and become a big, strong man who cares for others?"

Another nod and a shy look upwards from big dark blue eyes.

Will gave the child an assessing look. "I have a task for you," he said. "I have a mind to gift my lady the queen with a guard dog for her chamber door, but he is still only a pup and he is missing his own mother. I want you to be responsible for taking care of him while he is still very small. Do you think you could do that?"

Adam stared at him, his gaze growing round and wide. "Do you have him here now?"

"No, but I will send him from the kennels before the week is out, I promise you. One thing you should know about me is that I always keep my promises." He looked at Adeliza as he spoke and she looked back at him with moist eyes. He lifted a warning forefinger. "It is a very important duty; I would not give it to just anyone."

The boy nodded and straightened his spine in a soldierly fashion. Will responded to the gesture with a firm nod of his own to seal the matter. An instant later, a plump woman bustled up to them and began clucking over the boy like an agitated mother hen. This, then, was Hella.

After she had hurried him away to be cleaned up, Adeliza turned to Will. "That was kindly done."

He gave an embarrassed shrug. "Something to care for helps to take one's mind away from grieving—or so I have found." He knelt to her again, rose, and turned to his horse.

She watched him mount the beast: a handsome pied animal, powerful and solid like him, with a kindly eye.

"Thank you," she said. "...for everything."

He made a gruff disclaimer and, with another salute from his saddle, rode out.

Adeliza watched the porter close the gates and listened until the clop of hooves and the jingle of harness faded to bird-song. Then she returned to her chamber. William D'Albini's vigorous masculine energy had disturbed the air, and it had a completely different scent and feel now, as if the season had changed in a moment.

❖ ❖ ❖

Stephen eyed the golden bundle of puppy squirming in Will's arms. "This is a gift for the dowager queen?" He looked both dubious and amused. "It will chew her shoes and piss on her dress and you know how finicky she is. I would think there are better things to take her if you desire to win her favour."

Will raised his chin and the dog followed him with a fast pink tongue, destroying all his dignity. "It is a gift I promised to a child under her care at Wilton," he replied.

Stephen raised one eyebrow. "A leper child?"

Will shook his head. "He's an orphan my lady has taken into her household."

"I see." Stephen gave him a keen look. "But you are taking the whelp yourself, not entrusting it to a servant?"

Will put the pup down and it immediately attacked his shoes. He drew a deep breath. "Sire," he said, "I ask your permission to court the dowager queen with a view to making her my wife."

Stephen's eyes widened. "God's blood, you are ambitious!" His amusement remained but mingled with wariness now. "Just how long have you been brooding on this notion?"

Will gave the puppy a gentle side shove with his foot and it growled at him. "I have always honoured the dowager queen and thought highly of her, sire. She has been in mourning for two years and it seemed to me that if she was not set on the cloister, I could offer her an honourable marriage."

"And the way to a woman's heart is through deeds of kindness, especially when you cannot hope to compete with what she had as a queen?" Stephen said with a knowing smile.

Will was uncomfortable with that assessment because while it was partly true, it also made coarse cloth from fabric he

considered very fine. There were many things he could give
her that had not been hers as queen of England. But he said
nothing, merely set his lips.

Stephen shook his head. "You are a dark horse, Will. I
would never have thought to witness such audacity in you, but
I am discovering that men are seldom what they seem, and your
request at least is harmless ambition."

"Sire, I gave you my oath at your coronation and my loyalty
is to you."

Stephen grunted. "So you say, and so, in your case, I believe.
Well then"—he waved his hand—"go and court your queen,
and if the lady consents to your suit, I will give you an earldom
as a wedding present to make you a worthy consort."

"Sire!" Elation sparked in him, but caution too, because
while Stephen was generous, he would want something in
exchange.

Stephen rubbed his chin thoughtfully. "It is perhaps of benefit
that the dowager queen should have a new husband to give her
direction. She has too much time to brood in that nunnery, and
cling to the past." His eyes lit with a hard gleam. "If you marry
her, I trust you to keep her occupied and out of trouble. She
has been overly concerned with her rights in Waltham Abbey,
which belong to a reigning queen, not a dowager. I would
expect you to set her right on the matter. By all means let her
indulge in good works, but in her own sphere."

Will inclined his head. That at least seemed simple enough.
"I will do so, sire."

Stephen nodded approval. "I often thought that Adeliza was
wasted on my uncle. He never saw her delicate charms the way
others did."

"Sire." William scooped up the puppy and bowed from the
chamber, feeling smirched and elated at the same time. He had
been granted permission to ask for Adeliza's hand in marriage,

and he had the verbal promise of an earldom and in exchange for very little. All he had to do now was win Adeliza's consent.

❖❖❖

Adeliza had not expected Will D'Albini to return quite so soon, but she took his arrival in her stride, and thought well of him that he not only brought the pup for Adam, but spent a while with the lad and his new pet to see them settle into the relationship. She watched him tussle and play with boy and dog as naturally as a child himself.

"You like children, my lord," she said as eventually they walked to her lodging to take refreshment.

He smiled and shrugged. "They are easier to deal with than adults. As are animals. If you love them, they will love you, and their needs are easily read. I enjoy them for that wholesome simplicity."

She felt a pang at his words. There was very little of that in the world.

"I have something to ask you," he said as they reached her door.

"About the leper hospital?" She looked up at him and was trapped in his bright hazel stare. No, not about the leper hospital, she thought, because that subject would not fill his gaze with such intensity or bring such a flush to his face. Adeliza stumbled on the threshold and he caught her arm to steady her. She felt the span and strength of his grip.

"No," he said, "or not directly."

Adeliza had Juliana take his cloak and pour wine, and then dismissed all of her women, telling them to wait within call. Folding her hands in front of her like a nun, she said, "What do you want to ask?"

His complexion was fire-red by now. He gathered himself, and spoke in a rush. The words emerged like a speech, so she knew he must have been rehearsing them for some time—probably since riding away last week. "I have long admired and esteemed you," he said. "If it would be an honourable estate for you, then I offer my hand to you in marriage. I have the king's permission to pursue my suit, and should you agree, he will bestow an earldom upon me so that you shall not be disparaged."

Adeliza opened and closed her mouth. She had been queen to one of the greatest kings in Christendom for fifteen years, and had known what to say on every occasion, but now she had no voice, only a stare.

"I have shocked you," he said. "Forgive me; I am too blunt."

She struggled to draw her scattered wits together. She had suspected this was coming ever since he said he had something to ask her. Wilton was a safe haven where she could hide from the world and coddle herself. His masculine vitality frightened her. When he entered the room, he filled it with earthy life and she had grown accustomed to spiritual delicacy. And yet she had asked God to give her a sign, and perhaps this man was it. Not a shining miracle, but something spun of everyday cloth—something she had never had. "I am honoured, my lord," she said and had to clear her throat as her voice caught, "but I cannot give you an answer now. I must consult with my heart and with God and pray upon what you have asked."

She saw his face fall, but he swiftly mastered himself. "I understand," he said. "I was hoping you would give me an answer now, but I was not expecting it. I have thought upon the matter for a long time, but I know you have not." He made a face. "In truth, I would not want you to think for as long as I have, but I have the patience to wait on your reply."

She gave him a bemused look. "Why me, my lord? Why choose me?"

He flushed. "To choose anyone else would be to look at second best. You are beautiful and gracious, and a queen. You are no termagant. With you at my side, I could build great castles and found monasteries and hospitals. I could sit by the fire at night and be content to talk with you and watch you sew...or hold our child in your lap."

Those last words shot through her like a fiery arrow and her knees almost buckled. She wondered if he knew the effect such a speech would have on her and thought he probably did.

"And," he added in a voice that was soft but filled with knowing, "were you to ask why you should choose me, I would answer that I will protect your lands. I will fill your life with companionship—and your lap with children."

"Only God can do that," she replied unsteadily. "He did not see fit to grant me that privilege with my first lord husband, despite him having many children with other mothers. What if I am a barren wife?"

A spark kindled in his eyes. "I doubt that very much."

"But if I were?" she insisted. "What then?"

"I am prepared to take that risk, and I will still have you, and all that you are."

She felt as if she were drowning in a shallow sea. The talk of children made her loins heavy as if the potential was already curled within her, waiting. She was pragmatic enough to know that the statement "all that you are" involved more than just her physical person. It was the glamour of her former position as England's queen that attracted him, and the wealth she possessed. Arundel, Shrewsbury, Bicknor. For the moment she could please herself, but if she remarried, she would have to obey a husband again. "What did Stephen say when he gave his permission?" She could not bring herself to call him the king.

He looked down, but she caught a flash of something in his eyes—chagrin? Embarrassment? "He wished me success."

Stephen would, she thought. This man was his loyal supporter and promoting him would be useful.

Will cleared his throat. "I will leave you to your talk with God," he said. "Send to me when you have decided. I hope it will not be too long, but I am prepared to wait."

She could see that he was. But whether it was the persistence of a hunter outside a burrow or the gentler patience of a farmer attuned to the seasons remained to be seen.

Once more she saw him to the stables. Adam emerged, carrying the licking squirming bundle of puppy, christened Rex because he had come from the royal kennels. Will ruffled the boy's hair, tussled the pup in similar wise, bowed to her, and turned to his horse.

When he had gone, Adeliza felt a momentary surge of relief, followed by a shiver, as if she had forgotten to don her cloak on a chilly day. Biting her index finger, she turned towards the church. She tried to envisage being married to Will D'Albini and felt awkward. It was like having a new dish on her plate that was so different, she could barely pluck up the courage to taste it.

❖ ❖ ❖

Riding away from Wilton, Will squared his shoulders and kept his head high. She had not refused him outright; she had said she would think on the matter, and while there was hesitation, hope remained. She was so fine and rare that he felt like a foolish, shambling bear in her presence. He wished he had the urbane refinement of Brian FitzCount and Waleran de Meulan, or the pugilistic arrogance of the Earl of Chester, but neither were a part of his steady, cheerful nature. She would go and pray to God for an answer and all he could do was pray in his turn that God gave her the right one.

On his return to Winchester, he was dismounting in the courtyard of his lodging house when his knight Adelard came running to tell him they had received news that Robert of Gloucester had renounced his oath to Stephen. "He's declared for the empress and shut Bristol against the king!"

Will was dismayed but not surprised. Everyone had been expecting Gloucester to renounce his oath ever since the Normandy campaign when Stephen had returned to England and Robert had stayed at Caen, nursing his grievances. It would give impetus to other rebellions, and because Gloucester had lands on either side of the Narrow Sea, both areas would be destabilised. It was bad news, yet, at the same time, Will felt a twinge of excitement. The onus on the king to reward the men who remained loyal to him would be keener still, and who knew what other riches lay in store beyond an earldom and marriage to a queen?

Twenty-seven

MATILDA SAT DOWN ON THE BED IN HER CHAMBER AT Carrouges. Her crown was making her head ache. It might look a delicate thing, but she been wearing it for most of the day amid formal ceremonies and celebrations; the weight was beginning to tell on her neck and the band was squeezing her temples. Even so, she had no intention of taking it off, because while she wore it, she was a queen and an empress and she had authority.

Fetching his small stool, Henry wandered over to the sideboard and stood on it so that he could look at the two engraved silver cups standing there. They had been presented to him and his brother by the people of Saumur in exchange for a charter. "When can I drink wine out of mine?" he asked, looking round.

"When you are a man," Matilda replied. "They are no ordinary drinking cups, but tokens of an agreement between our family and the people of Saumur." Her voice held a warning note. If she knew Henry, he'd be having his dogs drinking out of them or worse. "And you are not to touch William's either," she added as she watched his hand stray towards his youngest brother's cup. The reason there were only two, not three cups was that Geoffrey, her middle son, was being raised in the household of her husband's vassal Goscelin de Rotonard.

It did not do to keep all of one's eggs in a single basket. William would go for fostering too when he was older but for now, at not quite two years old, he was still kept close in the women's chambers. Henry ignored him because he was only a baby and Henry knew he was the heir and the most important.

Geoffrey entered the chamber. A gold coronet embraced his brow, not as ornate as Matilda's but still a symbol of his rank, and he was wearing a blue silk tunic embroidered with small gold lioncels. Henry's tunic had been cut from the same piece of fabric. Geoffrey unbuckled the sword he had been wearing for ceremonial purposes and hung it over the back of a chair. Moments later, Matilda's half-brothers Robert and Reynald followed him into the room with Baldwin de Redvers.

Robert went to his nephew and admired the silver cup with serious interest. "If you drink from a silver cup, you will never be poisoned," he said.

Henry gave him a severe look. "Mama says this isn't a drinking cup. She says it's a token of agreement."

Robert's lips twitched. "She is right, but it is still true that you should always put a silver coin in your flask to keep your drink sweet. Did you know that?"

Henry shook his head, but absorbed the detail as he absorbed all knowledge, sucking it up like a sponge drawing up water.

"You are a fount of knowledge, Robert," Geoffrey said drily.

"My father believed in educating us all." Robert leaned his elbow on the sideboard. "Why be at the mercy of priests and charlatans when for the sake of a little study you can be armed to the teeth?"

Matilda said, "When you are a woman, having an education makes you realise how much at the mercy of priests and charlatans you are."

"So are you saying you would rather have remained in ignorance, wife?" Geoffrey asked with a sardonic gleam.

"I am saying it is twice as important that a woman should be educated, and twenty times as difficult for her to be heard." She looked round at the menfolk of her family and knew they would never understand, much less want to do so. That her place was above theirs, that she was the only one of them born of a ruling king and queen, was cause for envy, not worship. Had she been male, she could have led the discussion about to begin without a second thought. As it was, although she was a figurehead, they did not expect her to contribute to the dialogue, any more than they expected her to gird on a sword and don a mail shirt. Geoffrey was here with his army, amply fortified by the two thousand marks Stephen had given to him the previous year. He wanted to talk tactics with Robert, not her.

Matilda cleared her throat. "I have drafted letters to the pope, to my uncle of Scotland, and to my stepmother." She held up the sheaf of parchments lying by her right hand. "We must lobby the pope to reverse his ruling on Stephen's right to the crown; I will be working closely with the bishop of Angers on that matter and Brian FitzCount is writing a treatise from a secular perspective on my right to rule."

"But we need more than words," Geoffrey said and turned to Robert. "Will FitzCount go so far as to renounce Stephen?"

"Yes," said Matilda firmly. "He will."

Robert nodded in confirmation. "FitzCount will help however he can. He is being circumspect for the moment but as soon as we set foot in England he will declare for us. We can count Wallingford as ours. Miles FitzWalter has indicated he will come over too, and John FitzGilbert the marshal. He has control of the Kennet Valley with Marlborough and Ludgershall."

Geoffrey eyed Robert keenly. "Tell me," he said. "If Stephen had proved himself a model king and promoted your interests, would you be here today?"

Robert flushed. "I am not proud that I broke my oath to my father and to my sister; indeed I deeply regret it, but sometimes circumstances overtake the best of intentions. I thought perhaps it was God's will, but I was wrong." He looked at Henry, who had stepped down off his stool and was now playing with his toy wooden knight and horse on the floor. "I will not renege again."

The company settled around the fire to discuss their plans. The time was not yet ripe time for an invasion of England; there was still much to be done in the way of preparation and recruiting allies, but the following year seemed a possibility.

"You say you are in contact with the dowager queen," Robert said to Matilda. "I had heard she had retired to a nunnery and was occupied in succouring lepers."

Matilda nodded. "Yes, but it is no more the entirety of her life than being a patron of Bec is mine."

"A little more than that, since she lives amongst them. I even heard it suggested when my father died that she intended taking vows."

Matilda shook her head emphatically. "That is far from the truth. She is still concerned with what happens at Arundel and her other estates. The only trouble is this." She handed Adeliza's most recent letter to her brother, who studied it and, with pursed lips, handed it on to Geoffrey.

"D'Albini?" Geoffrey raised his brow.

"His father is one of the royal stewards and lord of lands in Norfolk, including the castle at Buckenham," Robert said.

"Will he be willing to swear for us?"

Robert frowned. "I do not know. If you saw him, you would think of a big friendly dog. He is intelligent and strong, but not complex."

"Meaning?"

"Meaning I would not mark him down as a man for subter-fuge and I would say he will do what he must while hoping for a quiet life. I suspect he will stick to his oath to Stephen, and if he becomes lord of Arundel, that could be difficult for us."

Matilda gnawed her lip. From her slight acquaintance with him she knew William D'Albini was good-natured and amenable. Despite his size and strength, he was agile and light on his feet and had a delicate touch at mixing wine. Women liked him. He exuded an earthy, wholesome virility, but seemed not to notice it himself or use it consciously, and thus it was not a threat. Even so, it was difficult to imagine the ethereal Adeliza sharing a marriage bed with him. "How good a strategist is he?"

Robert shook his head. "I doubt he has ever been tried beyond bringing the Albini men to the king to perform feudal service, but that only tells us he is inexperienced—it does not mean incompetent. He is an unknown quantity and that could be dangerous."

Matilda sighed. "I will keep writing to Adeliza. Whether she marries D'Albini or not, she has no love for Stephen. She will do what she believes is right."

"Well then, have a care what you do write," Geoffrey said. "We cannot afford to have our plans brought to naught by women's gossip."

Matilda glared at him. "Do not worry, my lord," she snapped. "I intend any 'gossip' I exchange with Adeliza to be of benefit. You do not understand how much the wheels of your endeavour are greased by such exchanges. Deal with your campaigns and your men, but leave this matter to me. I know my stepmother as you do not."

He exhaled down his nose with irritation. "Do as you will," he conceded, "but be cautious."

"I know my business," she retorted. "Do yours and leave me to mine."

For a moment the atmosphere was strung with tension. Then

Robert clapped his hands together and rubbed them. "We still have much to plan," he said. "This is only the beginning." He flicked his gaze between Matilda and Geoffrey. "The first thing I propose is a lasting truce."

Twenty-eight

ADELIZA TOOK THE LETTERS SHE HAD JUST READ AND CARE-fully fed them to the fire in her chamber. She watched them until they were ash and then turned away, hugging herself. Outside it was a hot August afternoon, but the chill was in her soul, not her bones.

Matilda wrote that she was preparing to come to England and challenge Stephen for his crown. The plans were still in the making but, when the time came, she wanted Adeliza to admit her to Arundel. Adeliza bit her lip. Matilda was the rightful queen and little Henry the heir to the throne. Adeliza would not dream of turning down the request, but she was frightened of what such a stand might cost. She was still struggling to come to terms with the recent happenings at Shrewsbury. The castellan there had risen against Stephen, who had marched to put down the revolt and hanged every last member of the garrison. There had been no leniency. She knew such things happened in warfare, but Shrewsbury was her town, given to her in dowry when she had married. To know she had been unable to intervene and save lives filled her with a terrible burden of guilt. There had been other uprisings round the country too, all stamped out like small bonfires, but still new areas kept flaring up. A Scottish army had invaded and been defeated in a fierce battle at Northallerton. King David had narrowly escaped with his household guard. She had known him well when she was queen and had counted him a good friend. One of his scribes had written a history of Henry's reign for her. To think of him now as the enemy made her feel sick.

The last of the parchment flaked into ash. Adeliza left the hearth and, drawing a deep breath, went to look out of the door that faced on to a courtyard with covered walkways and benches surrounding a grassy area with a cherry tree planted at the centre. Juliana and Melisande sat on a bench, talking to each other as they worked on chemises to go in the clothing chest for the leper hostel.

She heard young Adam's voice raised in bright chatter, and a moment later the boy hurtled round the corner, attached by a lead to a large adolescent dog galumphing at full speed. A little behind boy and hound came Will D'Albini, his stride long, but measured and deliberate. Adeliza suppressed the urge to run away. After all, she had summoned him here.

"Madam!" Adam attempted a bow while the dog strove to lunge after a cat that had been sleeping in a flowerbed. "I have brought you a visitor!"

"So I see." She faced Will with a pounding heart, but her tone was calm and gracious, betraying no sign of her flustered state. "Messire D'Albini, you are welcome."

He performed a small, serious bow. "Madam." He smiled and indicated the dog and child. "Both have grown beyond measure."

"Indeed, they are thriving." Adeliza dismissed Adam with a word of thanks, and as he and his charge ran off, dragging each other by turns in their preferred directions, she walked along the path and sat on a bench away from her women. He joined her side, and as he took a moment to adjust his cloak out of the way, she cast a swift glance at him in profile and noticed the healing cut along his jawbone. He had lost weight and his hair was shorter, although it still retained its curl.

"Your letter reached me in the field with the king," he said. "This is almost the first time since midsummer I have been out of my armour—and I do not suppose it will be for long."

An attendant brought them wine and napkins containing dainty hot wafers sprinkled with rose water. The breeze ruffled the leaves of the cherry tree and the scent of lavender and gillyflowers wafted from the borders.

"Were you at Shrewsbury?" she asked in a tight voice. "Is that where my letter found you?"

He grimaced. "Yes it was. I know your connection to the place, and I am sorry. The king had reached the end of his patience." He stared into the distance, and his eyes grew bleak. "These are difficult times. I want to protect you and keep you safe."

Adeliza looked down at her cup. "But the walls of Shrewsbury castle were no defence for its garrison, were they?"

"They were soldiers who took their chance, not women," he said. "They had rebelled against the anointed king."

A usurper king, she thought, but said nothing. Something must have shown in her expression, because he said, "You wrote to say you had decided to accept my offer of marriage. Have you then changed your mind?"

She could feel his tension and her own matched it. Even now, even when she had committed herself in written words, she was still unsure.

"I swear if you accept me, I will do everything I can to be fair and just." He took her hand in both of his, making a warm, enclosing shell.

She shook her head. "I have not changed my mind. I have asked God for His advice and He has sent you to me. I have thought about taking holy vows, but there are things beyond the cloister that I must do." She gave a troubled frown. "It is such a difficult step to leave these walls and take up the reins again."

He stroked her captive hand with a gentle movement of his thumb. "My own choice was very simple," he said.

After a moment, she raised her free hand to touch his face in a gesture as light as a breath. "Then I hope you have made the right one."

"I am certain of it." He took one hand from hers and curved his arm around her shoulder, and she felt herself fit into the cup of his palm as if it was meant to be. Tentatively, she leaned against him.

He continued to stroke her hand as he gazed across the tranquillity of the sunny courtyard. "We will have days like this, together," he said. "You and me, and our children. I promise you that."

She made a small sound in her throat. "If you can give me those things," she said, "then indeed I will know my choice is the right one."

❖ ❖ ❖

Adeliza gazed down at her shoes. They were of soft lilac fabric with fashionably pointed toes and were stitched all over the surface with silver thread and gems. The shoes of a queen. She had not worn them since the last occasion she and Henry had sat together in state at a court feast before he left to go hunting and never returned.

She had spent the morning in prayer with Herman her chaplain before the altar in the chapel at Arundel and, although she had risen from her knees, she was still praying now. "God help me in this," she whispered. "Help me to heal my heart and do the right thing." She was still uncertain about becoming a wife and mate again. At the time, she had not fully appreciated how Matilda felt when she was sent to marry Geoffrey of

Anjou, but now she understood a little more, and it wasn't a comfort, because she had seen what had happened to Matilda and Geoffrey's marriage.

She took a step, and then another, watching her shoes appear and disappear beneath the flaring hem of her silver silk gown. This was the path God wanted her to take, or else He would not have sent Will to her. He was a good man, even if he was loyal to Stephen. It was up to her, with God's help, to find a path through this. Will had promised her days of peace and offspring to fill them. The notion of the latter both spurred her forwards and held her back. She was desperate to conceive and at the same time terrified she would not. Fifteen years of being a barren wife to a man who had been siring bastards almost until the moment of his death had flattened her expectation and left her with terrible scars.

Will was waiting for her at the church door with the barons and knights of the Albini household and a host of gathered wedding guests, including the king. The bishop of Worcester was present to conduct the ceremony, his surplice shining as white as a gull's breast in the sunlight and flashing with thread of gold. Head high, eyes downcast, Adeliza made herself keep walking.

Will stepped forward to take her hand in his and, as in the garden at Wilton, she felt the warmth and vitality emanating from him and surging into her. When she raised her eyes to his, the intensity of his stare was almost too much to bear. Henry had not once looked at her like that.

"You will always be a queen," he said, his gaze leaving hers to rest upon the delicate crown set upon her veil of light silk.

She felt herself blush like a girl despite being a mature woman of five and thirty.

The marriage took place outside the church door in full public view, and then the guests entered within to celebrate the wedding mass. Many of the same people who had attended her marriage to King Henry were present now. The same faces had been at Reading for his funeral, but she would not think of that. Today was a time of celebration.

At the formal feast following the mass, she accepted the congratulations of the guests, and wished she were somewhere else. She wondered if the smiles on people's faces were genuine. Were they happy, or was it just an act for them too? When they turned their backs did they still smile?

"I am pleased for both of you," Stephen said, kissing her on either cheek. "William D'Albini is a fine man and you will be well protected by my new Earl of Lincoln. Eh?" He gave Will a slap across the shoulders.

Well guarded was perhaps closer to Stephen's meaning, she thought, concealing her antipathy behind a wan smile. Well, they would see. He might have Will's oath of fealty under his belt, but he did not share his life, his bed, and his board as she was about to do. She looked into Stephen's face. His geniality was strained and his features wore new lines of tired experience. Perhaps he was discovering that wearing a crown was a heavier burden than he had expected. Perhaps he did not sleep well at night. Whatever he did, he would never fill Henry's shoes in terms of ability. "Indeed, sire," she said.

Stephen's wife, Maheut, small and dumpy, kissed her too. "Life will seem very different to what it was before," she said. "But I know you have the fortitude to adapt."

Adeliza murmured a bland reply, her stomach tightening. Once Maheut's power had been hers as queen of England, but now it was all diminished. Of the things particularly dear to her that had been taken by this small, tenacious terrier of a woman, the patronage of Waltham Abbey was still the main hurt. Maheut now had it as a reigning queen's privilege, and Adeliza no longer had the influence to fight that corner.

More people spoke to her informally and she smiled until her cheeks were stiff and she felt as if that smile would drop off and be trampled underfoot.

Brian FitzCount was kind to her and one of the few to understand how difficult it had been for her to leave Wilton and rejoin the world. "I often think I would have taken to a life in the cloister," he said. "My father was in two minds whether to give me to the Church when I was a boy, but then the king took me because he wanted youths to raise as companions for his son. If not..." He spread his hands.

Adeliza managed another smile, this time less strained. "You would doubtless be an abbot by now—or a bishop."

He shook his head and his peat-brown eyes were pensive. "I am not sure I would be worthy of such robes."

"Then that in itself makes you fit."

He looked wry. "Madam, you always think well of people." He lowered his voice. "I am glad you will be at Arundel. Perhaps, if you are still a patron of the arts, you will permit me to write to you sometimes?"

Adeliza dropped her gaze. She knew what he meant and he was not talking about the books and works of poetry she had sponsored in the past as queen of England. Brian was a skilled poet and writer of tales that had been read out at court of an evening, but he was not intending to send her stories or poems now. "Providing the content is suitable," she said.

"I would send you nothing of which anyone could disapprove." He inclined his head and still in a lowered voice asked, "Do you ever receive news from the empress?"

Adeliza risked an upward glance and saw the anguish in his eyes. "Yes," she said. "She is my family still." She laid a sympathetic hand on Brian's arm. "I know your loyalty, but keep your vision clear."

"Madam." He bowed to her, his colour high.

His wife arrived fresh from a conversation with Waleran de Meulan about hunting dogs. Her face was as shiny as a new apple, and wisps of grey hair escaped out of the side of her wimple, which was slightly lop-sided. "My lord of Meulan says he has a fine black alaunt dog that he'll lend us to breed greater size into the pack at home," she said, loud with enthusiasm. "Two of the bitches are due in season any day."

Brian looked mortified. Unabashed, his wife addressed Adeliza. "Do you hunt with hounds, madam?"

Adeliza shook her head. "I do not have a pack," she said faintly, "but I believe my husband does."

"Well, if he needs advice on breeding, you must let me know."

Adeliza promised she would and made her escape. Brian FitzCount's quiet request had flustered her. For the moment she knew she must keep it to herself until she had had time to work upon Will. And then there was the troubling matter of allegiance. She had vowed a wife's loyalty to Will, but before that, such loyalty had been to Henry and she had sworn an oath before God to uphold his daughter.

During and after the wedding meal, there was music and entertainment. There were tumblers and jugglers, singers of songs, tellers of tales, and dancing too. For Adeliza it was like being at court again but it was also very different. She could almost feel Henry standing just beyond the reach of fire- and candlelight and it gave her a frisson of unease as she imagined what he might think of all this—none of it positive.

The time arrived for the bedding ceremony and suddenly Adeliza's hands were icy and her chest so tight that it was difficult to breathe. Memories of her first wedding night surged over her. The crowds in the chamber, the stares, the comments. She sensed the current speculation, and branching off from it, the curiosity and voyeurism of people wanting to see her unclothed. She could not bear to think of being thrust naked into a bed with Will D'Albini in front of all these people. She was a dowager queen, yet she felt as powerless as a chicken being chased round the yard because someone wanted it for the pot.

As she and Will were tumbled into their chamber by a merry crowd of revellers, she seized his arm. "Get rid of them!" she hissed. "I cannot bear this. It is too much!"

He gave her a perplexed frown. "They are not causing harm."

Adeliza shook her head. "I cannot," she repeated. "I will run mad. They have escorted us here, and they have all seen the bed. Let that be enough. What else is there to see?"

"It is tradition," he said, eyeing her as if she was making an unnecessary fuss. "It will soon be over."

She tightened her grip. "Please. For my sake."

He looked at her a moment longer; then his gaze softened and he sighed. "For my sake too," he said with a small shake of his head. "I do not want a madwoman in my bed tonight."

Turning, he spread his arms and began gathering up and ushering the guests from the room, thanking them for their good wishes, being by turns assertive, polite, jesting, and rueful, but never taking no for an answer until the cloak of the last one had flipped out of the door and he was able to close it behind them and shoot the bar across. Leaning against the wood, he folded his arms. "There," he said. "Is that better?"

"Thank you, yes." She gave him a wan, grateful smile. "I thought it would not matter, but suddenly I could not face the thought of them all staring at us. It brought back too many memories." She shivered and, rubbing her arms, went to the hearth.

"Now they will speculate to themselves," he said, adding wryly, "undoubtedly led by Lady Maude of Wallingford. Small wonder that my lord FitzCount used to spend so much time at court."

"You should feel sorry for her too," Adeliza said. "She and Brian FitzCount are as mismatched a pair as were ever yoked to an ox cart."

"And what of our own ox cart?" He checked that the door was secure and took a few steps towards her before stopping again, as if she were a wild creature and he was unsure how best to approach her.

"If I did not think we might manage to draw a straight furrow between us, I would never have consented to wed you."

"I want to make new memories for you," he said softly. "If you will allow me...but I do not know where to begin."

She looked at him standing there, doubtful now, when a few moments ago, for her sake, he had driven everyone from the room with authority. "Then let me help you." Facing him, she unfastened the brooch at the neck of her gown, and then the one lower down. She lifted her arm and showed him the tight lacing from armpit to hip.

"My hands are too big for such a delicate task," he said gruffly, but nevertheless came to unfasten the ties.

She did not ask him if he had ever done this before because she did not want to know. "No, see, they are not. You are deft when you choose to be." She gave a little laugh and tried not to flinch as he accidentally tickled her. "There." Easing the gown off her shoulders, she stepped out of it.

Very gently he removed her crown so that he could unpin the veil from her long, ash-brown hair; but then he replaced it on her head and took a backstep to look at her. "I have never seen anything so beautiful," he said softly.

Adeliza stood very still beneath his scrutiny. His swift breathing and flushed complexion kindled a glow in the pit of her belly.

"I am glad you asked them all to leave," he said. "Because otherwise I would not have seen you like this." He came closer again, cupped her face using one hand, and kissed her. His lips were warm and she could feel the heat and strength of his body. It was a good thing, she thought. Women's humours were known to be cold and to sap a man's strength. They needed a man's heat to complete them, and if one's mate was not sufficiently hot in his humours, then his seed might prove ineffectual. She had read every medical treatise she could while trying to conceive with Henry. She gave herself up to the kiss, and it was pleasant, as was the strength of his arms; yet he held her as delicately as he had held the crown, and she felt protected and secure.

With great ceremony he left her and, going to the bed, drew back the sheets, opening the covers for her like a gentleman. When she was settled, he sat on his own side and turned discreetly away to remove his clothing. He had broad shoulders and the relaxed loose muscles of a quiescent lion. Nothing like Henry, who had been stocky with a hard paunch and age-crêped flesh. This was a young man, virile and eager. He turned towards her, and she almost gasped at the sight of his broad chest and the stripe of hair feathering down his body and curling at his groin. Very virile and eager indeed. She did not know whether to avert her eyes, or stare in wonderment. And then the sheets fell across and she was rescued from her dilemma.

"I have a sin to confess, if sin it be," he said as he leaned towards her.

"Then you should see a priest," Adeliza whispered. Fascinated by the sight of his smooth, bare skin, she reached out to touch his shoulder and arm. His muscles had the gleam and definition of youth. Her fingertips encountered the glossy dark coils at his nape and her senses began to swim.

"A priest could not help me," he said. "I want you to be my confessor and listen to what I have to say."

"What if I cannot grant you absolution?" She wound her index finger round a cluster of his curls.

"Then I will be lost." He set his palm at her waist. "I confess I have loved you and desired you for a long time. You are so beautiful. I confess to envy of the king your husband even while I knew you were as far beyond me as the stars. And now I have you, I cannot believe my good fortune. How many men wish for the stars and have their wish granted? You shine, and I am dazzled."

She traced the outline of his lips with her fingertips. Such words were gems. Henry had never spoken thus to her. The times they had bedded had been a matter of business. Henry's preference was for buxom, big-breasted women who looked fecund and ripe.

"You are so slender and small," he said, his eyes following the path of his hand up and down her flank. "I fear that if I breathe out too hard, I will blow you away."

"I am strong enough to bear your weight," she said, feeling as if she would dissolve within the intensity of his stare. "I absolve you." She rolled into his arms and set her lips against his collar bone and hid her face. Above her, she heard him hiss through his teeth.

With Henry the act of procreation had often been uncomfortable. His needs had been bullish and practical. He expected her to please him and for her the experience had been a duty— one that she had performed gladly because it was God's will and her responsibility as a wife, but she had never understood why it should put a sparkle in people's eyes and lead them into sin. Indeed, sometimes it had been so painful, she had wept into the pillow afterwards, knowing it was all her fault. Men of science said that for a woman to conceive, she must release her seed, and the outward sign that such a release had happened was that she would shudder in a crisis of pleasure. Adeliza had never experienced such a thing with Henry, but now, tasting Will's skin, feeling it so supple and warm under her fingers, hearing his soft groan, she began to shiver with feelings that were utterly delicious.

She wanted to explore his body, and he was equally keen to investigate hers. "Mine," he whispered as he cupped her breasts and thumbed her nipples, then bent his head to stroke them with his tongue. "My queen now." She arched towards him and gasped. She had never imagined that a man's mouth and hands could work such alchemy on her body. It was like a poem; it was like the Song of Songs. The sensuality, the beautiful tension. And the act itself, for which she had learned to hold herself rigid against the pain, was a fluid thing of give and take, although she had never felt so full in her life. He took his weight on his arms so that he would not crush her and he did not lunge with the full force of his body but treated her with delicacy, and he called her his queen again, and his light and his joy.

She cried out beneath him and shuddered in his arms, overcome by ripple upon ripple of sensation. She clutched him, and felt him stiffen against her and buck. That part of the act was familiar to her, and yet at the same time it was wondrously different. And still he held his weight off her while he dipped his head into her shoulder, and gasped for breath as if he had run across a field in his mail shirt. After a moment, he withdrew from her and fell on to his side.

She drew her legs together and bent her knees towards him and he reached for her hand, kissing her knuckles and then her palm. "That was very fine," he said with a broad smile in his voice. "Very fine indeed."

"Yes," she said. "It was." She was still assimilating what had happened and marvelling. Small, pleasant aftershocks continued to undulate through her body. Earlier she had watched people laughing and had wondered if they were happy, and what it felt like. She had wondered what was wrong with her, but now she thought she knew a little of what they did. If the wonderful sensations she had just experienced meant that her body had released its seed to join with his, then the first part had succeeded. Perhaps this would be the time. Maybe now, with this new man and marriage, God would favour her with a big belly. Closing her eyes, she imagined herself in that condition, proud and fecund.

He left the bed and went to investigate the food and drink that had been left out for them under a cloth. Through half-closed eyes, Adeliza studied his loose-limbed grace and was again reminded of a proud male lion.

He brought her wine in a green glass, and a platter of delicate rose-water pastries, presenting them in a white napkin. Adeliza smiled at the incongruous contrast. He was so big, and yet he could be so precise and delicate too.

"We must make the best use of this time together to come to know each other," he said. "It won't be long before we have a full nursery to disturb us."

Adeliza flushed and wondered if he had said it deliberately, or whether it was of the moment and his own needs. He was a newly created earl, and an heir would be high on his list of priorities. "Indeed, I hope it is true, my husband," she said, and the last two words were as sweet as the rose-water pastry on her tongue, because of what he had given her now, and what might be in the future.

Twenty-nine

MATILDA WATCHED WITH A MINGLING OF AMUSEMENT AND sadness as Robert the hauberk-maker covered Henry's russet-red hair with a linen bonnet, and then fitted over it a child-sized coif of lightweight mail rivets. There was one too for Hamelin, Henry's half-brother.

"I'm a great knight now." Drawing his toy sword, Henry struck a pose. He was wearing a miniature version of the quilted tunic sported by the serjeants and men-at-arms.

"Indeed you are."

"Just like my papa."

Matilda quirked her brow, but forbore to comment. One day her son was going to be greater than his father, and his grandfather. She intended to make sure of that.

"I'm going to be just like Papa too," Hamelin said. He was two years taller than Henry and sturdy. His hair was not as vibrant as his younger brother's and his eyes were a wide-set mottled hazel like his mother's. Matilda had accepted him into her household without malice. The child would be what he was moulded into. A companion, help-meet, and loyal military servant for Henry was her intention for him.

"But I'll be the duke and the king and you'll be my vassal,"

Henry said. "You will have to promise to obey me and fight for me, and I will give you lands and gifts in return."

Hamelin frowned. "What sort of gifts?"

Henry waved his hand. "Castles, and swords, and horses, and armour."

Hamelin fingered the coif and the green glints shone in his eyes. "I want a big black horse," he said. "Like Papa's."

They ran off to play their game of capturing a pretend castle and were joined by some of her brother Robert's younger sons. Matilda pursed her lips. She would have to watch Henry and quash any inclination to profligacy. She did not want her son growing up to become a weak man at the mercy of barons who would milk him dry and then desert him. He needed to learn how to be shrewd and build affinity, and how to divide and conquer as necessary. She curled her lip, thinking of Stephen. He had no notion of how to rule a kingdom. All the wealth her father had accumulated was pouring out of the coffers like blood from a slashed artery as he strove to hold together the factions at court. Being a king was not about pleasing people. It was about controlling them.

A messenger was ushered into her presence and, kneeling, presented her with a bundle of parchments. Her eyes lit on the seal of Ulger, bishop of Angers, as she dismissed the messenger. This was the news she had been waiting for, and her breathing quickened. The bishop had been in Rome at the Lateran Council, petitioning to have Stephen overthrown. Matilda had sent rich gifts to the delegation along with her pleas: reliquaries, a gold pyx, boxes of frankincense, and a robe woven with cloth of gold and embroidered with rubies from the treasure store she had brought with her from Germany. Stephen had sent his own delegation there to argue his case under the auspices of the dean of sees and she knew he would have sent similar gifts and left nothing to chance. She read rapidly, repeating the words to herself. It was written in Latin, in which she was fluent. As she read, her cheeks began to flame and she felt so sick with rage that she heaved.

"Sister?" Robert, who had entered the room in the messenger's wake, hastened over to her. "What is it?"

"Have you seen Stephen's argument?" she choked. "Have you seen why he says I have no right to be queen of England?" She thrust the parchment at him. "He argues that my parents were never legally married—that my mother was a nun, a bride of Christ, who had taken the veil! I expected him to make much of the lie that my father absolved men of their vows to me on his deathbed, but this…this reeks of the gutter! Yes, she dwelt in a nunnery before she wed him, but she did not take vows."

Robert read the letter and his expression grew grim. "That is a desperate argument," he said with contempt. "The marriage was performed by Archbishop Anselm, and he would never have sanctioned it if he believed for one moment your mother had taken the veil." Robert read further and then said bleakly, "The pope has upheld Stephen's claim to the crown."

She controlled her anger. "I did not expect any different from Innocent." She gestured to the letter. "Many of his cardinals disagreed with his decision. It is they we must foster, and we shall look to the next pope for a better outcome. Innocent is an old man and not robust. This only makes me the more determined. All the time my father was heaping largesse and privilege on Stephen, he was fostering a viper in his bosom."

"Stephen would not have done it without advice from his inner council," Robert said. "He allows men of stronger will to govern him, and in turn they fight among themselves over who is going to be the power behind the throne. The Beaumonts are trying to undermine the bishop of Winchester's influence with Stephen. You know how much our cousin wanted to be an archbishop, but they've stopped him in his tracks."

Matilda exhaled with bleak amusement. Cousin Henry had supported Stephen all the way to the throne of England, expecting to become his chief adviser and archbishop of Canterbury in due course, but his plans had been thwarted by the Beaumont brothers Waleran and Robert. It was their candidate, Theobald of Bec, who had been elected to the archbishopric. Adeliza had written that Bishop Henry was fuming at what he saw as an insulting slight.

"So you think he can be further weaned away from Stephen?" Matilda asked, thoughtful now. Her rage had become a dark sediment in her blood. "I would not trust Henry of Blois further than I could throw him in all those glittering robes of his, but he could be useful to us."

"I will write to him in general terms," Robert replied. "A little diplomacy to grease the wheels and some flattery to soothe ruffled feathers will not come amiss, and may even be of great benefit."

Matilda gave a curt nod. "Do what you can." She tried to put the news from Rome aside. She had always known the road would be strewn with obstacles, and each time she came across another one, she set herself to clear it because right was right and she had a son to fight for. Stephen's use of underhand tactics and false oaths merely put iron in her soul and made her even more determined to bring him down.

❖❖❖

At Arundel, Adeliza sat on the window seat in her sun-filled confinement chamber and stroked the wonderful curve of her belly, round as a full moon. Even now, in the middle of her ninth month, she still had to reassure herself that she was not dreaming, that there really was new life growing inside her. She had conceived within the first weeks of her marriage during the honey month. God indeed must be shining His light on them, she thought. After fifteen barren years with Henry, Will had got her with child at a glance. Her fluxes had ceased straight away. And the strange thing was that Will had no bastards to his name, and Henry had had more than a score.

Will was due home from court any day, having attended a gathering at Oxford to discuss matters of government with the king.

Adeliza's belly hardened under her palm and a small pain lodged in the small of her back. She shifted her position in the window seat to make herself more comfortable, easing her spine with a large pillow. A pile of sketches lay on the cushion beside her and she picked them up to study again. Now that Will had a substantial income through their marriage, he had embarked on various building projects. Arundel had received a new round keep of stone that had reached completion a fortnight ago, its foundation having been laid in the first month of their marriage, and work had begun to build an ornate castle on his manor of Rising in Norfolk. The latter was mainly sheep pasture and park land because the agricultural soil was poor, but Will thought it an ideal place for a hunting preserve and retreat that would also be fit for a queen. They had visited Rising on a freezing January day to study the ground and discuss plans. The first stones had been laid in late February as the evenings started to lengthen, and work, so she heard from regular reports, was continuing apace.

She shifted again as the pain returned, meandered vaguely around her hips and loins and vanished again. Turning her head, she looked out of the open window and saw two of Will's outriders cantering through the gate. That meant he would not be far behind. She stood up, intending to send one of her ladies with a message to the steward, but as she turned in the window seat, she felt a strange sensation deep inside her body, followed by a gush of biblical proportions between her thighs, drenching her chemise and gown and puddling the rushes. The pain strengthened and her belly grew as hard as a drum.

She cried out to Juliana who dropped her sewing and hastened to her, while Melisande ran to fetch the midwife.

❖ ❖ ❖

"You will wear out the floor," said Joscelin of Louvain. He was Adeliza's younger half-brother, born out of wedlock, and had joined Will's household at Christmas, arriving from Brabant to take up the post of castellan. He was lithe and slender like Adeliza, with laughing grey eyes.

Will swung round and paced back the way he had come. "It has been a full day and night," he said. "Why does birthing a babe take so long?"

Joscelin shrugged his shoulders. "You would need to ask a woman that," he said with a rueful grin. "They always take their time whatever they decide, and then they're apt to change their minds on a whim."

"I always thought I was a patient man until now. It's almost as bad as being at court," Will said. The waiting, the pacing, the not knowing what was happening behind closed doors. There were many similarities. He began to pace again, then stopped himself and unclenched his fists.

Joscelin eyed him thoughtfully. "What will happen now that the bishop of Salisbury has been attacked by Waleran de Meulan's men?"

Will grimaced. "Your guess is as good as mine. It's an enormous mess and no mistake. I am glad to be here and out of it."

"Stephen lost control, didn't he?"

Will shook his head. "Not exactly. The bishop of Salisbury has been stockpiling riches for himself and his relatives for many years, even back in the time of the old king. Something should have been done long ago. When it happened, it just got out of hand, that's all."

Joscelin arched one eyebrow. "That's an understatement."

"Stephen knows what he is doing," Will said hollowly. In Oxford, there had been a quarrel over lodgings between the household knights of Meulan and the bishop of Salisbury. A vicious fight had broken out, blood had been spilled, and the bishops of Salisbury, Lincoln, and Ely had been accused of fomenting a riot and subjected to arrest and arraignment.

"I wouldn't call laying hands on a bishop a good way of garnering support from the Church."

"It could have been done with more finesse, I grant you, but the amount of silver Salisbury has been creaming off is beyond a jest."

"I agree, but Church discipline is a matter for the archbishop of Canterbury and the rest of the bishops, not the king."

Will heaved a sigh. "Done is done. It is not the wisest move the king has ever made, but we have to go on from here. I—" He looked up as a midwife entered the room with a wrapped bundle in her arms.

"Sire," she said, "you have a son."

The words struck Will such an emotional blow that it was hard to breathe. "And my wife, the queen? Is she all right?"

The woman gave him a broad smile as she placed the baby in his arms. "Your wife is well indeed, sire, and sends you her greetings and your heir."

Will gazed into the tiny crumpled face amid the folds of soft blanket. Suddenly there was a tight lump in his throat. "I have a son," he said in a choked voice to Joscelin. "A prince because his mother is a queen. A son to carry my line." The feel of the baby's weight took his breath away and filled his chest to bursting. He passed him to Joscelin, who took his nephew gingerly and having murmured appropriate words, and held him long enough to be polite, returned him to Will with relief.

Will was torn. He was so proud and besotted that he could have carried the baby round with him all day, but he also knew that the child should be kept safe in the haven of the women's apartments, not in the public arena. With great care he returned him to the midwife. "Give him to his mother," he said, "and tell her I will visit as soon as she is ready to receive me. Tell her also I will arrange to have him baptised tomorrow morning."

When the woman had gone, the blanketed bundle cradled along her arm, Will put his head in his hands and wept a little with pent-up joy and release. "The world has changed," he said to Joscelin, who was looking at him askance. "I have a son in it now, and I must safeguard his future as much as my own."

❖ ❖ ❖

Later in the day, he visited Adeliza in her confinement chamber. She was sitting up in bed looking radiant, her hair a gleaming braid falling forwards over her shoulder. Her gown had a deep opening secured with brooches so she could feed the child herself, which she intended to do until she was churched, after which she would employ a wet nurse. Her face was tired, but her eyes were glowing and her smile was radiant.

Will leaned over and kissed her very gently, feeling big and awkward. "I am so proud of you, and our beautiful son," he said.

"And I am so grateful for God's great mercy that we have him," she answered with a tremble in her voice.

Sitting on the low chair at her bedside, he presented her with the small carved box he has been hiding under his cloak, and looked at her with anxiety and expectation.

Mystified, she took it and ran her fingers over the exquisitely chiselled leafwork on the top and sides, before unfastening the clasp. Inside was a book, its jewelled ivory cover a stunning contrast to the red silk lining. "Aesop!" she exclaimed with bright pleasure. "I love those stories!"

"I used to listen to you tell them at court years ago, and

saw how you engrossed everyone." He gave a wide smile at her delight.

She turned the pages, marvelling at the illuminated capitals and illustrations. The crow dropping his cheese for the fox to gobble; the ant and the grasshopper; the fisherman piping.

"I had the monks at Wymondham make it for you. I thought you could read it to the little one when he is older."

Adeliza's eyes were suddenly brimming.

"Ah, beloved, don't cry," Will said, alarmed. "You will make me weep too. What will my men say if I come from your chamber red-eyed and sniffling."

She laughed and wiped her eyes. "They would not dare say anything, and a strong man's tears are perhaps the strongest thing about him."

He clasped her hand in his, marvelling again how small and fine-boned she was. The sight of her fingers encompassed by his large paw filled him to the brim with protective love. She had been through such an ordeal.

"I never thought I would be this happy," she said. "You do not know the gifts you have given to me." She reached her free hand to touch the soft cheek of the slumbering baby. "This is worth more than any earthly crown."

They sat in contented silence, neither of them inclined to talk in depth, because what was felt was enough without words. Although he had been apprehensive at first, Will was now reluctant to leave this wonderful, incense-scented room. He could have gazed at his Madonna-like wife and son all night, but he had duties elsewhere and the women were becoming restless at his lingering presence. It was time to leave. He kissed Adeliza again and the baby on his soft little brow, then reluctantly departed.

As the door closed behind him, Adeliza gave a contented sigh and, settling down in the bed, opened the Aesop, her fingertips exploring the intricate carving and smoothing over the small cabochon gemstones. It was a rare and beautiful thing. Will was not a man of many words, but he could be thoughtful and delicate when the occasion arose, and sometimes, as now, he was capable of surprising her deeply. He did not always understand her, nor she him, but they had enough to live on, and sometimes, as now, a glittering feast.

Thirty

ARUNDEL CASTLE, SUSSEX, AUGUST 1139

ADELIZA STOOD BY THE DOUBLE ARCH OF HER CHAMBER windows at Arundel. It was late August, the harvest white in the fields and the dusty scent of high summer hanging in the air. The wet nurse sat in the window seat rocking little William and crooning to him. Adeliza was momentarily distracted by her son's gurgles and turned to look at him, a sunburst of pure love lighting her from within. He was her little miracle and she still found it difficult to believe that God had granted her such grace.

After a moment, a smile on her lips, she turned back to the window. Will was in the courtyard, hands at his hips, the wind ruffling his dark curls around his head as he discussed the building work on the keep with the master mason. Adeliza felt blessed by the depth of his steady affection. It was like balm on a wound that had been raw and open for a very long time, and only now was healing.

Will was about to leave to attend a council at Winchester to discuss the issue of the bishops of Salisbury, Ely, and Lincoln. Roger of Salisbury and Alexander of Lincoln were under arrest and Nigel of Ely was in rebellion in the Fenlands. Adeliza thought it disgraceful for a king to take up arms against God's representatives. There were better ways of resolving issues between Church and State.

Her expression grew pensive as she dropped her gaze to the letter a messenger had recently brought to her chamber. The oval wax seal on a green cord was Matilda's. She hadn't told Will about it yet and was toying with the idea of not showing him until he returned from court because she was worried about what the letter might contain. With all the unrest brewing in England, Stephen was keeping a close watch on the coastline because he feared an invasion from Normandy. Adeliza knew a storm was coming, and she would either have to act or look away.

Making a decision, she left the window, broke the seal on the letter, and began to read. The writing was in Matilda's firm personal hand and in German, which they both understood, but which denied the casual observer, Will included. Matilda expressed her delight that Adeliza had borne a son and praised God that she and the child were well. She added that her own sons were growing apace and she was much pleased by their progress, especially Henry's. He was so clever and astute. The next words bore signs of having been erased many times, for the surface of the vellum was thin and rough, which was out of character for the usually decisive Matilda, but as Adeliza read, she began to understand why, and her hand went to her mouth. Matilda wrote that it was a long time since she had seen her beloved stepmother and she would like to visit her at Arundel if Adeliza would bid her welcome. She also wanted to enter into discussions with Stephen concerning the future of the crown of England and the ducal coronet of Normandy.

"Dear God," Adeliza whispered. The letter was like a burning brand between her fingers. What was Will going to say from his position as a staunch supporter of King Stephen? If she agreed, she would be welcoming the king's mortal enemy into her household. Yet it was a queen's duty to be a peace-maker, and Matilda was her kin, her daughter by marriage. And Stephen was a usurper, whether Will served him or not.

Hearing Will's voice on the stairs, Adeliza swiftly folded the parchment and stuffed it into her writing coffer. She needed time to consider what to say.

Will was breathing strongly from his climb, but not out of breath. He went to his son, kissed him, and chucked his chin, making him crow, then turned to Adeliza and took her in his arms. "The men are ready," he said. "Will you come down and bid us farewell?" Then, with a frown, he stepped back and touched her face. "What's wrong?"

"Nothing." She forced a smile.

"Look, we'll be back in a few days and you are well protected here. There is no need for concern."

Adeliza felt terrible, knowing he had misconstrued her guilt as worry. "I know I am safe. Have a care to yourself, my husband." She gave the whiskery side of his face an affectionate pat and kissed him.

When she had seen the men on their way like a good and dutiful wife, she returned to her chamber, took out Matilda's letter, and pored over it for a long, long time. And then she put it in the fire and watched it burn until she was certain that it had all turned to ash.

❖ ❖ ❖

It was teeming with rain when Will returned from court four days later. "It has been like riding through pottage these last few miles," he told Adeliza as he shook himself like a wet dog. "A good thing we didn't take a baggage cart or it would have bogged down."

She chivvied the servants and hastened him out of his wet garments and into dry replacements. Sitting him down before the fire, she brought a towel to rub his hair. ·

Will leaned back and closed his eyes. "You will never guess what the bishop of Winchester has been hiding up his sleeve," he said.

"I do not suppose I will," she replied. "Henry of Blois is a man of great cunning and knows how to hide things he does not wish people to see."

"Indeed," Will said grimly. "You know how angry he was about being passed over for the see of Canterbury in favour of the Beaumonts' candidate?"

"Yes." She finished drying his hair and fetched a comb to tidy his curls.

"We all sat down to discussion and suddenly he produced a papal bull he'd been sitting on since April, if you please, to say that Innocent has granted him the position of legate, which effectively puts him over and above Theobald of Bec."

Adeliza lowered the comb, her gaze wide and astonished. "Since April?"

He nodded. "For four months the king's own brother has been biding his time, and now flourishes this thing like a tumbler producing fire in his hands. There is no one above the king but God, and who is God's representative on earth but the pope, and directly beneath him are the cardinals and the legates. If Stephen is a secular king, then his brother has set out to match him, and not in a harmonious way. Winchester says Stephen must make reparations for arresting the bishops and that he had no right to do what he did to Salisbury, Lincoln, and Ely."

Adeliza left his side to bring him a cup of hot wine and a platter of wafers and pastries. "What does Stephen say?"

Will shrugged. "Stephen says maybe so, but that the castles held by Salisbury and the wealth within them is a matter for the Crown, not the Cross."

She made her voice casual. "Is it a serious rift then?"

"Difficult to say. If Henry of Winchester can keep his appointment as papal legate secret for four months, then what else does he have up his sleeve? His nose has been put out of joint by the Beaumont brothers. They are becoming a danger to Stephen because their power games are dividing the court."

"Are they a danger to you?" she asked with concern.

Will took a pastry and bit into it. Honey oozed out and he licked the golden stickiness off his fingers and took the napkin Adeliza handed to him. "They have no interest in me because I keep my distance and I have no desire to seek power by whispering in the king's ear. The Beaumonts have their eyes upon others who are far greater rivals than I will ever be—men who support the archbishop, and men who would follow Robert of Gloucester if he were in the country. The Beaumonts think I do not have the wit to cause upheaval. That you are my wife amuses them—as if a pet dog has stolen a juicy marrow bone off a butcher's stall. I am nothing to them. All that matters is that I am loyal and steady and wag my tail like a good hound." He looked at her. "If the Beaumonts ignore me, it is because I make sure I am no threat to them. But others are in deep danger and that is a pity, because they are strong men whom Stephen should retain in his service rather than cause by his inaction to take their swords elsewhere. FitzCount at Wallingford has as good as declared for the empress and now it looks as if John the marshal will turn rebel too. The Beaumonts begrudge him Marlborough and Ludgershall, and think that Stephen values him too highly. If they push him further he will rebel and cause great damage. They are doing the same to Miles FitzWalter, because, again, he is a threat to their power. In the end, they will ruin all."

Adeliza allowed the food and drink to mellow his humour; he was never out of sorts for long. Then she sat on his knee and played with his hair and stroked his face. "After what you have said, I hardly dare speak, but I have something we must talk about."

"Surely it cannot be anything that bad," he replied, his tone indulgently amused as he settled her more comfortably in his lap.

Adeliza drew a deep breath. "Matilda has written to congratulate us on the birth of our son. She wants to visit us and asks us to welcome her to Arundel."

His body had been loose and relaxed, but now she felt him tense. "Have you given her an answer?"

She wrapped a curl of his hair around her index finger. "It would not be fitting without consulting you first."

"I doubt she wants to pay us a visit for the sake of love alone," he growled. "All the south coast ports are on alert against assault from Normandy."

"But she is hardly going to arrive wearing a hauberk."

He snorted down his nose. "You think not?"

She curved her arm around his neck. "She has never been able to mourn at her father's tomb. She should be granted permission to visit Reading at least. That is only Christian and decent."

"But it is not the reason she wants to come to England, and you know it. Do not play me for a fool."

"I would never play you for a fool!" she said vehemently. "What harm can she do if she comes to Arundel? You are Stephen's man and not about to change that stance. What better surety could there be?"

He shook his head. "It would be dangerous and foolish to agree to her request. The best surety is keeping her the other side of the Narrow Sea."

"But she will be under our eye and Stephen can watch her movements." She gave him a pleading look. "Now I am settled with a husband and a baby son, I want her to see that life can still be good. I have a duty to her, one I took on when I wed Henry, and it does not end because he is dead. I do not expect you to understand, but it is about the ties of women. Matilda is like a jewel in my crown—part of what made and still makes me a queen. Would you deny me that?"

"You would have me risk all for the 'friendship of women'?" he asked on a rising note. "Are you mad? What do you think Stephen will say when he is doing his best to keep her and Robert of Gloucester out of the country?"

She raised her chin. "What do you think my first husband, Henry the King, would say if he knew I had refused to admit his daughter to the castle he gave me when I became his queen and Matilda's stepmother? That bond is sacred." She moderated her voice. "I am not fomenting war or rebellion, but I want to see Matilda and talk to her, and perhaps talk sense into her. We can act as mediators. Stephen trusts you, and Matilda is my daughter and my friend." She curved her body round his so that she could press a kiss to the frown between his eyebrows, and then another on his set lips.

"I do not know what to say." Will's tone was bleak. He had either to believe that Adeliza was being naive and ruled by her womb, or that she was playing the game of politics with an agenda of her own, and neither option was palatable. He could refuse her, but there was some truth in what she said. There had been many time over the past few years when he thought Henry must be turning in his grave and this was one of them. What Henry would have made of him marrying Adeliza in the first place, he preferred not to contemplate.

"She will find a way to come to England whether we refuse her or not," Adeliza pointed out. "I ask this as a boon of your love for me...I have asked little enough until now."

"It is more than a boon," he muttered. "I do want to please you, and I love you dearly, but I must consider the consequences. Do you think Stephen will stand by and not act if I do agree?"

"But I am within my lawful rights to welcome her."

Abruptly, he put her from his knee and stood up. "I need to think about this, because I have to keep everyone safe."

He dug his hands through his hair, rumpling the curls she had just untangled. "If I do agree, then the moment she arrives at Arundel, I will send to the king and tell him she is here, because it is my own duty and obligation to do so. I will have no subterfuge and no secrets."

"No, my lord." Adeliza swept him a deep curtsey and bowed her head. She knew she had won, but it left a sour taste in her mouth. She was playing a role, to influence a man who was no actor and she felt as if she were cheating him. She knew that when Matilda came, there would be repercussions. But what else could she do? Will owed his fealty to Stephen, and she owed her wifely duty to Will, but beyond those oaths, older loyalties and vows had their claim, sworn on the finials of a royal crown, and they were the greater.

Thirty-one

MATILDA DREW A DEEP BREATH AS SHE ROSE FROM HER KNEES before the devotional in her chamber and blew out the candles in their enamelled stands. Then she instructed her servants to set about dismantling and packing the items she needed for her imminent journey. Within the hour she was setting out for England to make a play for the crown that was hers by right.

Going to the table near the bare bed frame, she picked up the letters she had earlier been reading and tucked them away in a satchel to peruse again later. There was one from the constable at Bristol, assuring her that all was in readiness for when she and Robert chose to arrive. Another was from Adeliza at Arundel, with the all-important confirmation that she was welcome as kin should she choose to visit. And then there was Brian's letter, assuring her of his support at Wallingford—to the death if necessary. His words were like a strong steel rod down her backbone, stiffening her resolve. Others were waiting to rally to her cause, promising their commitment when she had landed safely in England. Miles FitzWalter, constable of Gloucester, Humphrey de Bohun, John FitzGilbert. With good fortune, the south-west and the Marches would soon be hers. Then too, there was the bishop of Winchester, her cousin Henry.

Too wily to commit anything to parchment, he had sent a messenger with a few cryptic words that might mean anything or nothing. He spoke of conciliation and the role of the Church as mediator. Matilda was wary. A man who went behind his own brother's back was not to be trusted.

"You can't go there, you're trapped!" piped a child's voice.

Matilda turned and fixed her gaze on her eldest son. He was sitting in the window seat, playing a board game of fox and geese with his half-brother Hamelin and he was concentrating on defeating his opponent. She felt a surge of fierce maternal pride as she watched him. He was fully focused but not in an exclusive way. He was observing all the activity around him, even while engaged with the game. It was a formidable trait in a child just six years old, and what it would be like when nurtured to manhood gave her cause for optimism. He was tenacious too, because Hamelin was a bright boy, older, and determined not to give ground. She had to swallow as her throat tightened. She might never see him again after this morning because who knew what was going to happen if and when she reached England. She had put everything possible in place to support him and her other sons in her absence. The best women to care for them; the best pages and squires as companions. Excellent priests and scholars to nurture their education and teach them to walk a true path with God. She could do no more, and still she was anxious. She was going to miss them so much, especially Henry. She had even considered staying in Normandy and seeing it conquered first, but knew she had to make her challenge in England before it was too late

Geoffrey entered the chamber and looked round, hands on hips. He had ridden to Domfront to see her on her way and to take charge of their sons, something Matilda did not want to think about. She could not deny that Geoffrey was a good father, but she had had the greater part in raising their boys and it was a wrench to hand them over to him.

"Everything is ready for you," he said, stepping aside to let the servants carry out the box containing the last items.

She waited impatiently while her maids clasped a thick cloak around her shoulders, and then she turned towards the light streaming through the open shutters. "Henry," she said. "Henry, come here. It is time for me to go."

He left his game and crossed the room, following the path of the light, until he stood in front of her, looking up solemnly. His eyes were grey, but flashed with green in their depths like Geoffrey's.

"Attend to your lessons and do as your father tells you," she said. "I need you to be big and brave and grown up."

Henry gave a stout nod. "Can I come to England soon too?"

"As soon as you are old enough. One day you will be king there, and it will be very important for you to know the place and the people." She stooped to his level and smoothed his vibrant hair. "Look after your brothers. I will write to you often and your father will tell me of your progress." She kissed him on both cheeks and stood up, her pride swelling to almost unbearable proportions because Henry was not crying or making a fuss. Even in the small boy, she could see the king he might one day become—but only if she gave him that chance.

She went to make her farewells to his brothers. Today, they were all present to bid her farewell, but usually little Geoffrey was with his tutors in Anjou. It had been a conscious decision not to keep the children together; that way there was more chance of survival if there was sickness or foul play. Thus Geoffrey was a solemn stranger and the farewell kiss she gave to him was tinged with sadness that she did not know him. Her third son, at only three years old, was not really sure what was happening and accepted her hug with a grimace and a wriggle.

Matilda knew if she let emotion in, she would weep and grieve, and she made herself as hard as stone. She had learned as a child herself that life was a series of partings governed above all else by duty.

She turned to her husband, who was watching her with an enigmatic look in his eyes. She half expected him to mock, but he said quietly, "You are an empress and a true queen. Only you can do what has to be done. Now is your opportunity to prove yourself." He took her hands in his and gave her a formal kiss of peace on both cheeks, as she had done to their sons. And then his grip tightened and he claimed her mouth in a lingering, hard intimacy. As the salute ended, he said with a strained smile, "I will miss you."

"I wish I could say the same," she retorted, more disturbed than she cared to admit, not least because she could see he was guarding against emotion too, "but I will hold you in my prayers."

Geoffrey snorted. "As you should. You might not want me, beloved wife, but you do need me to conduct your affairs in Normandy and raise our sons. I will hold you in mine also."

Drawing herself together, Matilda went down to the court-yard and allowed Alexander de Bohun to assist her into the saddle. When she picked up the reins, it seemed as if she were picking up her destiny too. She gazed at her children in final farewell, her eyes lingering on Henry, then she faced forward and although her heart was aching, did not look back.

Thirty-two

THE AUTUMN TIDE WAS RUNNING FAST ONSHORE AND SURGING up the estuary of the river Arun as Matilda's fleet navigated the channel at full flood. She gazed at the approaching shore, land of her birth, ignoring the sting from the hard, salty wind. It had been eight years since she had last set foot here. Then her father had been alive and men had knelt at her feet and sworn to uphold her as future queen of England. Now she came to claim her crown from them.

She looked round as her brother Robert joined her. "Soon enough the warning beacons will be lit, and Stephen will know I am here," she said.

"Already he is too late." Robert gave a confident smile. "There is nothing he can do."

Matilda compressed her lips, feeling queasy. She told herself it was seasickness, but in truth she felt she was being dragged into the deep by riptides of doubt. Supposing Stephen was waiting for them close by? He had his spies, after all, even as they had theirs. Supposing Adeliza had been unable to prevail on her husband to open Arundel's gates for them? What if William D'Albini forbade them to land the troops, horses, and equipment they had brought from Normandy?

The river Arun wound and looped inland like one of

Adeliza's silver hair ribbons. Although autumn was advancing, the grass was still green and the fields were full of grazing sheep. In other circumstances, Matilda would have taken interest and pleasure in the journey, but for the moment she was too tense and impatient.

By the time they moored at the wharf near the castle mound, the silver of the river had become sunset gold and a party was waiting to greet them. Matilda stiffened as she saw the soldiers lining the bank, spears held at the upright and shields bearing the Albini rampant lion on a red background. Beside her, Robert came to attention. As the mooring ropes snaked out to the bollards, a bellowed command from the shore sent the men to their knees as one in a clatter of mail and weaponry. Matilda saw Adeliza, and her new husband kneeling at the front, and her heart leaped with relief. The first barrier was down; they had an uncontested landing.

The moment she disembarked, Matilda went straight to Adeliza, raised her to her feet, and tearfully embraced her. "I am in your debt," she said against her ear. "Thank you for keeping the faith."

"Nothing would have stopped me," Adeliza said fiercely. "You are kin, and I have missed you so much, and been so worried for you."

Will D'Albini turned from greeting Robert and knelt again to Matilda. "Empress," he said. "Be welcome at Arundel."

Matilda gazed down at his broad shoulders and glossy dark curls. She knew little of this man personally beyond the detail that he had given his oath to Stephen. Yet his honour was unquestioned and she was certain that while she was under his roof, he would protect her with his life. But beyond these walls and the etiquette of the kinship bond, it was a different matter, and she suspected he was already wondering how soon he could be rid of her and Robert.

❖❖❖

The chamber appointed to Matilda was comfortably luxurious, furnished with embroidered cushions on the seats and benches, fine wall hangings, rich textiles, and clean, clear light from beeswax candles and oil lamps. A subtle scent of incense filled the air and there was even fine pale glass in the windows. Adeliza might no longer be queen of England, but she still surrounded herself with regal trappings and an atmosphere of tranquil grace.

Matilda walked around the room, familiarising herself, and then paused by the painted cradle that a maid had brought in. A swaddled baby lay on a soft lambskin cover, its face pale rose-pink, its lips making small smacking sounds as it slept. Matilda felt a pang at the sight of such innocence. "Isn't he beautiful?" she said, smiling at Adeliza. "I am so pleased for you. I know how much you grieved for your childlessness when you were married to my father."

Adeliza's own smile was full of tender pride. "I was in doubt about leaving Wilton, but God answered my prayers and showed me it was the right decision. I have such cause to bless His bounty."

"And your husband?" Matilda's voice held a note of caution.

Adeliza's complexion grew rosy. "I am content," she said. "Married to your father I was queen and Lady of the English, but Will has given me what I could not have—and he loves me." She looked at Matilda. "He has opened our gates to you on the understanding that you are visiting as my kin, and that somehow a peaceful settlement can be negotiated from this. While you are under our roof as a guest who is stepdaughter to his wife, he will succour and defend you, but do not expect more. Even this was a great step for him to take and I had to fight very hard to persuade him. That he admitted you at all is as much a miracle as that baby lying in the cradle."

"Then how do I make men such as your husband change their minds?"

"I am not sure you can," Adeliza replied.

Matilda went to the window and touched the panes of pale green glass with their wavy stretch marks, and gazed at the luminous tinge reflected on her skin. "Stephen stole my throne, and no one tried to stop him—save Baldwin de Redvers. Now others are thinking twice about following Stephen, but only because they dislike the politics of his court and that they must play underdog to other men. They will come to me to punish Stephen, not because they honour me and the oath they swore and then cast away like latrine rags. They will come because they think to have greater influence at my court and that I will give them the rewards Stephen will not. After all, I am a woman and can be more easily manipulated—no?" She grimaced. "I can use such men, but I can never trust them."

"Some will honour you," Adeliza said. "You spoke of Baldwin de Redvers. There is your brother Reynald too. He will stand firm. You can look also to Wallingford for aid that will not waver."

Matilda turned round, her heart quickening, and met Adeliza's quiet stare. Her stepmother said, "I have seen little of Brian FitzCount since your father's funeral, but you have in him a loyal servant unto death."

Matilda felt warmth rise in her cheeks and turned again to the window, seeking a cool draught. She had to guard her heart from all blows. She dare not let Brian inside because he would break it from within. "I should be downstairs with Robert," she said abruptly.

"No," Adeliza said firmly. "There is time for all that in a while. It has been so long since I have seen you and soon you will be fully occupied with the business you have come about. We have so much catching up to do. I want to know about your sons and everything you have been doing. Just for a moment, let everything be as it was before. I will send one of my women to prepare you a warm footbath. I refuse to let you play the warrior queen for this moment with me."

Matilda gave a strained smile. "As you wish, 'Mother.' I will not deny you."

"Indeed not, for then you would gain a reputation for being contrary," Adeliza said with a mischievous twinkle.

The curve of Matilda's mouth grew less strained. "We couldn't have that, could we?" she replied as she joined Adeliza at the hearth.

❖❖❖

Will felt a pang of trepidation as he watched Robert's troops and their supplies march into Arundel. This was not the baggage of a friendly visitor on a diplomatic mission, but the spearhead of an invasion. But what else had he expected—that they miss the opportunity and come with nothing?

Robert turned to him. "We are grateful for your succour," he said. "It will not be forgotten. We will repay you in full measure when we are in a position to do so."

Will gripped his belt either side of the buckle. "I have taken you under my roof out of love for my wife and obligation to her kin. I do it so that negotiations may be opened to discuss a lasting peace. I am not your enemy, as I know some members of the court are, but my fealty is to Stephen. I guarantee your safety under my roof because of the kinship tie, but I must tell the king you are my guests. In truth, it is safe for neither of us if you remain here."

Robert nodded curtly. "That is understood, but we are still indebted to you for this landing and for your hospitality. I will not abuse or outstay my welcome, be assured. Only let me rest here and organise my men and I will be on my way to Bristol as soon as I may."

A feeling of sweet relief ran through Will. "And the empress?"

"Let her stay for a few days more with your lady wife. She is under your protection, and since she is visiting her stepmother, the king has no legal grounds for objection, and it is no detriment to you. I know she has missed Adeliza's company."

Will suppressed a grimace. He would have been greatly pleased to see the empress depart as soon as possible, and he was less sanguine than Robert about the damage her presence might to do. "So be it," he said.

Having shown Robert to his quarters to refresh himself after the journey, Will returned to the courtyard. He felt like a grain caught between two millstones. He was Stephen's vassal, but was giving houseroom to Stephen's enemies, including the commander of Matilda's troops. He knew he should be playing the host with Robert, and that Adeliza would be annoyed with him for shirking that duty, but he could not in good conscience be the welcoming host. He told the groom to saddle up his horse, and rode out to check the fields, the river, the roads, fixing them in his mind's eye as they were, because it seemed to him that everything was going to change and that he was about to lose things that were very precious to him.

❖❖❖

Two days later, at dawn, Robert left Arundel. A wet sea mist was rolling off the coast and cloaking the land. Watching the low grey clouds swallow him up as he rode out of the castle, Matilda thought that it was almost as if he had disappeared into another world.

She had not accompanied him. She knew Stephen dared not harm her while she was under Adeliza's roof, and was determined to exercise her right to visit her kin. She had expected a warmer welcome from her stepmother and her new husband. She had thought they might offer military aid or at least promise moral support, but William D'Albini had made it clear that she was welcome as a domestic guest, nothing more.

"I cannot make Will change his mind," Adeliza said as they sat before the brazier in Matilda's chamber when Robert had gone. "He is sworn to Stephen and I am bound as his wife to obey him. I will do what I can for you, but Will has a sticking point beyond which he will not go, not even for me. I would not have you think I love Stephen. He has taken so many things not rightfully his. He only consented to this match between me and Will because he wanted one of his own men in control of Arundel. He wants to render me powerless—or his wife does."

Matilda grimaced at the mention of Stephen's dumpy little wife. It was going to be a long battle to dislodge the usurpers.

The warning notes of a horn blared from the battlements and the women looked at each other in alarm. Moments later, Joscelin came to the chamber door and announced that King Stephen was pitching his tents outside Arundel's walls. "My lord is going out to speak with him," he said and, message delivered, hastened out again.

"Stephen would not dare besiege us." Adeliza's eyes were wide with anxiety. "I still hold the title of queen and I am his aunt through my first marriage. He will not breach that etiquette."

"But your husband sent for him in the first place," Matilda said curtly.

Adeliza flushed. "He was honour-bound to do so, even as he was honour-bound to grant you entrance and succour. You know that."

A nauseating brew of anger and pain churned Matilda's stomach. She rose abruptly to her feet and started towards the door.

Adeliza said sharply, "Let Will deal with this. Stay here."

Matilda turned. "How am I to be queen of England and

regent for my son if I shut myself in this chamber and let a man speak for me?" she demanded with icy contempt.

"You have no choice. Do you think I want any of this?" Adeliza's chin wobbled. "Do you not know how frightened I am? Not for myself, but for my child, for my husband, and most of all for you—for what will become of you, and what you will become."

Her words struck Matilda like a slap. "I am an empress and a queen," she snapped, "and I will be no one's pawn."

"But I am a queen too, and you are my daughter," Adeliza pressed. "And you are God's child and His subject above and beyond all." She reached a slender hand towards Matilda. "Please, leave it to Will—for my sake."

Matilda felt like screaming at Adeliza, but knew it was pointless. "Very well." She made a determined effort to control her frustration. "But I will have the maids pack my baggage, because whatever happens, it seems I have outstayed my welcome."

❖❖❖

Will dismounted outside the king's recently pitched campaign tent and handed his reins to an attendant. The morning mist was slowly clearing to expose a fuzzy halo of sun, although there was no warmth in the atmosphere. Will inhaled deeply to steady himself and followed an usher into the king's presence. Stephen was standing by a brazier, warming his hands and drinking hot wine, steam curling from its surface.

"Sire." Will knelt on the thick fur rug. The king's brother, Henry, bishop of Winchester, was also present and extended his hand for Will to kiss his sapphire ring. He too must have recently arrived, for he was wearing silver spurs and the hem of his cloak was muddy.

Stephen gestured Will to rise, irritation obvious in the abrupt waft of his hand. "What do you mean by succouring Robert of Gloucester and the Countess of Anjou at Arundel?" he demanded.

Will cleared his throat. "The Earl of Gloucester is no longer at Arundel, sire."

"And you did not see fit to detain him?" Stephen's gaze was dark with displeasure. The bishop looked down and fiddled with his episcopal ring.

"Sire, I deemed it honourable to let him go on his way without interference."

Stephen's brows arched in astonishment. "Did you indeed?"

"He is my stepson by marriage and the son of King Henry. I am honour-bound to respect the kinship bond and give him houseroom. It would have been dishonourable to make him my prisoner. Had you arrived while he was still under my roof, I would have had to choose between my oath to you and my duty to a family guest."

"But why grant them houseroom in the first place?" Stephen snapped. "Why in God's name give them a safe landing place and admit them into the castle? What is the point of having everyone on alert, watching the coast, if you are going to open the back door? Either you have soup for wits, my lord, or I should add you to the list of the faithless."

Will's shoulders tightened. "They would have landed no matter what precautions you took. My wife thought that by talking to the empress as a mother to a daughter, she could make her see sense."

Stephen looked sceptical. "And has that happened, my lord?"

Will grimaced. "She has fixed notions, but Adeliza is continuing to counsel her."

"And may as well talk to the wall for all the good it will do. You should not have let Robert of Gloucester leave Arundel." Stephen drained his wine and banged his cup down. "If I order you to hand over the empress will you defy me?"

Will was alarmed, but remained outwardly impassive. "Sire, if I give her to you, I will be breaking a sacred bond."

"If you do not, you compromise your loyalty to me," Stephen growled.

Henry of Winchester stepped forwards. "You cannot afford to besiege Arundel," he said to Stephen. "It will take too long, and while we are pinned down here, Gloucester will be carving himself an empire with Bristol at its hub. He is the one you should pursue. If you lay siege to Arundel, you will lose respect and men. The dowager queen was much loved at court and everyone knows she would not act out of defiance to you, but from the softness of her heart—and she is within her right. My lord D'Albini's only sin is that of being too fond a husband."

Stephen glowered at Winchester. "Then what am I to do, because I dare not leave Matilda here, whatever you say about womanly visits and the role of honour. I cannot ignore this threat and just ride away."

Will wondered why the bishop of Winchester was giving Stephen a dove's advice when usually he was all for seizing the moment.

"Give her safe conduct to Bristol to join the Earl of Gloucester," the bishop said. "Return her to his custody. While she remains here, she is a woman acting of her own volition. Sent to Bristol, men will see that she is in her brother's keeping, and will be reminded that he is the power behind her presence, and would rule England in all but name. How many will bow to that? I will gladly go as her escort. That will leave you free to deal with insurrection elsewhere. With the Countess of Anjou and Robert of Gloucester pinned in one place, you will only have to focus on one objective—and men will commend you for your great chivalry." He gestured to Will. "It will also liberate my lord D'Albini of the burden of his obligations."

Stephen's mouth twisted. "Men might also commend me for great folly."

Winchester shrugged. "Since the alternative is a long siege that might see you surrounded in your turn by Gloucester, you have no choice."

"It is a way out, sire." Will had never thought to find himself grateful to the bishop of Winchester. "Otherwise we are at an impasse."

"Very well," Stephen growled, "but I will have renewed oaths of fealty from you and your wife, my lord D'Albini, before I ride from here."

"Gladly, sire." Filled with relief, Will knelt to Stephen; but he felt as if he has been bruised and battered in a hard fight and that he was still on the battlefield.

❖❖❖

Matilda stared at Will in disbelief and contempt. "You are giving me up to him?" In that moment she could have killed Adeliza's upstart dolt of a husband, standing there in his muddy boots, legs planted wide, telling her of the deal he had made with Stephen.

He reddened. "I am doing no such thing, domina. You are being offered safe conduct to Bristol where you will be protected without causing harm to your stepmother and those beholden to her. I ask you to see sense and agree to the truce terms the king has offered."

"And if I refuse?"

"Then you destroy us all and you leave me no room for manoeuvre." He extended an imploring hand. "Please, I ask you to accept the terms and go to Bristol. The bishop of Winchester and Waleran de Meulan will escort you."

"It seems I have no choice," Matilda said bitterly, hating to be powerless. She faced Will with angry pride but inside she was weeping with frustration.

He shook his head. "I do not have a choice either, and for that I am sorry." He bowed to her, exchanged an unhappy glance with Adeliza, and left the room.

Thirty-three

*T*HE FOLLOWING MORNING, MATILDA DRESSED FOR TRAVEL IN a red wool dress embroidered with thread of gold and sparkling with jewels. A gold cross set with rubies lay on her breast, and her fingers glittered with rings of sapphire, ruby, and pearl. "I will not leave here as a fleeing woman, but as a queen and an empress," she said to Adeliza as her ladies fastened her ermine cloak with gold clasps.

"You must see that we are caught between two millstones." Adeliza's gaze pleaded Matilda to understand.

"Had everyone followed my father's wishes, there would not have been any millstones," Matilda said curtly.

"I agree, but since they did not, everyone has had to make unpalatable decisions." Adeliza bit her lip. "You must write to me. I will worry about you."

Matilda was tempted to ask if Adeliza would share the letters with her oaf of a husband and pass the notes on to Stephen, but she bit her tongue. "If I can," she said shortly, and turned to the door. "No," she said. "Do not come with me."

Adeliza's eyes filled with tears. "I cannot bear to part like this. Will you not at least let me embrace you?"

Matilda was still angry but allowed her to do so, and as she felt Adeliza's arms around her, a sudden tug of emotion made her hug Adeliza in return. Before the feeling could turn to tears, she pulled away and stood upright like a soldier.

"God keep you safe," Adeliza whispered. "I will be praying for you."

In the courtyard, the bishop of Winchester and Waleran de Meulan were waiting for her with Will D'Albini. Since Henry of Winchester was not only a bishop, but also a papal legate, Matilda had to kneel to him. She knew he was sizing her up like a spider with many flies stuck on his web, his own brother among them, and wondering if he could entangle her too. Waleran de Meulan on the other hand was a wolf, ready to run down his enemies and rip out their throats.

"Cousin," said Henry of Winchester. "Would that we were meeting in happier circumstances."

"Indeed, my lord," Matilda said. She did not acknowledge Meulan beyond a curt nod. He knelt to afford her the courtesy due her rank, but rose again immediately so that his knee barely skimmed the ground. Matilda compressed her lips.

Will assisted her into a covered wain that had been part of the negotiations. It contained her baggage and was covered by a rich tent cloth painted with golden lions that had belonged to her father. It meant she would not be seen by Stephen's soldiers as she journeyed past the enemy camp and was a symbol of peaceful travel rather than military briskness.

Will knelt to her again, with full honour, and then stood up. She expected him to look away in embarrassment or shame, but he met her gaze with a troubled, steady look. "God speed you, domina. I wish you no harm."

"But you do wish me gone, do you not? Well, you have your way, my lord, may it not trouble your slumber." She climbed into the wain and dropped the curtain, then sat down amid the cushions and furs padding the sides. Light filtered through the red covering, dipping everything in dark crimson like the back of a closed eyelid on a sunlit day. Briefly Matilda put her face in her hands, and a tremor shook her body, but she made no sound.

❖ ❖ ❖

Will found his wife standing in the room that had been Matilda's for her brief stay. He was uncertain how she was going to receive him, but when she turned at his entrance, there was no anger in her eyes, just troubled sadness. "I fear for her," she said. "I fear for us all."

He put his arms around her and kissed the top of her head. "When I married you, I swore I would protect you and keep you safe, and no matter what happens, I will do that." His voice strengthened with a hint of anger because he felt as if his word of honour had been impugned. "I am a man who keeps my promises."

Adeliza leaned her head against his chest. "I know that, but I am sorry you cannot protect her in the same way you protect me."

"She can look after herself," he muttered, remembering her wide grey eyes on him in the moment before she climbed into the wain. The contempt. The pride. The anger.

"No," said Adeliza. "You are wrong, my husband. She cannot, because she is her own worst enemy."

❖ ❖ ❖

The escort party stopped for the night at Rowland's Castle, a small keep on the road to Winchester. The lord was not in residence, but his bailiff and steward, forewarned by outriders, had lit fires and prepared chambers. Matilda's room, set two floors above the main hall, was draughty from the ill-fitting shutters over the window loops, but heat from braziers kept the worst of the chill at bay and her ermine cloak was heavy and warm. She felt as if she had been shaken about in a bag of logs after her day in the cart.

Her women made up the bed in the chamber with good linen sheets and woollen blankets. When the legate's usher came to request that she attend on his lord, Matilda was tempted to refuse for the pleasure of putting Winchester's nose out of joint, but she was intrigued too, and wondered what he was up to. He was not the only one who could spin webs.

When she arrived at the legate's chamber, he was standing by a brazier reading a piece of parchment but looked up as she entered. A youth was setting out a flagon and cups on a sideboard, and arranging a white cloth containing small stuffed pastries. Patting the lad on the head, the bishop dismissed him with a pastry for each hand and gestured the other servants to leave too.

"Is my lord of Meulan not joining us?" Matilda enquired as the door closed.

"The Earl of Worcester has retired to his chamber with some wine and an accommodating companion," Henry said with a wave of his hand, making sure the light flashed on the intaglio ring adorning his middle finger. "I see no need to disturb him."

"You have done well for yourself despite Stephen's efforts to hold you back," she said. "It must gall him that you have acquired the position of papal legate."

He gave her an assessing look. "I would not say that. My brother accepts that it is so."

"But you left it many months before you told him."

"A man who exposes everything inside his jewel casket is asking to be robbed and deceived," Winchester said over his shoulder as he went to pour wine for both of them.

"It seems to me your brother is just such a man, and in consequence his jewel casket is almost empty."

"But I hazard you are not such a woman."

She realised with concealed amusement that he was flirting with her, both in the physical sense and as they danced around delicate political issues. "No, I am not." Her gaze hardened. "But I have been robbed and deceived anyway."

"That is a matter for debate. Some would say oaths made under duress have neither validity nor value. Some would say being absolved of an oath is reason enough not to retake it." He handed her a cup so smoothly that the surface of the wine barely rippled.

"Some would also say that the Church should know its place and not involve itself in secular affairs," she said. "Those who speak of absolution have robbed and deceived me and will continue to feather their own nests at the expense of others. Your brother's coffers are woefully light these days and he has had to rob the church to keep himself from penury. In my father's day, the treasure chests were always full. Now it is the Beaumonts who drip with gold, and the mercenaries who have been paid for their loyalty who wear the jewels and the power. Who rules your brother's court, my lord? Not your brother, for certain, and not you."

Henry's cheeks reddened above his thick bush of beard. "I admit that my brother has been misled by bad advice, but as papal legate, I have influence to deal with such matters." He put delicate emphasis on the word "influence."

Now they came to it, she thought. Here was the spider. A man who would be king in all but name. A man who would play both sides to his own best advantage. She took a sip of the wine, noting its quality. The bishop did not believe in stinting himself even when travelling. "So." She set her cup down. "You have not asked me here to socialise before retiring. Let us be frank. What do you want?"

He looked slightly pained. "You are my cousin whether we stand on opposite sides of a divide or not. And you are my daughter because of my position as a priest. I am worried about you on all counts."

Matilda arched her brow. As far as she was concerned, the family feeling could remain in its crypt. "But that is not the sum of it. I do not believe my lord of Meulan would be pleased to know we are having this conversation."

Henry made a gesture of dismissal. "He will know anyway in the morning. His spies are everywhere."

"And Stephen will know too."

His expression said without words that he was not unduly bothered. "He would expect me to report back all that I can find out."

"Or all that you are willing to tell him, because even with his spies, Waleran will not know what was said between us."

Amusement curled his lips and she realised how much he thrived on this intrigue.

"So, what are you willing to do for me and at what price, my lord legate?" she said. "Let us be precise on this. What would be the price of a crown?" She reached for her wine again, took a deliberate sip and swallowed slowly. "An opportunity to weave policy? Or the head of Waleran de Beaumont on a platter perhaps?"

He said nothing, but his eyes narrowed.

"I am here to fight for that crown. Some have already risen to join me, and others are waiting their moment. Your brother may have followers, but how many will remain loyal when he has spent all the money in the treasury—some of it stolen from the Church? I have a son, my lord; he is growing fast and he will be a king. I see it in him; it is not just a mother's fondness. You have more reason than one to look to the future."

Henry pursed his fastidious lips. "We both have matters to consider, I agree, but let us not be hasty lest we repent at leisure. My brother is not well versed in policy, but he is still an anointed king and nothing can change that."

Matilda said quietly, "I have often thought that changes cannot be made, and often been surprised."

She did not trust her cousin; indeed, without him, she suspected Stephen would not have been king in the first place, but he would prove useful as long as he thought there was something in it for him. She knew he was probably thinking the same about her. Her task was to play upon his self-importance and his desire for power. Stephen was his own worst enemy and the Beaumont twins were busy digging him into a deep pit while he stood by and let them. Sooner or later he was going to fall in—either by accident or design—and when that happened, she wanted no one throwing him a ladder.

❖ ❖ ❖

The mist was still low the next morning as they continued on their way, and it was like travelling through a swathe of grey cerecloth. The bishop exchanged an eloquent glance with Matilda as she climbed into the covered wain, but he said nothing. Waleran de Meulan was keeping himself to himself and plainly nursing a headache to judge from the frown between his eyes and his greenish pallor. Of his nocturnal companion there was no sign. Matilda suspected that the key to dealing with Waleran lay in his extensive Norman lands and that it would be her husband's policy to deal with the issue by seizing them and holding Waleran to ransom. For the moment, however, let him cause unrest at Stephen's court.

Shortly after noon they arrived at the boundary marker where it had been agreed that Robert would meet the party and escort Matilda the rest of the way to Bristol. Leaving the wain, Matilda alighted on to dank, straw-coloured grass. The marker was a stone in the shape of a bent old man with calluses of yellow lichen growing on the long curve of his back and she shivered as if ancient fingers had traced a pattern along her own spine.

Within moments she heard the jingle of harness and the soft thud of hooves. Riders appeared out of the mist, wraiths becoming solid shapes. Matilda saw Robert at the head of a group of knights and nobles. As one they dismounted and knelt to her in the wet grass beside the marker stone. The hair rose on the nape of her neck and her eyes filled. Suddenly being a queen did not seem so far away, yet they were in the middle of nowhere with the mist swirling around them and the sodden grass soaking into their shoe soles and cloak hems, when all this should be taking place in a hall filled with candle glow, incense, and the bright gleam of regnal gold.

She drew herself erect and raised her voice. "I have come to claim what is rightfully mine and that which my father willed to me. You all swore to me thrice, and if what a man says three times is true, then how much more when uttered by a king? I am your sovereign lady, and I thank you all for your true support."

Waleran de Meulan made a sound in his throat. Ignoring him she went to Robert, took his hands, and gave him the kiss of peace on either ruddy cheek. Let Meulan and Winchester stare their fill and report back to Stephen as they chose. The fight for England's crown had well and truly begun.

She turned to take the oath of the next man, who was kneeling awkwardly because he was so tall. His head was bowed and a few fine strands of silver threaded his mist-dewed hair. The sight of that silver when before it had been midnight-dark sent a pang through her. He took her hand and kissed the ring upon it, and then pressed his forehead there.

"Forgive me, domina," he said. "You must do with me as you see fit; my life is yours. I did not have enough faith."

The pang intensified as affection mingled with exasperation. "Certainly you are of no use to me down there," she said and gestured him to rise.

He shook his head. "Not unless my queen tells me she forgives me. Otherwise treat me like a traitor and strike me dead."

Matilda tapped him briskly on the shoulder. "Get up, you fool." Her voice was terse with the effort of concealing her emotions. "There is nothing to forgive. I need every sound man willing to swear to my banner and what use are you to me dead?"

Slowly, he unfolded to his full height, and now she had almost to crane her neck. There was a sheen in his dark eyes and his throat was working. "None, unless you profit from it, domina," he said hoarsely.

Her lips twitched. "Can you still put up a tent?"

He answered with a faltering smile. "With the best of them, domina."

"Then for the moment, that is all I need to know." She looked round. "I will ride now," she said imperiously. "I have had enough of carts."

A groom brought Matilda's mare from the back of the wain. Henry of Winchester and Waleran de Meulan turned their party back to Arundel, the bishop saluting both her and Robert with a meaningful look as he reined his horse around.

Brian assisted Matilda into the saddle and saw her feet securely settled on the riding platform. His touches were brief and impersonal, but there was an underlying restraint that gave them greater meaning. Without looking at her, he bowed his head and turned to his tall black palfrey. She was glad that he still had Sable. In a world of shifting quicksand, it was good to have anchors of mundane familiar detail.

Thirty-four

MATILDA CONSIDERED THE MAN KNEELING BEFORE HER making his obeisance and swearing to take her as his liege lady. Miles FitzWalter, constable of Gloucester Castle and lord of Hereford, was a tall, sandy-haired man with a freckled complexion and eyes the colour of green mud. He was quiet and laconic, but that did not mean he was slow-witted or easily dominated, rather the opposite. When Miles prowled through a room, men stepped aside. As with many of the disaffected here to pay her homage and swear allegiance, he had fallen foul of the scheming of the Beaumont brothers who were determined to bring down any man who might prove a threat to their power. Miles had never been on particularly good terms with Waleran and Robert and the antipathy had increased after Stephen's coronation to the point where Miles's position had become untenable. The same was true for John FitzGilbert, Stephen's former marshal, whom Matilda had now taken as her own. He was another who prowled the court like a leopard among domestic cats. His brother William, made in a less predatory mould, was already her chancellor and a priest of the household. She had accepted the oaths of allegiance, but she had not smiled on the men. First they had to prove themselves in her service.

"Domina, I swore for Stephen," Miles said, "because I thought he would be strong and honourable and you were far away in Anjou. But now I have seen how he conducts business and the men he favours, and you are here, I swear that from this day forth you have my absolute loyalty."

"And I accept that loyalty," Matilda said, "but deeds are worth more than words."

His head remained bowed but he looked up at her through his sparse sandy lashes. "I offer you Gloucester Castle and my protection, should you wish to hold your own court away from Bristol. Whatever resources I have are yours."

Matilda inclined her head. "I will indeed consider your offer." She had been going to suggest it herself, but was pleased he had offered of his own accord. She needed to separate from her brother and take power into her own hands. It also meant that Stephen would have to look in several directions at once.

Once the allegiance-swearing was over and dinner consumed, Matilda took a moment to herself and, with only a maid for company, went for a walk round the castle precincts to freshen her mind. The air was cold and dank and she could smell the pungent waters of the estuary rising from the moat and hear the mournful scream of gulls. Bristol Castle was nigh on impregnable and easily supplied and protected by the rivers Frome and Avon, and able to conduct trade without hindrance. Stephen had tried to take it the previous year and failed abysmally.

The sound of closing shutters came from several of the chambers as useful daylight faded and the sky turned from ash to charcoal with a single glimmer of red like a dying ember.

She was turning back towards her chamber, when she saw Brian FitzCount coming from the direction of the stables, skirting the puddles to avoid miring his fashionable curl-toed boots and the hem of his cloak. He hesitated when he saw her, as if to change direction, then set his shoulders and continued walking.

"Domina." He bowed.

"My lord FitzCount." She gave him a questioning look.

"I was checking my horses to make sure they are ready to take to Wallingford tomorrow," he said. "Stephen will strike at me next now I have renounced my fealty and I must see to the defences."

"It is a little too late for shoring up," she said sharply.

He gave her a reproachful glance. "I have been preparing ever since your father died, but when I think about the future I need to reassure myself that all is in order."

Matilda watched her gown flare and fall back as she walked with him to the domestic quarters. "If Stephen comes to Wallingford, he will not stay camped there for long. He cannot afford to because others will rise against him."

He drew a deep breath. "What if there do not have to be battles? What if we can negotiate a settlement?"

She eyed him sharply. "What kind of negotiation?"

"What if Stephen were to acknowledge your son as heir to Normandy and England?"

Matilda snorted. "Is that likely? Even if he did, his wife would refuse. I know my cousin Maheut. Stephen may have sat on the throne, but Maheut has her teeth in it."

"But let us say this suggestion did come to the table. Would you be willing to negotiate an agreement based on that premise?"

She arched her brow. "Forgo my crown you mean—the one you all swore you would honour?"

Brian gestured. "But your line would succeed, and everything would meld back together as it should have been."

"I am not so certain of that."

"But would you consider it?" he persisted.

"Yes, I would," she said after a long pause. "But you will not find Stephen willing to do so, believe me." They were nearing the hall door. He extended his arm in a courtier's gesture and she laid her own hand lightly along it. She looked at his fingers. "I am glad to see you still have your ink stains."

"Writing preserves my sanity. Sometimes the only thing holding me steady is that line of ink between my mind and the point of my pen." He lowered his voice and dipped his head towards her. "Sometimes I write words that I send to God in smoke and flame, because if I left them on the page to be seen they would consume the reader."

Matilda believed in looking people straight in the eye, but she dared not look at Brian now. "I think you are wise," she said. "Let the words become ash."

"I do, domina, but it does not mean they were never written. Their imprint stays in my memory, and all you need do is ask me for them. My life and my honour are yours to do with as you see fit."

"Then keep them both intact if you would serve me," she said. "Other than your loyalty, that is all I want."

"Is it?"

She stopped and turned. Her own voice was pitched low so as not to carry. "Do you think you are the only one with a pile of ashes in your hearth? I burned my dreams to build my nightmares." Removing her arm from his, she swept indoors, walking briskly so that it looked as if she was moving on to the business in hand rather than running away.

❖ ❖ ❖

Her sewing unattended in her lap, Adeliza gazed into the fire, watching the flames and trying not to think. It was a raw morning in early November with the trees almost bare of leaves and icy rain in the wind. Helwis the nurse was changing Wilkin's swaddling while singing a nonsense song to him and blowing on his tummy, making him squeal.

Will arrived in a flurry of cold air. He was dressed for travel in his sturdiest boots and a thick wool tunic, with a heavy cloak over the top. He was also wearing his sword. The cloak sparkled with rain and his hair had twisted into tight curls. Adeliza gnawed her lip as she watched him stoop to their son and tickle him under the chin. The baby giggled and waved his little arms. Will straightened and turned to her. The softness in his eyes and the broad smile given to the baby faded into caution.

Adeliza left her sewing and came to him. Last night they had lain together and it had been the sweetest thing. Now, in the cold, drizzly morning, he was leaving her to ride with Stephen in order to besiege Brian FitzCount at Wallingford. She was finding it difficult to reconcile these two parts of her life: lying with this wonderful lover, the father of their son, fulfilling her duties as a wife, all the time knowing he was going to war to prevent Matilda from claiming her rightful throne. He would be facing men with whom he had once been friends at court, and where an army went, death and destruction inevitably followed, usually of the innocent.

"I know you do not want me to go," he said, "but it is my duty, even as you felt it yours to welcome the empress in the first place. My oath is to Stephen and I must obey his summons."

"That does not make the situation less deplorable," she replied. "When Henry ruled we had peace, and no one dared to break it."

"But he left a legacy of bitter strife, and now we all suffer the consequences." He touched her face. "All will be well, don't worry." They both knew it was a meaningless platitude. Words to glide over a surface of broken shards without repairing the underlying damage. She did not agree with him, but she was his wife and she would not send him off with sharp words and recrimination. Instead, she kissed him and bade him look after himself, but it was a pale imitation of the sensuous intimacy of the night and she hated the feeling of distance.

She accompanied him to the courtyard to bid farewell, playing the formal role of chatelaine. She knew it looked to all their retainers as if she was endorsing all this, and it made her feel sick.

Thirty-five

*B*RIAN STOOD IN THE GREAT UNDERCROFT AT WALLINGFORD Castle with his constable, William Boterel, and gazed at the piled stores he had been amassing ever since King Henry's death. Even as he had been kneeling in homage to Stephen, his household officers were buying in stores and making plans to conserve supplies. He eyed the piled bales of dried stockfish, hard as stone.

"You could build walls with them and they wouldn't fall down," Boterel said, plucking one of them out of the bale and slapping it against his palm. "Last for years." A faint fishy-smelling dust drifted under their noses and Brian grimaced. Stockfish had to be one of the most evil foods on earth, but as a basic store for times of privation and siege, there was nothing better.

As well as the stockfish, there were barrels of beef in brine and sausages smoked and dried in long loops. Crocks of honey; bladders of lard, tallow and beeswax, butter and cheese. Oats and grains. Two stone querns stood in a corner, ready to hand-grind flour should the mills be destroyed. And then there were the weapons. Barrel upon barrel of arrows were stacked against the far wall and the fletcher was busy making more. There were mail shirts, many of them given to him by Matilda, fashioned by the famed hauberk-makers of Argentan and transported in leather sacks as part of the ballast on the ships that had come from Normandy. Matilda had given him one as a personal gift, the rivets black as midnight and hemmed with bronze. It was a beautiful, deadly thing, sinuous as snakeskin, with a helm of the same colour. He had donned it to check the fit and had seen the admiration in men's eyes and he had not known himself. From boyhood, despite being trained to fight, his clever fingers had worn only the ink stains of the written word, never the blood of other men.

"We have enough for years to come, should it be necessary," William said grimly.

Brian made a face. "I hope it will not come to that." Leaving the undercroft, he stepped out into the smoky autumn air. His wife was returning from the henhouse with a basket of eggs. At this time of year the birds were not laying in large quantities, but there were enough for the lord's table. Her dress was spiked with straw and her figure resembled a lumpy sack with a knot tied in the middle. She cast an assessing look at the men. Earlier she had eyed Brian in his fine armour, humphed, and said that looks were all very well, but it was what lay within that mattered.

"Two of the hens have stopped laying," she grumbled. "Time to neck them. We cannot afford to keep anything that does not work for its living."

Brian bit the inside of his mouth, uncertain whether this was a dig at him or just her natural thriftiness coming out. "I will look forward to chicken frumenty then," he said with a courteous smile. "I appreciate your skills in using all our resources to their best advantage."

She gave him a hard glance "Someone has to. Fine hauberks, especially when given as gifts, come at a price."

There was a shout from the walls and a serjeant came running across the bailey to Brian. "Sire, it is King Stephen's army," he panted as he arrived. "Here, outside the walls!"

Brian set off at a run for the battlements with William hard on his heels. Gazing out between the merlons at the approaching silver line of soldiers, with Stephen's banner snapping in the wind, his dark imagining became reality. It was not just an undercroft stuffed with supplies and weapons, it was an army spreading out on the opposite bank of the Thames and he felt as if someone had punched him in the stomach because he could not breathe.

His wife joined him on the battlements, still clutching her basket of eggs. "Let us hope Waleran de Meulan does not hold it against you that you kept him prisoner here," she said, eyeing the fluttering banners.

"I care not if he does," Brian snapped. "They won't take Wallingford. I have known this day was coming ever since Stephen usurped the crown."

"But are you ready?" He gave her a hard look, which she returned with aplomb. "I am a soldier's daughter," she said, "and my first husband was as tough as horseshoes. You talk fine words, and you write them too, my lord, but can you stand? That is what we will find out now. You had best go and put on that fine hauberk of yours." With a curt nod to drive her words home, she left with her basket of eggs. A feather floated in her wake and gently drifted to the ground at Brian's feet.

He watched it land, and then raised his head to the besieging force. He had no choice but to stand, because he was doing this for Matilda, and he had promised.

❖❖❖

A raw wind blustered through the king's camp. The soldiers had laid down pathways of straw between the tents because the intermittent rain and the constant tramp of men, horses, and siege equipment had churned the ground to mud.

In Stephen's pavilion, Will stood around a brazier with several other barons. He was whittling at a piece of wood, working it into the shape of a toy horse for his infant son, keeping his hands occupied. They had been bogged down for a week now, assaulting Wallingford to no avail, like little boys trying to knock down a wall with shingle. Brian FitzCount had made it plain he was not going to be lured out by acts of burning and pillage on the surrounding lands and it was also plain that the place could resist their assault for longer than they were willing to sit.

"I cannot afford to stay here." Stephen testily plucked at his beard. "Wallingford is the key to London. We must either capture it, or render it useless to the rebels. FitzCount was building this up all the time he was playing the loyal servant at court. He never intended keeping his oath to me."

"You could construct watchtowers to prevent provisions coming through," Will said, "and garrison them with men to harass the supply route."

Waleran de Meulan glared at Will "That woman and her brother should never have been allowed a safe landing in England."

Will blew shavings off the little horse. "It was a matter of honour," he said, refusing to rise to the bait.

"There is honour and there is folly," Waleran snapped.

"Enough." Stephen made a chopping gesture with his right hand. "D'Albini is right, although I could have wished for a better outcome. Next you will be saying I was foolish to let the Countess of Anjou join her brother in Bristol, when it was the only decision I could have made."

"She is not in Bristol now though, is she?" Waleran sneered. "She is holding court in Gloucester and encouraging all manner of rabble to join her. We should have taken her when we had the chance."

A messenger drew rein outside the tent and swung down from his sweating horse. Entering the tent at Stephen's command, he knelt and his gaze flicked to Waleran. "Sire,

Miles FitzWalter has sacked Worcester. He has burned the suburbs and seized captives and herds."

"What?" Waleran's face suffused. He lunged to his feet and hurled his cup at the side of the tent. "The whoreson! I will rip him apart with my bare hands."

Will stared at the heaving, frightened messenger. Worcester belonged to Waleran and this was more than just political strategy by the rebels; it was a personal attack on Waleran by Miles FitzWalter, who hated him. The war was spreading, like coals dragged from a fire and scattered abroad by a pitchfork.

"This confirms my decision to move," Stephen said grimly. "We shall ride to deal with this insurrection now and leave a detail here to build watchtowers. I want the garrison at Wallingford pinned down like a snake with a forked stick."

❖❖❖

It was very late. Brian stood on the wall walk and gazed out across the river. The night was moonless but there was a glimmer of cold starlight and the pin-prick wink of torches from Stephen's watchtowers. Their garrisons were preventing new supplies from getting through, although they could do nothing to touch Wallingford itself. Brian had managed to send the occasional messenger out and receive information back in, but it was a dangerous and haphazard business. Two of his men had been caught and tortured before being hanged on a gibbet in full view of the Wallingford garrison.

Brian had ordered food to be rationed although they had plenty, because who knew how long this state of affairs was going to last? He was out on a limb here, cut off from communication, and it drove him mad, because communicating was his main skill, over and beyond his weapon play. They had begun to call him "the Marquis" because he was out on a March here, Wallingford pointing like a finger into enemy territory.

Maude said nothing, but her expression was enough. He

knew he was out of his depth. When instructing the men on watch, he was firm and decisive, but he wondered if anyone guessed how much doubt lay beneath the surface.

The bitter evening chill seeped through his garments and he abandoned the wall walk, going to his chamber to write letters he knew might never arrive and documents that might never be read. Yet, while his mind was connected to the parchment through the flow of the ink, he felt control and stability settle upon him and the sense of dread retreated a little.

When the words began to blur on the page and his eyes to burn with the strain of staring, he sought his bed and curled up, drawing the blankets and furs around his ears. Inside his mind he was still writing, could still see the tip of the quill scratching over the parchment in line upon line of oak-gall ink. Defending his position, defending Matilda. The quill bit deeper and the ink, turning red, ran like blood from the blade of a sword. He tossed and turned, trapped in sweaty visions. He heard chanting, and saw a lone ship hoisting a sail against a carmine sky that might have presaged either dawn or sunset. Behind was loneliness; ahead lay solitude.

The sound of a fist pounding on wood jolted through his dream. At first he thought it was the clunk of the oars in the rowlocks, but it grew louder and suddenly his chamber door banged open. He shot upright, gasping, and fought to free himself from the sour sheet that had tangled around him as he fretted in his nightmare. He stared in bewilderment at Miles FitzWalter, who stood at his bedside clad in dark clothing, filthy with mud from head to toe.

"I heard you were in need of reinforcements," Miles said with a broad grin, his teeth very white in his dirty face. "I think it is time to do something about those towers, don't you?"

Brian staggered out of bed and clasped Miles in a hearty embrace, partly to make sure that he was not a figment of the dream. "I was praying you would come, but I did not know when or even how you'd achieve such a thing!" he said, his voice raw with relief.

"Hah! It takes more than a shallow king and a gaggle of piss-proud hangers-on to stop me!"

Brian scrabbled around, donning his crumpled tunic, raking his hands through his hair. He shouted for servants to bring food and wine, which Miles devoured with gusto.

"In plotting to bring me down, they have fomented their own ruin," Miles said with a feral gleam in his eyes

Brian's spine tingled. Miles FitzWalter was like a deep, cold pool. The shallows at the edges were safe enough, but go any further and you risked drowning.

Miles dusted his hands. "My men are awaiting my signal outside. It was easier for just a few of us to sneak past their guards and reach you. I will need some pitch-soaked arrows and your best archers. You've got your Welshmen?"

Brian nodded and strove to gather his wits.

"Good." Miles grasped Brian's arm. "Put on your hauberk and summon your men. I'll meet you in the hall."

He strode from the room with a brisk air, leaving Brian opening and shutting his mouth.

❖❖❖

In the bleak dark preceding the November dawn, Brian handed his stallion's reins to a squire and studied the black outline of the right-hand watchtower he had been designated to take. Miles was to deal with the left using the men he had brought with him. Brian's stomach was queasy; the wine he had drunk earlier lay sour in his gut.

Miles gave him a fierce grin. "Good fortune," he said.

"And you," Brian replied hoarsely.

"It will be like a day out at a fair with the ladies after Worcester," Miles said, and was gone like a wolf on the hunt: light, swift, and focused. A detail of Brian's Welsh bowmen accompanied him, and several serjeants. Brian turned to those remaining with him: more serjeants, archers, and his own knights from the garrison. His breath was a pale vapour in the air and his chest shook on each exhalation. To the east the sky was a touch paler than it had been at the blackest part of the night.

"Now," he said, swallowing. "Now or never."

They loped across the marshy ground, crouching low. Grapnels attached to rope ladders soared over the stakes of the outer palisade and men began to climb at speed. An alarm note blared on a hunting horn, summoning the defenders to arms. Brian's archers shot blazing arrows into the compound. Brian muttered a prayer under his breath and took his turn on the swaying grapnel ladder. His hands burned on the rope as he pulled himself upward, all the time fearing that he would be speared like meat on a skewer or crushed by a falling stone. And this was only the first obstacle. The main tower lay beyond. He gained the top of the palisade, pulled himself over on to the walkway, and, with sword drawn, ran towards the gates. A defender came at him with a hand axe. He avoided the downward chop of the blade and with a side-swipe, knocked his assailant off the palisade. The soldier struck the bailey floor with a solid thud and Brian suppressed a heave. The world had run mad, and this was hell.

In several places the palisade was burning. Brian caught a lungful of hot smoke and turned aside, coughing. Someone else came at him and he dodged and cut and struck and felt sick. An arrow slammed into the side of his coif, spinning him to the ground. Blood filled his right eye.

"Sire!" William Boterel leaned over him. "Sire…"

"Take the men!" Brian gasped. "Get that gate open. We can't lose the impetus! Go!"

Boterel did as he was bidden, leaving Brian to be attended by a serjeant. "Just a surface wound, sire," the man said. "Arrow's lodged in the mail. You'll have a red stripe tomorrow, no worse." He snapped off the shaft with a grunt. "Lucky though."

Brian removed his helm and coif and gazed at the arrowhead, his vision blurred with blood. The serjeant produced a strip of bandage and used it to wipe Brian's eye and stanch the wound. He strove to his feet. The broken shaft and arrowhead on the walk reminded him of a snapped quill pen. Picking up his sword, he drew a shaken breath. He had to carry this through, and write his will in blood and fire, because how else was he going to be a leader of men, keep his word to Matilda, and give her a crown?

The thatch on the outbuilding roofs was ablaze and men fought amid swirls of smoke and stinging sparks. Brian strode among his soldiers, shouting encouragement, urging them on, and forcing himself forward. "For the empress!" he bellowed, wiping a fresh trickle of blood from his eye corner. "For the rightful queen of England!"

As dawn paled the eastern horizon, Brian and his men over-came the last resistance on the outer works and tore down the gates. Then it was on to the tower itself. No scaling here, just brushwood and pitch and flaming arrows. Some defenders tried to escape by ropes from the battlements and were shot down by Wallingford's archers. Those who reached the ground were taken for ransom if wealthy enough. If not, they were stripped of their weapons, purses, and clothing and sent on their way in their underwear. Brian had the booty, such as it was, piled up outside the gates while the tower burned, surrounded by a ring of fiery palisade. His right temple throbbed as if a small drum was being beaten against his orbit and brow bone. He could only half see out of his right eye.

Facing the gateway, he watched Miles FitzWalter come towards him. The man's surcoat and face were freckled with soot and blood, but his smile was incandescent.

"Success!" he cried. "Stephen's going to be too busy running hither and yon to return and rebuild these for a very long time, if ever." He cocked his head and considered Brian's injury. "Close one," he said.

Brian reached up to touch the clotted line at the side of his eye. "It was one of our own arrows," he said. "Taken up and shot back."

"Always the most dangerous." Hands on hips, Miles turned in a slow circle and nodded with satisfaction. "A good night's work. That, my lord, is how you run rings around your enemy."

Thirty-six

GLOUCESTER CASTLE, SPRING 1140

MATILDA PACED UP AND DOWN HER CHAMBER IN AGITATION. "It is intolerable," she snapped at Brian, who stood by the hearth looking wary. "I will not stand for this!"

He avoided her gaze. He had been at court since Christmas, working tirelessly on arguments supporting her right to be queen and her son's right to inherit. Negotiations were about to take place in Winchester, brokered by Bishop Henry, the proposal being that Stephen would acknowledge Matilda's claim to the crown in right of her descendants and grant her the rule of Normandy in her lifetime. Her son Henry would be brought to England and sworn in as heir to the throne. The difficulty was that Stephen and Matilda were to be represented by intermediaries, and Stephen had appointed his wife to speak as his—a shrewd move that stole a march on the opposition.

She reached the end of the room and flung round. "Where is the right in allowing Stephen's wife to negotiate on his behalf, while I may not speak?"

"It is the role of a queen to be a peacemaker," Brian said. "And Stephen has nominated her to represent him. We can do nothing about that."

"Hah! With my 'beloved' cousin Maheut in charge, the

outcome is a foregone conclusion. You won't prise her jaws off the throne."

The atmosphere between them bristled with tension and was broken as Matilda exhaled on a hard breath and waved her arm in a gesture filled with angry dismissal. "If because of this 'sacred tradition' I am barred from attending in person, I expect you and my brother not to yield an inch of ground."

He rubbed the pink scar at the side of his eye, legacy of the fight to take down the Crowmarsh siege towers that had threatened Wallingford. Miles had commended him at court as a fine compatriot in battle, but whenever the subject arose, Brian shrugged it off, and moved on to other things. "You can trust us, domina."

"Can I?" Her tone was weary and sceptical. "I sometimes wonder if I have any trust left to give."

❖❖❖

Brian shifted his buttocks on the bench and folded his arms as he listened to Robert of Gloucester advancing proposals for a peace that would end the fighting. He knew Stephen's party were unlikely to agree to them, but the suggestions were not outrageous and Robert's eloquence lent weight and credibility to the argument.

Stephen's queen, Maheut, was leaning forward in her seat with a pained expression on her face as if she was struggling to hear what Robert was saying, her attitude patronising and authoritative. Beside her, dwarfing her own chair, stood an empty throne as a reminder that, even without his presence, the king was a part of the process and would see and hear all.

Maheut was small and sturdy, with close-set shrewd eyes set beneath heavy, dark brows, her prim mouth concealing small, pearly teeth. Matilda often called her a terrier and the comparison was apt, but beyond his amusement at the analogy, Brian knew her tenacity was dangerous. She was utterly loyal to Stephen, and her brisk, motherly manner engendered loyalty in others. When with Stephen in public, she kept her eyes lowered and her mouth closed, cultivating the persona of a modest, submissive wife, but Brian suspected it was a different matter behind their bedchamber door.

The empress had no such maternal image to temper her own abrasive nature. If she thought a man was a fool, she said so to his face in front of others, and gave no quarter. She was tall, slender, beautiful, desirable—like a mistress, and while few men would ever strike their mothers, he knew many who would take a fist to a mistress, or leave her for another woman.

"You ask the impossible, my lord," Maheut said to Robert. "My husband is an anointed king, elected to his throne by the barons and bishops of England. He will neither share power with your sister the Countess of Anjou, nor acknowledge her claim."

"She is the only surviving legitimate child of my father," Robert asserted calmly. "All swore to her before they ever swore to your husband. Moreover, she is the only claimant born of a reigning king and queen, and she is owed that respect and acknowledgement."

"Her father absolved his barons of that vow on his deathbed," Maheut replied with equal firmness. "We could argue that point all week and get nowhere. We might concede the dower castles in Normandy that the Countess of Anjou was granted on her marriage, but the Countess would have to quit England, and all warfare in Normandy would have to cease forthwith."

"You cannot grant what is already acknowledged as belonging to the empress," Robert said. "My sister has a right to England's crown and the coronet of Normandy. She will settle for rule in Normandy while her son grows to manhood, and in the fullness of time, he will inherit England. To that end, he will be brought here and the barons will swear him their allegiance."

Maheut sat back, hands gripping the finials of her chair. "That is out of the question. One of the reasons men swore to my husband was that they knew him and his stock. England and Normandy have no wish to be ruled from Anjou by a woman who has spent her life in foreign courts and has no knowledge of our ways. If King Henry had wanted his daughter on the throne, he would have said so on his deathbed!"

"Likely he did and it went unreported," Robert retorted. "Oaths are bought and sold these days like cheeses at a market. Perhaps England and Normandy do not want to be ruled from Blois and Boulogne...and France. Perhaps England would rather a king of the true blood sat on the throne, a grandson of King Henry and the king of Jerusalem."

Maheut's spine was as rigid as the back of her chair. Her eldest son had been betrothed earlier in the year to the French king's daughter. "You would have people swear for an untested child?" she scoffed. "You would further disrupt the country? People will swear to him and then perhaps think they no longer need to be loyal to their rightful anointed king. I say no and no."

The bishop of Winchester had been watching the proceedings with sleepy eyes that nevertheless missed nothing. Now he rose to his feet and opened his broad, bejewelled hands in an encompassing gesture. "This entails a deal more discussion," he said in his rich, carrying voice. "Time now to take stock and refresh ourselves. We must think upon these issues and gauge what to do in order to have a binding peace."

Brian did not trust the bland, urbane bishop of Winchester. He was consummate at playing one side off against the other, all for his own gain. It seemed to Brian that whoever offered Bishop Henry the most power would be the one to win his support and influence.

"I believe we must widen the discussion and take further consultation with our neighbours, and the Holy Father,"

Bishop Henry said. "He may have more to say on this issue now that each side has put its case."

Indeed, Brian thought cynically. Rome was for sale just as much as Henry of Winchester. With jewels and bribes, with promises of profitable deals from trade and commerce. With gifts to the Church and enticements of lucrative appointments. The sacred manipulating the profane. The Church would claim to be a peacekeeper and arbiter of the rules, but only inasmuch as it suited those in ecclesiastical power. It made Brian feel smirched and unutterably weary.

Thirty-seven

WYMONDHAM PRIORY, NORFOLK, AUTUMN 1140

KNEELING BEFORE THE ALTAR OF WYMONDHAM PRIORY, Adeliza felt the baby kick, and pressed her hand to her womb in gratitude for the new life growing there. Her second pregnancy was as much a miraculous gift as her first. Today they were attending a mass followed by a feast to honour Will's father, who had founded Saint Mary's more than thirty years ago and now lay enshrined in the choir. Will had presented the priory with a silver chalice and candlesticks for the altar, his own weight in beeswax for candles, and five marks for distribution to the poor.

Following mass, Adeliza doled out more silver pennies to the folk waiting outside to see them in the bright November cold. Many hailed her as queen, which made her glow. It was so peaceful here that it was hard to believe there was so much strife in other parts. Three days ago, they had heard about the failure of the latest round of negotiations. The bishop of Winchester had returned from conferring with the French and his older brother Theobald, Count of Blois. All had agreed that the empress's son, Henry, should be acknowledged as the heir to England and Normandy, but Queen Maheut had refused to countenance such a future, and, supported by her backbone, Stephen had dug in his heels too.

Now the fighting would escalate. Adeliza hated it when Will went on campaign with the king. He had spent the summer fighting rebels in the Fens. She did not understand what Will saw in Stephen. Will in his turn was impatient with her attitude towards Matilda, and it created considerable friction between them.

Hands on hips, Will was looking at the priory. "My father often brought me here to watch them building this place," he mused. "He laid some of these stones himself and I helped him, although I would only have been three or four years old. I want to do the same with my own sons. I want to build things and know that they will last beyond our lifetime. I want to enfold and protect what I have, and I will fight tooth and nail to do so."

"I know," Adeliza said, and shivered, because his words were both a comfort and a reflection of the times.

Immediately he was all concern, folding his arm tenderly around her shoulders. "You have been out in the cold too long. Come, we should go within."

She was glad of his support, but insisted on completing her duty of doling out the silver to the poor, who she knew had been standing in the cold for much longer than she had, and with less protection.

In the Prior's lodging, Father Ralph, eager to please his patrons, had laid a fine table. The surplus pigs had recently been slaughtered and the main dish was pork garnished with apples from the priory orchard. Servings of stew, barley pottage, and blood sausages were sent out to the poor.

"We hear grave news from further south." Prior Ralph dabbed his lips with his napkin. "The sacking of Worcester and the siege of Hereford are shocking. These are godless times when men desecrate graveyards to better position their siege machines and turn churches into fortifications when they are not burning them to the ground."

"It is indeed appalling," Will agreed diplomatically. "Be assured, no harm shall come to the Church by my hand, on my honour. I will so vow at the altar before I leave."

"I am glad to hear it. You are a good man, my lord."

"I am not," Will said gruffly, "but should I tear a cross from an altar or defile a grave, I would be dishonouring God, and I would never be able to look my wife in the eyes again or be at peace with myself." He reached for Adeliza's hand and squeezed it.

A young monk approached the table to announce that a messenger had arrived with urgent news for the Earl of Lincoln. Adeliza exchanged a worried glance with her husband. Urgent news these days was seldom good. Will stood up with an apology to the prior for the interrupted meal. "I will see him in the guest house," he said as he assisted Adeliza to rise.

The messenger was waiting for them and, kneeling, removed his cap. "Sire, madam, grave tidings. The Earl of Chester and his half-brother have seized Lincoln Castle and declared ownership."

Adeliza stifled a gasp. Lincoln Castle was Stephen's property but Will was Earl of Lincoln with administrative rights and privileges.

"Go on," Will said.

"The earl and the sire de Roumare sent their wives into the castle to visit the constable's wife and talk as women do. Then the earl and his brother returned with just a few men to escort the ladies home; but, once inside the castle, they overpowered the soldiers on the gate and threw the doors open to their own troops."

Will absorbed the news with a set jaw. He dismissed the messenger, telling him to find sustenance and a fresh horse ready to set out again within the hour. Then he entered the guest house and breathed out hard. "Well, this makes my earldom a complete laughing stock, does it not?"

Adeliza shook her head. To her, it was just another sign of Stephen's unfitness for kingship. Men walked all over him because he had no authority.

"Stephen will have to nip this in the bud," Will said. "He cannot allow Chester and de Roumare to do this to him—or to me."

"It looks full blown already to me," Adeliza replied. "As you say, this makes a mockery of your power in the shire." Her exasperation overflowed. "None of this would have happened when Henry was king. He would have dealt with Chester and de Roumare long before now."

"And well he might, but he left enough of a mess that we are all suffering for it," Will snapped. "He was no saint for all you are forever making him out to be one. He should have left Matilda in Germany or married her to a Lotharingian prince and left England to Stephen. If there is war now, then Henry's decisions and selfishness are the root causes of it."

Adeliza recoiled as if he had struck her. "He was my husband and he was a great king." She tried to steady her voice. "I will not be disloyal to him or to his memory, and you should not speak ill of him."

"It is not disloyal to say he had faults. Were you never hurt by the number of bastards he sired on the string of women he took to bed under your nose? Did it never trouble your sleep that he blinded his own grandchildren because their parents rebelled against him? Or the manner in which he manipulated his daughter without a thought beyond his own schemes?" He gave her an exasperated look. "He was great because he was ruthless. Stephen for all his faults would never have done any of those things, and that is part of the reason I follow him. Henry exacted a price from us all, and we are still paying." He made an abrupt gesture. "Enough. I will take you to Arundel and then I will go to the king and all this will be set to rights."

Adeliza's throat was painful with tears. Stephen was incapable of setting anything to rights, whatever Will thought, but she held her tongue. Too much damage had been done already. She pressed her hand to her belly, her emotions a solid, heavy block. "I beg your leave to retire," she said shakily. "I need to rest." With a gesture to her women, she left his side and disappeared behind the screened-off partition at the rear of the room where her travelling bed and chest had been set up.

Will rubbed his face and softly groaned. This news was a serious blow to his prestige and to Stephen's authority. Chester and de Roumare were half-brothers and similar to the Beaumont twins in their ambitions. They were a disruptive element when at court, and bad enemies to make. Thus far he had managed to avoid involvement in the power play of the Beaumonts and had scrambled his way through the issue of opening Arundel to Matilda while still supporting Stephen. But now he risked being caught in the riptides involving the Chester faction. If he sank, his family sank too; his wife, much as he loved her, did not understand.

His favourite dog, Teri, padded up to him and licked his hand. He stooped to tousle the silky ears. Dogs were faithful and demanded nothing of you but food, exercise, and affection. Sometimes he found himself wishing he had been born a common kennel boy. Instead he had married a queen and climbed so high on fortune's wheel that the distance to the ground was dizzying.

❖❖❖

The green wood in the hearth of Lincoln Castle's great hall gave off gouts of smoke and aggravated Will's hacking cough as he huddled over what heat there was, feeling decidedly unwell. The raw damp of the early December weather seemed to have permeated every crevice of the walls, and every joint and sinew in his aching body. He folded his arms inside his cloak and shivered so hard, he felt as if his flesh might leave his bones. King Stephen was pacing the room like a caged lion. The half-brothers Ranulf, Earl of Chester, and William de Roumare watched him with steely eyes. De Roumare was playing with his dagger, tossing it end over end.

"Our mother's family has a hereditary right to the custody of Lincoln Castle," de Roumare said, jutting out a pugnacious jaw pocked with acne scars. "It should be ours. We have only taken what we are entitled to."

Stephen whirled, the hem of his cloak flaring at his ankles. "Lincoln Castle is a royal one even if its constables have served in the past by heredity," he snapped. "You have no automatic right." He gave de Roumare a hard glare. The latter sheathed his dagger, but continued to play suggestively with the hilt.

Ranulf of Chester pulled on his long, auburn moustaches. "Then give us what we are due, sire. We have upheld your reign thus far, but you ignore us at your peril. Would you deny us our patrimony?"

"You have had lands and privileges from me in plenty already, without Lincoln," Stephen said tersely.

De Roumare pivoted and stabbed his finger at Will. "Why make him Earl of Lincoln and not one of us?" he demanded. "He is nothing but a jumped-up hearth knight who has ideas above himself because of his marriage to the dowager queen."

Will started to his feet. "You insult me!" he said, his chest burning with the need to cough.

"No more than my brother and I am insulted that you are Earl of Lincoln and claiming the third penny of a shire that should be ours," de Roumare spat. "You act like an amiable big dog with no brain between its ears, while all the time you are lying under your master's table, taking the bones that belong to better men. No matter how many fancy castles you build, you are still nothing."

Rage flamed through Will's body. "But at least I am faithful," he snarled, and then had to turn aside to cough and then spit into the fire.

"Oh indeed," de Roumare sneered. "This is why you harboured the empress in your bosom last year."

"Peace!" Stephen roared. He glared at the brothers. "Since you feel so greatly aggrieved and I value your fealty, I shall heed your argument. De Roumare, you can take the title of Earl of Lincoln if my lord D'Albini is willing to accept that of Earl of Sussex instead."

Will's gut curdled. He felt insulted and humiliated, but was too sick and feverish to argue.

"And you will give me the right to Lincoln Castle?" pushed de Roumare.

Stephen ground his jaw. "Providing you swear me fealty and stay within bounds."

The way that the brothers were staring at Stephen made Will apprehensive. His dogs had that air when they fought each other for dominance of the pack.

After a long pause, de Roumare stepped forward and bent his knee. "I do so swear," he muttered. Chester followed suit.

"Oh get up," Stephen snapped. "We will make it official tomorrow before all, and let this be an end to it. I will yield no further!"

The tension was palpable. This wasn't the end, Will was certain, because appeasement was not control, and no one in this room was satisfied.

❖❖❖

Will lay in bed beside Adeliza, lazing in delicious warmth, the furs drawn up to his chin. He did not want to move to get ready and go to the Christmas court at Windsor, but knew he must. Stephen was expecting him, and he was to kneel and pay homage for his replacement earldom of Sussex. There was a bitter taste in his mouth over the arrangement, although in truth, it made sense and should have been given to him as his earldom from the outset.

He could hear the nurse in the anteroom cooing to their son as she changed his wet linens. Against his body, Adeliza's womb was round and full with their second child. She was soon to go into confinement, and it gave him pleasure to feel the baby kick against the palm of his hand. Adeliza had said nothing about his change of title, and he was grateful for her silence even if her looks had been eloquent and knowing.

Eventually, aware of his duty and prodded by the increasing sounds from the antechamber, he left the cosy nest of their bed, shoved his feet into his shoes, and, scratching and yawning, ambled to use the latrine. Then, wrapped in his fur cloak, he went to see his son. Wilkin squealed and held out chubby arms, demanding to be picked up. Will swept him into his embrace and nuzzled the baby's pale brown curls. He smelled of fresh, warmed linen and sleep. "Pa!" he said and pulled his father's whiskers.

"Well, my little man," Will chuckled, "what shall I bring you from court? A silver spoon? A golden cup? Bright silver bells? Or perhaps a new earldom, hmm?"

"Sire…"

He glanced up to see Milo Bassett, one of his senior knights, hesitating in the doorway. "What is it?" Will beckoned him into the room.

"A messenger's just ridden in." Milo's expression was tense with two fine creases between his eyes. "William de Roumare and Ranulf of Chester have just gone the full distance and declared for the empress. They've closed Lincoln against the king."

Will stared at him. "I knew this would happen," he said grimly. "I told Stephen he should not trust them, but he would not listen. He gives too many the benefit of the doubt."

"You're summoned to meet the king at Lincoln, not

Windsor," Milo continued. "I've set the grooms to harnessing more packhorses and told the steward to increase the provisions."

Will nodded briskly. "Give me a moment to dress and I'll attend you. Find Adelard and tell him I'll need my hauberk and weapons."

As Milo strode off, Will returned the infant to his nurse and went to tell Adeliza he was not going to Windsor as planned, but north to Lincoln and war.

❖❖❖

Matilda was holding court in Gloucester when a hard-travelled messenger brought her the news about Lincoln, together with the information that Stephen had abandoned his Christmas court at Windsor and was riding north to deal with the situation.

"Now is our chance to take on Stephen and bring him down," Robert said, his eyes full of a hunter's light. Ranulf of Chester was his son-in-law and he had long been working at dividing him from Stephen.

Matilda frowned and pursed her lips. "Ranulf de Gernons and William de Roumare are wily dissemblers and they will exact a high price for their loyalty. Just because they have seized Lincoln does not mean they have had a complete change of heart. All they see is their own opportunity."

"But if they can run Stephen off, then by coming to their aid we gain at least a nominal hold on Lincoln. Hugh Bigod is wavering in his support of Stephen, for all that he was one of the first to swear for him. It will only take another push. It might be worth offering him the earldom of Norfolk to secure his help. He's an untrustworthy self-seeker, but if we can work on him to abandon Stephen, then to the good."

Matilda rubbed her aching forehead. Even though the news held promise, she still felt as if she were trying to swim across a cold, dark lake with weights on her ankles. There was never enough money, and she was well aware that men who knelt to her and smiled one day would as likely stab her in the back and abandon her on another. Those who stayed with her had nothing left to lose. Sometimes she wondered if it was all worth it, but would then shake herself. This was for her son, and for his sons (God forbid they would be daughters), stretching in a line that travelled so far she could not see the end of it, and if she gave up, that line would not exist. "Do whatever you can," she said.

Robert pressed his hand to her shoulder and left the room. Brian, who had been listening silently, a little to one side, said, "You will win this, domina."

"Will I?" She went to stand before the hearth, rubbing her arms.

"Assuredly, domina."

"Your voice carries platitudes," she said irritably.

"I hope not, because then I would be deluding myself."

She turned to him. "I want to succeed, Brian," she said, vehemently. "I want this so much that I could set the world ablaze with what I feel inside." She pressed her hand to her stomach in emphasis. "Sometimes I think it will consume me and there will be nothing left. You tell me 'assuredly' and I want to rage at you because it is the slick word of a courtier."

"That is all I thought you wanted from me," he answered woodenly. "If you desire me to say I will go through that blaze for you, I will do so, gladly."

Matilda retreated behind her shield again. What she desired of him she could never have, and she was far too sensible to ask what he desired for himself. "Do you not have matters to deal with outside of this chamber?" she asked curtly.

There was a taut silence. Then he said, "Domina," and left the room, the cold air lingering on the tail of the closing door. She stared at the hearth for a long time; then she moved away from it, and set her mind to the matter of Lincoln and what defeating Stephen might mean.

Thirty-eight

WILL STOOD AMID THE THRONG OF STEPHEN'S BARONS IN THE
nave of Lincoln Cathedral where they had all gathered
to celebrate the Feast of the Purification of the Virgin Mary. It
was so cold that his breath emerged as white vapour. The only
difference between here and outside was the absence of the
bone-chilling wind and occasional flurries of icy rain. The interior of the cathedral blazed with the light of numerous candles
and lamps as befitted a celebration of light. The honeyed scents
of incense and beeswax overlaid the musty smell of winter stone
with the haunting, evocative perfume of God.

King Stephen had been besieging Lincoln Castle for several
weeks, and was making slow progress, but each painstaking
advance was costly in terms of time and finances. With his
architectural and building skills, Will had been commanding
the siege machines that had been pounding the castle walls.
Thus far, the garrison was holding out. No great breaches had
been made in the defences and it was clear that Chester and
de Roumare had used the time to hoard men and supplies and
were not for yielding.

This celebration of the Virgin's churching had a deeper
resonance than usual to Will because he had recently heard
that Adeliza had been safely delivered of their second child, a

daughter this time, christened Adelis. As he joined the procession to carry a lighted candle down the nave to the altar, he fixed his prayers upon his wife, his new baby, and his small son.

In front of him, Stephen stumbled upon the trailing hem of his cloak. Molten candle wax dripped over the king's hand and he dropped the candle on to the stone flags of the nave, where it broke in two and extinguished itself in a pale thread of smoke. Men glanced at each other with unease. A young knight darted forward and handed his own candle to the king, and a chaplain hurriedly removed the broken one, but the damage was done and although Stephen shrugged it off as nothing, the tension was palpable.

The sense of doom was compounded moments later when the delicate silver box holding the communion wafers fell from its hanger chain, struck the side of the altar, and tumbled on to the steps, scattering the wafers abroad and breaking many. Several members of the congregation crossed themselves and a low mutter of unease percolated throughout the nave. The hair rose on Will's nape because this was God's own house and the communion wafers were the body of Christ. He was not given to flights of fancy, but he was perturbed. Stephen, however, acted as if nothing had happened. He remained calm and prostrated himself before the altar in submission while priests hastened to rescue the pyx and the fallen wafers and bring new ones.

The remainder of the service continued without incident and the tension eased, but did not entirely dissipate. As they emerged from the cathedral into the bitter February weather, William D'Ypres remarked flippantly that Stephen should think about shortening the length of his cloak, but no one smiled.

Will returned to the siege machines and quelled the speculation among his troops. "A candle broke, and so did the link in a chain," he growled. "Such small things happen around us every day and if we saw portents in them all, we would be paralysed by our fears."

A squire brought him bread and cheese and he ate while watching the men setting up the trebuchet, their fingertips and noses red with cold. He imagined a roaring fire and Adeliza reading to him from one of her books in her gentle voice, or singing a lullaby to their son and the baby, and he felt heartsick and wished he was at Arundel.

A horn sounded on the town battlements, and then another, and another, all along the walls. Will swallowed his mouthful of food and sent the squire to find out what the noise was about. He was buckling on the sword he had removed to attend mass when the lad returned in a high state of excitement.

"Sire, it's the Earls of Gloucester and Chester. They've been sighted across the Witham looking for a fording place." The youth's Adam's apple bobbed in his throat. "It's the whole Angevin host—cavalry and Welsh levies and all!"

Will stared at him. It was foolhardy to risk all on a single battle, but perhaps Robert of Gloucester felt it was all or nothing.

"It's a sign from God," one of the siege-machine crew gabbled. "First the candle and the pyx; now this."

Will rounded on him. "Gloucester was bound to come here; the only question was how soon. Get back to work until I say otherwise."

Lowering his eyes, the man turned back to the trebuchet.

Having given interim orders to the men, Will went to join the king at Bishop Alexander's lodging. By the time he arrived, a heated discussion was already in full flow. Stephen wanted to ride out and face the approaching Angevin force and bring them to battle. His barons did not.

"Sire, it is unwise," counselled William D'Ypres, shaking his head. "Their numbers are greater than ours. Surely it is better to withdraw or stay behind the town walls and wait them out."

"No!" Stephen snapped. "I will not yield an inch of ground to Robert FitzRoy or Ranulf of Chester and his hellspawn brother. I am the anointed king and I am sick of these men. Let God decide."

"Sire, even God needs help," said D'Ypres to nods of agreement from the other barons. "Perhaps what happened in the cathedral is a warning. You should reconsider."

"I said no!" Stephen banged his fist down on the trestle. "We will fight and put an end to this insurrection once and for all. I am the anointed king of England and I will be listened to!" His gaze flashed around the room, striking each man and nailing him to his duty. "Are you weak, superstitious fools and women that you baulk? Go and ready your men. If they cross the Witham, then we will meet them."

As the barons left the chamber to begin the muster, Stephen called Will to him. "I want you to stay back with the siege machines and prevent the garrison from assaulting from the rear..."

"Sire," Will said and, with a grim set to his lips, left for his position.

❖❖❖

"He's going to make a full fight of it then," said Adelard le Flemyng, Will's senior serjeant, as Stephen led his assembled army away from the siege camp and towards the city gates.

Will grimaced. "It appears so,"

Adelard looked dubious. "Is that wise?"

Will shrugged. Stephen had never been one to sit and ponder the wise alternatives. They were the realm of his brother the Bishop of Winchester from whom the King had become estranged. When something bothered Stephen he would up and deal with it in a physical way. "Perhaps not, but Gloucester is taking a similar risk. His Welsh levies may give him advantage of numbers but they are not seasoned and they won't stand."

"Even so, to risk so much…"

"The king will not retreat because of his father," Will said.

"His father?" Adelard looked bemused.

"He was accused of cowardice while fighting in the Holy Land—of fleeing from a battle and not standing his ground. Stephen would rather die than have such an accusation levied at him. Whatever happens, he will not yield."

"But what if he loses?"

Will gazed round his camp. He had been thinking that himself. He was no deserter, but he was pragmatic and he had a responsibility to the men under his command, not all of whom were wealthy enough to be worth ransoms, should it come to that pass. It was as well to be prepared. "Tell the men to have their weapons and equipment to hand," he said. "Make sure they have food in their packs and that their water costrels are full."

❖ ❖ ❖

Brian was in the thick of the fight when a massive roar went up. Stephen's centre had collapsed. The backbone that should have stood, including the forces commanded by William D'Ypres and five senior earls, had fled the field, leaving Stephen marooned on foot and horseless at the hub of an assault from all sides.

Brian brought his sword down in a slashing arc and as it bit through flesh, he felt sick; and because of that, he increased the pressure, trying to expunge the feeling and push forward. Again and again his blade flashed and he urged his men on in an aggressive voice that disguised his fear and disgust but sounded like battle rage. It was as if he were outside his body watching a stranger in black armour trample and hack and destroy. It was like slaughter day in a butcher's shambles. Blood ran down his sword blade and the men opposing him were as cattle. He was doing it for Matilda, he told himself, for a promise he had made that he had to keep. All this was happening for a purpose, for the greater good. And when it was over, he could wash his hands and the building of a proper reign could begin.

He swung his sword again. His stallion stumbled on a body; Brian grabbed the rein to steady him and, as the horse regained his balance, heard a massive roar erupt from the centre.

"The king is down, the usurper is taken!"

He watched the royal standard toppling beneath a surge of troops. Stephen's men were either falling or fleeing. Brian glimpsed Stephen on his knees, surrounded by the dead and wounded of his own side and by opponents he had brought down in a final, desperate flurry. Blood crawled from a wound under his helmet and his mouth was open as he gasped for breath.

Gloucester arrived to take him into custody and Stephen, dazed and mumbling, yielded to him. Having converged on the person of the king and his banner, the Angevin army began to spread out again, and the pursuit and punishment of the vanquished began.

Brian checked his men and was relieved to discover that the wounds were mostly shallow cuts, bruises, and broken fingers that would heal quickly. For himself, he felt as if a heavy dark-ness was pressing down on him, winding black tendrils through every orifice in his skull. The roars of victory only served to aggravate the burning nausea in the pit of his belly.

Miles FitzWalter joined Brian as he rode towards the city walls. "I sometimes think you a bit of a courtier," he said, a hard grin on his face, "but you fought out of your hauberk just now."

Brian said nothing. Miles did not realise how close to the truth he was. Brian was still not sure he was back inside his hauberk, and in fact he didn't want to be because of the terrible weight of it, as if it were a coat of sins.

"God has well and truly spoken. Did you see de Meulan and Bigod fleeing the field like cowards? And even D'Ypres?" Miles bared his teeth and laughed.

Brian could almost see the battle heat rising off him. "Stephen should have stayed behind those walls and waited for reinforcements," he said.

"Useful for us that he did not. Now we must keep him securely locked up and see to it that the empress takes her rightful place as queen."

"Indeed." Brian's thoughts turned to Matilda. Already a messenger would be galloping to Devizes with news of their victory. Would it light her with joy, or would the news settle a burden across her shoulders, like this hauberk across his own?

Miles rode off to see to his affairs, and Brian made his way into the town. The gates hung wide and the stench of smoke from blazing thatch filled the air. There was going to be retribution aplenty for the citizens who had supported Stephen and not the beleaguered garrison. Everywhere he looked people were fleeing, trying to avoid the incoming troops.

His destrier started to limp. Brian dismounted to look, and discovered the stallion's knee puffy and hot from a strain sustained in the fighting. Not wanting to ride on and worsen the injury, Brian ordered his squire to fetch his remount from the back of the ranks.

A band of soldiers rounded the corner, their manner one of clandestine haste. Brian's men drew their freshly sheathed swords and pointed their spears. So did the other group, their fear palpable. Brian stared at Will D'Albini, who returned the look and drew himself to his full height.

Brian swallowed his gorge and made a swift gesture. "Go," he said. "We have not seen you. Stephen is taken and your cause is defeated. Make haste and watch your road because if Miles FitzWalter catches you, he will have you in irons or turned to corpses faster than the bishop of Winchester can say a paternoster."

D'Albini's hazel eyes narrowed with suspicion. "Why would you do this for me, my lord?"

"Because I am not your enemy, Will. Before all this happened, we were friends. You allowed my lady to land at Arundel and that deserves acknowledgement and recompense. I have seen a surfeit of bloodshed today and victory is won. What difference will taking you make? Just go, and be swift about it!"

"Thank you," Will said stiffly. "I will not forget." With a curt nod, one soldier to another, he moved on.

"Will they escape?" asked a knight.

"I do not know, but I have given them their chance." Brian heaved a troubled sigh. "I have often shared bread and company with Will D'Albini, and we were companions sent to meet the empress when she came home from Germany. I will not raise my sword against him now, nor barter him for ransom. Enough is enough. I gift him to his wife and his family." A little of the darkness eased, but only to grey, and the weight remained.

Thirty-nine

LINCOLN, FEBRUARY 1141

*S*TEPHEN WAS PUT ON A HORSE THE DAY AFTER THE BATTLE and taken south to Gloucester. He was concussed, bruised, and shivering, even though wrapped in a heavy fur-lined cloak. There had been serious debate as to whether he should ride in a cart, but that would have slowed the journey and Robert wanted him in their stronghold territories as swiftly as possible. Stephen too had insisted he would ride because only women, the infirm, and servants rode in carts. In the end, they had given him a bay gelding, strong and sturdy with an even stride.

"I am an anointed king," Stephen told Brian, who was riding beside him to make sure he did not fall. He was certainly in no condition to attempt an escape. "Whether you kill me or imprison me for life, it does not alter that fact. Nor that my army is still intact and will regroup to sweep you aside."

"They deserted you," Brian said.

Stephen gave Brian a shrewd glance from a livid purple eye socket. "They expected me to leave the field too," he said. "They will continue the fight, and so will my wife. Your empress will never cast down the crown from my Maheut's head. I may be your captive, but this is far from the end of the matter."

"It is a matter that should never have begun in the first place, sire. I do indeed pray that this is the end."

Stephen looked scornful despite his battered countenance. "You do not like to soil your hands, do you, Brian, but warfare is a dirty business. My cousin will use you up until you are dust trickling through her fingers, and then she will say it was only her due, and you will have no one to blame but yourself for your choice."

Brian said nothing, but he was unsettled by the prophetic wisdom in Stephen's words. Yesterday's battle was still working its way through him both physically and mentally and his thoughts remained bruised and dark. When he told himself that this was the beginning of Matilda's rightful rule, he felt satisfied and vindicated, but when he thought that it might be the beginning of even harder fighting, he felt sick. He had promised to give her his life, but sometimes he wondered what he had set upon himself.

❖❖❖

It was dark outside; the February dusk had closed in an hour since and in the chapel of Gloucester Castle, the pools of candle flame were the only source of light. Matilda looked up from her prayers to Saint James, Saint Julian, and the Blessed Virgin Mary and regarded her chancellor and chaplain, William Giffard. His face was naturally laconic and difficult to read even without the candle shadows casting deep hollows in his cheekbones and eye sockets.

"Domina," he said, "there is news from Lincoln. The Earl of Gloucester's messenger is here."

She was aware of the cold tiles beneath her knees, the heat of the candle flames, and the chill beyond their ovals of light. Her heart began to bang against her ribs. Ever since Robert and her commanders had taken the road to Lincoln, she had been poised on the edge of a precipice.

"Domina, he says the Earl has won a great victory and Stephen is taken prisoner. He is being brought to you."

"A great victory?" Her voice caught in her throat.

"Yes, domina." A faint smile broke across his features. "The king's earls deserted him. Even William D'Ypres fled the field, but Stephen would not, and he was struck down and captured."

The words filled her mind but grasping their meaning beyond the superficial was impossible. Robert had won. Stephen had lost. For a moment she stood in a void. She had been striving for so long, pushing and pushing, and now suddenly, out of her sight and her presence, victory had been secured and a crown was hers for the taking.

"Domina?" Giffard touched her arm in concern.

She drew herself together. "Bring the messenger to my chamber," she said. "And gather the household together in the hall so that I may talk to them."

When he had left on his errand, Matilda lit another candle to add to those already burning, and knelt to give thanks and pray for the strength she would need in the months to come.

❖❖❖

Robed like a queen, her gown glittering with precious stones, her imperial crown set on her head, and her father's sapphire ring glowing on her finger, Matilda gazed down at Stephen who had been brought to kneel before her in Gloucester Castle's great hall. His head was bowed and she could see where his hair was thinning at the crown, exposing the freckled pink scalp. The bruises from Lincoln mottled his face in varied hues of purple, magenta, and yellow. He was robed in a plain tunic of brown wool and the only jewellery about his person was a gold cross at his breast and the garnet brooch pinning his cloak. He was a man, just a battered, ordinary man, and he was in her power. She sat above him on a throne and he was at her feet. This was a moment she had been anticipating yet somehow the reality did not measure up to her expectations. Somehow she felt as if she had been waiting too long. This diminished, bruised man evoked little emotion in her beyond irritation and contempt, yet she had wanted to feel so much more.

"God has spoken," she said imperiously to Stephen. "You took what was not yours, and when offered a treaty, you refused the terms that would have secured peace. Now, by the will of God, you are brought before me in your defeat."

Stephen slowly raised his head. "I am justly humbled by God for my sins," he replied in a rusty voice, "but accepting the crown of England is not one of them. God has shown his displeasure in my deeds as king by delivering me to my enemies, but I have faith that He will yet have mercy and that He has spared my life for a purpose."

"Perhaps to repent for the rest of it," Matilda said coldly. "You are to be taken to Bristol and kept there for the rest of your days, however long or short that span might be." She could see Stephen's body shaking with rigors and his complexion under the rainbow of bruises was grey. "You will be given what you need for sustenance and prayer."

His lip curled. "Do not be misled by the sight of my condition. It is only temporary and will abate sooner than you think. I am answerable to God, not to you, and I am an anointed king, chosen by the barons of this land. You will not move me from that position whatever you do to me."

Matilda looked at her father's ring on her hand and felt the weight of the diadem on her brow. These had far more meaning than Stephen and his empty words. He was unimportant. She was a queen now, and she would use the formal force of the law to deal with this. "You will leave on the morrow for Bristol," she said, as if he had not spoken, "and there you will stay—for the remainder of your days." She looked at him and then straight through him, and, rising from the throne, walked majestically from the room, not waiting to see him taken away.

❖❖❖

Henry FitzEmpress, almost eight years old, was testing the paces of his new mount, Denier. The dam's Spanish breeding had given the little chestnut fire in his feet. Henry loved the feel of the wind streaming past his face, even though it was cold enough to sting his eyes, because it gave him a feeling of speed. On a swift horse, he was invincible.

His father had started taking him hunting, and Henry had also begun his military training, fighting with a shield made to suit his size, and a wooden sword. He loved every minute. Indeed, the only thing he ever found difficult was staying still. It was always a trial when he was in church and expected not to fidget in the presence of God. By contrast, flying on a horse was easy.

His father was waiting in the stable yard to greet him when he returned from his ride, his groom following several paces behind. Henry showed off by drawing rein in a dramatic slide of hooves, and leaped from the saddle almost before the pony had stopped. He flashed his father a broad smile, exposing gaps at the front where new teeth were growing in.

Geoffrey's lips twitched. "That was fine riding, my son." He plucked a burr out of Henry's cloak.

Henry flushed with pleasure. "Yes, sire." Much as he was enthralled by the swiftness and grace of Denier, what he really wanted to ride was a destrier like his father. His new pony was just another point on the road towards that accomplishment. "I could have made him go faster, but Alain wouldn't let me." He scowled over his shoulder at the groom.

"Alain was wise; you should listen to him," Geoffrey said. "And to your horse. Always be bold; never be heedless."

Henry pursed his lips and said nothing.

His father folded his arms. "I have been waiting for you because I have received some great news from England, from your mother. Stephen the usurper has been defeated in battle and captured by your uncle Robert and others of your mother's kin and allies. Your mother is to become queen."

Henry stared at his father while his stomach gave the same kind of swoop that it had done while he was galloping Denier. He had not seen his mother in almost a year and a half and memory of her features had blurred at the edges, but she wrote to him often and sent him things from England: a writing tablet with an interlaced design on the ivory cover, and a fine penknife. Things she had sewn, which held her scent. Bells for his harness. Numerous books. And always the promise that one day he would be a king because England was his.

"Can we go there?" He was suddenly consumed with eager impatience. Had a ship been present in the courtyard, he would have boarded it there and then.

"No, no, no," his father laughed. "Rein back your horse a little. It is early days yet. Your mother will send for you when it is time."

"But when will that be?"

"Soon," his father said. "But not quite yet." He ruffled Henry's hair. "One battle does not a victory make, even when the enemy has been captured. Once your mother has been crowned, she will send for you."

Henry frowned and wondered how close "soon" actually was. When adults said such things, it was usually simply to pacify— and it was always a long time. He did not see why he could not go immediately. He knew he could help, and it was his destiny.

His father said, "My first task now your mother has succeeded is to go into Normandy and secure the duchy. Many barons will want to pay homage to the winning side." He looked at Henry. "And no, you cannot come there either for the time being. Your task is to stay safe and learn and become a man."

Henry grimaced, but knew better than to protest. As far as he was concerned, he was a man, and years were only numbers.

Following a night of blustery wind and rain, a bright March morning dawned over the city of Winchester. Matilda knelt to her cousin, Bishop Henry, in the great hall of the castle, and kissed his papal ring, her emotions a mixture of relief and wariness. Yesterday he had agreed a pact of peace with her and promised to hand over the castle and the treasury. These were fine concessions, but she still did not trust him and suspected he had yielded because either he was unprepared to fight, or because, like all the others, he thought he could manipulate her because she was a woman.

She had conceded to him that all ecclesiastical appointments in England would be under his sway and she would be governed by his counsel. In exchange he had sworn to uphold her right to the throne and announce in public that she was queen designate. He had promised also to bring the rest of the Church into allegiance and had formally given her custody of the castle.

Now, as he raised her to her feet, his knights came forward, bearing the treasure chests. For show and ceremony, the most magnificent articles had been placed on silk cushions: an orb and sceptre; rings set with precious stones. A ruby the size of a hen's egg, and two enormous teardrop pearls. A staff set with garnets and sapphires; a goblet of gold and sardonyx; and a pyx enamelled in blue and crimson. The chests contained embroidered robes of cloth of gold, and one in royal purple, heavy with pearls. There were sacks of money, and a pair of swords with ornate fittings. Superficially it was a glorious sight, but Matilda suspected that much had been creamed off into the coffers of her legate cousin. He was already wearing a fortune on his back and his fortified palace outshone the castle.

"I expected more," she said.

"I am sorry for that," he replied blandly. "This is all that remains."

She pressed her lips together and looked instead at the final cushion. A crown was set upon it, the one her father had worn at his coronation, and that Stephen had usurped. Gems glittered about the band and the finials were adorned with small golden spheres. She took it in her hands as she had once taken Heinrich's crown in Speyer. She felt Henry's watchful stare, as if he expected her to put it on her head. How little he knew her. "I am not your brother," she said curtly. "I know the proper ways."

Winchester's cheek muscle twitched. "I know you will govern with wisdom and the sound advice of your councillors."

"I will do my best to honour the role that my father intended for me." Her voice gained depth and authority. "But I will not be a cipher for power-hungry men. I have seen what happens when a sovereign is weak."

"Indeed," Henry replied, his tone neutral and his expression guarded.

In slow and dignified procession, they walked from the castle to the market cross in the High Street, the bishop and Matilda side by side under a palanquin, supported by Brian FitzCount, Miles FitzWalter, Robert of Gloucester, and Reynald FitzRoy. A crowd of citizens had gathered to listen to what their bishop had to say and Henry's knights opened a path through the people so that he and Matilda could mount the steps beneath the cross and be seen by all.

Henry struck his crosier on the ground three times and filled his lungs. "Here before you stands the Empress Matilda, daughter of King Henry and the only surviving child born to him of his Queen Edith, of an ancient royal house!" he cried in a powerful, charismatic voice. "Here she stands among you! Give allegiance to your rightful queen!" He stooped to the lower step to take the crown from the priest holding the cushion. "Behold," he said. "Matilda, the Empress, King

Henry's true successor, and Lady of the English!" With slow exaggeration, he placed the diadem on Matilda's head. The gesture was symbolic and not a true crowning, but nevertheless it had a potent impact. "Let us do proper homage to her power that she may bring peace to our lives and bounty back to our lands. Let her come to us redoubled in glory for the courage and fortitude she has expended and let us follow her that we may be blessed. And let her take wise counsel and rule in justice and wisdom and grace!"

The sound and sight of a thousand people kneeling all at once filled Matilda with triumph, yet at the same time she was irritated at Henry of Winchester's orchestration of the event, playing at kingmaker, even if she needed him. Winchester might be the old capital of England and the place where the treasure was stored—such as it was—but Westminster was the new hub, and not until the full ceremony had been performed at the abbey there and her brow anointed by Theobald, archbishop of Canterbury, would she truly be queen, whatever was said and done today.

Forty

ARUNDEL, APRIL 1141

ADELIZA SAT BY THE FIRE IN HER CHAMBER, EMBROIDERING pearls on to a cope intended for Bishop Simon of Worcester, who had once been her chaplain. Juliana was reading aloud from the copy of Aesop that Will had given her, but Adeliza was not really listening. Outside the rain was fierce. Although spring had supposedly arrived, the season had turned back to winter for several days.

It was two months since the Battle of Lincoln: a disaster for Stephen's forces and a triumph for the empress. Receiving the news, Adeliza had felt as if she were stranded on a shore at the water's edge, neither on dry land nor in the sea. Will had not returned to Arundel, although she had received a disjointed letter from him to say he was safe and lying low at his keep at Buckenham. She was to remain vigilant but do nothing and they would wait and see what demands were made. As yet there had been no word from either side, but she knew that state of affairs would not last. Either the tide would roll in or it would recede. She had heard that Stephen's wife was rallying supporters and William D'Ypres, deeply penitent at having fled from Lincoln, had vowed to restore his honour and was commanding her troops. Stephen might be a prisoner, but the war was far from won.

Adelis whimpered in her cradle and Adeliza went to pick her up. Her complexion, eight weeks from her birth, was pink and cream like new roses. She blew bubbles at Adeliza and gurgled. Adeliza laughed and tickled her chin, thinking what a miracle she was.

Her chamber door opened to a knock and Rothard her chamberlain put his head around it. "Madam, the earl is here," he announced, and had barely finished speaking when Will pushed past him into the room. Adeliza gasped because he was dripping wet, his clothes hanging on him like sodden sacks.

"Dear God, why did you not send word?" Replacing Adelis in her cradle, she turned to her women. "Towels and dry warm clothes for my lord immediately." She went to him but stood a few paces off because he really was soaked to the skin.

"Because I..." He made a pleading gesture. "Because I was unsure of my welcome and because it was safer not to broadcast my movements. We have been travelling by back roads at night and picking a careful route. I..." He palmed his face. "I was not sure until I rode through the gates that I was coming here, and even now I do not know if I should stay."

Adeliza's gaze widened. "What do you mean, you do not know if you should stay? Where else would you go? Come, get out of those wet clothes before you take a chill." She unfastened his cloak and handed it to a maid. His tunic and shirt were damp too, and his boots, light fawn when dry, were the colour of ancient oak and slick with water.

"My presence here might endanger you." He pressed the napkin to his wet face and she wondered for an appalled moment if he was crying.

"Come," she said again briskly, "let me have your boots, and get you into some warm shoes." She knelt to remove his footwear, tugging at the sodden lacings.

Adelis wailed in her cradle. Will lowered the napkin and

looked round like a deer hearing a hunting horn. Then he went to the crib and gazed down at his daughter, unborn when he had ridden out to Lincoln. Water dripped from the tips of his hair on to her swaddling. He leaned over and touched her cheek with his forefinger and she rooted towards it hungrily and gave a fretful cry. Beyond the crib, a nurse held the hand of his son who was out of smocks now and wearing a miniature version of an adult tunic. He was staring at Will with big eyes, and sucking his lower lip uncertainly.

Abruptly Will turned and strode from the room, his shoelaces trailing dangerously. Adeliza stared after him with concern and astonishment. Then she rallied. Telling her women to continue with the preparations for Will's comfort, she grabbed her cloak off the wall peg and ran after him.

❖❖❖

Will knelt in Arundel's chapel, shivering so hard that his stomach ached. He felt wretched; he knew he should not have come here. He had taken refuge at Buckenham after the battle while he awaited developments. News had been scanty, but what had arrived was demoralising and suggested that the empress was consolidating her grip. He had desperately needed to see Adeliza, but knew that, with her sympathies towards the empress, she was in a better position at Arundel to negotiate without him. The ground had fallen from under his feet and he felt powerless, and that made him a lesser man in his own eyes. "I am facing my own nothing," he said to the painted wooden image of the Virgin and Child standing on a marble plinth to one side of the altar. "I know you can take away just as you bestow. I want to do what is right, but how can I when I do not know what is right any more?"

"Husband?"

He turned at the sound of Adeliza's voice. "Leave me alone," he said. "Do I interrupt you when you are at your devotions?"

She came and knelt beside him and clasped her hands. "Whatever has happened and whatever is to come, no burden is so terrible that God will not listen."

"Was I so wrong?" he asked after a moment, his head still bowed. "I followed my honour and did my best, and now I am lost, because my best was not good enough. I feel as if I am falling down a long, dark tunnel with only more darkness at the end of it."

"Never that." She was shaken to see him so defeated and low when she was accustomed to his bluff optimism "Never think that!" She set her arms around him protectively, uncaring now of his wet garments. "You are a fine man, a good man."

He clung to her, his body shaken by tremors, and she held and shushed him as if he were one of their children until eventually he pulled away and cuffed his eyes on his sleeve. "I do not deserve you," he said hoarsely. "I have never deserved you."

"Hush." Adeliza kissed his cheek and rose. "Let there be no such talk between us. Say your words to God and seek His help and forgiveness, then come and bathe and eat and sleep. Tomorrow is time enough to decide what we must do."

When she had gone, he clasped his hands and bowed his head again and tried to concentrate on the smiling Virgin in her blue robe, but nothing came into focus beyond his sense of failure.

❖❖❖

"Why did you marry me?"

Adeliza looked across the hearth at Will. He had eventually come from the chapel, grey with cold, shivering and barefoot, his shoes in his hand. She had renewed the bath with fresh hot water and made him eat a bowl of mutton and barley pottage washed down with hot spiced wine. Colour had gradually returned to his face and although his eyes were still heavy, they were less haunted. She had dismissed their attendants and they were alone in their chamber with the hangings drawn across the shutters and the fire a comfortable glow of ruddy embers in the hearth. Teri, his favourite dog, stood on his hind legs and sniffed at the almost empty pottage bowl. Will held it for the dog to lick out, which told Adeliza he must be feeling more at home with himself.

"Because I chose to," she said.

"But why?" He fixed her with a puzzled stare. "You were a queen. You could have had anyone you wanted." He put the bowl on the floor.

That was not quite true, she thought. Any man she took as a husband would have had to have Stephen's approval. "You offered me an alternative life," she said. "You made me realise that I was not quite ready for the cloister."

"I never thought you would consent. You are as far above me as the stars."

"But you dared to ask—and I dared to answer, and I do not regret it. You have given me gifts of far greater worth than any number of crowns."

"I thought it was another gift to stay away from you," he said in a low voice. "That is why I said I should not be here. My absence will keep you and the children safe. If I am not at Arundel, there is no cause to besiege it."

Adeliza raised her brows. "You are not going to acknowledge the empress?"

"I swore my oath to Stephen. Should I disavow it because he is a prisoner? What does that say about my honour? Until he renounces his kingship I have a sworn duty to support him. Yet if he is truly overthrown, I have a sworn duty to protect my family also."

Adeliza bit her lip. "No one has come to Arundel of either faction yet, so I say we do nothing and wait and see. We should tend our estates and keep them orderly and secure. We should succour those who have suffered through no fault of their own." She took his arm. "Come, it is late and this can bide until the morning."

She led him from the hearth to their bed and helped him to disrobe, kissing him as she unfastened ties and laces, offering him reassurance and comfort, encouraging him with little touches and signs. Then she removed her own garments and pressed her body against his. "Husband," she said tenderly. He uttered a soft groan and his arms tightened around her and suddenly, with appetite awakened, he started to kiss her in return.

She had had her women remake the bed with clean, fresh sheets, scented with lavender and thyme, knowing that to him, the perfume was associated with her and with home—with coming home. She drew him into her with desire, with compassion, and with the urge of a nurturer to make him whole again in any way she could. At the climax, Will pressed his face into her neck and gasped that he loved her and needed her. She was his heart and his world. She was his queen. Adeliza held and soothed him while he fell into a deep, healing slumber on her breast, and then she wept a little too, and, despite her reassurances to him, wondered what indeed was going to happen to them.

❖ ❖ ❖

Matilda set her hand upon her father's tomb in the choir of Reading Abbey, her composure as hard as the chiselled stone. She was cold and her stomach was hollow with hunger both physical and mental. She had faced death many times but confronting her mortality in the shape of her father's tomb, knowing his remains were under her hand, intensified her awareness. She needed to make good use of every moment on this earth that God gave her. The last time she had been in her father's presence, they had argued fiercely over her dower castles. Not wanting to dwell on that memory, she thought of her childhood instead. She had a vague recollection of running to him and how big and alive he had seemed. How real. How he had picked her up and carried her through the court in his arms, proud of her. He had given her a honey sweetmeat to eat and silver ribbons for her hair...and then told her she was to go far away to her marriage. When she tried to think of him after her return from Germany, the sting of grief and bitterness was so strong, she could not visit those memories.

He had the resting place he desired and the monks to pray for his soul. She too would lie in a tomb one day and she had much to accomplish before that time. Easing to her feet, she crossed herself, and left the church, her pace dignified but decisive, and she did not look back.

From here, from her father's resting place, the road now lay towards London, and Westminster...and her crown.

Forty-one

*I*N HER CHAMBER AT THE WESTMINSTER COMPLEX CLOSE BY the abbey, Matilda prepared for a formal feast to celebrate her forthcoming coronation. Her ladies were combing her hair with scented lotion. She was aware of the wiry grey strands coarsening what had once been a shining, dark waterfall and knew she was no longer a young beauty but a woman entering her middle years, with lines of strife and tribulation carved for all to view. These days she preferred not to look in a gazing glass and see what time had wrought.

The women patted her hair dry and rubbed it with a silk cloth, before combing it and plaiting it tightly. Then they covered it with a fine white veil, edged with pearls and gold. Her gown was embroidered blue silk; her cloak was lined with ermine as befitted a queen and an empress. The trappings of royalty. A headache throbbed at her temples. Her flux was imminent and she was irritable and on edge. Men had no such burdens to bear.

A few weeks earlier, the Londoners had refused to acknowledge her as their queen, but had changed their minds when Geoffrey de Mandeville, custodian of the Tower of London, had switched allegiance and agreed to support her, bringing with him de Vere of Oxford and Gilbert, Earl of Pembroke.

The citizens had tendered their grudging submission, but she knew there was a large faction among them still eager to have Stephen back on the throne. They had only capitulated because they had no choice. It galled her that they snubbed her and refused to pay tribute, yet they had eagerly welcomed Stephen as king when her father had died and had paid him without demur. She despised them, and since pretence was not within her scope, she was finding it difficult to conciliate. They had even given Stephen's vile little terrier of a wife the money to hire mercenaries. Those troops were now pillaging the lands outside London, and the citizens were wringing their hands and blaming Matilda for it rather than themselves and the woman who was actually responsible.

"You should not frown, domina," said Uli. "You will create more lines."

Matilda fought her irritation. She was certain that no one had ever said that to her father, or to Stephen. As if a smooth forehead were the ultimate goal. Even with England's crown on her head, she knew she would have a constant battle to rule. The earls and barons who supported her took decisions among themselves and held their own meetings, treating her as a figurehead rather than heeding her voice. Their bluff, masculine camaraderie excluded her by the very fact of her gender and was something she could not change. They saw her as a member of the weaker sex, too soft to rule; yet when she showed a hard face and acted in a stern manner, they muttered that she was going against nature. Whatever she did, she was damned, and it led her to think damn them all too.

She completed her adornment by wearing her favourite German crown with the gold flowers. Gathering her women around her, escorted by knights and ushers, she left her chamber and processed to Westminster's great hall. It had been built by her uncle King William Rufus more than forty years ago, incorporating the existing hall of the time. Her uncle had complained that the structure, despite being more than 240 paces long and the largest in Christendom, was too big for a chamber and not large enough for a hall. She could remember running between the bays as a little girl, and admiring the bands of chequered masonry along the walls. She had played hide and seek with her brother, and skipping games with girls whose names she had long forgotten. Later, on her return from Germany, she had sat in this hall and dined at her father's side in the place of honour at the high table. But this was the first time in her life that she would sit here and preside as lady of the English and queen designate.

Fabric hissed and belt fittings clinked as people knelt to her. She took their obeisance as her due but noted amongst all this fine rustle of silk and cloth of gold that there was no sign of the bishop of Winchester's elaborate cope, even though Bath, Ely, and London were represented.

"My lord of Winchester appears to be still sulking," Brian murmured to her as he assisted her to her seat on the dais. "Apparently, he has not been seen this morning."

Matilda pursed her lips with irritation. She had had a long argument with her cousin of Winchester about her decision to appoint her uncle David's candidate William Cumin to the see of Durham. Bishop Henry had disapproved of her choice, saying angrily she had promised him full jurisdiction over Church affairs and he had a different man in mind for the task. But she owed much to her uncle David and felt more beholden to him than Cousin Henry. Besides, it would not hurt Henry to be put in his place. "Let him sulk," she said curtly.

"Better to have him in your sight," Brian warned.

"I do not care if he is here or not," she snapped as she settled in the chair. It had once been her father's in the days when he had presided over feasts here. That Stephen had sat upon it too, she put from her mind.

"Even so, it might be wise to conciliate with him for now."

"Brian is right," said Robert, who had been listening to the conversation with a troubled expression. "We should keep him sweet at least until you are more established."

"I do not see why we must pander to his every whim," she said bad-temperedly. "Taking his advice is one thing, but giving in to him all the time just to prevent him from stamping his feet is another. I will not ruin this feast by talking of him. There are plenty of other churchmen present to say grace."

Stewards brought bowls of warm water and towels to the dais and she washed and dried her hands, her movements vigorous and annoyed. In lieu of the papal legate, Bishop Nigel of Ely gave the benediction and the first course was served. There were dishes of delicately spiced frumenty and crisp fried elderflowers, quails' eggs, dyed different colours, and small spicy cheese tarts; all dainty items, designed to whet the appetite for the roasts to come. Matilda began to relax a little as she gazed out over the diners and listened to the babble of eating and conversation.

"I have a gift for you," Brian said. Taking her hand, he placed in it a small silver coin, the size of her index fingernail. On one side was depicted a woman's head, and around the rim the legend read, *Matilidis Imperatrice, Domina Angliea, Regina Anglia. Wallig.*

"I had the die made and the silver stamped at the mint at Wallingford," he said. "I wanted you to have the very first one, but soon there will be many more because this will be the currency of all England."

Matilda gazed at the silver disc in her hand and her throat was suddenly tight. "Thank you," she said hoarsely.

He flushed and made a small gesture of negation. "All of my garrison there have your name on their pay now."

She started to answer him, but paused as the clamour of numerous church bells ringing came through the window aperture. Others were raising their heads from their food and looking round.

"Probably practising for the coronation," Brian said nonchalantly, although his gaze flickered. Now that the sound had intruded on their dinner, there was no ignoring it. The bells, some near, some distant, were being rung with vigour.

Moments later, John FitzGilbert her marshal walked briskly up the hall to the dais table. "Domina, the Londoners have risen against you." His voice was low pitched but terse. "There is an armed mob on its way to Westminster from the city. For your safety, we must leave."

Matilda closed her fist over the silver coin in her hand and felt the thin rim bite her flesh.

Brian leaned towards FitzGilbert. "Perhaps the bells are ringing in salute and rejoicing."

"No, my lord." The marshal's blue gaze was hard and direct. "The reports of a riot come from our supporters in the city, who are fleeing before the mob. The bells are ringing to muster the people and to tell Stephen's wife that she may enter London with her army of Flemings and receive support. I have given orders to saddle the horses. If we do not leave now, we will be overrun."

Feeling sick with fury and frustration, Matilda glared at her marshal and vented her spleen on him because he had direct command of her household knights and responsibility for military order. "I refuse to be driven out of my rightful territory—my own father's hall!—by a mob and a rabble army of mercenaries. Any man who says we must leave is a coward."

He stood ramrod straight. "Domina, I would kill any man who called me a coward. I deal in reality and I tell you we cannot stay here. We are not equipped to fight and when Stephen's wife arrives we will not hold our enemies. Better to pull back to Oxford or Devizes and deal from there."

Matilda jutted her jaw. "No," she said.

"Are you certain of this?" Brian demanded. "This is not just idle rumour that has got out of hand?"

The marshal looked at him with incredulous contempt. "Sire, if I doubted the information, I would not have interrupted your dinner." He made a sweeping gesture towards the door. "However, if you want to talk to a mob, then do as you please, but you will find they desire to parley with spears and swords."

Robert, who had been listening closely to the exchange, rose to his feet. "We should heed the marshal's concerns," he said to Matilda. "As he says, we are ill equipped for a fight and we cannot afford to have you captured. John, you will ride rearguard?"

"Sire." The marshal bowed, and even as he left the dais was shouting orders.

Shaken, utterly furious, Matilda removed her coronet and folded it up with her golden cup and spoon into the embroidered cloth at her place, including the silver penny that Brian had given to her. She could not believe this was happening. As Robert and Brian bundled her out of the hall, she refused to look back because that would have been like bidding farewell. In the city the church bells tolled and tolled. From every parish and quarter, they rang their rejection of her.

A groom had readied her mare and Brian helped her into the saddle before turning to Sable. All around them people were grabbing their hastily saddled horses and making their escape. Servants fled, some astride, some afoot, many of them clutching aprons and knotted cloths full of the food that had been intended for the banquet. Matilda could still barely comprehend this was happening, but her marshal was in deadly earnest as he whacked her mount's rump, and Sable's, making both horses leap into a startled canter. Matilda swayed in the saddle, grabbed the reins, and clung on. In the distance, there was a shout and an ominous clash of weapons, followed by a scream.

"I will not let them push me out. I will not," she said through clenched teeth, even as she shot out of the gateway on to the road. She imagined turning her mare around, but the plan went no further than her mind, because she could not row against the tide.

The marshal rode up, forcing his sweating white stallion alongside the mare. "Madam, we must increase the pace!" he shouted above the pounding hooves. "If we do not, we will soon be engaged in bloody battle."

"I will not ride out like a fugitive from my father's hall and what is rightfully mine!" she spat.

"Then you will be captured, and every man with you. Is that what you want?"

She threw him a fulminating glance, but struck the reins down on the mare's neck to urge her on. The greater speed made it impossible for her speak because she had to concentrate on her riding, but inside she was sick with rage.

Forty-two

MATILDA DREW BACK TO OXFORD AND SET UP HER COURT in magnificent splendour in order to expunge the humiliation of London. She held formal feasts in the great hall there and at each mealtime and when conducting business she wore her crown and sealed her charters as Lady of the English. She made men earls of the realm and dealt out largesse in titles and honours, even though she had little to spare in terms of money and power. She dealt with all matters as if presiding over a royal court, but deep inside, in her soft and vulnerable places, she ached with frustration and misery. She had had several stormy exchanges with Bishop Henry. Having avoided the debacle in London, which she suspected he had been fore-warned about, and perhaps even involved in, he had ridden off to Winchester and she was highly suspicious of what he was fomenting there. He had come briefly to court on behalf of Stephen's wife and her eldest son, asking Matilda to recognise the youth's rights to his father's lands. At the time, Matilda had still been smarting from her flight from London, her flux had been upon her, making her ill with cramps and headache, and the bishop's slippery prevarication had been the final straw. She had refused his request and in a backlash of white anger had ordered Stephen to be put in fetters in captivity at Bristol.

Bishop Henry had departed in a fury of his own, and refused all summonses to come back to court.

In late June, a detail of Angevins arrived in Oxford, sent to her aid by Geoffrey and headed by his close friend Juhel de Mayenne. Matilda welcomed the group cordially enough, but was wary because although the extra men were useful, it meant Geoffrey had an increased presence and influence at her court. Nevertheless, she was pleased with Juhel's news about Geoffrey's successful progress in Normandy.

"Since hearing about Stephen's imprisonment, the Norman barons are arriving daily to treat with the Count of Anjou and sue for peace on his terms," he told her. "Stephen's grip is weak and each day brings new adherents."

Matilda was delighted at de Mayenne's report on her sons. "Growing well, domina," he said. "My lord Henry keeps pestering the count to let him come to England. He would have sailed with us given half the chance. I would not have been surprised to discover him stowed away in one of our baggage carts." De Mayenne smiled. "Your son is so eager to wear a crown and rule England you might find yourself with a new challenger from inside the family. He is so bright, he could do it."

Matilda glowed at his words. "But likely not tall enough yet," she said. It was good to feel her spirits lift with pride and humour. "What of my other sons?"

"They are fine strong boys, domina, although with Master Geoffrey being fostered I have seen less of him. I hear he is progressing well with his lessons and his training and the count is pleased. The lord William is swift to learn and reads fluently."

She bit her lip. When she had left for England, William had scarcely been out of smocks, his wrists and hands still chubby with baby fat. And now he was a scholar. She could not call this fight for their future time wasted, but it was time lost that she could have spent watching her sons grow while supervising their development, and that filled her with bitter sorrow.

Waleran de Meulan arrived in Oxford to tender his submission on a thundery, sweltering August afternoon. Receiving his request for an audience, Matilda was interested but cynical. He had always been one of Stephen's staunchest followers, even if he had fled at Lincoln. Many of her own supporters had changed their allegiance to her as a result of the machinations of Waleran and his brother Robert. For him to be here now was akin to having a live snake thrown into the middle of her private chamber.

She changed her everyday gown for a regal one of blue silk and bade her ladies arrange her flower crown over her veil. She called for her sceptre and adorned the middle finger of her left hand with her father's ring. In the great hall, she took her place on the high dais in the great chair where she was accustomed to sit and render judgement. Bronze statues of lions stood on either side of her seat, and on the wall behind was a cloth of red samite embroidered with golden leopards. Only then did she bid the ushers admit de Meulan.

As he entered the hall, the atmosphere thickened with tension. He still walked with a swagger as if he owned the world. Matilda watched him with narrowed eyes and thought how easy it would be to ram her sceptre through his treacherous heart.

Standing at the side of her throne, de Mayenne muttered, "He has no choice but to make his submission, domina. His lands in Normandy are about to be swallowed up by your lord husband."

De Meulan knelt and Matilda felt vengeful triumph. "I see you have accepted the inevitable and come to yield to me," she said haughtily, but after a moment gestured him to rise.

"Domina, I am here to tender my allegiance," he replied but gave her a hard upward look out of light green eyes.

"As you did before?" She gripped the armrests of her chair. "Three times you swore your oath to me, and when my father died, you went back on your word. Why should I trust you now or treat well with you?"

"Because I will no longer oppose you in England. Because I will swear to be your vassal in Normandy and fight for your son's cause." He spoke in a carrying voice in which there was no submission. "Because I am a pragmatist. If I stay with the queen and with Stephen, I will lose all of my lands in Normandy and my English estates are not enough compensation, burned and harried as they are. My support in Normandy will be invaluable to you."

"You are here because your position in England is untenable," she said icily.

He did not give ground. "I am here to strike a bargain. Whether you accept it is up to you, but even my enemies here will advise you to do so, although of course," he added, his lip slightly curled in contempt, "you might not want to take their counsel." His expression and body language suggested without words that he was referring to her contrariness.

"Why should being rid of you not be to my taste?" she retorted. "I can think of few things I would like better in this world, my lord. What of your brother? Where does he fit into your schemes?"

"He will stay in England and keep his allegiance to Stephen on his own lands." De Meulan spread his hands. "It is a sensible division."

Matilda would have liked to string him up but she recognised that de Meulan's words were sensible. She was irritated that he had only come to tender his submission after Geoffrey had sent reinforcements. It might seem to some as if he respected Geoffrey's authority above hers—which she suspected was his intention. Nevertheless, if she sorted this out now, it would leave her free to deal with the bishop of Winchester should it prove necessary. Waleran knew it too; she could see it in his eyes and disliked him even more because, whatever happened, he could not lose.

"Very well," she said, "on those terms, I accept your submission. It is a great pity you did not bring your brother to submit too, but that would have been too much to expect."

Meulan bowed. "Indeed, domina," he said archly, "it would."

❖ ❖ ❖

Once de Meulan had gone, Matilda retired to her chamber to remove her crown and change back into a less ornate dress. She had not invited de Meulan to stay at court, but had let him depart in the teeth of a heavy thunderstorm. She hoped he got soaked to the skin and caught a chill.

She pressed her hands against her face for a moment. Outside, the thunder was growling away towards the west and fresh green smells curled tendrils through her window. She ought to be buoyed up, but everything seemed such a struggle and she felt as if she could sleep for a week. Forcing herself to focus, she began to read the correspondence awaiting her attention, one of the items being a letter from Adeliza, who wrote that her husband was keeping to his lands and recovering from Lincoln, which had laid him very low. He had not ridden to join Stephen's queen, but neither was he disposed to swear for Matilda, although she believed in time he might come round. For the moment they were concentrating on their family and their religious foundations because in these times, there was need of charity and compassion for the suffering people.

Matilda made a face as she put the letter to one side. Adeliza was doing her best, she knew, but it did not alter the fact that there would be no help coming from that quarter beyond prayer and she had hoped for so much more. With prayer in mind herself, she summoned her ladies and went to the castle chapel, hoping to find God in a receptive mood to her entreaties.

Brian FitzCount was already there, kneeling before the altar, his head bent on his clasped fists, and his lips moving in an impassioned whisper. She hesitated, wondering whether to leave, but he raised his head as he sensed her presence. "Domina," he said. His voice was hoarse and his eyes were suspiciously wet. "I should leave."

"No." She made a swift gesture. "I have interrupted your prayers, and the house of God is for everyone." She touched his arm. He hesitated for a moment, but as she sank to her knees before the altar, he bowed his head once more. She wondered what had brought him to such a pass of emotion, but knew she could not ask, and suspected he would not speak of his own accord.

Eventually she rose and went to light a candle. He followed her example, and for a moment they stood side by side, linked by flame as he lit his from hers. His hand shook slightly and wax dripped in small clear circles that swiftly cooled and turned opaque on the iron surface of the stand.

"I have heard from Adeliza," she said. "D'Albini refuses to come over to us, but she thinks she can keep him neutral for the time being."

Brian grimaced. "I could have taken him prisoner, but I did not count him a threat."

"The ransom would have come in useful," she said with a frown.

"Perhaps, but there had been enough fighting and bloodshed that day." His expression grew bleak. "I—"

They both turned at the sound of rapid footsteps. Moments later, Robert strode into the chapel with Miles of Gloucester and John FitzGilbert hard on his heels. Her heart began to pound because she could tell before anyone spoke that the news was bad.

"It's Winchester," Miles said grimly. "The bishop has turned on us and is besieging the castle."

She stared at him in consternation and as the words took on meaning, her anger began to burn. The bishop of Winchester had handed the castle over to her not three months ago, promising her his loyal support and that she would be queen. "How dare he!"

"He never had any intention of yielding to you unless you made him the power behind your throne," Robert growled. "I know what he is about. He is trying to take the castle to use as a bargaining piece to buy himself back into favour with Stephen's wife."

"Then we must go to Winchester and stop him," she said, urgency mingling with her rage. "Go and muster everyone you can and make haste."

Robert departed to issue orders to the men. Brian swept her a bow before departing with the marshal, and Matilda returned to the hall so that she could be at the centre of the hub as preparations were made to ride on the city and deal with the perfidious bishop.

❖ ❖ ❖

Arriving in Winchester, Matilda discovered that the bishop's troops had drawn off and shut themselves inside his palace beside the cathedral. Whether Bishop Henry was there or not was another matter. Matilda hoped he was, but suspected he had pulled back to better safety. What was evident was that he had reinforced his palace extensively since March and turned it into a fortress. With grim determination, Robert settled down to besiege the new stronghold and Matilda took up residence in the castle.

On the morning of the third day, Brian came running to

tell her that the soldiers defending the bishop's palace were catapulting flaming balls of pitch over their walls and had set fire to the adjacent Benedictine Abbey of Hyde and the nunnery of Saint Mary's. "Our scouts are reporting that Stephen's wife and William D'Ypres are bringing up an army from Kent and we are likely to be encircled and besieged in our turn," he panted.

Matilda hurried with him to the castle battlements and looked out in dismay at the gouts of smoke and flame that were spreading from the nunnery to the suburbs as thatched roofs and timber buildings, dry from the summer, caught light. All was chaos with the monks, nuns, and citizens desperately trying to quench the flames and still the catapults shot out more fireballs to add to the destruction and confusion.

"A townsman reported seeing the bishop riding out with his entourage," Brian said. "I suspect he has gone to join his sister-in-law."

"I had to yield London." Matilda clenched her fists. "I will not give them Winchester too."

Brian shook his head. "It may not come to that, but we should pack the baggage in readiness. All this burning and wasting means we are being denied ground cover and supplies, and the closer D'Ypres and the Countess of Boulogne come to Winchester, the greater the problem becomes. There will be more hungry mouths to feed and homeless folk with nowhere to find succour."

"While we have Stephen in chains at Bristol, we have the upper hand," she said curtly, but her heart sank, because for every gain, there seemed to be a corresponding setback. At midsummer she had been one day away from wearing the crown of England. That day had become weeks and months and she could see the opportunity fading into darkness and becoming never.

❖ ❖ ❖

She was in her chamber dictating letters to a scribe when Brian came to break the news that the forces assembled by Stephen's queen were making a concerted assault upon Winchester from the London road, while mercenaries under the command of William D'Ypres were heading down from Andover, which they had sacked.

"We must leave now," he said urgently. "If D'Ypres gets past the marshal's outpost at Wherwell, we are trapped. The Londoners are already in the suburbs. Robert will create a diversion, but Reynald and I have to get you out." He was breathing hard. "We'll make for Ludgershall and then on to Devizes, but we have to cross the Test at Stockbridge, and we must do it before the trap closes. You will need stout clothes and shoes; it is going to be a hard ride."

The look in his eyes was bordering on fear and it gave her a jolt. She had the bitter experience of being driven out of Westminster to tell her that she dared not stay. Without a word she hastened to change her clothes. By the time she reached the courtyard, her horse was saddled and Brian was waiting for her clad in his black hauberk.

Robert strode up to her as she was gathering the reins on her mare. "Ride hard, sister," he said. "Miles and I will protect your rear. We'll meet you at Ludgershall and ride on to Devizes."

She leaned down and they clasped hands and exchanged a swift kiss. Then she reined about and set her heels to the mare's flanks. Brian had sent soldiers ahead to scout the way and give them early warning of trouble. He set out at a rapid trot but he was tight-lipped because he knew the pace was not fast enough. The north gate out of the city was the most direct route, but would lead them straight into the jaws of the enemy troops coming down the Andover Road, unless the marshal had held them at Wherwell, and he doubted that, because even with his formidable fighting skills, John

FitzGilbert did not have sufficient men to hold back an entire army of Flemings.

Brian knew they had to clear the causeway at Stockbridge before D'Ypres did and before they were seized by the troops overrunning Winchester. His upper chest was tight and it was difficult to breathe. Recognising panic, he was ashamed. The sensations had been coming upon him with growing frequency as the fighting continued and increasingly difficult burdens were laid upon his shoulders, including those of dependency and expectation. He was not the brave soldier and hero people thought he was. He could stick a lance in a man if he had to, he could kill, but it was not natural to him; the images stuck to his brain like scale to the side of a sewage chute and sickened him.

Behind them, he heard yells, screams, and the clash of battle, and acid burned his throat. "We must press on, domina," he shouted, almost gagging. "Go in front!"

She slapped the reins on the mare's neck and swayed in the saddle as the pace increased. She was a fine horsewoman, but could only go so fast riding side-saddle and if their pursuers reached them, all was lost. The ford was eight miles away and they could so easily be caught by hard riding troops. "Domina, you must ride astride," he shouted. "We are losing ground!"

Reynald sent some men back to watch the road and hold up the pursuit. Brian dismounted and put Matilda up on Sable. Fumbling in haste, he discarded her side-saddle and mounted her mare. There were no stirrups, but the saddle cloth was secure and he could grip the breast strap as well as the reins. "Hah!" he shouted, digging in his heels, and they were off again at a hard pace.

Tight-lipped, Matilda urged Brian's big black. Now that she was astride, she could indeed go faster and it was like galloping to the hunt, but the pace jolted her limbs and strained her thigh muscles and her flesh rubbed against the hard sides of the saddle.

She dared not think about what was happening in Winchester and how Robert's rearguard was faring. She had taken him for granted for so long but he and the handful of men defending her retreat were her backbone. She prayed under her breath, asking God to keep them safe and to strike down Henry of Winchester with a thunderbolt. A brief look over her shoulder showed her plumes of smoke in the city, but no sign of imminent pursuit. Easing the black down to a fast trot, she turned to Brian. "We should conserve the horses, because we are not going to find remounts along the way."

He shook his head. "We have to reach Stockbridge ahead of the Flemings if we are to escape." He leaned across to Sable and unfastened the costrel hanging from the saddle and brought out a silver goblet from the baggage roll on the crupper. The sight filled her with bitter humour. She was an uncrowned queen, drinking at a jog trot from a silver cup on the road to God knew what future with her enemies in hard pursuit and her dreams of a coronation in flames.

The wine was potent and revived her strength. "One day I will make you a great earl," she said to Brian, returning the cup.

"Domina, I want no such lustre," he said in a choked voice.

She raised her brows. "To serve me is enough?"

"What would I do with a title except encourage envy? Where would be the point when I will never have an heir? Your father raised me from the dust and all that I have is his daughter's." He lashed his reins down on the mare's neck, thereby terminating the conversation, and once again they galloped for the ford.

Several times, looking over their shoulders, they saw pursuers in the distance. Matilda had to use her spurs on the black, but when they reached the causeway at Stockbridge at a lathered canter, the way ahead was still clear and they were able to cut off and take the track across the Downs where they swiftly vanished amid the grassy humps and hollows. They had covered eight miles at a punishing pace but still had fourteen more to reach the precarious refuge at Ludgershall and another twenty after that to the greater safety of Devizes.

❖❖❖

By the time Ludgershall came in sight, Matilda was clinging on in a state of exhaustion. Her thighs were chafed raw against the saddle, her spine was screaming for respite and she was unable to think beyond the engulfing pain and despondency that had encroached on her as the heat of the chase dissipated. When she drew rein in the courtyard, she could barely move. The horses were staggering and almost foundered. Summoning the last of her will power, she managed to swing her leg over Sable's back to dismount. Reynald and Brian caught her, otherwise she would have fallen.

The castle of Ludgershall belonged to her marshal, and its constable, like its lord, was efficient, and swiftly provided them with food and succour.

"You should lie down, sister," Reynald said anxiously.

"No!" she said with vehemence. She could not be found lacking. To be a queen and rule men, she had to prove she was as strong as they were.

"At least put your feet up," Brian urged, gesturing to the padded bench and footstool the servants had brought. "It is no disgrace to rest." He stooped to plump the cushions himself and she caught the acrid scent of his sweat and saw the dark circles under his eyes. In the dull candlelight, his features were almost cadaverous.

"I must be strong." Her throat constricted on the words.

"Tomorrow, yes," Brian said, "but there is nothing you can do for the moment save rest. You have to know when to delegate." He took her hand and gave it a squeeze, and then tucked it under the blanket. "I will return in a moment."

She watched him leave the room. He was right that each person had their duties, but she should be giving the orders, and by not doing so, she felt a failure. Something was troubling Brian. She could sense it in him, although he was trying to hide it. It was as indelible as those ink stains on his fingers, but more difficult to interpret. And she was tired, so tired.

❖❖❖

Brian climbed to the wall walk with Reynald and the constable and stared into the late dusk. He sought signs of pursuit: camp fires that might speak of an enemy drawing in on them, or torches and lanterns borne by night travellers, but there was nothing, and no sound to be heard beyond the walls but the bleating of sheep and the sough of the wind through the grasses of the Downs.

"We should never have come to Winchester," Reynald said bitterly. "The bishop lured us into a trap. He wanted us to advance and be destroyed. He besieged the castle to draw us there and then set the fires himself so that he could escape and at the same time signal to the queen."

"It is easy to be wise after the event," Brian said.

"But why should he turn his allegiance now?" Reynald asked in bewilderment. "Surely his quarrel with my sister could have been mended."

"He did it because Waleran de Meulan has yielded to us and gone to Normandy, so at one fell swoop an influence and an enemy is gone from the other court. With Stephen in prison, he can take over and rule England on Maheut's behalf. Maheut will forget his transgressions and lean on him because of his skills. He has the knack of making expedience look like the common good." Brian strained his eyes in the darkness and turned to Ludgershall's constable. "You should post lookouts at every window with two people to a window, one an observer, one a back-up."

"Sire, it shall be done." The knight bowed, and after a hesitation added, "You have no news of my lord FitzGilbert?"

Brian shook his head. "No, but he must have succeeded in holding off D'Ypres at Wherwell because we were not caught on the road."

"There is no sign of my lord though."

"He would not come here. He would draw the enemy away from the empress, not towards her." Brian did not add, "If he still lives," but the unspoken words hung in the air.

"And what of Robert and Miles?" Reynald asked, his eyes straining in the darkness. "They should have been here by now. And my uncle of Scotland."

"There are many reasons why they might be delayed," Brian said, for his own reassurance as much as Reynald's. "They may have split up because it would be unwise to bring a large number of men here. Ludgershall does not have the same defensive capabilities as Devizes or Oxford. While there are but a few of us divided in many directions, it keeps the enemy guessing and chasing hither and yon." It also meant they were scattered and ineffectual, but Reynald must know it.

The young man chewed his lip. "The horses will be in no condition to ride on to Devizes tomorrow."

"We have little choice. The marshal has a few stabled here we can use, but we dare not stay. Ludgershall is not strong enough to hold against Stephen's wife and D'Ypres." He bunched his fists on the wall. Every time he started thinking of ways out of the dilemma, he realised he was only tidying it round the edges, and making it smaller did not make it better. Doing so merely showed their predicament in its true, desperate light.

With halting steps he returned to the main chamber. He did not really want to be there in Matilda's presence, because he felt he had failed her. She was asleep, covered by her cloak and a blanket. Her face was careworn with deep frown lines between her brows even in slumber. She should be ruling England as its queen, not huddled on this bench, a wretched fugitive.

Brian slumped by the fire and put his head in his hands. He had a terrible feeling they were all doomed, and there was no way out. In his mind's eye, he saw a deep chasm before him with a crumbling edge. The darkness beyond was clean and calm—and terrible. It lured him and terrified him at the same time because it would be so easy to plunge into it. But she needed him, and she thought he was strong, and he couldn't let her down.

Matilda was woken just before dawn by Brian gently shaking her shoulder. She was so stiff and sore that she could barely move and was unable to stifle a groan. Aware of his anxiety and the unease of the other men, she tried to rally. If she had been able to ride away from Geoffrey after he had beaten her, she could manage this. The servants brought warm water for her to wash her hands and face and she ate some bread and honey, washed down with buttermilk, even though she was not hungry. Conscious of Brian watching her every mouthful, she gave him a hard look. "Will you cease staring at me the way people do when gathered around a deathbed," she snapped.

Brian swiftly lowered his gaze. "I am concerned, that is all. You are our lady and our queen. I have selected one of the marshal's horses for you to ride. It is fresh but placid and has a smooth gait."

In her turn, Matilda dropped her gaze. It would be so easy to cry. "Thank you," she said, and hoped her aching body would stay the distance.

It was still barely light as the small, battered party prepared to leave Ludgershall. Her horse was a pale dun with the fluid stride of an ambler. Although a compact horse, Matilda still struggled to mount him and had to stifle her cry of pain as her raw thighs touched the saddle again. Letting out her breath on a hard gasp, she hung over the reins for a moment, recovering.

"Are you sure you are—" Brian began.

"Yes," she cut him off. "Get on with it." She looked up at a shout.

A knight was clopping through the gate on a salt-caked, exhausted horse. She recognised him as one of Robert's men, Alain de Caen. He was swaying in the saddle, his face streaked with blood and dirt. Drawing rein, he slid from his mount and then leaned against it briefly to recover his balance before falling to his knees. "Domina," he croaked.

"Bring him a drink," she commanded. "Quickly!"

When the wine arrived, the knight gulped it with clumsy desperation, the liquid spilling down his chin like blood. "Domina, grave news. My lord of Gloucester has been captured and taken prisoner. I know not what has happened to the Earl of Hereford and the king of Scots, save that their men have scattered and fled. I escaped by the skin of my teeth and hid in the woods until I thought it safe…"

Cold shivers ran through her at this fresh news of disaster. She could see the dismay on the faces of her escort; her own emotion was despair. With their chief military captain taken prisoner and no knowledge of the whereabouts of the others, what were they to do? She had suspected last night when Robert did not come that something was wrong, but had hoped against hope he had found a bolt hole somewhere. At least he was still alive; that was a small mercy.

Reynald, ever the optimist said, "But the empress is free and clear and so are we, and Stephen is still a prisoner in Bristol. Even if it is a setback, a battle is not the end of the war. We are not defeated."

But it felt like defeat to Matilda. She told the young knight to seek food and rest and join them in Devizes as soon as he was able. And then she drew herself up and put on a brave face. "We shall win through," she said. "I promise you." And knew her words were so much chaff in the wind.

She rode out of Ludgershall sitting tall in the saddle. She was still lady of the English; nothing could ever take that from her. But inside, as they rode along, beneath the bandage of pride she was bleeding. With Robert a prisoner, her plans were in ruins because none of her other commanders were of his calibre. She had lost London; she had lost Winchester and in so doing had failed herself, her allies, and her son. It was too much to bear, yet bear it she must. Her vision blurred and whitened. She swayed in the saddle and heard Brian's shout of alarm. She was dimly aware of him catching her, of the feel of his arms around her. She tried to tell him she was all right, that she had just fallen asleep in the saddle, but she couldn't speak. If not at the end of her courage, she had exceeded the last frayed strand of her bodily endurance.

Her escort constructed a litter for her, woven from willow branches piled with blankets and furs. They strapped her to it and bore her back to Devizes almost as if bringing home a corpse and Matilda tumbled into an exhausted darkness that was both a wasteland and a blessed relief.

Forty-three

ADELIZA CLUNG TO WILL, RISING TO MEET THE SURGE OF HIS body, pleasure flooding her loins. He gasped her name and called her his love, his queen, his soul, and she clung to him all the tighter, because in this moment they were as one, giving and receiving each to the other without conflict.

When it was over, he lay down at her side, stroking her body, until their breathing had eased and their hearts ceased thundering. Then, sighing, he eased to his feet and began to dress. She watched him from the bed. Perhaps it was a little bit sinful to have made love in broad daylight, but she had needed the affirmation of the bond between them. "Will..." She bit her lip.

He turned and placed his foot on the coverlet to tie the thongs on his shoe. "What?"

"Can you not stay here?"

His gave her a look from under his brows. "You know I have to go. It would be disloyal of me not to greet Stephen on his release. I owe him my allegiance while he is our anointed sovereign. If God had intended Matilda to be queen, she would be on the throne by now."

Adeliza looked away. "There will be more bloodshed," she said bitterly. "More pointless killing and burning."

"If I stay here, how can I help make policy? I cannot be a force for good if I am not in the council chamber. If I shun the court, then it isolates us. To be a good lord, a good husband, and a good father, I must go out into the world, not retreat from it. He leaned over, took her face between his hands, and kissed her. Then he left the bed and, fastening his belt, went briskly from the room.

Adeliza rose, draped a cloak over her chemise, and went to look out of the window.

Will had reached the courtyard and was talking to his groom. She loved him deeply, but he frustrated her with his stubbornness. For a time after Lincoln she had thought he might change his mind and bring himself to swear for Matilda. But then the Londoners had driven her out of Westminster, followed by the debacle at Winchester and the capture of Robert of Gloucester. Matilda had escaped but everything had fallen apart. She still ruled her areas of influence from her court at Devizes and she still held Oxford, but the greater power had slipped through her fingers.

They had heard terrible things about Winchester. Parts of the town had been razed to the ground. The abbeys of Hyde, Holy Cross, and Wherwell were ashes. Numerous ordinary folk had been killed, or rendered homeless and destitute. Everywhere she looked outside of her own lands there was chaos and death and destruction. That she and Will had thus far succeeded in maintaining stability in their parts of Sussex and Norfolk was by God's grace and their own efforts, even if there was often friction between them. But she knew it could change any day and nowhere was truly safe. Robert of Gloucester was being exchanged for Stephen and the fighting could only escalate.

❖❖❖

Three weeks later, Adeliza stood in the nave of Westminster Cathedral, feeling sick as she watched King Stephen receive his crown from Theobald of Canterbury in reaffirmation of his kingship. She would rather have stayed at Arundel, but Will had wanted her with him, and as the former queen of England, it was her duty to attend. Stephen's queen had worn her own crown throughout the ceremony, a delicate affair of gold spires and lilies set with pearls that looked incongruous adorning her matronly form. She carried her head high, a look of satisfied pride on her face. As well she might, Adeliza thought, even while feeling resentful. Maheut had managed to keep that crown on her head through thick and thin and, in so doing, prevent Matilda from gaining the throne.

Everywhere Adeliza saw reminders of her own life as a queen. Once it would have been her playing a major part at the ceremony and the feast. Smiling graciously, speaking and mingling; receiving petitions. Now it was Maheut's role and Adeliza was part of the background. Any attention paid to her was in deference to memory.

Stephen looked unwell, she thought. His face was gaunt and his gaze darted watchfully between his courtiers. His captivity had sucked out the bluff good humour that had lightened his personality. So many attendees had abandoned him during the months following Lincoln and pursued their own advantage that he must be wondering whom he could trust. The camaraderie was shattered. And men must wonder whether a once-defeated king might not be defeated again. Stephen was not steadfast. He would sway like a grass stalk in the wind. Matilda had angered people with her brusque ways, but she had always been resolute. Will could talk all he liked about it being the natural order to have a man on the throne, but what kind of man? No matter what ceremonies were performed, the gleam of his crown was forever tarnished.

In the Rufus hall at Westminster Palace after the ceremony, Adeliza sank in a curtsey as Stephen and Maheut paused to speak with her and Will. She kept her eyes lowered, fixing them on her gown, which was one she had worn when she had been England's queen and lady of the English.

Maheut raised her to her feet and gave her the kiss of peace. "It is good to see you here. It has been a long time since we have shared company."

"Without a doubt," Adeliza replied, thinking that it was not long enough.

"At least today is a time for celebration and peacemaking," Maheut added. "We can begin restored and anew."

"Indeed," Adeliza said. "The birth of the Christ Child is always an occasion for joy in the world whatever our sorrows and tribulations. I pray that peace will prevail for the sake of all who suffer."

"Amen to that," said Maheut, a little narrow-eyed now. "By our actions and our prayers should these things come to fruition." She and Stephen moved on, and although Maheut followed her husband it was by her will that they paced forward, like a snail with its shell.

Adeliza knew she was going to vomit, and pressed her hand to her mouth. Blessedly Will noticed her predicament and hurried her from the hall. She stooped over in the bitter winter cold and heaved and heaved, feeling utterly wretched.

Will supported her as she straightened, and offered her a napkin to wipe her mouth. "What is wrong?" he said anxiously.

Adeliza pressed her hand to her belly. "I think I may be with child again, although it is too early to be certain."

Immediately he was all tender concern. "You should have said. I will take you to our lodgings."

"I only began to suspect when we were on the road. I knew you wanted me to attend this crown-wearing, and it is so long since I have been to Westminster. I wanted to see the palace again and worship in the abbey." She shook her head sadly. "Perhaps it was not so fine a notion after all. We can never go back, can we?"

Forty-four

MATILDA TAPPED HER FINGERS ON THE ARMS OF HER CHAIR and scowled at the men gathered around her. Beside her, a scribe had just finished reading out a letter from her husband responding to her request for his aid in which he had declined to send her extra men and supplies without knowing more, and had refused to come himself. He said he was not averse to providing aid, but had no intention of setting his foot on English shores until fully informed. However, if Matilda wanted to send the Earl of Gloucester to him for consultation, he would listen to what he had to say.

She was furious with Geoffrey for procrastinating and playing shy. She needed him here, now, to turn the tide. Stephen had recently been very ill. For a while it had seemed as if he might die, but her spies reported he had rallied and was improving daily. It would not be long before he was actively campaigning again and the last thing she needed was to lose Robert in Normandy for a month if not more.

Robert threw up his hands. "Perhaps I should stay here," he said. "I do not want to leave you unguarded with strategies unprepared and I have no desire to ride through hostile territory and risk being captured again—for both our sakes."

"We have few supplies," said John FitzGilbert. "We cannot

fight without men and horses and money. I can only stretch the resources so far, and they are close to breaking point. We do not have time to send a different envoy to the Count of Anjou only to have him refuse us again. Someone has to go and persuade him, and it is best if it is the man he asked for."

Matilda forced herself to face her marshal. During the fierce fighting around Winchester, he had taken a desperate stand at the nunnery of Wherwell and lost one eye when lead from the burning abbey roof had dripped down and terribly scarred half his face. Looking at him was like looking at the living and the dead combined in one man. She would do him the honour of not pitying him, nor showing compassion, because he had never pitied himself nor asked for favours. "I am aware of the situation," she said curtly, because he was right. Geoffrey would refuse to talk to anyone but Robert because he had that petty streak within him, and because as far as he was concerned, his own campaign in Normandy was more important and a success, whereas hers was in ruins.

Robert heaved a sigh. "If that is what is necessary then I shall go. I can understand his point of view, even while I do not condone it."

❖ ❖ ❖

Geoffrey of Anjou fixed his brother-in-law with a cold aquamarine stare. "The key to England's crown is Normandy," he said. "Until I have a secure grasp, it is folly for me to come to England and divide my attention."

They were sitting in a sunlit chamber in Robert's keep at Caen on a glorious afternoon in early September. Swallows stitched the sky, gorging on the last flies of summer before their departure. Geoffrey glanced at his nine-year-old heir who sat at a lectern in the golden light, busy with quills and coloured inks while the men talked strategy. His hair sparkled like fine-spun metallic thread in the rays slanting through the window arch.

Only a week ago, Geoffrey had taken the castle of Mortain from Stephen's constable. It had been a good campaigning season. Tinchebrai and Vire had fallen too, and more than half a dozen others. "One more effort will see Normandy secure for my son and his heirs," he said. "If I widen my focus now, I will undo all my work—all that I have achieved, and surely we have had enough of that already." He watched Robert's lips tighten. Geoffrey did not dislike his brother-in-law. He found Robert rather wooden and staid, but he was intelligent, a decent battle commander, as proven on their recent campaigns around Normandy this summer, and staunchly loyal to Matilda. Such endurance and tenacity was to be admired. "I am not finding fault with you," he said smoothly. "I know how contrary and difficult my wife can be when she takes the bit between her teeth, and you have had your share of ill luck and treacherous barons and prelates to contend with. However, it is pointless for me to come to England, and dangerous. The English barons will mutter about an Angevin upstart, and while my wife might welcome the men and money I provide, she won't welcome me. If you are having problems keeping men's loyalty, how much more difficult will it be if she has her Angevin husband in tow?"

Robert scowled. "If that is your stance, then it was foolish and pointless to summon me to Normandy. You could have said all this by letter. Each day I am gone makes the situation in England more precarious."

Geoffrey shrugged. "I needed to know what was happening, and who else should I ask but my wife's own brother? Letters and messengers are all very well, but they do not tell the whole of it. I have had no direct contact with Matilda for three years, in which time she has had her fingertips on the crown and by all accounts lost it through her own obstinacy, so who then is the fool? I must know that if I commit men and money to England I am not throwing everything into a bottomless pit. Besides, having seen you as a commander here, it does not dispose me to come to England."

Robert stiffened.

"You take me the wrong way," Geoffrey said, although with a gleam in his eyes to show that he had been deliberately baiting Robert. "You are an accomplished general, and you would object to my interference in your theatre. If we are being honest with each other, you no more desire me in England than I desire to go there."

"I could go," Henry piped up from his lectern. "I am going to be king of England and I should be there. It's not fair that Mama should be fighting when I'm not."

Geoffrey eyed his precocious son with amused pride. "Think you so?"

Nodding, Henry left his window seat and brought his parchment to his father and uncle.

Geoffrey studied the sketch of a castle under siege with arrows flying towards it across a ditch. Bodies bled copiously through their mail shirts, and men were hurling stones off the battlements. A ribbon of blue was evidently water because there were fish swimming through it. Henry started pointing out the weaknesses of the defences and how he would go about the siege and capture. "It's the Tower of London," he said.

"But you have never seen the Tower of London!"

"Then I need to."

Geoffrey chuckled, but then he sobered and shook his head. "England is a dangerous place. It would be unsafe to let you go."

"No place is safe," Robert replied harshly. "Bringing him to England might just tip the balance. We need to show the people that this child is their brightest hope for the future. He shines with kingship."

Geoffrey frowned, reluctant to take the conversation further. He had often been told of England's magnificence in the days of the old King Henry, the peace and fertility of the lands, the brimming treasure chests, but that was all gone. Stephen had squandered the gold on his mercenaries and his cronies, and what he had not spent, his bishop brother had stolen. There was war, and the fields were black with a barren harvest of ash. It was no place for a sane man to go, much less a vulnerable child. While Henry was here, he was under his eye, his influence and his tutelage.

"I want to go," Henry said with a stubborn jut to his chin and a steely glint in his eyes that reminded Geoffrey entirely of his wife. "I want to learn about war."

"Have you not learned enough about it in Normandy?" Geoffrey demanded. "I can show you everything you need to know, and explain it."

"But it does not come with a crown," Henry replied with inarguable logic. "I want to see Mama, and I want to see England."

Geoffrey tightened his lips.

"I will look after him," Robert said earnestly. "I swear on my life that he will come to no harm. Only give me the men and supplies to help us through this. You are right that Normandy may be the foundation for your son's victory, but what point is a foundation if you do not build the house?"

"That is up to you and my wife, and thus far whatever you have built, you seem determined to raze the next day," Geoffrey snapped.

"And your wife and I know that we need aid from Normandy and that it would be greatly enhanced if Henry returned with me—since you will not come yourself."

Geoffrey gave Robert a strong look, but eventually sighed. "Very well. I will give you three hundred men and sufficient provisions to fill fifty ships. I expect you to provide for my son and guard his safety with your own life as you have sworn. You will return him to me the moment I ask for him. And on those conditions alone, you may have him for a brief while."

Joy shone from Henry's eyes as he uttered a whoop of triumph, and immediately dashed off to tell his brothers that he was going to claim his kingdom.

Robert's face sagged with relief. "Thank you," he said. "You have made the right decision."

"I hope so," Geoffrey said grimly. He was far from relieved himself because he knew that, even with the most rigorous safeguards, England was a dangerous, difficult place and Robert could not protect Henry from everything, and that began with the sea crossing. It only took one mistake from the helmsman and one rogue wave. What really made his heart sink, though, was knowing how much he was going to miss the daily presence of this bright, vibrant child, who lit his world like the sun.

Forty-five

ARUNDEL, AUTUMN 1142

FEELING EXHAUSTED BUT TRIUMPHANT, ADELIZA GAZED DOWN at the infant nestling in the crook of her arms, clean and freshly swaddled. The birth had been hard work because he was a large, robust baby and had taken his time and a deal of effort to push out, but she had him in her arms now and the miracle was as fresh as the first time: a golden moment that made a triviality of the pain and blood and danger. She had been barren; now she was fecund. She only wished Will could see him, but he was away on campaign. Having recovered from the serious illness that had laid him low throughout the spring and early summer, Stephen had once more taken to the field.

She and Will had spent the first six months of the year in Norfolk, at their new castles at Rising and Buckenham, watching the progress of the builders and attending to matters of estate, dealing with business pertaining to the Church and their various foundations and patronages. She had watched her eldest son turn from a pudgy infant into a proper little boy with strong limbs and the speed of a deer. His sister Adelis had become an imperious toddler with pink cheeks, riotous golden curls, and her father's wide candid stare. But in August, Stephen's summons had broken their idyll and, once again, she had watched Will ride away to war, to fight for a man she regarded as a usurper.

Juliana went to answer a knock on the door and Adeliza heard her speak to Rothard the chamberlain. Then she came over to Adeliza. "Madam, the earl has just ridden in," she said with a curtsey.

Adeliza gasped and struggled to sit up in the bed. "What?"

A firm masculine tread sounded a fast beat on the stairs outside her chamber, and Will entered, still clad in dusty travelling gear and wearing his sword.

Flustered at his sudden arrival when she was unprepared, Adeliza pulled the covers up around her body. "I did not know you were coming!" she said. "You should have sent word!"

He made an awkward gesture. "I knew you were in your confinement chamber and would only fuss if I did. This way was better." He advanced to the bedside and she inhaled the odours of outdoors and pungent hard travel on him. His lips were cold and his whiskers sharp as he kissed her. Then he looked at the swaddled baby.

"Another son," she said proudly, but with a slight frown of exasperation. She had not decided whether his not telling her was thoughtful, or thoughtless. She placed the baby in his arms. Watching him trace the delicate little eyebrows with his forefinger and stroke its cheek, her expression softened.

"You are well?" he asked.

"The better for having you home," she said, "whether you choose to tell me or not."

He looked up from the baby and his eyelids tensed at the corners. "I can only stay a little while," he said.

She searched his face. "How long is 'a little while'?"

He hesitated. "It depends on circumstances, but I hope to be here for your churching." He returned the baby to her arms. "You should rest; I will return later and we'll talk." He kissed her again and left.

Adeliza knew he was keeping things from her, but the birth

had exhausted her and all she wanted to do was sleep. He was right, however. They would certainly talk later.

❖❖❖

In the morning, Will bore his new son to Arundel's chapel and had him baptised and christened Godfrey, for Adeliza's father. Her kinswoman Melisande and her husband Robert stood as godparents. Following the ceremony, Will returned his son to the confinement chamber. Even as he walked up the stairs, he was still undecided about telling Adeliza his news. Her health had been challenged enough by the birth, and he knew she would fret.

When he entered the room, she was out of bed, sitting on the window seat dressed in a loose silk robe. Her chamber attendants had set out food on a trestle—bread, honey, warm curd tarts, and a jug of hot wine—so he knew she wanted him to stay awhile. "Young Godfrey has the voice of a bull calf," he said with a chuckle as he kissed the baby's cheek and handed him to his nurse. "I thought he was going to roar down the roof when Father Herman baptised him. He is certainly going to be heard across a battlefield."

"Pray God that he will not need to utilise such a skill," Adeliza replied with a shudder. "Better he should use it to sing God's praises than for fighting."

Will prudently held his tongue and escorted her to the trestle, making a fuss of her and ensuring she was comfortable. He poured her wine and served her himself with bread and honey.

Adeliza ate well but daintily and as always Will was fascinated by the way she managed not to let drop a single crumb. He sucked honey off his own fingers and surreptitiously fed crusts to Teri under the table.

Adeliza rinsed her mouth with wine and then turned to him. "Tell me what you did not tell me yesterday," she said. "I know you were holding something back."

He thought wryly he should have known he could not hide anything from her. He picked up his own cup and turned it round. "Stephen is besieging the empress at Oxford."

Her eyes widened in dismay.

"We crossed the Thames last week. A local guide found us a fording place, although we had to swim the horses across. The garrison tried to stop us, but we had their measure and they were unable to close the gates against us." He spoke without inflection, avoiding her gaze.

Adeliza felt queasy. She knew what happened to the people when the gates were forced open by the enemy.

He opened his hands, palms spread outwards. "With Robert of Gloucester away in Normandy, it is Stephen's best opportunity to take her and end all this. Oxford's castellan died three weeks ago, and there is no one of sufficient military standing there to take the fight to Stephen. It will be over as soon as the castle runs out of supplies."

"And then what?" she demanded. "What will happen to Matilda?"

"I do not know. He may send her back to Anjou, or make an arrangement with regards to Normandy, because he cannot win that back from the Angevins now."

"Or he may imprison her."

"Yes," he said wearily.

"What of Robert of Gloucester and Brian FitzCount?"

"They are powerless. FitzCount does not have the resources, and even if Gloucester returns with an army, he will have to organise a campaign." He took her hand in his. "Her back is to the wall, my love. I am sorry to give you this news because I know how much you care about her and feel responsible for her, but, truly, there is nothing you can do."

"And did you come away so you would not be a part of it?"

"Stephen cannot keep his entire army in the field for months on end. I have leave to come home to Arundel until after your churching, but then I must return to him." He gave her a troubled look "I hope Oxford falls in my absence. I would rather not be there when Matilda surrenders."

Adeliza set her jaw. "She will never surrender. God has always seen her safely out of danger before."

"She has never been in so difficult a corner, my love, not even at Winchester. At Arundel, Stephen let her go. He will not make the same mistake again." He shook his head. "Enough. I do not want you to dwell on such thoughts when you are so recently out of childbirth. What will be, will be."

"Whatever happens is God's will," she said, "not Stephen's. I shall pray for Matilda. I want you to bring Father Herman to me."

Will wiped his hands on a napkin and stood up, relieved to have got off more lightly than he had expected. "I will go and do it now."

"And I ask you to pray for her too." She fixed him with a steady look.

"Willingly." He was happy to pray in a broad sense for Matilda's soul, and to ask God to give her the good sense to negotiate a surrender and return to Anjou.

Forty-six

MATILDA SHIVERED IN HER CHAMBER AT OXFORD CASTLE. A bitter freeze had begun at the end of November with day after day of bone-chilling cold, each one hardening upon the other until the earth was like iron and the water in the moat as solid as rock crystal. Two days ago it had snowed heavily, draping the scars of warfare in a thick white blanket, and the sky was leaden with the threat of more. Stephen's blockade of the castle meant that neither aid nor news nor supplies could reach the beleaguered defenders, and the deep snowfall served only to emphasise their isolation from the rest of the world. The city was occupied by Stephen, who had taken over the old royal residence outside the town walls. His soldiers were billeted in Oxford with access to the food and warmth that Matilda and her garrison lacked. Here in the keep, they had almost run out of wood to fuel the cooking fires and heat the hall. They had already demolished two storage buildings and a goat shed—having eaten the goats. Now they had begun on the castle furniture and everyone was shivering in one room, trying to keep warm under a huddle of clothes and blankets. The only sustenance was soup made with meagre handfuls of barley, a few onions, and chunks of stockfish, chewy as rawhide even after pounding and soaking for hours on end. Matilda had insisted on eating the same as everyone else, and felt the same blend of ravenous appetite and queasy revolt as she forced down the disgusting fish broth. At least for the moment it was hot.

The battering of the castle walls had continued day in and day out and the garrison was becoming too weak and cold to resist. Unless she could find a way to escape, Matilda knew it was the end. Every day she prayed for Robert to arrive and lift the siege, and every day her prayers went unanswered. She did not know where he was or how he was faring because the blockade was complete.

"The only option is for me to escape Oxford and make my own way to safety," she told Alexander de Bohun, chief of her household knights. "Without me, Stephen has an empty fishing net."

"And just how are you going to get out?" De Bohun gave her a sidelong look. "Stephen has us surrounded."

"There are gaps between his guard posts, and the weather is so bitter that he will not expect anyone to leave the castle at night."

"At night?" De Bohun's eyes widened.

"Stephen's men will be huddled round their fires. There will only be a skeleton watch on duty. The river is frozen solid— there are no boats and no fishermen. I can escape over the wall with a small escort, and we can make our way to Wallingford."

De Bohun continued to stare at her as if he she had grown two heads. "Without horses and in the snow?" he said. "In the dark? It's as cold as a witch's tit out there."

She fixed him with a resolute gaze. "I would rather trust myself to the elements and God's mercy than kneel to Stephen. I know I must yield Oxford because we are at the end of our endurance, but without me his victory is as hollow as his crown."

"There will still be guards, even if reduced in number. What if you are seen and caught in the open? Prayer alone will not make you invisible."

"Of course not. Do you think I have not thought this through?" She glared at him. "We will go clad as if we are made of snow, and Stephen's men will see only what they expect to see."

He raised his brows.

"Bring me whatever white material we have," she commanded. "Sheets, tablecloths, blankets."

De Bohun hesitated for a moment, as if he really did think she was mad, but then bowed and went to give the order.

As servants returned from turfing out the contents from various coffers and garderobes, Matilda studied their finds. "The undyed blankets can be made into mantles by cutting a head hole," she said. "These sheets will make good hoods."

Matilda and her women set to with a will while the escape plans were discussed. She chose Alexander de Bohun, Hugh Plucknett, and two other strong knights to accompany her, together with Ralph le Robeur who was one of her messengers. He had been born in Oxford, knew the roads and pathways well, and would see them safely to Wallingford.

"We should go by way of Abingdon," he said. "That's about six miles all told. We can stop at the priory to warm ourselves and borrow horses."

Matilda agreed with him. She knew Abbot Ingulph well. He would succour them in the name of God. With each stitch she took, her determination solidified. Better to die of cold and exhaustion than yield.

She gave orders to relax the food rationing and told the cooks to boil up full portions for everyone, and to broach the last barrels of wine. As the dim winter afternoon darkened into dusk, everyone sat down to make a feast of the last of the stockfish, onions, and barley, augmented with plenty of pepper from the spice cupboard to add increased heat. Matilda was not hungry, but forced down her portion, knowing this was her last meal before she went out into the biting cold. She tried not to think about what was to come, but her mind was locked on to a treadmill and she kept returning to the same place time and again. There was a postern door she could go out of, but it attracted too much scrutiny from Stephen's guards. The more dangerous way physically, but which held much less chance of being seen, involved climbing down from the window of the domestic chambers by rope.

Her women dressed her in men's woollen hose and three layers of gowns. One of the garrison donated his spare gambeson to her because of its stuffed, quilted warmth. Her ankle boots were lined with unwashed sheepskins, and the outers were slathered in rancid goose grease to try and water-proof them. Once clad in their white sheets and blankets the travellers resembled shapeless, living mounds of snow. One of the knights carried a stout rope, another a lantern, although it would be kept unlit so close to Oxford. Besides, there would be cold blue snowlight by which to navigate.

"It is snowing again," said Ralph le Robeur as he and Hugh Plucknett secured a stout rope around the central mullion of the window arch.

Matilda peered out at the white flakes dancing in the dark blue. "The better to hide us," she said, but inside she was quaking with terror. *I am going to die,* kept running through her head. "In God's name, let us be about our business," she said harshly.

Ralph dropped the rope out of the window and slithered after it like an eel over a weir. He made it look so easy. Hand over hand down the knots. Fluid filled her mouth. Alexander de Bohun followed, more bulky and less agile than the messenger. His sword chape scraped on the sill with a loud rasp and she could hear him panting with effort. She began to shake her head, to say no, she could not do this thing; but still her feet carried her forwards and Hugh lifted her up. "Hold tightly," he said. "Let yourself down slowly and they will catch you. Have courage." She felt the gritty stone beneath her feet and the fierce grip of the rope under her hands. The bite of the wind. The frozen air burning in her nostrils. The soft white touch of snow on her face like the wing feathers of a plucked angel. Inside she was screaming in terror, but her jaws were locked and the sound stayed in her chest and throat as a solid ball of pain. She closed her eyes, committed her soul to God, and started down the wall, hand over hand, legs sliding down the rope. Dear Christ, dear Holy Virgin. Her arms burned with the effort of holding on and bearing her weight as she swung in the blackness.

Suddenly hands gripped her thighs and steadied her, and for a brief moment she was clasped breast to breast with Alexander de Bohun as he set her on her feet in the crunchy, powdery snow.

"Domina, you have given me a memory to keep me warm throughout this journey," he said with a forced smile as she staggered and clung to him.

Matilda managed to laugh as she straightened up, but the sound seemed to come from far away and someone else because she was still locked into her terror and it was as if a part of her was still hanging against that outer wall in dark mid-air. Hugh and the other knights shinned down the rope in turn, Hugh giving it a tug as he landed. The watchers at the top untied it and cast it down and the escapees knotted themselves together, so that should one fall through the ice, the others could pull him out. It also meant they would not lose each other if the weather worsened. Matilda strove to secure the rope around her waist but her hands were shaking so badly that de Bohun had to do it for her.

They set out with Matilda in the middle, protected from the elements by the men. The moat was the first obstacle and although they all knew it was frozen, still their steps were tentative, for they were afraid of slipping and instinctively crying out, thus alerting the enemy. Worried too that they might be seen anyway by Stephen's guards.

Matilda crunched ankle deep in the snow until her boot soles rested on ice. She took a tentative step and then another, her eyes wide with fear and the effort to see in this monochrome world that was absorbing her, her ears straining for a raised alarm. But there was nothing but snow whirling in the wind and darkness. They navigated the moat, shuffled their way off the ice, and began trudging towards the greater stretch of the frozen Thames that lay between themselves and Abingdon. The drifts were knee deep, and without a path to follow, they had to make one of their own. The knights took turns forging a way for the others to follow, lunging like horses on the rope. It was tiring, difficult work, but at least it kept their muscles warm and each step took them further from Oxford and closer to sanctuary. Matilda felt her scarf grow warm and wet from her exhaled breath as they snaked a route between Stephen's picket posts. Her stomach clenched as they passed between two shelters, but there was no sign of any guards. A fox crossed their path, streamlined and swift despite the deep snow, and was gone. "Further north it would be wolves," Ralph said cheerfully.

After what seemed like hours of trudging, they arrived at the riverbank. Bits of tree branch were frozen in the water like skeletal hands adorned with icicles. The snow was silvery in places and opaque white in others. Birds had scribbled tracks amid the stiff sedges. Matilda stared out across the white swathe of the river, her breath clouding the air with pale vapour.

"Well," said Ralph, pointing to the row of paw prints leading into the night. "If the fox came this way, then he must be our portent." He forayed gingerly on to the ice with de Bohun following, and as the rope paid out and Matilda felt the tug, she had no option but to follow them, terrified that she was going to hear the creak of strained ice, feel it shatter, and fall through a jagged crack into black, icy water to drown as her brother had done when the *White Ship* went to her doom. Snow continued to twirl down as they stepped like clumsy dancers across the frozen water, step after step sinking through the powdery surface until the snow compacted underfoot with a soft crumping sound, and each time that happened, she felt another surge of fear.

Then suddenly they were once more amongst frozen sedges and willows and clambering through the tangle on to the opposite bank. Panting, Matilda turned to look over her shoulder. Their churned tracks were obvious, stretching away to the opposite side, but the way the snow was falling, all signs would be covered by dawn.

"Drink," said de Bohun, offering her a flask. The wine had been hot when they set out and a residue of warmth remained, enhanced by added pepper and spices. Matilda felt it burn down her gullet. De Bohun produced bread and dripping from a cloth in his satchel. The bread was so hard he had to smash it into pieces with his sword hilt. Matilda pouched a morsel in her cheek and sucked on it until it softened. They still had six miles to walk to reach Abingdon, and another fifteen to Wallingford. Climbing down from a castle window and crossing the frozen moat and river was only the start of their journey. As they set out once more, forcing a path through the snow, Matilda knew she would never again use the phrase "When hell freezes over" without remembering this night.

❖ ❖ ❖

Will sat before the hearth in Abbot Ingulph's parlour at Abingdon enjoying the heat from the flames on the front of his body. The part facing away from the fire was protected from the cold by a thick fur-lined cloak. Teri lay at his side, his nose between his forepaws, his brows cocking occasionally in his master's direction. Will had brought a gift to the abbot of nuggets of frankincense and two silver censers in which to burn the precious resin. He had also brought the abbot a cover for a book of the New Testament he wanted to give to Adeliza. The monks had been copying the work over the past several months and now the book was to be bound with carved ivory plates set with rock crystals, garnets, and chrysophrases.

Will's errand was a welcome relief from duty with Stephen's army besieging Oxford. He knew the defenders must be at the end of their resources and that surrender was close. They could not survive much longer in these bitter conditions. Stephen was expecting to be master of Oxford before Christmas. Will had been trying not to think about Matilda trapped inside the castle with her garrison because her kinship with Adeliza—and, by association, with himself—agitated his conscience. He knew that when Matilda was taken, Stephen would incarcerate her for the rest of her life.

"War is a terrible thing," Abbot Ingulph said quietly. "We see so many dispossessed and homeless folk at our gates and through no fault of their own. All the burned crops and slaughtered animals bring famine and suffering, but not to those who make the war."

Will flushed at the abbot's gentle chastisement. "I do what I can on my own lands and foundations to succour them," he said, "and it is my lady's main cause."

Ingulph steepled his hands under his chin. "The ordinary people are being severely hurt by this war between those who should be offering them good governance. It is your duty and responsibility to sort out a lasting peace, rather than fighting each other and everyone else into the grave."

"I agree," Will said. "Your advice is sound."

Ingulph opened his hands. "Then act upon it," he said.

When Will had finished his wine, he clicked his fingers to Teri, took his leave of the abbot, and made his way to the guest house. He liked Ingulph, even if the old man did tend to lecture like a sorrowful parent to a sinful child. He was right. There had to be a lasting peace, but in order for that to happen, there had to be the will for it too, and that was less in evidence.

He hunched into his cloak as a fresh flurry battered him side-on. Teri suddenly stiffened, his hackles rising and a low growl rumbling in his chest. Will stopped abruptly and stared at the bedraggled group staggering towards the guest lodge from the direction of the gatehouse. All wore strange white robes that flapped in the wind like wings and for a moment he was filled with gut-lurching fear as he wondered just what he was seeing. Angels perhaps, or souls of the dead in their shroud cloths. Two of them, seeing him, moved to protect a slighter figure in their midst and laid their hands to their swords. The hair rose on Will's nape. He was not wearing his own sword because he was on monastic lands and had come with peaceful intent. Then the slighter figure pushed the guardians aside and came forward, putting down her hood and ignoring the growling dog.

Will was stunned and shocked to see Matilda—an apparition indeed. "Domina." He bowed. She was pinch-faced with cold and exhaustion, but her eyes were fierce. "This is an unexpected meeting indeed."

Her jaw was taut. "A meeting that never happened," she said, "unless you make it so."

He could see her shivering as fresh flurries of wet snow spun across the courtyard. What in God's name was she doing here? "Never mind that," he said. "You should come inside before you freeze."

Matilda hesitated. Her knights exchanged worried glances.

"This is a house of God," Will said brusquely. "Neither I nor my men will harm you; you have my word."

She inclined her head. "Then I accept because I know you for a man of honour, whatever your loyalties."

While they had been speaking, a monk had run to fetch Abbot Ingulph, and he arrived as Matilda and her escort were gathering around the guest-house hearth, although not too close to the fire because of the pain in their frozen hands and feet. Ingulph was plainly disconcerted, but did his best to appear composed. "Be welcome in God's name, domina," he said. "This house embraces all travellers, especially on a night such as this. I will see that you are fed and given beds."

"Thank you, Father, but we will not be staying for long," Matilda replied. "Just let us warm ourselves for a while, but hot food would be most welcome."

"The loan of horses, would be appreciated too," said de Bohun. "We have some distance still to travel."

Ingulph's brow furrowed. "Most are out at the grange. There are only two cobs in the stables, and my old mule, and his riding days are long over. You are welcome to the cobs, providing you return them as soon as you may."

"Thank you," Matilda said, although her heart sank at such news. "We are grateful for whatever you can provide."

Ingulph offered Matilda and her escort his lodging in which to revive themselves because it was warm and more private. Since there were things he needed to make straight, Will went with them. "I am lodging at the abbey tonight," he said as they entered Ingulph's house, "but tomorrow I shall be returning to Oxford."

Matilda sat down on the bench before the fire and opened and closed her fingers, encouraging them to thaw. "Tomorrow it will not matter," she said, "because the castle will surrender to the king."

"But you will not be inside it."

"No." She gave him a thin smile. "Whatever he steals, it will always lack its true worth in his hands—like his crown. All glitter and no substance."

"You will forgive me, domina, if I beg to differ."

"Will I?" she said, barely smiling at all now, and changed the subject. "How is Adeliza?"

"She is well. We have another son, Godfrey." He added after a hesitation, "You are often in my wife's prayers."

"As she is often in mine. I will write to her as soon as I am able."

Will concealed a grimace. "Is it worth it all?" he asked.

She drew a deep breath. "I know you will never abandon your oath to serve Stephen, but what happens when he is gone? Would you bend the knee to that brat of his, Eustace? Or would you look to my son?"

Will considered this woman, sitting before the fire, her fine bones sharpened by the cold and dark smudges of exhaustion under her eyes. Even if he thought her misguided, he acknowledged her courage and resolution. "As much as his breeding, it would depend on the kind of man he becomes, and the same could be said for Eustace."

"But you would consider?"

"Yes, domina, I would, but very carefully indeed." He bowed to her and turned to leave, but on the threshold he paused, torn between his duty to Stephen and the obligation to Matilda born of the kinship bond between her and Adeliza. Before he could think better of it, he said, "If they are of use to you, you may take three of my horses from the stables. The chestnut is sturdy and will bear two of you with ease; the bay with the white star is steady, and the grey bites, but he's a worker."

"Thank you." Her eyes glinted with moisture, and her expression dared him to notice.

"It is the most and the least I can do," he said.

She swallowed. "I ask also of your goodwill and for the kinship your wife bears to me that you intercede for the garrison and those of my household who are still trapped inside the castle."

"I will do what I can." He left the room and returned to the guest lodge, and when his men asked him what had transpired, he put them off with a bland comment and, retiring to his mattress, put his back to them.

In the morning the empress and her party had gone. A fresh fall of snow had obliterated all tracks beyond those of monks going down from dorter to chapel in the dead of night. Were it not for the fact that his chestnut stallion and the bay and grey geldings had gone from their stalls, he could have believed it all a dream. As it was, he faced a long trudge back to Oxford.

Forty-seven

MATILDA DROOPED IN THE SADDLE. EVERY MUSCLE WAS aching and tight with cold and she felt as if the marrow had been sucked from her bones and replaced with ice. They had been struggling through the snow for most of the night, trying to cover the ground between Abingdon and Wallingford before dawn. The light was grey in the east with a streak of oyster white low on the horizon. It had stopped snowing an hour ago and the world was hushed and colourless, the only sound the crump of the snow under the horse's hooves and the jingle of harness.

Now, finally, the walls and towers of Wallingford Castle rose out of the dawn in lime-washed stone and timber like a sketch on an embroiderer's linen cloth. Relief coursed through her at the sight, but there was misery too, because although this place guaranteed safety, she did not want to be here, and the circumstances driving her were of defeat and failure.

At the outer works, a herald rode out to greet them and establish their credentials. Matilda realised what an odd party they must look, sharing horses and still clad in their disguising white robes for warmth. The moment the herald recognised them, he raised the horn he was carrying and blew three strong blasts, and the guards hastened to open the gates.

As Matilda entered Wallingford, folk were shovelling pathways through the night's fresh snowfall. A groom hastened to take her bridle. De Bohun dismounted and turned to help Matilda from the saddle, but Brian was there before him to claim the privilege.

She felt the hard grip of his hands as he lifted her down, and for an instant they stood as close as lovers. Then he stepped back, putting a body's distance between them, even while their breath mingled in the icy air.

"Domina, I do not know what you are doing here," he said, "but I thank Christ to see you, and know you are safe." Falling to his knees, he bowed his head.

Matilda wanted to weep aloud, but suppressed her emotion with rigid control. Beyond Brian, everyone else was kneeling too, so that in this bleak courtyard, piled with snow, muddy straw underfoot on the walkways, she was queen of all she surveyed.

"All that is here is yours," Brian said, as if reading her mind.

It began to snow again in light, fine flakes. She saw the relief and raw anguish in his eyes, and all the tally of the things so long unsaid between them. She swayed on her feet. "All I want is to be out of this bitter cold," she said, her voice cracking.

Immediately he was contrite. "Come within. I will send a messenger to Cirencester, to my lord of Gloucester, immediately. He will not yet have marched on Oxford."

"He has no need," she said wearily. "It is too late; the castle is lost."

"Then how did you..."

"I do not know." She blinked hard and rubbed her forehead. "Dear God, Brian, I do not know."

He beckoned and his wife stepped from the throng and curtseyed. "Domina," she said. "Let me show you to a comfortable chamber."

Matilda summoned the last of her strength and followed

the lady of Wallingford to a room on the upper floor of a fine timber hall. A large, warm fire burned in the hearth and a bed with a soft blanket of red and green stripes, topped by a folded silk quilt, was pushed against one wall. A pleasant scent of incense and beeswax filled the room. There were numerous shelves lined with scrolls and parchments tied up with ribbons, and there were books too. A lectern stood under a window to catch the best light,

"This is the warmest chamber in the castle," Maude said. "I hope you find it fitting, domina." Her gaze was closed and wary.

Matilda just wanted to lie on the bed and fall asleep, but would not do so in the presence of Brian's wife. "It will suit me very well," she said.

Servants arrived bearing fresh bread and hot wine. Maude directed them to set it down near the bed. A woman brought in a ewer of hot water and a towel.

"You should remove those wet boots or you will catch a chill," Maude said with a cluck of her tongue. "Come, sit."

Matilda was reminded of her old nursemaids. The woman had that deferential but bossy air about her and, apart from a gold brooch on her dress, was garbed like a peasant. Turning her back, Brian's wife straddled Matilda's legs to pull off her boots, grunting and tugging with effort, but eventually succeeding. Maude then bathed Matilda's icy feet in the warm water with thorough efficiency, all the time keeping her eyes lowered and her mouth set in a straight line. She brought some soft shoes lined with lambskin from their warming place at the hearth.

Matilda pushed her feet into them and the feeling was utter bliss. "Thank you," she said with a more genuine smile for her hostess.

"I may be a simple woman," Maude said, "but I know the things that matter. If you will excuse me, I have arrangements to make."

She left the room, followed by the maid with the used water. A different girl arrived with a fresh bowl, a chemise of clean linen, and an old-fashioned gown of dark red wool with a simple braid belt. Matilda removed the various layers of garments in which she had travelled, washed, donned the chemise and gown, then sat down on the bed and put her face in her hands. She wanted to cry, but her eyes were dry, and besides, tears were a waste of time. She had to think her way out of this. What was going to happen to her? What was she going to do now? Wallingford was a safe haven but she could not stay here indefinitely. She could do nothing until Robert arrived, but what after that? She could see no way out of the forest.

Leaving the bed, she sought distraction by drinking a cup of wine and looking at the books and scrolls of parchment on the shelves. Some of the writing was in the hand of a scribe, but she recognised most of it as Brian's neat, swift script. She realised that this was Brian's chamber—his private place—and the notion both disconcerted and comforted her. She picked up a small book bound in plain leather and found herself gazing at a copy of a treatise expounding her right to be queen of England. She put her hand to her mouth as she read the erudite Latin. Brian argued with the incisiveness of a lawyer, the simplicity of a monk, and the elegance of a man whose lifeblood was ink. Reading the words, feelings of grief and love assailed her in equal measure. She was in his chamber, at the heart of the man, and she was between the words and the fire.

She lay down on the bed with the treatise clasped in her arms, curled her knees towards her chest, and closed her eyes. Breathing in she inhaled his scent from the sheets, mingled with a faint aroma of incense.

❖ ❖ ❖

"She is still asleep," Maude said to Brian. She stooped to pick up the newest version of Rascal and fondled the pup's silky ears. They were standing in the hall before the fire and the servants were setting up trestles for the main meal of the day.

"Leave her," he said. "She will wake when she is ready." He looked at her with his eyes full of wonderment. "Do you know what she did? Escaped out of a window at Oxford Castle by rope, crossed the frozen moat and the river, walked to Abingdon, and then made her way here through the night."

"Indeed, she has great fortitude and courage," Maude said, and pressed her lips against the top of the dog's head.

"More than anyone I have ever met."

She gave a small sniff. She admired the empress for fighting for what was hers by right, but Brian never stopped to think that those same qualities had to be applied to the daily grind. To portion out rations and keep a level head whilst constantly surrounded by enemies and with the castle in a state of semi-siege. Month upon month; year upon year. Sometimes she felt like a donkey, staggering along under a heavy burden of firewood, while Brian ignored her to look at the fancy glossy horses prancing past on the road with bells tinkling on their harness. Her own fortitude was about to be severely tested by the arrival from Cirencester of Robert of Gloucester and his entourage. Providing food and lodging for such numbers was no simple matter and she loathed all the pomp and ceremony. "How long will the empress stay?"

"For as long as she has need," Brian said, giving her a sharp look. "She is entitled to all the help we can give her."

Maude said with quiet conviction, "She will destroy you. I can see the hunger in your eyes."

Brian gave her an impatient look. "No," he said. "You do not understand. She is what keeps me alive."

"Then you should find other sustenance before it is too late," Maude retorted and, the dog in her arms, walked briskly from the hall.

Brian watched her leave and clenched his fists. He did not want any other sustenance and it was already too late. Either she would feed him, or he would die, and be glad to do so.

❖❖❖

Three days later the snow was still thick on the ground, but the wind was less cold and there had been no fresh falls. Standing in the outer bailey Matilda studied the selection of horses milling in the enclosure, their winter coats plush and thick and their breath clouding the air.

"Choose any you want," Brian said.

She perused the animals with a keen eye. Most were in the slack condition of winter stalling, but she considered the underlying conformation. She wanted a horse that had stamina, a good pace, and even temper.

"Just one?" She gave him a half-smile.

His mouth curved in reply. "You may have them all, but you can only ride one at a time."

Matilda indicated a mare with a rich golden coat and pale mane and tail. "That one," she said

Brian had her tacked up and fitted with a lady's saddle. Matilda mounted from the block in the yard and took the horse on a circuit of the training ground. The mare was smooth-paced and strong, but tugged to the right and Matilda felt her spine twist and jar. Unsuitable for a long journey, she thought. Returning to Brian, she accepted his aid to dismount and, stepping out of his grasp, indicated a grey gelding. "Now this one," she said.

Brian gave a wry smile. "So you do intend to try them all?" He gestured to the groom and the men set about changing the tack.

"At least until I find the right one." She gave him a sidelong look.

Brian was relieved to see that sudden gleam. Oxford had taken so much out of her. Despite all the sleep she had had, her eyes were still ringed with exhaustion. The look she had given him was at least a sign that somewhere deep within her spirit still burned.

Matilda tried out several horses, but finally returned to settle on the grey. "Definitely this one," she said, riding back to Brian and patting the horse's neck. "The roan is too headstrong. A man might say such a horse can be mastered with whip and curb, but why ride something unruly when you can have a good mount that will not cause you trouble?"

Brian patted the grey and ran his hand down its shoulder. "A pity this horse is not England."

"Indeed," she agreed.

Taking the bridle, Brian led the grey back to the stable with Matilda still mounted, then he tethered the horse to a post and helped her dismount. For an instant they stood pressed closely together with his hands either side of her waist. She touched the side of his face, and he turned so that his lips kissed her palm. He grasped her fingers to hold her there.

She closed her eyes for a moment. "Brian," she whispered. "Dear God…" She tugged her hand free and pulled away from him. Her limbs felt weak and heavy. She wanted to kiss his mouth and the place beneath his ear where his hair lay in a vulnerable curl, but knew it was crossing a boundary, and once it happened, there would be another step and another on the forbidden side and no turning back. Already they stood on the cusp of scandal. "This can never be," she said. Making a tremendous effort, she turned away and walked swiftly towards the keep.

"I wasn't tempting you," Brian said wretchedly to the space where she had been. "I was torturing myself."

❖❖❖

Matilda retired to her chamber, washed her face and hands, and changed her stout boots for soft indoor shoes. She was trapped here, she thought, and in this room which was Brian's through and through and gave her neither respite nor tranquillity.

Riding the horses had lifted her spirits for a short while, but knowing she could not just leave as she chose, knowing that her every move was being observed and judged, made her feel like a prisoner.

The lady Maude entered the room. Her dark gown was flecked with dog hairs as usual and she smelt faintly of the kennel. "Heralds from the Earl of Gloucester have arrived, domina," she said. "He will be here by noontide."

A great wash of relief swept through Matilda and she felt as if a crushing weight had lifted from her chest. "Thank God, thank God! That is great news!" With Robert here, Wallingford would feel more like a court and she could begin the business of governing again in earnest. She needed to talk to him and find out what had happened in Normandy, and especially how much aid Geoffrey had sent, even though he had obviously not come himself. They could take stock and regroup; recover and evaluate.

Maude made a stiff curtsey. "If you will excuse me, domina. The castle is going to be full at the seams and there is food and accommodation to prepare."

Her voice was neutral, but Matilda sensed the resentment lurking in the impassive gaze. "Thank you," she said quietly. "I know this is a hardship for you."

"It is my duty, domina." Maude raised her head proudly. "I am lady of Wallingford, and have been since well before your father of blessed memory was a crowned king."

"Nevertheless, you have my gratitude."

Maude curtseyed again, woodenly, as if Matilda had offered her an insult.

❖ ❖ ❖

Matilda prepared for Robert's arrival. She dressed in one of the gowns she had brought from Oxford, worn as an underlayer that snowy night. It was of red wool, the sleeves and neck trimmed with silk of the deep royal purple that was the hue of a western sky at midnight, and stitched with jewels. She wore her father's sapphire ring and a large glossy ruby that matched the gown. She had brought her crown of gold flowers from Oxford, and she set this on her head, over her silk veil. The feel of the band across her brow reassured her, carrying as it did the pressure of regal authority.

An usher came to tell her that the Earl of Gloucester and his entourage had arrived and were dismounting in the outer bailey. Matilda smoothed the dress and, with mingled feelings of relief and apprehension, went to greet her brother.

There was no sign of Brian, who had gone out to meet the party and escort Robert to the hall in honour, but Maude was there, and she too had changed her dress for one of plain but clean blue wool. Jugs of wine had been set out on a table together with baskets of bread and pastries.

Robert entered the hall with his customary vigour, the manner of his stride emphasising his height and his strong body. However, there were tired pouches beneath his eyes and far more grey in his hair than Matilda remembered. She hastened to embrace him, but stopped in her tracks as she saw the boy standing a little behind him and to one side like a squire. He was sturdy, with golden-red hair, freckles, and brilliant grey eyes. "Henry," she whispered, close to disbelief. "Henry?"

"I have brought you a rare and precious Christmas gift," Robert said, smiling.

"My lady mother," Henry said and knelt to her.

Matilda stared and stared. She wanted to bend down and scoop up the little boy she had left behind, but in his stead was this older being, self-contained and already marked for manhood. It was as if she had put down a precious object and returning to it a while later had discovered it utterly changed. All the emotion she had been suppressing as she battled to survive and keep hope alive now threatened to flood up and overwhelm her. Her chin wobbled and her mouth moved in different directions as she tried to control herself. She had a position to uphold, and knew she should not be acting like this in public, in front of her son. People were gazing at her in consternation.

"Mama, don't cry," Henry said, looking at her askance. "I am here now. All is well. I will protect you."

She tried to hold back her tears and failed. "I am so pleased to see you, I am overcome," she choked. "Let my lord FitzCount show you to your chamber and I will come and talk to you in a little while."

Henry blinked for an instant, then adapted his mental stride and bowed to her again, and when he stood up, gave her a smile as bright as the sun.

"Come, sire." Brian gave Matilda a worried look, but smoothly dealt with matters. "There is a fine chamber prepared for you and my lord of Gloucester, right up near the battlements."

"Can I see the dungeons too? And the armoury?" Henry's voice filled with excitement, his meeting with his mother already losing its importance in the face of more interesting, masculine fare.

"You can see the entire castle and I will show you where everything is and answer as many questions as you can ask," Brian replied, "but first your chamber. Give your mama a moment to herself."

As Brian left with Henry and Robert, Matilda allowed Maude and her women to help her to her room, but once there, she shrugged them off, furious at her own weakness. She gestured everyone to leave, and lay down on her bed with the curtains closed. Dear God, she thought. What sort of example was this to set to her son? She wrapped her arms around a pillow and held it against her body with her fists, trying to stem the spasms as other memories welled to the surface. All the things she had dammed behind the façade of being the empress now poured out of her. The flight from Winchester; the jolting over rough ground; the pursuit and the terror that she might be caught. Climbing down from the tower at Oxford into the bitter air. The long, dark drop and the fear that she was going to die. The moments with Brian when she had pulled back from intimacy and denied herself that comfort, choosing to walk alone. The nugget of concentrated emotion she had felt on seeing Henry so grown up had breached the flood banks and suddenly she had become a mother and a person. She couldn't let Henry see her thus. He must not think she was weak.

At last the spasms subsided, leaving her like the survivor of a shipwreck cast up on a beach, wrung out and exhausted. She lay on the bed for a while, but eventually rallied enough to rise and wash her face. Then she drank a cup of wine and summoned the women back into the room.

"Are you feeling better, domina?" Maude enquired.

"Thank you, yes," Matilda said stiffly. "I have not seen my son in more than three years. Small wonder I should be overset." From the middle finger of her left hand she removed her ruby ring and gave it to a chamberlain who was standing in the doorway. "Take this to the lord Henry," she said. "Tell him I will talk to him in a little while, but that this comes to him with all the love of a mother's heart." *And the red of a woman's womb,* she thought as the man bowed and departed.

❖ ❖ ❖

Henry looked at the ring. It was far too big for any of his fingers and he had set it around his neck on a length of thin gold braid. The ruby was as big as his thumb and glowed like an illuminated drop of blood. It was a gift fit for a king, not just a trinket. He had decided it was going to be part of his regalia when his turn came to rule, and such a time could not be far away because it was the reason he had been sent here—to finish his education and to learn what he needed about becoming king of England. As far as he was concerned, he was already the uncrowned ruler of the country. His mother had done what she could, helped by his uncle Robert, but she was a woman, while he was growing into a man—albeit too slowly for his patience. The way she had wept in front of him and had to retire had been a little disconcerting, but that was just a part of her womanhood. His own eyes had tingled in response to the moment, but he had not cried, because he was a man, and there was nothing to cry about.

Wallingford Castle fascinated him and once he had been shown his chamber and where he was to sleep, he had been eager to be about the fortress, exploring the defences, the chambers, and all the nooks and crannies. He enjoyed himself at the kennels, making the acquaintance of various dogs, thus earning the approval of Brian FitzCount's wife, the lady Maude. She patted his head and said if he wanted he could have a puppy when he left. Henry had been delighted. Having a puppy was not as good as having this ring, but it all added to the excitement and the largesse being poured on him. Vassals often gave hawks and dogs in tribute. He had been taken to see the huge storage barns and undercrofts with their supplies laid down for years of siege. He screwed up his face as he recognised the bales of stockfish. It was one of the hazards of Lent, and of course people under siege, although you had to have a plentiful water supply in order to soften the stuff.

"How long could you hold out?" he asked Brian and his uncle, who were examining the stores.

"For as long as the enemy chooses to lay siege, sire," Brian said.

"How long would that be?"

"It depends. Might be days or weeks or months, but they would break first."

Henry was thoughtful. "Will Stephen follow Mama to Wallingford?"

His uncle shook his head. "I doubt it. He has bitten off more than he can chew, especially when he cannot trust his teeth." He ruffled Henry's red-gold curls. "You need have no fear, lad."

"I'm not afraid. I want to fight him. It's my crown." Henry was aware of the adults casting amused glances over his head and was affronted.

"All in good time," his uncle Robert said. "But first you have more learning to put under your belt and some growing to do if you are going to fit into your hauberk, hmmm?"

That was true, but the eagerness bubbling up within him was impossible to contain. He wanted it now, not in several years' time.

"I promised your father I would keep you safe, and that is what I intend to do. You will be dwelling in Bristol and learning what a king needs to know in order to rule."

Henry tucked the ring back inside his tunic. The stone and the gold were cold for a moment, but gradually warmed against his skin. He returned to the great hall with his uncle and FitzCount and found his mother waiting there for him. She was composed now and smiling, albeit in a strained way. Henry knelt to her again as he had been taught.

"I am sorry for weeping earlier," she said a little breathlessly. "I did not realise how overwhelmed I would be to see you." Raising him to his feet, she embraced him; with an effort, she kept her touch light. "How you have grown!"

He puffed out his chest. "I am here to help you, Mama," he said. "It's my turn now."

Her eyelids tightened, but her smile became less strained. "Indeed, and I am glad, because I have an important task for you."

Henry swelled further.

She set her hand on his shoulder. "Your uncle has told you that you are to go to Bristol and continue your studies there?"

He nodded.

"But first you will come to court at Devizes, and everyone will swear fealty to you as my heir, and acknowledge you as the heir to England. Everyone will know you are the future for which they must hold firm. You have taken oaths before in Anjou and Normandy with your father. It will be similar to those times, but more important."

Henry's breathing quickened. "Will I wear a crown?"

Matilda's expression warmed with proud amusement. "You will indeed," she said. "If you are to rule England, no one must be in any doubt, but you have to act like a king as well as look like one."

Henry raised his head. "I can do that."

The words and the tone of voice were adult and serious, and a pang squeezed Matilda's heart and womb. She had failed at so many things, and the terrible grief was still close to the surface, but she could cope; and this child was a precious shining light on the path to the future even if there was still much to do to educate and steady him. The fight was only going to grow harder the nearer he came to being of an age to rule the kingdom. But rule it he would, of that she was certain, even if her own time was slipping away.

Forty-eight

ADELIZA KNELT ON THE ALTAR STEPS OF THE CHAPEL AT Arundel with her eldest son and supervised his prayers. He was two months short of his fourth birthday and every day he brought her joy with his questions, his brightness, and his existence. His hair was a tousle of warm brown curls and his eyes were a bright tawny hazel, like Will's. He had lined up his collection of toy wooden figures on the altar step together with a representation of the Virgin Mary wearing a painted blue cloak. There was a little manger too with the Baby Jesus and a wooden donkey.

"You were once a tiny baby in the cradle," she said. "Just like your brother Godfrey, and just like little Jesus."

He wrinkled his nose. "But Jesus was born in a stable," he said. "I wasn't born in a stable, was I, Mama?"

Adeliza swallowed a smile. "No, my love, you were born in the bedchamber with many attendants and soft feather pillows. But Jesus only had a poor manger for a bed. You should never judge people by how much wealth they have. The poorest person may have the greatest gift. If you ask Jesus he will help you and sustain you and look after you all of your life, although he was born in a manger and you were born in a feather bed. He is the Son of God, and yet he chose the path of humility."

Wilkin nodded and sucked his bottom lip, the way he did when he was unsure about something. Adeliza gently stroked his head.

"If I pray to Jesus to bring Papa home soon, will he make it happen?" he asked.

Adeliza's stomach gave a small leap. She had been praying for that herself. There had been no word from her husband for several weeks. He had come home after Stephen's Christmas court in a subdued frame of mind and had told her about his meeting with Matilda at Abingdon, and how he had let her go, instead of taking her prisoner. "I could have stopped the conflict at a stroke, but I did not," he said. "Nor did I tell the king what I had done, but perhaps I should."

She had kissed him and put her arms around him. "You did what was right and what your conscience told you to do."

He had shrugged and said nothing. A few weeks later, when it thawed, Matilda had returned the horses he had lent her with words of gratitude and a long letter for Adeliza. She said that her son Henry was in England to further his education, and to learn more about the kingdom to which he was heir. Adeliza had wondered if she could persuade Will to swear allegiance to Henry, but he was a stubborn ox when the mood was upon him. He said that Henry was a child and he had no intention of jeopardising himself or his family by stepping out on such a precarious limb.

"Mama?" Wilkin tugged on her sleeve. "Will he? Will Jesus make Papa come home?"

Adeliza shook herself. "Yes," she said. "Yes he will." She set her hand lightly on her son's head and sent up her own silent prayer.

❖ ❖ ❖

Seventy miles away, on the outskirts of Wilton, Will was attending to his own prayers in the chapel of the leper hospital of Saint Giles at Fugglestone. He had given four pounds of silver to the master to help sustain the brothers and sisters of the establishment, and also given them a cow he had brought from Arundel. She was in calf and would provide the inmates with good sweet milk come full spring when she gave birth. Adeliza would be pleased, he thought, and put from his mind the knowledge that she would certainly be a deal less pleased to know her nunnery of Wilton, less than half a mile away, had been invaded by Stephen and was being used by him as a camp from which to attack Robert of Gloucester at Wareham. Fresh from his success at Oxford, Stephen was in a bullish mood and determined to retake the port and thus deny the Angevins a secure landing with easy crossings to their supplies in Normandy.

Indeed, Will thought, his wife would be furious, which was one reason he had not written to tell her where he was, although of course she would find out and he would have to weather the storm when he returned home.

He had tried to dissuade Stephen from taking over the abbey, but the king had been adamant. He said he would compensate the nuns in due course, but he needed the buildings. It had been pointless to argue because the bishop of Winchester had been present and had made no protest, and since he was the papal legate, and had ultimate authority, it was a lost cause.

Will had billeted his own troops at Fugglestone, sufficiently removed from the leper hospital to assuage the fears of his men, but not on the nunnery site. It was making a silk purse of a sow's ear, but at least it had mollified his conscience, as had the four pounds of silver and the cow. He was not afraid of the lepers, as many were, and he did not revile them because all men were sinners and Christ taught that one should have compassion for the afflicted. Adeliza had always concerned herself with the sick and the poor in practical ways and he loved her dearly for her compassion and dedication. So he talked to the lepers, listened to their stories, and cherished his own good health with renewed thanksgiving.

Back at the camp a summons had arrived from Stephen to attend a council at the abbey. The summons was delivered by Serlo, one of Adeliza's clerks, who was serving Will on campaign as his scribe. Serlo had been conducting routine business with Stephen's clerks and reacquainting himself with his birthplace. "It has all changed," he said morosely. "The house where I was born is no longer there. There's a new one of stone with a tiled roof when it used to be all timber and thatch."

"Is that not a good thing?" Will asked, sending a groom to fetch Forcilez.

Serlo grimaced. "I suppose it is, but I always thought my house would be there, even if my parents were not. I expected to see something familiar, and for a moment I did not know who or where I was."

Will shook his head. "I have come to the conclusion that there is no point dwelling on the past or worrying about the future."

"There was talk at the clerks' tables that they've sent the boy to Bristol."

"What boy?" Will said with mild exasperation at Serlo's habit of leaping from one thought to another.

"The empress's son. She and the Earl of Gloucester have employed tutors for him—Adelard of Bath no less." Serlo's eyes gleamed with admiration. "They have set him up with his own household, so it seems that he is staying for the moment."

"It is to be expected if they want him to be recognised as heir to the throne, but they have to keep him safe too."

"The empress's barons have sworn to recognise him as king when the time comes," Serlo said. "They held an oath-taking in Devizes at Christmas."

"Is there anything you do not know?" The groom arrived with Forcilez and Will turned to mount the stallion.

"I try my best not to leave gaps in my knowledge, sire."

Will grunted with sour amusement.

"Would you swear for him?" Serlo asked curiously.

"Not to the detriment of the king," Will replied as he swung his leg across the saddle. "Besides, swearing allegiance to an untried child would be leaping out of the cauldron into the fire, would it not?" He wondered if Adeliza had asked Serlo to work on him concerning that particular subject, and thoughtfully eyed the little clerk as he went off on some business at the leper house.

He turned Forcilez towards the abbey, then drew rein as he heard the sound of shouts and the clash of weapons from the direction of the nunnery. His men came hastening from their tents and cooking fires, eyes wide and bodies tense with alarm.

"Arm up and get your horses!" Will commanded. "Martin, see if you can find out what's happening but don't take risks."

"Sire." A young serjeant saluted and ran to his horse.

Will dismounted and gave Forcilez to the groom. "Hold him while I put on my hauberk." Cursing under his breath, Will ran to his tent and, with the aid of a squire, swiftly donned his padded undertunic and mail shirt. As he buckled his swordbelt, he ordered the youth to harness up the baggage ponies and pack the valuables, just in case.

Outside, Adelard had assembled the Albini troop into tight formation. The sounds of battle had escalated and as Will was remounting Forcilez, the smell of smoke began to waft on the evening wind from the direction of the abbey. He leaned down to take his shield and spear from the squire.

"There is only Robert of Gloucester in the vicinity," Adelard said grimly.

"You think he is preempting the king's strike at Wareham?"

"Could be, sire."

Will nodded. "It is what I would do, and Gloucester is always ready to seize an opportunity."

"But what about the king?"

Will compressed his lips and urged Forcilez out of the leper-house gates on to the road that led one way to Wilton and the other to Salisbury. Dusk was closing in, the sun sinking in a yellow pool, smudged by long streamers of charcoal cloud. The smell of smoke was thicker now and Will could hear the crackle of flames. As he picked up the pace, Martin came galloping back towards him and drew rein in a swirl of dust.

"It's the Earl of Gloucester, sire," he panted. "And Miles FitzWalter and William of Salisbury. They've fired the village and the abbey!"

"The king, did you see the king?"

"No, sire, but one of William D'Ypres's Flemings said that he and the bishop of Winchester have fled under hard pursuit to the legate's castle at Downton, and everyone should scatter as best they may!"

Several fleeing horsemen burst out of the dusk at full gallop. "Go!" one of them bellowed at Will. "Gloucester has overrun the abbey—flee for your lives! The roads south and north are cut off!" He reined his horse around Forcilez and spurred away.

Before Will could turn to give orders, more soldiers arrived at a hard gallop in pursuit of those who had just raced through. He barely raised his shield in time to ward off a vicious blow from the mallet wielded by a knight on a roan stallion. He groped for his sword, drew it, and twitched the reins. Forcilez half reared and struck out at his opponent's horse with pawing forehooves. The other stallion shied, and Will was able to land a blow on his adversary's unguarded leg. Blood spattered and the man screamed and reined away. Will pivoted Forcilez to take on another opponent, this time slashing through the reins and clipping the destrier on its neck. The knight retaliated, his blade nicking Will's cheek.

"Sound the retreat!" Will bellowed to Adelard, aware that reinforcements could arrive from Wilton at any moment. A flail connected with his ribs and the blow shot the air out of his lungs. Forcilez turned and lashed out and turned again, and he praised God for the stallion's courage, training, and implacable nature. He rallied enough to strike again and heard the blare of the horn. Once, twice. His knight Milo Bassett came to his aid and they hacked themselves free and clapped spurs to their destriers' flanks. The Angevin knights hurtled in pursuit, eager to capture an earl. Forcilez lacked speed but was sure-footed and strong, and this paid off as one of the chasing men drew level. As he reached to seize hold of Will, his horse stumbled. There was a sickening crack as the destrier's foreleg snapped, and the man was thrown and hit the ground hard. Two other pursuing knights were too close to swerve and were brought down, and the others, now lacking superior numbers, drew back.

Will and his men rode on hard, using the last of the light to put more distance between them and their enemy. Looking over his shoulder Will could see the glow of fire from the direction of Wilton. The village and abbey were well and truly alight, and it was obvious that the Angevins had carried all before them. He put his hand up to his face and brought it away red-fingered. Most of his men bore superficial wounds. A couple had deeper cuts that needed binding and stitching, and there was one empty saddle where one of his serjeants had died in the skirmish. They had some of their baggage, but all the tents and food supplies were lost.

He turned swiftly at the sound of hooves on the track to his left and, with pounding heart, drew his sword. Moments later, a white mule emerged through a narrow gap in the hedgerow with Serlo astride. Will slumped with relief. "You fool, I could have cut off your head," he snapped.

Looking aggrieved, Serlo gestured to the panniers attached to the mule. "I have clean bandages in here and ointments, and needles for stitching flesh if anyone is in need of attention. I thought you would be pleased to see me."

Will exhaled hard. "Indeed I am. If nothing else this night, you at least are a godsend."

Serlo glanced back towards the glow from Wilton. "My lady the queen is not going to like this," he said.

Will grimaced and felt the sword cut tug along his cheekbone. "No," he said, his heart sinking further. "She isn't."

❖ ❖ ❖

Adeliza tiptoed into the bedchamber to look at the sleeping children. The soft glow from a lantern set in a niche near the open bed curtains illuminated Wilkin spread-eagled on his back, his chest lightly rising and falling and his face flushed in slumber. Two-year-old Adelis was curled up like a little hedgehog, her thumb in her mouth, and Godfrey, five months, was making soft snoring sounds in his crib. Sarah, his nurse, was gently rocking the cradle and working wool from her distaff to her spindle, a task that could be done in dim light. Watching their innocent and vulnerable slumber, her eyes prickled with tears. It grieved her to think of the many children unable to sleep safely in their beds because of all the strife in the world.

After a while, she crept out and, in a pensive mood, sat down by the open window in her chamber to work on some plain sewing by the last of the light. She glanced at the length of sheeting draped over two trestles. Earlier, Wilkin had constructed a campaign tent for himself and a couple of playmates. They had pretended to be soldiers at war. Listening to the martial talk of little boys still firmly tied to the apron strings but fiercely practising their future roles had saddened Adeliza deeply. She knew that, to survive, they had to learn to be warriors, and how to control and command, but it was as if nowhere was free from the taint of violence, even her own chamber.

Hearing a shout from the walls and the sound of the gates being opened, she set down her sewing and gazed out of the window.

Melisande joined her. "Who is it?"

The servants were kindling torches and she could hear the jingle and clatter of mounted men. "It's the earl!" Adeliza said in astonishment. "Will's home!" She clapped her hands, and bade servants bring food and prepare a tub. Remembering Wilkin's prayer in the chapel earlier, she praised God for answering so promptly, but at the same time felt worried. To return at this late hour suggested they had pushed the horses, which could mean either good news or bad.

Arriving in the great hall to greet the returning men, she recoiled from the powerful stench of sweat, blood, and hard-ridden horses. Will, clad in his mail, was staggering with exhaustion. A clotted cut slashed one cheek and his eyes were glassy.

"We have wounded," he said. "Do what you can."

"Wounded?" She stared at him in consternation and dismay.

"Robert of Gloucester caught us unawares," he said. "We escaped by the skin of our teeth." His gaze slid from hers as if he was unable to bear the weight of contact. "Stephen is free and clear, thank Christ, but others have not been so fortunate..." He broke off and rubbed his forehead with his cuff, leaving a black smear. "Martel's been taken prisoner by Robert of Gloucester..." He staggered again. Frightened, Adeliza called two burly menservants to support him and bade them bring him to her chamber, but he pushed them off. "No," he said. "I must see to my men first."

She gave a slight nod because she knew about duty and responsibility. However, she bade the servants stay close as she accompanied him to see what she could do. Most of the injuries were cuts and contusions and small broken bones. The main need was clean water, bandages, sustenance, and rest. These things having been provided, together with words of comfort, she eventually managed to persuade Will to their chamber. Food and drink had been set out, and water was heating in two cauldrons over the hearth, which attendants now poured into a tub, mixing in jugs of cold to adjust the temperature. Will's squire helped him to remove his armour and Will hissed through his teeth as he bent over so the youth could pull the garments over his head.

"You are injured!" Adeliza reached to him in consternation.

"Cracked ribs," he panted. "I took a blow from a flail when we were fighting our way out."

The armour removed, he dismissed the squire and let Adeliza finish helping him undress. She gasped at the sight of the purple and red mottles flushing his right side. "Dear Jesu! And your face!"

"It could have been much worse, believe me." He stepped gingerly into the tub and eased down into the hot water.

"Where was this battle? You have not said?" She tried to keep the panic from her voice, hoping it was not close to home.

He clenched his eyelids. "It was at Wilton."

Adeliza went rigid. "Wilton?" That was very close to home indeed.

He uttered a soft groan. "I wish I did not have to tell you. Stephen wanted to capture Wareham from Robert of Gloucester and bade us muster at the abbey."

"You did not tell me that when you left to join him."

"I did not want to upset you, and all I knew was that it was the muster point. I did not know he was fortifying the nunnery until we arrived."

"He put soldiers in the nunnery?" Her voice rose in outrage. "He used Wilton to make war?" She felt as if she had been stabbed. "To occupy a nunnery is against God's holy word! How could Stephen do such a thing—and how could you let him?" Her voice was harsh with disgust.

"I didn't let him." Will snapped. "He was already in occupation when we arrived. I made my camp at Fugglestone—and before you rail at me about that, I gave alms to the lazar house, and my men made their billets in a field away from the chapel."

She turned away from him and, in a fruitless attempt to calm her anger, began fussing with a pile of towels. He spoke as if he thought his actions made everything all right.

"Stephen might have taken over the nunnery to billet his men and discuss his strategies," he said in a hard voice, "but it was Robert of Gloucester and Miles of Hereford who threw torches into the buildings and burned the place to the ground."

"Wilton is burned?" Adeliza whirled to face him, and now she truly was furious.

He grimaced. "Gloucester's troops sacked the abbey and set it alight. I heard that they even seized men who had claimed sanctuary at the altar."

Adeliza pressed her hand to her mouth and sat down abruptly as the strength left her legs. "Dear God," she said with revulsion. "There is no end to this, is there?" Wilton. She tried to envisage the sanctuary in flames. Her retreat from the world after Henry's death. The nuns who had been her comfort and her support. She thought of the rough tramp of soldiers' feet in the cloister, and imagined the torches whirling through the air and landing in the thatch. "What happens now? What of the people burned out of their homes? They cannot turn for succour to secure castle walls and the arms of a waiting wife. How can the Church help them, when the Church itself is naught but ashes? It does not matter who set the torches, husband, the result is the same."

He continued with his ablutions, his movements slow and painful and his shoulders rigid. She wondered if he was trying to cleanse himself of more than just the grime of hard riding and battle.

"You may not have thrown the torch, but you have dwelt in the house of God with a sword in your hand," she said, hurling her words against his silence.

"Peace, wife," he replied in a dull voice. "What has been done to Wilton is a terrible thing and a sin, I agree. I am no callous warmonger to be ignorant of the desperate plight of the people caught up in this battle."

"Peace? How can I be at peace when my house has been razed by the man my husband follows and honours?" Bitterness scalded her throat. "What is going to happen to all of us if we continue to burn and rend and destroy? What will be left for our sons and daughters but a wilderness of ashes and bones, bereft of all moral worth?"

"I said peace!" he snarled. "I have enough bruises and cuts without taking more from your tongue!"

"As you wish, sire." She plucked her cloak from the peg in the wall and flung it on. "Have your peace!" She spat the last word as she swept from the room. Once outside, she put her face in her hands and allowed herself a brief shudder of tears, and then felt guilty because tears were not going to help Wilton.

She felt as if a hard splinter had entered her heart. Was this how Matilda felt? Was this how it began, before gradually everything solidified as the splinter worked its way inwards and there was no longer any flexibility and no joy from which to fashion a smile?

She made her way to the chapel to kneel in a holy place that had not been defiled by war and pray for the nunnery. The warm colours and the soft light in the darkness comforted her. She counted her prayer beads through her fingers and asked God for strength and guidance.

She was still kneeling when she heard a soft footfall. A moment later, Will eased himself down at her side and crossed his breast. An herbal scent of bathwater wafted across the space between them and his hair was a tangle of short damp curls. The space between them was stiff with silent emotion as they each rendered their devotion to God.

Eventually Will raised his head and picked up the wooden horse that Wilkin had left on the altar step. It was the figure of Forcilez he had whittled when on campaign with Stephen several years ago.

"What's this, an offering?"

The toy served to break the silence between them. "I expect it is," she said. "I was teaching our son to honour all God's creatures and all God's people, whatever their station in life."

He turned the piece over in his big hands.

"He was praying this morning for your return."

Will eased painfully to his feet. "Well, he got his wish." He took her hand in his free one. "I have always tried to do my best and be honourable. I freely acknowledge I make mistakes, but I have never acted out of false intent or malice."

She looked at him. The cut on his cheek was an angry red stripe and his breathing was shallow. His gaze beseeched her for clemency. "I do not doubt your honour, or your intention," she said, "but when I think of what has been done to Wilton by men on both sides of the divide, who hold their own honour on high as an example to all, then I despair."

He screwed up his face. "There is nothing I can do to restore Wilton to what it was or change the past, but I swear to you, and to God, that those who wish it may take shelter at Arundel, or Rising, or Buckenham. I will see to the building of the shelters and hostels, if you will see to the people." He made the sign of the Cross. "At least I can offer refuges and new homes on lands that are unlikely to be attacked." He set his arm around her, still clutching their son's wooden image of Forcilez. "Do not turn against me," he muttered against the top of her head, and she heard his voice choke. "I could not bear strife at the heart of my home. You are my only sanctuary."

She drew her head back to look at him and even as earlier she had seen the man inside her eldest son, now she saw the child inside his father, seeking comfort and reassurance, and felt the shard in her heart slip and dissolve, even though there was a scar where it had been. "Come," she said. "It is late and dark and the only sanctuary we should be in other than a church is that of our bed. Let all else wait until the morning."

Forty-nine

THE DEEP OF WINTER WAS A TIME TO STAY INDOORS BY THE hearth and play chess. Matilda sat over a board with Henry in her chamber at Devizes and watched his gaze dart in swift thought before he picked up the chunky ivory bishop and moved him two spaces. Then he smiled at her. He was not yet eleven years old, but already he understood the complexities of the game and was offended if anyone suggested he play the simpler popular chance version of dice-chess.

She sought to work out the trap she knew he was planning. Think ahead. Always think ahead. His tutoring at Bristol under Master Adelard was intensive and all bent towards moulding him into a king capable of ruling England and Normandy as her father had done. She had come to the bitter but inevitable realisation she would never be queen of England, no matter what men had sworn to her, because, in the end, it was beyond their capabilities to follow a woman. But a woman could still rule and advise from behind a throne. She moved her queen to block Henry's bishop. That would give him food for thought. Strange how queens had so much power in chess, yet kings had none.

The year had been one of advances and retreats, successes and failures. Her resources were thin on the ground but at least she knew the core of men around her were dedicated and unlikely to desert. Her cause had been aided by the death of Pope Innocent in September, which meant that the bishop of Winchester no longer held the position of legate. And with a new, more sympathetic pope, the way was open for fresh negotiations on the matter of who had the right to England's crown.

Henry had spent longer this time pondering the board, his eyes narrow and his hand cupping his chin. She was pleased with his progress. When he had come from his father, he had had difficulty in sitting still for even a moment, but these days he could focus if he was given a task that demanded concentration and thought—for the time it took, at least.

He made his move, sweeping decisively down the flank with his rook, and expending some of his cooped-up energy. Matilda made her own reply swiftly. Henry had obviously anticipated what she would do, for he immediately struck with his knight, his grey eyes shining. Once again, she saw the trap, but it was now double-edged and she was only a few moves away from defeat whatever she did.

"Oh, very clever," she laughed. "I concede you the victory— but you had to think hard, didn't you?"

Henry grinned. "Yes, but I like thinking," he said, "and I like winning."

"Indeed!" The competitive urge in her son was as bright as his hair, and had been deliberately fostered, together with the ability to focus on the goal while keeping an eye on peripheral dangers. "But you must learn to weather the times you do not win and be prepared to endure."

"Papa says that too."

"Well, your papa is wise," she said neutrally. Rising from the board she went to look out of the window on the stark winter landscape. She often had occasion to deal with Geoffrey through formal letters and discussions about their sons and the state of Normandy, but she no longer felt any emotional attachment, and the long separation had weaned her off the corrosive but compelling physical desire she had felt for him. And with the waning of that dark need, other volatile feelings had died. She no longer hated him; she could be detached and impartial, because he meant nothing to her beyond the need for his soldierly qualities and his diplomatic skills. She saw him every day in Henry, but more strongly still did she see the royal blood of Normandy and England. Henry was the son of an empress and the grandson of a great king. Beside that, the blood of his father was a thing of no consequence—in that, at least, her father had been right.

Henry left the chessboard and came to stand at her side, stepping up to the embrasure so that he could see out of the open window and sniff the cold, damp air.

"One day all of this will be yours." She set her arm around his narrow shoulders. "You must rule it wisely, like your namesake, your grandfather and his father before him, who was brought here by God. God has ordained that you should rule this country in honesty and humility, tending always to its needs and administering with justice. That is a big lesson to learn and a great responsibility."

"I know, Mother." He jutted his jaw. "I will govern as king, and I will do it until I die and nothing will hold me back." The earnest tone of his voice made her look at him fondly and smile and ruffle his hair because he was a child, and yet he spoke like a man and she was proud of him.

"I mean it," he said with intensity.

She gave him an assessing look and pursed her lips. A feeling of recognition settled in her stomach. She knew how he felt because she felt that way too, and it was as if the spark had passed one to the other.

She turned at a sudden touch on her arm, and faced her

brother Robert. At the sight of his grave expression, her pleasure vanished. "What is it?"

Robert's gaze flicked to Henry and back to her. "Prepare yourself for bad tidings," he said.

"How bad?" Her arm was still around Henry's shoulder and she cupped her hand protectively. "Has Stephen...?"

Robert shook his head. "It is nothing to do with Stephen. Miles FitzWalter is dead, God rest his soul."

Matilda stared at her brother in shock. "How?" Miles was a senior commander and good friend. He had opened Gloucester to her when she first came to England. He was a constant. He couldn't be dead.

"Hunting deer," Robert said. "One of his own knights shot wildly and struck his lord instead of the stag. He died almost instantly."

"I should have kept him at court," she said, feeling sick. "He would have lived then."

Robert shook his head. "You could not have prevented this. If you set a fence around him, he would have broken out. He lived his life as if it was one long hunt."

"But such a waste, God rest his soul." She crossed herself and her voice shook. "He was a brave man and a loyal vassal." *And how will I replace him?*

Robert looked at Henry who had crossed himself too. "Do you remember Miles FitzWalter, lad?"

"He gave me sword lessons," Henry said, his eyes wide. "He promised to take me hunting."

"Thank Christ he did not." Matilda resisted the urge to hug him to her breast. How vulnerable they all were. Who knew when death would strike and scatter all their plans like straws on the flood?

Fifty

BRISTOL, MARCH 1144

MATILDA PATTED HER MARE'S NECK AND INHALED THE DANK air of late winter as she trotted along a forest path with Brian. Ahead Henry cantered along on his grey pony, dogs running at his side as he chased small game through stands of oak, ash, and elm, their branches stark and black in the early spring afternoon. Various members of the court rode ahead and behind and the atmosphere for once was relaxed and informal. Earlier in the day, Henry had jointly witnessed a charter to Humphrey de Bohun and another to Reading Abbey.

Matilda had come to Bristol to celebrate Easter and discuss Henry's education. His progress thus far pleased her greatly and although times were difficult, his presence had put new heart into their cause. Henry's charm, his fierce energy and obvious deep intelligence had won over her own supporters and convinced them that this was indeed their future king. Watching him yell and spur faster, she smiled with pride at his fearless vitality, and tried not to think that he might take a tumble.

"He rides better than I did at that age," Brian said.

She glanced at him. He looked weary, with deep lines carved in his cheeks and seaming his eye corners. In the pale light his complexion still wore winter's indoor grey. She was concerned for him. He had recently been sick with a heavy cold. They were all exhausted from the long drag of war, and this time of year was never easy with its endless dark days and sparse rations. The evenings had started to draw out, but as yet there was no sign of spring greenery to alleviate the grey. She had intentionally come on this ride to raise her spirits and sweep away the cobwebs. "I wager you were a fine boy though," she said to him.

He raised his brows. "What do you mean by that, domina?"

"I imagine you were as active as my son and ranged far and wide before my father took you into his household."

The lines at his eye corners deepened, but in the direction of a smile. "Yes, I did enjoy roaming free, and even at your father's court I was allowed to do so. He let us all off the leash now and again. He knew how to train unruly pups, did your father." His expression sobered. "Of course, in those days anyone in the land could roam free in safety and not be bothered. It was a different world when your father was alive."

"Yes," she said, "sadly it was, but those times will come again."

"Will they?" He looked grim. "I have had to turn robber to keep my men and horses fed. I raid merchant trains. I steal horses and sacks of grain. I waylay anyone who looks as if they might have wealth about their person and I rob them down to their braies. I never imagined I would do such things to survive, but I have to, and it sickens me."

She knew he was referring to an incident before Christmas when he had intercepted some merchants on their way to the bishop of Winchester's fair and confiscated their goods and chattels. The bishop had threatened to excommunicate Brian, who had written a blistering response to the effect that the good bishop had changed sides more often than the wind changed direction, and that had his support of Matilda stayed constant and had he upheld her as queen, the raids would never have taken place because there would have been no need.

She gave him a firm look. "We have all been forced to act in ways we would not choose."

Brian said quietly, "Your sire was a father to me. I honour his memory in the best way I know—by honouring and serving his daughter to the best of my ability, and while there is breath in my body, I shall do so."

She put out her hand to his across their horses and touched his sleeve in a brief gesture. He swallowed and set his jaw.

Henry arrived in a flurry of dogs and galloping pony. As she withdrew her hand, Brian raised his own to rub the back of his neck as if at an irritation, but when he saw her looking, he redirected the movement to check that the neck brooch of his tunic was secure.

On their return, a messenger from Geoffrey was waiting for them, his eyes alight as he knelt and handed her a sealed letter. "Great news, domina!" he cried. "Rouen has surrendered to the Count of Anjou. Normandy is won!"

Matilda hastily broke the seal and opened the letter. Triumph coursed through her, and joy, but mingled with it was a thread of vile darkness because Geoffrey's success emphasised her own inability to take and hold England. Her golden husband had achieved what eluded her. "That is wonderful news!" she said, swallowing the bitter and celebrating the sweet. Gesturing the messenger to his feet, she took a ring from her finger and gave it to him in payment for the tidings.

Henry had been listening to the exchange. "Papa has won?" His grey eyes shone. "I knew he would!" He drew his toy sword and saluted the air. Robert had heard too, and Brian, and they were smiling broadly. The news spread through the hall like fire and with the same warming effect. England might still be a frozen struggle, but Normandy was achieved. Matilda turned away while she composed herself, because the letter contained other news that cut her heart.

She heard Robert calling for a tun of the best wine to be broached in celebration. Tonight there would be feasting and toasts and she would wear her jewelled silks and furs to honour Geoffrey's success—which was her success too, and Henry's. She would rejoice with a glitter so bright and hard that no one would see how she bled.

❖❖❖

Henry was supposed to be preparing for bed, but when Matilda entered his sleeping chamber, he was still clad in the tunic he had worn to the feast. His bedcover was strewn with an eclectic jumble representing his interests: a bridle, a hawking gauntlet, a gaming board, two books, several pieces of parchment with diagrams and bits of untidy writing…and Rumpus, the terrier Maude of Wallingford had given him. Rumpus had spread an inscription of muddy paw and belly marks across the embroidered quilt. At the sight of Matilda, he began thumping his tail on the bed as if beating a drum, and she hastily looked away before she became the recipient of his enthusiasm. To add to the detritus, Henry's clothing chest was open, spilling entrails of garments across the floor.

"Where is your chamberlain?" she demanded. Henry was too old to need a nurse, but there should be servants to attend to him.

"I said I could see to myself." He gave her a mulish look. "I am old enough."

"Are you indeed?" She looked round. "This place is a pigsty."

"I was going to tidy it, but I had to take Rumpus for a piss first."

That explained the muddy paw prints and why he was still in his clothes. "Do you often wander about the castle at night?"

He shrugged. "I talk to the soldiers if I can't sleep, or I walk about and think. Sometimes I read or I write things, or I play chess with myself."

Given his prodigious energy, she suspected he did not spend much time in slumber. She wondered how well she really knew this child of hers. For certain he had the will and intelligence to be a king, and the education and the curiosity. She was unsure where his inclination to tear through life like a whirlwind came from, unless it was a trait that had been her father's as a child and had become weighted down with time and the burdens of kingship.

"Your father wants you to return to Normandy," she said. "Now that you have spent time in England and have come to know the men who will help you rule when you are king, he needs you with him, because even as you will be a king in England, you will be a duke there and the barons need reminding."

She watched him weigh up her words thoughtfully in a way that spoke of a calculating man, not an eleven-year-old boy, and, as she studied his expression, she knew it would not be long, irrespective of his years, before he truly was capable of governing a country. "When must I leave?" he asked. There was no regret in his voice but neither did she receive the impression he was eager to go.

"As soon as the wind is set fair for a sea crossing and your baggage packed." She gave the wreckage of his room a meaningful look.

He jutted his jaw. "And when I come back to England again, it will be to rule it."

Matilda swallowed. She might never be England's queen, but she would be the mother of the greatest king Christendom had ever seen, of that she was certain, even if for the moment he had an unbroken voice and only came up to her shoulder.

"Yes," she said. "That is your destiny."

Fifty-one

I CAN SEE THE CASTLE, MAMA, I CAN SEE THE CASTLE! I WAS the first!" Wilkin leaped up and down on the ship, and pointed to a distant gleam of white, his voice shrill with excitement. Will had been telling him for a while to look out for the castle and he had been leaning at the prow, eager to be the first.

"Yes, indeed you were," Adeliza said, and picked up two-year-old Godfrey in her arms to show him too. "See the castle."

"Cackle," said Godfrey.

"Almost there," Will said to his three-year-old daughter, who sat on his shoulders, her pale gold curls ruffling in the stiff sea breeze.

Across the flat sandy heathland, the new castle at Rising stood like a gleaming white tooth in a gum. The surrounding ringwork was low and offered little defence, but that had not been his intent. He wanted Rising to proclaim itself and be an aesthetic haven amidst the chaos of war.

In the basketwork travelling cradle, six-month-old Reiner had started to wail like a little gull. The nurse picked him up, but Will gestured. "Give him to me," he said.

"Sire, his swaddling is wet."

"No matter. Give him to me while you find fresh."

Taking his youngest child in his free arm, ignoring the heavy dampness of the swaddling clouts, Will faced him towards the shoreline and the lime-washed gleam of Rising's walls. He wanted all of his children to see this, whether they understood or not. Scaffolding still caged the edifice and not all of the stone was painted, but enough had been to give a fine impression, especially against the deep blue of sky and sea, and the green of the reclaimed land dotted with grazing sheep.

As the ship navigated the river channel, Will handed Reiner back to the nurse and went to stand beside his wife. Adeliza had been unwell for several months following their son's birth and was still frail; he wanted to see the pink return to her cheeks and to give her something beyond the continuing conflict to think about. He had chosen to sail rather than ride because there was less chance of meeting opposition and the late August weather was fine and clear with a good breeze for the sails. The journey would be less wearing for his wife and the sea approach would show the castle to its best advantage.

There had been fighting in East Anglia earlier in the year as Stephen had subdued the rebellious Hugh Bigod, and there had been a skirmish at Lincoln with Ranulf of Chester, but for now the area was reasonably stable.

"You will see many changes since we were here last," he said, slipping his arm around her shoulders. "Before it was only dreams and plans built on scant foundations."

"Is that not the story of many a life?" she asked him with a smile.

His eyes sparkled. "Indeed, but not everyone sees them brought to fruition."

Adeliza felt a warm pang of affection as she leaned against Will's reassuring solid strength. He loved to plan and build. She would come upon him sitting at a trestle surrounded by heaps of parchment covered in drawings and sketches. He often entertained master masons at his board and exchange ideas with them. He would sit on the floor with Wilkin, constructing miniature buildings out of pieces of wood and stone, and his big hands would be sensitive and knowing—as they were on her body. His childlike enthusiasm always pricked a tender spot within her. Far better the builder than the warrior intent on destruction. She knew this visit was only a lull, that he would go to war again once the harvests were in the barns and his lands visited, but for a while she had him and the children to herself, and perhaps here she could find the space to recoup the energy she had lacked ever since Reiner's birth. She felt well today; the tingling sea air was rejuvenating.

Meandering upriver towards the castle, they passed a white dovecote with the Albini lion banner flying from its tiled roof. A flock of birds took off from the shingles and haloed the building, their breasts dazzling in the sunlight. Godfrey pointed to them with a squeal, and Adeliza kissed his soft cheek. The briny smell of the river filled her nose and mingled with the green of the land. Grazing sheep lifted their heads to watch the boat sail past and the shepherd's dogs ran along the bank, barking, which set Teri to barking too until Will silenced him with a sharp command and a click of his fingers.

The ship nudged in gently to moor at a landing stage that gave access to a small, moated building where grooms waited with horses and a two-wheeled cart lined with cushions for the nurses and children. Adeliza and Will had two matching grey palfreys, one adorned with a sumptuous padded ladies' saddle. Will helped Adeliza to mount and handed up to her a fat pouch of silver coins. "You will need this," he said.

He had been busy planning not just the castle, but a town to prosper around it, and also a leprosarium. The hospital of Saint Giles stood outside the town wall and consisted of individual dwellings for twenty lepers attached to a small chapel, where they could attend daily prayers. The timber houses, white-washed and neatly thatched, were ready to receive occupants. Adeliza's task while at Rising was to select the first ones.

The master of the hospital and five lay attendants waited before the church to greet Adeliza and receive the bag of silver in alms. She spoke warmly to the master and bade him attend her on the morrow to discuss plans for the leper house, and then rode on into the town, noting the neat plots and thoughtful layout. The decorated west front of the new church, dedicated to Saint Lawrence, filled her heart and she gave Will a look brimming with love because his efforts were much more than a token gesture; they showed a true desire and enthusiasm to give glory to God.

Beyond the town, a short ride brought them to the castle, and having crossed the ringwork ditch they entered under the arch of the gatehouse.

"Portcullis!" announced Wilkin proudly, pointing at the jagged teeth above their heads. "That's a portcullis!"

"Clever lad!" Will ruffled his son's curls.

"Portcullis!" Adelis aped her brother, shouting the word from the cart much to everyone's amusement.

Once dismounted, Adeliza gazed at the castle, perfectly framed in the gatehouse archway. The forebuilding was decorated with blind arcading and geometrical designs that echoed the church. Two rondels depicted amusing animal faces, the right-hand one having a distinct look of Teri. The great doors, banded in wrought-iron shapes and curlicues, stood open to reveal a long series of steps, rising under an archway and leading towards a vestibule.

"I wanted to build you a palace," Will said with anxiety in his eyes. "I hope you approve."

Her throat tightened with emotion. All the work on the

outside (except perhaps for the rondels) was designed to her taste, not his. "I am overwhelmed," she said. "Approve is not an adequate word." She wiped her eyes on the corner of her sleeve.

He held out his arm. Adeliza laid her hand along his wrist and processed with him in courtly fashion through the first door and up the stairs, the children following behind with their nurses. Passing under an arch with decorated columns, she came to a vestibule facing a splendid series of arches curving one over the other, leading into a great hall with a fireplace set on a stone slab in the centre of the room. A hanging bearing the gold Albini lion decorated the end wall, with two carved and painted chairs set on the dais below it.

Adeliza felt as if her eyes were not large enough to take in all the detail. It was like having a serving dish piled high with so many delectable foods that just by looking you could almost lose your appetite.

Beyond the great hall lay the chapel, embellished with ornate arches and more blind arcading. Painting had begun and the main colours were blue and white, for the colours of the Virgin's cloak and veil. A lamp burned above the altar, which was adorned by a silver cross and candlesticks.

Adeliza could only shake her head. Will opened his arms and she went into them and pressed her head against his breast.

"Why is Mama crying?" Wilkin demanded.

"Because this is a big surprise she was not expecting."

Wilkin frowned. "I like surprises," he said. "Doesn't Mama?"

"Yes, she does; her tears are happy ones. Go with Bernice and she will find you something to eat and drink. Your mother will talk to you later."

The nurses removed the children, and Adeliza knelt to pray. Knowing her foibles, Will knelt with her, waiting until she was ready.

At length she raised her head and wiped her eyes. "I will

have to explain to him now why sometimes people cry with joy," she said wryly.

"But not just yet," he said. "There is something else I want you to see."

Adeliza shook her head. "I am not sure I can bear any more surprises. My cup is already overflowing."

"You can bear this one, I promise." Smiling broadly, he led her by the hand from the chapel, back to the hall, and then through to a well-appointed living chamber with two recessed south-facing windows and between them a large fireplace. An ample bed stood at the back of the room, made up with mattresses, but as yet no hangings and covers.

Adeliza gazed round. "It is very fine," she said, relieved that there was nothing here to overwhelm her saturated emotions, but cautious because his grin was brighter than ever.

"And I will show you something finer yet." He gestured towards two narrow doorways set in the west wall. Her curiosity piqued, Adeliza went to the first one. Along a narrow, skewed passageway, she came to a door, and beyond that, a latrine with a small looped window giving air and light. There was a recess for a candle and a polished wooden seat. "You show me a latrine as a thing of wonder?" She eyed him askance.

He shrugged and gestured. "Now look at the other one."

Mystified, she did so, and found an almost identical garderobe, except that this one had a triangular urinal set into the wall.

"You always complain I splash the seat," he said. "That will no longer be a problem if we have one each."

Adeliza stared and her shoulders began to shake again. Tears filled her eyes. "Oh Will!" She was laughing so hard she could scarcely breathe and it was his turn to look askance. Clutching her aching stomach, she stumbled to the bed and collapsed on the mattresses. "You showed me a town and a hospital," she said, raising one hand to wipe her eyes. "I was expecting that. You showed me a church and a castle with fine decoration, and I thought you had excelled yourself. You showed me a chapel that is so beautiful that it hurts me in here." She pressed her hand to her heart. "And then you bring me here, and as if it is the greatest prize of all, you show me a pair of latrines!"

"Are you not pleased?" He looked anxious.

She fought to contain her hilarity because her stomach was aching, and she did not want to hurt him. "Of course I am pleased! It is a wonderful surprise and I bless your kindness. Not many husbands would be so thoughtful."

His colour heightened.

He seldom bought her fripperies such as silks and jewels. If she wanted those she had to see to it herself via her chamberlain. Will rarely noticed details such as the colour of her gown or if she had made a special effort to dress for him. He took it all for granted and she had to fish for compliments. But then he would suddenly surprise her by bringing her a copy of Aesop or an ivory-covered prayer book. He would build her a chapel beautiful enough to make her cry...and her own private latrine, revealing that, in his own way, he had been paying attention to her after all and all the time. It was something very rare and precious that Henry had never done, despite making her a queen.

He came and sat beside her. "I tried to think of the things you would like—or find appropriate," he said and kissed her, softly at first, and then with growing ardour.

"I am not certain this is appropriate, my lord," she said, but with a smile in her voice and quickened breathing. "We should have hangings on the bed at the least. What if someone comes in and finds us like this?"

He rose and going to the door, he shot the bolt across. "They won't."

Her blood turned to honey in her veins. Lying together in daylight did seem slightly sinful, but that very sense of daring was erotic and it was her duty to love her husband and procreate with him; and in that sense, it was very appropriate indeed.

Fifty-two

GRIPPING A HALYARD AND LEANING FORWARD, THE WIND ruffling his copper-gold hair, Henry watched the English coastline grow out of the haze and take on solid shape and knew it was a portent, because this land would one day be his. The sea slapping against the strakes of the ship was a choppy grey edged with whitecaps, and reflected the state of the sky, and the wind was so raw that his face was numb, but he was exhilarated, both by what lay on the horizon and by the sound of the soldier's banter behind him on the ship. He was bound for England with a small band of mercenaries. He had no ready money to pay them beyond a few coins and jewels of his own that he had scraped together, but had promised them rich pickings when they arrived. He was a week short of his fourteenth birthday, but he knew he was a man. Indeed, boyhood had always been a trial because he had never seen himself as a child and hated it when others did.

He had organised this mission without parental knowledge or consent, but he intended to show them that he was a contender now, and could do his part. Besides, he was needed in England. King Stephen had the upper hand and that had to change. He had to prove he was a leader of men and show the barons he was England's rightful king, especially as Stephen was attempting to have his own son Eustace crowned to succeed to the throne.

Thus far Rome and the archbishop of Canterbury were resisting, but Henry knew he had to make himself the only choice. He was not simply undertaking this voyage to stir up trouble with armed conflict. He intended taking a diplomatic approach too because a king had to be able to negotiate, as well as fight.

Gulls circled over the ship, crying their message of approaching land, and two fishing boats were casting their nets a little off the steerboard side of the bows. Very soon the news of his landing would be spreading like wildfire. Henry smiled a little and pinched his upper lip, where a soft coppery moustache was beginning to grow in. His first intent was to spread rumours, and watch them grow in the telling. Thus could fifty men become five hundred, or even five thousand.

❖❖❖

Will knelt in Arundel's chapel and prayed for the safe deliverance of Adeliza and their unborn child. The midwives had been with her all night and into this blustery March morning with rain spattering in the wind. She had not fared well while carrying, and except for the round swell of her womb and her engorged breasts, she was skin and bone, with exhaustion-shadowed eyes. Pressing his clasped hands to his forehead, he swore to God that if she survived this birthing, he would not seek her bed again, no matter how much she entreated him, or how much he desired her, because her safety and well-being far outweighed a few moments of intimacy, physical pleasure, and her driving need to prove she was fruitful.

When eventually he made to rise from his knees, the pain and stiffness was so great that he could scarcely move. He walked slowly round the chapel, easing feeling and movement back into his limbs, and then went to the door. Outside, the children were playing tag, their voices bright and eager. Wilkin, his light brown curls tamed by a recent haircut, was ducking and twisting as Adelis sped after him, her skirts kilted up like a peasant's. She was as fast and lithe as a boy, with vibrant, delicate features. Godfrey danced after them, shorter-legged but determined, and three-year-old Reiner ran along last, happy to be shouting and using his little legs, but not really involved in the game. Their youngest sister, Agatha, aged twenty-two months, and conceived on their visit to Rising, was asleep on a cushion, being watched over by her nurse. Will swallowed. Each of his sons and daughters was a precious gift. He thanked God for their lives and their good health, because he knew how precarious both could be. Not many families went unmarked by the loss of a child, or of a woman in childbirth. He and Adeliza had been blessed five times already and he was afraid that such grace was running out.

Glancing beyond his playing offspring, he saw Juliana coming towards him, and his stomach knotted. She had been bringing him reports throughout the morning and they had not been particularly encouraging. The baby was big, and Adeliza was struggling. Juliana's face was pale and serious and he did not want to hear what she had to say.

"Sire, the countess has been safely delivered of a son," she announced.

He stepped sideways so that he had the support of the wall at his back because he was shaking. "You speak truly? Adeliza... is she...?"

"She is weak, sire, and very tired, but God willing she will recover. The infant is strong and lusty." She gave him the ghost of a smile.

"Praise God." He had to pinch tears of relief from his eyes.

Juliana curtseyed and returned to her duties. Drawing himself together, Will cuffed his eyes and summoned the children from their game to tell them that their mama had given them another brother. With the nurses in tow, he brought them to the chapel to light candles in gratitude for Adeliza's life, and that of their new sibling.

Later, alone, Will climbed the stairs to the confinement chamber, hesitated outside, then, taking a deep breath, went in. Adeliza was lying in bed, propped up on numerous pillows. Her hair, stranded with grey, lay on her breast in a single braid, bound with a purple ribbon. She was awake, but her face was white and exhausted. The baby lay in a crib beside her, swaddled and sleeping. Gingerly, Will leaned over to kiss her. "I was worried about you," he said gruffly.

"God and Saint Margaret saw me through," she said with a faint smile."

"Perhaps, but we should have no more."

"When I wed you, I thought I might not bear any at all," she whispered.

He picked up her hand to kiss the wedding ring he had set there. "I never doubted you would."

"I would not deny any of them their lives. They are God's gift." She directed his attention to the cradle. "I want him to be named Henry."

He raised one eyebrow. "Henry," he said flatly.

"To honour my first husband, and be insurance for the future," she said. "Stephen cannot object because it is the name of his uncle and his brother, and fitting...and it is what I want." Fatigued, she lay back against the bolsters.

His expression softened. "As you wish." He leaned over the cradle to touch the baby's cheek. "I will attend to his baptism tomorrow. I..." He raised his head and looked towards the door where Juliana was conducting an urgent whispered conversation with Adeliza's brother.

"Joscelin?" Adeliza struggled upright again. "What is it?"

Juliana stepped aside and he entered the chamber, his expression sombre. "I do not want to trouble you," he said. "I will talk to my lord outside."

Will started to rise.

"No," Adeliza lifted her hand. "If the matter is urgent enough to bring you to my confinement chamber, I will hear what you have to say. I will only fret more if something is wrong and you will not tell me."

Joscelin grimaced. "Henry FitzEmpress has landed a large invasion force of ships and men at Wareham."

Adeliza gasped.

"What?" Will stared at him. "Who told you that?"

"A horse-trader. He says he heard it from a customer who saw them disembarking. One of them made a point of telling him they were here in full force and would be needing good mounts."

"Who is leading them?" Will demanded. "Surely not the Count of Anjou?"

Joscelin shook his head. "No, Henry FitzEmpress, as I told you."

"But he's barely fourteen years old!"

"That is all I have heard. If it is true, the king will be calling for support." Joscelin turned to the bed and opened his hands. "I am sorry."

"It is a good thing our son is being named Henry," Adeliza said faintly.

Will grunted. "Whether he's arrived at the head of an invasion fleet or not, it means nothing. No one is going to heed a boy. I doubt he has that many with him. To entrust an entire expedition to a child is madness and whatever Geoffrey of Anjou may be, he is not mad." He gestured. "I cannot see hordes of seasoned fighting men flocking to a boy's banner— nor to his mother's. In the end it will make no difference save to cause more destruction."

"It will make a difference because he is here," Adeliza contradicted, summoning her strength. "He is but fourteen as you say, and Stephen is forty years older. Experience may hold the day for now, but youth will eventually triumph, so who truly has the advantage in this?" The men looked at her, plainly startled. "You may not agree with me," she said as she closed her eyes, "but you should consider."

❖❖❖

Matilda watched her brother pace her chamber at Devizes Castle, his temper evident in his hard footfall and the deep frown lines scored between his brows.

"Henry is a young fool," he growled. "No good can come of this idiotic scheme."

"Indeed, but he has shown initiative and courage," Matilda defended her son. News had arrived of Henry's "fleet" landing at Wareham, from where he had marched inland and made an attempt on a castle at Purton and been beaten off by the garrison. She was anxious and cross, but unlike Robert she was also proud and amused by her eldest son's escapade. He had energy and daring.

"He is a danger to himself and others. If he comes to grief, then what of our future plans? What does it say to the opposition when they see his inept attempts at warfare?" Robert snapped. "They must be laughing up their sleeves."

"Or they may be watching with interest. Robert, he is born of lions. Do not expect him to be a mouse."

"I do not." He shot her an angry look. "I saw to his tutoring and training when he was here before. I know his abilities, but I also know that he wants to run before he can walk. We cannot condone this!"

"It concerns me as much as it does you," she retorted. "But it is not a disaster, and you should not act as if it were." She frowned at him. His second son Philip had recently let him down. The young man had been forced to surrender the strategic keep of Farndon of which he was constable, which had caused the first rift between father and son. Following a fierce argument, Philip had gone over to Stephen, and then abandoned everything to go on crusade. She knew Robert had been deeply upset by his son's actions, and his health and his temper had suffered as a result.

"Do you think his father had a hand in this?"

Matilda gave a vehement shake of her head. "Geoffrey would never allow Henry to do something so foolhardy." She felt slightly sick as she thought that at Henry's age, Geoffrey had been preparing for his betrothal to her. Where did the child end and the man begin?

"He has to be reined in and shown that we will not tolerate such recklessness. He cannot stay here in England. We do not have enough resources to support ourselves, let alone provide him with protection and a household." Robert's voice rose a notch. "Who is paying for the soldiers he has brought with him, if you say Geoffrey has no notion?"

"He is bound to come to Devizes," she said, "and we will speak to him then."

❖❖❖

The next morning she sat in the window embrasure in her chamber, reading various pieces of correspondence. As yet there was no more news of Henry's exploits. A letter had come from Adeliza saying she had been safely delivered of a son named Henry in memory of a glorious king and in salute to another who would surely follow in his grandfather's footsteps. That made Matilda smile but saddened her too. It was eight years since she had seen Adeliza, and of the six children, only the first had been born. Letters, while they warmed the soul, only served to point up the long separation.

She was pondering what to send as a christening gift when her chamberlain, Humphrey de Bohun, interrupted her. "Domina, the lord Henry and his men have ridden in with the marshal."

She was immediately filled with relief and apprehension.

What was Henry doing in the company of her marshal? "Very well," she said in a neutral tone. "Put him in the solar and tell him I will be with him soon, but bring the marshal to me first."

While she straightened her gown and added a few rings to her fingers, she considered what she was going to say.

Her marshal John FitzGilbert was swift to arrive, rapping briskly on the door with his rod of office and entering with a decisive tread. As always his manner was controlled and courtly, but she could sense an atmosphere around him—a simmer of anger like a heat haze on a hot day.

"I am told you rode in with my son," she said.

He fixed her with a hard stare from his undamaged eye. "Domina, I discovered him fleeing an unsuccessful attempt to take the castle at Cricklade, using my equipment and horses, purloined from my keep at Marlborough in my absence." He spoke with clipped control. "I thought it best to escort him here where he would be less of a danger to all, including himself."

Matilda could now understand the reason for her marshal's anger if Henry had been helping himself to his equipment behind his back.

"Cricklade," she said.

"Apparently Purton was a similar disaster."

"Thank you, my lord," she said sharply. "I am aware."

"His mercenaries are mostly untried youths and men down on their luck. I am astonished they have come so far with so few injuries."

The word "injuries" made her recoil. "The lord Henry?"

"Domina, he is well and in good spirits." There was an irritated edge to her marshal's voice. He shook his head. "He is courageous but foolhardy."

"You are a man of similar traits yourself," she said.

"Ah no, domina." He gave her an astute look. "I always

know the odds and I wager accordingly. What may look foolhardy to others has only been my road when I have had no alternative. I always weigh the odds."

"Sometimes you have to take a road even when the odds are against you."

"Indeed, but never without being aware of where you might tread."

"My son knows his destiny," she snapped. "He will be king."

He bowed to her, the hint of a dour smile on his lips. "Indeed," he said. "I believe he will."

Her marshal dismissed, Matilda heaved a sigh and went to talk to her scapegrace golden son. Entering the solar attached to the hall she found him pacing the room like a caged lion and stopped in shock. In her mind's eye, she had been seeing the image of the toothy eleven-year-old to whom she had bidden farewell three years ago, but here was an adolescent on the cusp of manhood. He had a fledgling coppery beard and his limbs had lengthened and grown strong. He was as tall as her and he had his grandfather's eyes, clear grey with a flash of Geoffrey's aquamarine in their depths. She could feel the energy whirling around him like a fresh breeze. His cloak was pinned high on his shoulder with a round gold brooch and he wore a sword at his hip, even though he was not yet knighted.

"Henry," she said as she came towards him, and the word held pride, censure, and affection all at once.

"My lady mother." He knelt to her and bowed his head. The copper-gold tangle of his hair filled her with a surge of tenderness. She stooped to give him a formal kiss of peace, then drew him to his feet and embraced him with joy. She knew she should be furious, but that was not the emotion uppermost. Taking his arm she led him to the embrasure so she could see him properly. "You are almost a man."

Henry's chest expanded. "I am a man," he replied with a

spark of indignation that he should be thought anything else. "And I am here to fight for my kingdom."

"So I am told."

He eyed her through his thick sandy lashes. "I would have taken Purton and Cricklade if I had had the resources. With the right men and money, I could make a big difference."

"Men and money." She gave a bitter laugh. "So could I, so could your uncle Robert, but we struggle for every penny. What does your father say about this?"

His complexion darkened. "He refused to give me aid and said I was not to go, so I raised everything myself."

"So you disobeyed him? Do you not have responsibilities in Normandy and Anjou?"

"They do not need help as England does," he said tersely. "My father will understand when I tell him."

She raised her brows at that. She suspected Geoffrey would be less than sanguine. "And Cricklade and Purton are your notion of helping?"

He bunched his fists. "If I had been properly equipped, I could have taken them easily."

The conversation had gone round in a circle. She was elated to see him but he could not stay, and in truth what he had done was rash and dangerous. "If the only money you have is that which you raised yourself, how are you going to pay your men?"

"I have brought them to you so you can use them under my command." He set his shoulders defensively. "I did not need the marshal's safe conduct here."

"He seems to think you owe him horses and equipment."

His eyes flashed with anger and irritation. "I want to help. Doesn't anyone understand?"

Matilda drew herself up. "You bring a rag-tag band of mercenaries here and make two abortive attempts to take a couple of small castles? How amused Stephen must be to hear of this. I cannot afford to pay for your men, or to set you up here, because you will have to be protected and given the means to live, and I do not have those means. You are creating difficulties for all of us. When you went back to Normandy, it was to finish your education and training and to be kept safe until the time was right."

"I did not think I would have a kingdom left to claim by then," he retorted. "I had to do something. By the time I am old enough by years of reckoning, it will be too late. I am old enough now."

Matilda reined in her anger and, sighing, went to sit down on a window seat. "I am glad to see you," she said, rubbing her forehead, "even if I am angry too. You fill my heart with joy, but you cannot stay; you must see that. I have no money to pay for your men, and whether you think you are old enough or not, you are not ready."

He gave her a long look and it jolted her to see the temper in his eyes; but beyond that temper lay a shrewd and determined mind. He might not have the maturity of experience yet, he might have made mistakes in his eagerness and impatience, but he was right. He was no child. "If I do return to Normandy," he said, "that would be expensive as well."

She rubbed her brow "How much?"

"I owe each man a shilling a day for following me, and their provender and expenses. We'd have to hire the ships to take us back too."

She made the calculations in her head. It was far more than she could afford without compromising her own people; it would be a huge drain on her resources and a total waste. "I cannot afford that kind of sum," she said.

He set his jaw. "My uncle Robert could."

"And he would have to take money out of another pot to do so. Ask him if you wish, but I can tell you what his answer will be. He is already heartsick over the defiance of his own son and he has no time for young men's rebellions." She took his slender young hands in hers, unmarked by years, not yet toughened by fighting. His narrow wrists were dappled with freckles and gilded with fine hairs. "Take your men home and ask your father to pay, and while you are about it, ask him to send me more money too, because I am in sore need."

His expression became set and still.

Geoffrey was going to be furious with him, she thought, but that was the price paid for disobedience. "Every action has consequences," she said, "and you must learn to deal with them and think everything through."

"Did you do that at Westminster, Mama?" he challenged.

"I am giving you the benefit of my wisdom in hindsight. Learn from your own mistakes and those of others. Sometimes the lessons are harsh indeed—as I have cause to know, and you are finding out."

He narrowed his eyes. Then he fixed her again with that knowing, calculating look. "I have been rash," he admitted. "I have some thinking to do."

Matilda received the impression that Henry had indeed absorbed a lesson from their conversation, but she was not entirely sure it was the one she intended. The look on his face was determined and wilful rather than contrite.

Fifty-three

WILL WAS PLAYING DICE WITH STEPHEN, ROBERT DE Beaumont, Earl of Leicester, and William Martel the steward. Outside a dark March day was drawing towards dusk and servants were lighting fresh candles and refilling the oil lamps. The shutters were latched against the bitter weather and the old man who tended the fire for a wage of four pence a day was keeping it well stoked with logs and charcoal. The venison stew and force-meats, the fruits in honey and spices, had left everyone feeling warm and befuddled. Stephen was in a genial, expansive mood. The threat from Normandy had proven to be so much piss in the wind, and there had been no sign of the Angevin lordling or his rabble since they had been put to flight at Purton and Cricklade.

Will threw a pair of sixes and, with a triumphant laugh, scooped up the pile of silver in the middle of the table.

"Will that be enough to build some more fancy latrines?" jibed Leicester. Everyone had been highly amused by the refinements Will was building at Rising.

"You are just jealous," Will said equably. "Or your wife is."

Leicester rolled his eyes. "I dare not tell her, or else we would be inundated with the things. Thank Christ you have built your little folly off the beaten track, D'Albini. At least she won't come visiting and covet everything she sees."

Will shrugged. "It is my haven," he said. "Somewhere I can create a thing of beauty to honour my wife, and not be disturbed."

"How is your lady?" Stephen asked.

Will was silent for a moment and Stephen's look sharpened.

"She is but recently out of confinement," he said. He was worried about Adeliza because she had still been very fragile when he left to come to court.

"You have named the boy Henry have you not?"

Will reddened. "It was my lady's choice, for the king her first husband."

"Of course," Stephen said blandly and picked up the dice. "Another game?"

An usher entered the chamber and hurried over to the gaming table. Bending to the king, he murmured in his ear.

Stephen's gaze widened. Then he gave a short bark of laughter. "Bring him," he said. As the usher departed, Stephen looked round at his companions. "Well, when I said another game, I did not quite have this in mind, but it seems that my nephew of Anjou is here to pay his respects."

They all stared at him in shocked surprise, but Stephen was still chuckling. "I will say this for him, the lad has nerve, even if he is a fool."

Moments later the usher returned, leading a handsome red-haired youth. He was not as tall as the usher, but his physique was robust and he had presence. He wore serviceable travel clothes without embellishment: a thick winter cloak and a quilted gambeson over the top of a fine but plain tunic, and stout hunting boots rising to mid-calf. To look at him, Will would have guessed he was well to do, but there was nothing regal about him. His expression was open, with a slight curve to his lips, and there was not an iota of tension in the language of his body or the set of his jaw.

"Dear God, he looks like the Angevin but without the gilding," William Martel muttered into his chest.

"He also resembles his grandsire, the empress's father," Will said. Despite Stephen's remark, he did not think this young man was a fool at all. Indeed, he thought it might just be the other way around.

"Sire." Henry went down on one knee to Stephen and bent his head. "My lord uncle," he said in a light, adolescent voice.

Stephen cleared his throat. "Nephew," he responded. "To what do we owe this pleasure?"

Henry gave them all a smile as bright as the sun. "I thought to pay my respects before I returned home," he said. "I have only ever been told my mother's side of matters and my uncle Robert's, and I want to find out for myself."

"Is that so?" Stephen said, but his lips were twitching.

Will was amused too, and taken aback at the youth's daring in walking into the lion's den. It was a rash move, but not without its merits. Will found himself approving of the youngster, even while he should have been appalled. It was good news that he was leaving, but the motive for being here, spoken with such an open, smiling countenance, was perhaps suspect.

"And what makes you think you will return home?" Stephen asked, but cleared a space at the trestle for Henry to sit. "Why should I not take you prisoner or dispose of you now that you have put yourself in my power?"

"Because I am your nephew and your guest and the rules of hospitality are sacred," Henry said. "Because I have come under a flag of truce to talk."

Stephen raised his eyebrows. "To talk about what?"

Henry shrugged. "You have only heard rumours about me from my own side. Perhaps you want to find out about me too. If I were you, I would."

"Perhaps Cricklade and Purton speak for themselves," Stephen said mockingly.

"That was folly; I realise that now. I should not have attacked them."

A servant arrived with food and drink for the "guest" and Henry set to with an adolescent's hunger and a complete lack of self-consciousness.

"Is this to spite your mother?" Stephen asked. "Or perhaps to make her pay attention to you?"

"Not at all," Henry said between rotations of his jaw. "She will be vexed when she hears about this, but I do my best to fulfil my duty towards her." He paused and rested his knife against the side of his dish. "And anyway, she is right; I should leave England."

❖❖❖

Henry displayed no inclination to leave straight away, however. Indeed, he settled his feet under Stephen's table, making himself agreeable and amenable to all. He took part in the roistering of the court at night with a ribald, masculine sense of humour that everyone appreciated, including Stephen, who rose to the challenge. Henry undertook wrestling matches with the older squires and displayed tremendous aptitude and skill. He conversed with the barons and chaplains, revealing the depth of his education and intelligence. He even proved an adept dancer.

Will wondered what Matilda had thought of his relaxed ways and mannerisms, the direct opposite of her stiff regard for propriety. Henry would sit on a stool, knees apart, cup dangling between them, and talk as easily to the pot boy as he did to the king. Henry had his own opinions but was eager to listen and learn, being deferential without ever losing face. And always the big smile and the constant energy. He sustained himself on very little sleep and wore everyone out. He would ride out for a day's hunting and still be fresh at the end of it despite many rigorous hours in the saddle. Beside him, Stephen's own swift energy appeared as a diminished trickle dwarfed by a strong silver waterfall.

On the third evening of his visit, Henry sat down in a window embrasure with Will to play chess. "How is my grandmother the queen?" he asked with a mischievous twinkle in his eyes.

"She is well," Will replied, not seeing any need to discuss Adeliza's fragile health.

"And all my little uncles and aunts?"

Will grunted with amusement. "All are thriving," he said. "Your youngest uncle was born just a few weeks ago on the feast of Saint Agatha."

Henry smiled and then said, "And your castles? I understand you have at least two projects under construction." He flashed a grin. "I even heard something about the latrines at one of them."

Will sighed with exasperation. "Who has not heard and mocked?" he asked, but under the influence of good wine and the youth's genuine interest in the castle buildings, he told Henry not only about Rising, but also discussed the fortress he was building at Buckenham on a more suitable site than the former one, which he had donated to the Benedictine Order as land for a priory. The new castle was a circular shell keep, set on a high mound with walls eleven feet thick. As with Rising, Will was in the process of building a village too and encouraging people to settle and work. Already there was a tannery on the outskirts of the fledgling plots.

Henry listened and absorbed everything like a sponge. "Are you not afraid that what you are building up will all be destroyed?" he asked.

"Indeed I am," Will replied, "but if I did not build and have faith in God's protection, what would remain? Rising is a palace to honour my wife, not a great fortress, so there is no reason for anyone to attack it, and the new keep at Buckenham poses no threat because it is purely for defence." He gave Henry a severe look. "All of my castles exist to defend my territory, not as bases to steal or encroach on other men's. Disputes have never been at my instigation. I serve the king because I am his sworn vassal and I will never go back on my word."

"But what of the future, my lord?" Henry said. "To whom will your own sons swear their oaths of allegiance?"

"I do not think this is a matter for discussion here," Will said curtly. "It is not something to be decided over a game of chess."

"Oh, but it is a game of chess," Henry said with one of his disarming smiles, "and we are both players."

Will gave him a dark look. "If you take my advice, you will be careful to whom you say such things."

"I intend to be very careful indeed," Henry replied with a glint in his eyes that left Will feeling uneasy. The youth had run rings around him but he was not quite certain how.

❖❖❖

The following day, Henry left Stephen's court, laden with gifts of horses and supplies. Stephen had given him silver for his expenses and paid off the mercenaries in his employ. Many of Stephen's barons had raised their eyebrows at such leniency and largesse. Some had muttered that it was like the time the empress had landed at Arundel all over again, but Stephen shrugged them off, saying he could not imprison the youth without risking an attack from Anjou and Normandy, and it was too dangerous to keep him here. People might start believing that Stephen was going to accept him as his heir.

Will considered these points as he counted the loss of the ten marks and a packhorse that had been his own contribution to the young Henry's departure. Everyone had been told by

Stephen to donate towards the youth's leave-taking so that the royal coffers did not have to stand the entire sum. Will suspected that the damage was done. Men had had a chance to assess the empress's son and had been impressed by his calibre. Stephen's own son Eustace had no such charisma to call upon; he was an ordinary youth of small talent, whereas Henry's personality blazed as brightly as his hair. Stephen was trying to have Rome acknowledge Eustace as the heir to England, but the pope was turning a deaf ear, as was the archbishop of Canterbury. No one here was going to desert Stephen; they had been with him for too long; but many had been given food for thought concerning the succession. Will wagered that the conversation he had held with Henry over the chessboard had been repeated many times throughout the ranks of Stephen's barons.

"It is suddenly very quiet, isn't it, Will?" said Robert, Earl of Leicester, joining him in the stable yard, where he was looking at the empty stalls left by the animals Henry had taken with him.

Will glanced at Leicester, whose brother Waleran de Meulan now served the Angevin cause in Normandy. "Stephen is certainly relieved."

Leicester smiled. "I think we all are, but a little flat too—if anyone dared admit as much." He approached a bay stallion tethered outside while the groom mucked out its stall. "So what do you think?" he asked, running his hand down the animal's neck.

"About the horse? A fine beast."

"Oh come." Leicester gave him a sharp look. "Do not play the wide-eyed fool with me, D'Albini. Neither of us is going to desert Stephen, but it will not be long until that boy is a man in body as well as in mind. How many here are likely to follow Stephen's heir, and how many that red-haired youngster, if it comes to the crux?"

Will made a face. "It is a great pity all this could not have been settled ten years ago without a war."

"In hindsight yes, but not at the time," Leicester said. "We were not to know what the empress's son would become, nor Eustace. Now we have been given a chance to judge." He gave Will an astute look. "Henry FitzEmpress knew exactly what he was doing when he turned up here. However disastrously his escapade in England might have begun, he has turned it to his advantage. How many others here are having the same discussion as us in quiet corners? The time is not right even now, but it is coming, and it is our duty not to squander it—for all our sakes."

❖ ❖ ❖

Matilda bit her lip as the messenger bowed from the room. She did not know whether to laugh or be appalled that Henry had gone to Stephen to ask for the money to return home.

"It is audacious, you must admit," she said to Robert, who had received the news in stony silence.

"That is one way of putting things," he growled. "You might as easily say foolish and wilful. What if Stephen had cast him in prison? What if he had been killed? This has been a hare-brained enterprise from beginning to end."

Matilda tapped her forefinger against her chin. "At the outset it was, I agree with you, but now he has been able to infiltrate Stephen's camp more deeply than we ever could even with the most accomplished of spies."

"And what sort of impression do you think Stephen's barons have garnered?" Robert said with a jaundiced curl of his lip.

"They will have seen his daring and initiative—that he was able to persuade funds out of Stephen."

"That would not be difficult. Look at the way Stephen drained your father's treasury in the early days."

"Yes, but his men will view it as a further example of his weakness, not largesse. By believing he is ridding himself of a bothersome gnat while showing magnanimous scorn, he has misread the situation."

"Then let us hope you have not," Robert said, then heaved a sigh and pinched the bridge of his nose. "I know Henry's presence has put new heart into our men, but he is not ready for full command." He gave her an exhausted look. "You may believe me to be hostile towards him, but in truth I am not. I will welcome the day when he is old enough to take this burden from my shoulders."

"I know you are not hostile." She came to embrace him, worried by how grey he looked. "I welcome it too. When I hold the imperial crown between my hands, it is Henry I see wearing it. But I am still the bearer and the custodian, and it is because of that duty I must carry on. It is like finding the final scraping in the bottom of the barrel when you thought there was nothing left."

"Yes," Robert said wearily. "The final scraping."

Fifty-four

DEVIZES, NOVEMBER 1147

BRIAN RODE INTO DEVIZES, HIS STOMACH CHURNING AND HIS lips pressed tightly together. Twice on the journey from Wallingford he had had to dismount and vomit at the roadside. He felt as if he was losing himself and becoming his own shadow. Matilda's people watched him ride by, their faces filled with trepidation before they looked at the ground or away. In a few eyes he saw sparks of relief, and turned away in shame, because he was here to add to the burden, not relieve it.

In the castle bailey, the grooms greeted him with mumbled words. The few people about hurried to cross the open ground and avoid the blustery spatters of rain. Brian dismounted from Sable and watched the old horse being led away to a straw-filled stall. He was showing his years, his muzzle silvering and his once broad rump beginning to resemble the bony rear end of a cow. After this, they had one more long ride to make, and then their journey was done.

In the hall, William Giffard, Matilda's chancellor, was working at a lectern by the light from a window. A brazier stood nearby, the heat keeping his writing hand warm. When he saw Brian, he stared through him for a moment, before recognition dawned. "Sire, I did not know you." Hastily he rose and bowed his tonsured head.

"Well, that is no surprise, because I do not know myself either these days," Brian said heavily. "I am here to see the empress."

Giffard gave him a pained look. "Since we heard the news about the Earl of Gloucester, she has kept to her chamber except to go to church. She has taken his loss very hard indeed."

"It is a grief to us all." Brian signed his breast, but the gesture felt empty, because he was empty. "Will you at least tell her I am here?"

Giffard swiftly set his quill back in the ink well. "Indeed, sire," he said. "I will bring you to her. She may even talk to you as she has not done to others."

He led Brian up a twist of stairs, along a gallery, and rapped on a closed oak door with his chancellor's staff of office. "Domina," he called out, "my lord FitzCount is here."

There was a long silence. Giffard looked at Brian and shook his head. Brian took the rod from him and banged on the door again with the brass knurl on the end. "Domina, I must speak with you and I would rather not shout my business through four inches of oak."

Giffard raised his brows but said nothing. There was another long silence. Brian leaned his head against the door and closed his eyes. "I am prepared to wait all day and night."

"Sire, you cannot stay here," Giffard said reluctantly.

Brian rounded on him. "Then fetch soldiers and have me dragged away, because I will not leave of my own accord. Do you think I mean harm to the empress after all I have done?"

"No, sire, but..."

The door opened and Uli stood to one side of it. She silently beckoned him into the chamber. Brian thrust the rod into Giffard's hands, turned, and stepped over the threshold.

Matilda was standing in the middle of the room, isolated like a lone tree. She was wearing one of her German court robes and everything was bound up and stiff and overlaid by jewels.

Her face was tight, her skin grey as stone, so she might almost have been her own effigy. She fixed him with an empty stare. "Robert is dead," she said in a distant voice. "How can that be? Why isn't Stephen dead instead? Why not me?"

Brian swallowed, feeling the sickness rise in him again. He wanted to embrace her, but feared she would push him away as she pushed everyone. And he would deserve it. Her knight Drogo had once said to him that she had a hard exterior sheltering softness within, but no one would ever knew how soft, because she refused to let anyone close enough to find out. His voice emerged as a hoarse croak. "It is the will of God you should live, domina. I too would more than gladly have taken his place."

"And why was it God's will that he should die?" Her chin trembled. "When last I saw him he was tired, as we all are, but still whole and strong, so I thought. To die of a congestion…I thought I would see him again and we would be together for our brother's anniversary and that of our father. He was supposed to be here to help and guide Henry and be his backbone…as he was mine. What am I going to do now he is gone?"

A shudder ran through Brian and he was suddenly riddled with guilt. What if she asked him to be her backbone when he did not have one himself?

"I brought him to this by relying on him," she said. "I should have seen beyond my own cares and known he was unwell, and now it is too late to do anything but say 'should have.'" She pressed her palm across her mouth.

"Don't," Brian said. "It was his cause too. He was never going to rest while Stephen was on the throne."

"I will have to be Robert now, as well as myself, but how, when he was the better part? No one can take his place. Those who remain with me were already here when he was, so how can we make up for what is gone?" She made a soft, anguished sound.

He came to her and set his arms lightly around her and for a moment she laid her head on his breast and they stood as close as lovers. Brian's grief deepened. He ached beyond belief with emotion for her, but it was part of a much greater pain. "I do not know what to tell you."

"And you were always so good with words." Her voice was brittle. "Have you none for me now?"

"They are all ashes in the wind," he said hoarsely. "I burned them as you bade me—all the ones that mattered anyway."

She drew back to look at him, then her gaze dropped to the base of his neck and sharpened with concern. She reached to touch his throat and he felt her cool fingers burn on the sores there before he could pull away.

"Dear Jesu, Brian, a hair shirt!" Her eyes filled with shock.

"It is between my conscience and God," he said tautly, "and no concern of anyone else's. Not even you."

"How long have you been wearing this?"

"Does it matter?" Leaving her, he went to the open window and stood in the cold draught. "It helps me stay sane," he said bleakly. "Sometimes I think the dark thoughts in my head will send me mad, but this keeps them at bay—after a fashion. While I have torment of the flesh, it lessens the torment of the mind."

She had suspected for a while that something was wrong, but his words alarmed her, as did his appearance. This was not the vigorous, bright-eyed man who had met her on the road when she returned from Germany and raised a tent on a windy night.

He said, "When I was a little boy in Brittany, I had the freedom to run wild. Then my father arranged for me to be raised at the English court by your sire. It would be a fine opportunity, he said. I would be educated and trained and if I worked hard, I might one day be a great and important lord. I wanted to please him and I wanted to learn; I was always eager then for new experiences. I loved my lessons and I loved your brother. I was even fond of Stephen then, when we sat drinking wine on long summer evenings and dreaming of our futures— of what we would become." He looked over his shoulder at her. "I do not think any of us imagined it would come to this, not even Stephen."

"Brian…"

"Is it worth it? Is any of this struggle worth the cost?"

"To do the right thing is never a waste." Her throat was tight with tears.

"But what is the right thing?" he demanded. "To put a sword through a man because he opposes you? To burn down a village because it lies in your path and its occupants are beholden to another lord? To ignore the screaming women and children as you throw torches into their thatch and put spears through their menfolk? To rob merchant trains because they are on their way to enrich your opponent's lands?" He raised and lowered both hands in a desperate gesture. "How does that benefit anyone? Does it make God smile? I have done all of those things and more, and my soul is sick." He turned over his right forearm and looked down at his wrist where the veins stood proud. "I swore to serve you to the last drop of my blood. I know what you think of men who renege on their oaths, and too many have done so…"

He hesitated and she felt a tightening of dread in her solar plexus. "And you are about to renege on yours? Is that what you have come to tell me?"

He shook his head. "No, domina. I will serve you for as long as you desire."

She did not want to see the desperate, hollow exhaustion in his eyes and turned away, rubbing her arms. She was so cold. "Then I have things to tell you also," she said. "The bishop of Salisbury is still badgering me to return Devizes to the see. I have promised him compensation and told him I will give the castle to him as soon as I am able."

"You are surely not handing it over..." She heard the ghost of the old Brian suddenly thread through his voice.

"Not in the near future, of course not, but I have to show I am willing to conciliate. I cannot dislodge Stephen from my throne; I no longer have the men or the commanders to do so. If I could not accomplish it with Robert, then how am I to do it without? Even keeping a stalemate is hard. I must hold fast until Henry is old enough, and that means fostering strong relations with the Church—other than that snake the bishop of Winchester." Her lip curled as she spoke of him. "Theobald of Canterbury is not inclined to crown Stephen's son as the future king, and I must strengthen and encourage his resistance. Everyone must look upon Henry as England's rightful heir. I have to keep up pressure on Stephen's lords too. Even if I cannot field an army, I can still undermine his position. It is a different kind of war I am waging now."

She paused to draw a deep breath. Behind her the fire crackled in the hearth and Brian was so silent, she only knew he was there because she could feel him. "My mistakes cost me my crown," she said, "but even had I been made queen, I would never have been accepted. A woman may be the power behind a man, but she is not allowed to take power for herself." She turned to look at him. Still clad in his dark travelling cloak, his hood pushed back on his shoulders, he resembled a monk save for the tonsure. "Once I have made arrangements and spoken to all, I am going to Normandy to raise support. I am not leaving the fray, but the military side must be overseen by someone else. Henry is almost ready and I can do no more here. I have been thinking about it for a while, and now, with Robert's death, it is time to let go of the rope and grasp it again in a new place." As she spoke of rope, she thought of her escape from Oxford in the snowy night. That had been a triumph wrung out of a disaster. She was swinging on that rope in the darkness now, afraid but still defiant and resolute. Brian's expression was unfathomable—or perhaps stupefied. "Have you nothing to say?"

"I thought you might ask me to take up the yoke of command," he confessed, looking at her and away again. "I would have done so because I have made a promise, but I fear I would have failed you."

"You have never failed me." She dared not think in that direction, because she would have to confront her own fear that she had let down not only him but also England and her son.

"I beg to differ."

"The differing is your choice, but I refuse to let you beg."

He swallowed. "Then let me ask you to release me when you sail."

She stared at him.

"I desire to make my peace with God and retire from the world." He bowed his head. "As I stand now, I cannot go before my maker on Judgement Day and expect His mercy. I have no heirs. My wife intends entering the nunnery at Bec. William Boterel will serve at Wallingford as he always has done. Nothing will change there."

"Where will you go?" She felt numb.

"Your uncle David has granted Reading Abbey the Isle of May in return for prayers and attending to pilgrims who come to worship at Saint Adrian's shrine. I shall go there and live out whatever time is left to me in God's service."

"And you will take vows?"

"If I am deemed worthy…and if you will release me."

"What use will you be to me if I do refuse?" she said with a break in her voice.

"No one rides a lame horse," he agreed.

Going to him, she took his hands in hers and turned them over. "Then go with my blessing when it is time, and commend me in your prayers, and ask God's grace that my son become king…" Her voice shook. "And write to me. I want to think of you with ink-stained fingers."

"But not putting up a tent."

It was meant to lighten the moment and make her smile, but her eyes filled. "You are wrong," she said. "I shall remember that of you first and always for the rest of my days."

Fifty-five

ARUNDEL, FEBRUARY 1148

ADELIZA WOKE TO THE SOUND OF SOFT CONVERSATION IN her chamber. Beyond the bed curtains pale winter daylight entered the room through the open shutters. A brazier twirled scented smoke towards the ceiling.

She knew she must have slept for a long time, because it had been twilight when she retired exhausted to bed, and now it was plainly morning. She still felt bone-weary—almost as if she had not slept—but her mouth was dry and her body ached with lying for so long a time. She had experienced bouts of debilitation before, but they had always eased after a short while. This current one, however, showed no sign of ending. It had been two months now, and was growing worse.

"Is there nothing you can do?" Will was asking on a pleading note.

The reply in a slightly higher tone came from Magister Vital, a physician who had been attending her ever since the lethargy had begun. "Sire, it is a wasting disease of the female embers. Sometimes the fire dies so low in the body that it cannot sustain the energy needed for life and there is nothing that can be done. I have tried to revive the flame with poultices and bleeding to make the blood rise, but to no avail."

"I refuse to believe there is no cure!" Will hissed. "I will not let this happen!"

"It is God's will, my lord. It is to Him that you should pray for a miracle. For the rest, she should have a regime of peace and quiet and contemplation, with food rich in hot elements to stimulate her humours. Ask others of my profession if you so desire, but they will give you the same answer."

"Get out," Will snarled. "What use are you to me if you do not have the skills to make her better? She is my life!"

"Sire, I wish I could help. She is a great and gentle lady."

Tears seeped from Adeliza's eye corners and trickled into the pillow. She heard the door close behind Magister Vital. Breathing raggedly, Will went to the window, pressed his head against the wall, and struck the stone with the side of his clenched fist. "I cannot bear this," she heard him whisper. "Why her?"

Beyond the window she could hear their children shouting joyously as they played. The sound of their brightness seemed to come from far away and she knew what she had to do. She had had plenty of time to think of late.

Will sighed and, leaving the window, came to the bed and looked down at her with eyes full of anguish and anger. She returned his gaze.

"I heard," she said, and her voice was hoarse and dry because she had been asleep for so long. "I cannot bear this either."

"I will not let you be like this," he said. Leaning over, he put his arms around her and helped her to sit up against the bolsters. Her stifled gasp of pain made him tense and draw back. "There has to be a cure."

She gestured weakly to the flagon at the bedside; he poured her some wine and then helped her to drink.

"Look at you. You are not even strong enough to hold a cup."

She swallowed and felt the liquid warm its way down to

her stomach. "I have asked myself what God is saying to me by visiting this curse upon me," she whispered. "What does He want me to know? What does He want me to do?" She wrinkled her forehead. "Why is He taking my energy back to him while my body is still here? I will willingly give Him my soul if He asks it."

He made a sound in his throat. "I do not want to lose you."

Adeliza touched his cheek, feeling the burr of stubble under her fingertips and the warmth of his skin. He was strong, healthy, bursting with life, just like their children.

"This is no good for either of us," she said. "What kind of a wife am I for you, and what kind of example as a mother to our children? I do not want them to see me like this."

"I will not have you say such things," he said fiercely. "You will get better."

"I have been sick for a long time and I am not improving," she said, and prayed she would have the strength to fight this through. "I cannot continue as I am. I would be better off elsewhere, so that the part of me that is still whole can do something of benefit."

"What do you mean 'elsewhere'?" He eyed her suspiciously.

She closed her eyes. "To the convent at Afflighem," she said. "I am still able to pray."

"No!" He instinctively recoiled because Afflighem was where her kin were buried, and it solidified the notion of losing her. "I will not allow it!"

"Then what will you do, my husband?" She raised her lids again and fixed her gaze on his contorted expression. "Watch me lie here and fade away before your eyes and those of our children day upon day? Let me at least end my time usefully."

He left her side to pace the room, digging his hands through his hair. He felt as if he would burst with pent-up emotion while she lay there like a wan and beautiful effigy. He thought of the struggle he had had to make her leave Wilton to marry him. Perhaps God had only allotted him this short time and it was at an end like a tree blossoming in springtime and shedding its leaves in autumn.

Her devotional stood under the window with its candles and crosses and one of her crowns: a delicate thing worked in spikes of gold adorned with pearls and small sapphires. Beside it was a jewelled cross he had given her not long after their marriage. He had been so proud to see her wear it. A beautiful object for a beautiful woman. His wife. His queen. The light of his life. Now she was asking him to let her go. He curled his fingers into his palm and looked at his clenched knuckles. "Strong Arm," some called him at court. But what use was such power in the face of this request? Whether he refused or consented, he was going to lose her.

He turned and came back to her, and slowly unfurled his fist into an open hand. "Very well," he said. "If that be your wish, go to Afflighem. Make your arrangements. We will tell the children that, as a patron, it is your duty to visit the nunnery, and that you are going there for contemplation and prayer. All those things are true, and I would not lie to them."

Her eyes flooded with relief. "It is for the best."

"Not for my best," he said. "I am losing the better half of myself."

"I will just be in a different place, and that is nothing new to our marriage. You are often away at court while I am here. Now you will be at court, and I will be at Afflighem."

"But you will not be here waiting for me within riding distance, or sharing my bed and my thoughts, or teaching the children..."

"No." She looked towards the window and bit her lip. Giving up this man was hard; giving up her children would break her heart, yet she could not stay. "That will be your task, and I trust you. They have Juliana and Melisande, and their uncle Joscelin. I will not allow them or you to watch me decline further than this."

He swore under his breath and took her hand, gripping it in his as if he would imbue her with his vitality. He would have drained himself for her, and he felt impotent that he could do nothing.

"Sire."

He turned at the interruption, ready to bellow at whoever dared disturb them, then bit his tongue as he saw that it was Rothard, Adeliza's chamberlain, and his expression was wide with concern. "There are heralds at our gate from the empress," Rothard said. "She requests leave for her and her household to bide here for a night. My lord FitzCount is with her too."

Will drew breath to snarl that he would not countenance having them under his roof, but Adeliza forestalled him, pressing her hand down on his and gathering herself to lift her voice. "Tell them they are welcome," she said.

Will stared at her in furious astonishment as Rothard departed. "Are you mad? I will not become embroiled again! Do you want Stephen descending on us with an army? Shall I lose Arundel as well as my wife? Is that what you want?" He made to pull away, but she continued to grip his hand.

"This will be the last opportunity I have to see her," she said. "She is not here with an army. This is a personal visit, and one she must have risked much to make, because this is not safe territory. It is not about war and political manoeuvring."

"You said that nine years ago," he snapped, "that it was just a visit between kin, and look where it led.".

"That was not the beginning, as well you know. What can she do now? She has no army and Robert is dead, God rest his soul. If you do not want her within the castle, then put me in a litter and I shall go to her. I mean it, husband," she added as he began to shake his head. "I may lack the strength, but I certainly have the will. Will you grant me this?"

His mouth twisted. "When have I ever refused you?" he said and, turning on his heel, banged out of the room.

Adeliza closed her eyes, summoned what small strength had trickled into her bones from the wine she had drunk, and had Juliana and Melisande help her rise and dress. Her clothes hung on her and the women had to draw the lacings to their tightest to fit her figure. She had them flush her cheeks with a tint of alkanet ointment, and placed a dab on her lips. She drank more wine and managed to eat a crust of bread while the maids put fresh covers on the bed and burned more incense on the braziers to freshen the room. Then she sent Melisande to organise the kitchens and prepare sleeping space for the guests, and prayed that she could hold herself together for the duration of their visit. Much as she wanted to see Matilda, she hoped her stay was going to be a short one.

❖❖❖

Matilda faced Will in the great hall. Last time they had been in each other's company was in the snowy courtyard of Abingdon Abbey.

"Domina," he said with a curt bow. He did not kneel and she let it pass.

"Thank you for opening your gates," she said, her tone gracious but frigid.

"Do not thank me," he replied. "I would have refused you, but Adeliza insisted and while I could so easily deny you, I cannot find it within me to deny her."

Matilda gave him a narrow look. "I will not stay long, but in the interests of all she has done for me and meant to me, it would be discourteous of me not to bid farewell."

He whitened and his hazel eyes shone with such antagonism

that Matilda recoiled and Hugh Pluckenett and Brian FitzCount hastened to her side, ready to defend her.

"Tact was never your strong point," Will said, "but that is crass even for you."

Matilda gazed at him in affronted amazement. "What is crass about wanting to see Adeliza before I leave for Normandy?"

Colour flooded back into his face. "You are leaving? I thought you meant…ah, nothing." He gestured towards the stairs. "Go, speak with her."

Matilda stared at him. "Thought I meant what? What is wrong with her? Is she ill? There has been no mention in her letters."

"She would not make a parade of it for others," he said, and turned his head, refusing to engage further.

Filled with apprehension, Matilda climbed the stairs to Adeliza's chamber and found her sitting in a chair by the hearth. Her cheeks were rosy, but the colour looked painted on and beneath it she was like a wilting flower.

"Forgive me if I do not rise," Adeliza said, "but you are welcome, whatever impression Will may have given to you in greeting. He is as grumpy as a bear just now."

Matilda hurried over to her and kissed her cheek, and felt the dusting of cosmetic against her lips. "Oh my love, why did you not say you were unwell?"

"What would be the point of telling you about something you could not change?" Adeliza shook her head. "It would only have added to your burdens, but I am truly glad to see you before I leave. I have a letter half written…"

"Before you leave?" Matilda looked at her in surprise. She had come here to say her own farewells, and this reception at Arundel had thrown her off balance. She had prepared herself for many responses, but not this one. Nor had she bargained for finding Adeliza in such a weak physical state.

As Adeliza told her about her decision to retire to Afflighem, she struggled to assimilate the news. "At least there I can pray and be of value, rather than lie here feeling like a useless husk. Will has accepted my choice, but it is a raw wound for him. I know it is the right thing to do, but he is not yet convinced." Her voice faltered. "The baby is but a year old. If there was another way, I would take it..."

"Perhaps there is another way. Have you tried—"

"The physicians have done everything they can," Adeliza said wearily. "Now it is in God's hands and that is why I must go."

"When will you leave?"

"As soon as arrangements are made. Will is likely to drag his heels, but I will find the strength to chivvy him."

Matilda shook her head. "I did not realise you were sick. I came to tell you I am returning to Normandy."

Now it was Adeliza's turn to stare. "Why?"

"I need to raise money and troops. With Robert gone, there is no one to command an army, unless Geoffrey or Henry take on the mantle. Henry is almost of an age to rule. Next month he will be fifteen; that is older than his father was when he married me and became Count of Anjou."

"It is still perilously young to govern," Adeliza said with concern.

"I agree, but he has abilities beyond his years, and even if I cannot lead an army, I can still advise him. There are many who will help him in the field, but he will be their uniting emblem." She looked at Adeliza. "Like you, I have little choice. Henry must come to the fore. I was furious with him when he crossed the Narrow Sea and made that foolish attack on Stephen's castles, but I was proud too. That was a year ago, and he has grown and matured in that time. He will be king, I know it with all my being. Men such as your husband will support him, where they would not support me. It is not defeat," she added, setting her jaw. To admit defeat would make this terrible, bloody war worthless and, at the same time, set its price beyond anything that could be repaid.

"No," said Adeliza. After a moment she said, "You could sail from Arundel with me. Your baggage is at Wareham, I know, but you have some things with you here, and I would welcome your company on the voyage." She bit her lip. "It also means Will would have to let me go instead of striving to delay me, which I know he will try to do."

Matilda looked taken aback, but then grew thoughtful. "I cannot tarry," she said. "I am not leaving England because I am abandoning it to Stephen but because I need to organise resources in Normandy, and I need to begin straight away."

"The sooner the better." Adeliza's chin dimpled, but she controlled herself. "The moment there is a fair wind for a crossing."

Matilda nodded. "In that case I will send word back to Wareham, and help you to pack what you need."

❖❖❖

By the castle jetty on the river Arun, a ship rode at anchor. The wind was strong and bitterly cold, but the weather was clear and the master had assured his charges that they would be safely ashore in Normandy well before nightfall.

Will stood with Adeliza, waiting for the sailors to complete their final preparations. She was wrapped in a thick, fur-lined cloak to protect her from the wind and sea spray. Above the bulk of the rich blue wool, her face was as wan as a lily and her eyes enormous. He kept striving for normality, telling himself that she was only going to Afflighem for a short time to pray and recuperate and that she would soon return, but it was like a bandage over a wound that would not stop bleeding.

He was glad Matilda was accompanying her on part of her journey. He had no love for the empress, but there was a special bond between the women and he knew, with Matilda's strict rules concerning routine and order, Adeliza would be well looked after, and at least the empress would be out of the country and his way. Even the blackest cloud had a silver lining.

He took Adeliza lightly in his arms. She was so fragile that he feared to use his full embrace on her. Grief engulfed him because he knew he was bidding farewell to something he would never have again. He cupped her face and stroked it for the last time. Her skin was still smooth despite her five and forty years. All the damage was on the inside.

"I have something for you," he said. "Something I want you to remember me by when you pray because we can be together in God if nowhere else." Opening her right hand, he placed in it a string of rock crystal prayer beads, adorned by a cross set with red gemstones, and then closed her fingers over it. "The bible says that a virtuous wife is more precious than rubies," he said hoarsely. "I will love and honour you all the days of my life, no matter how long I live."

She looked down at his gift, and then up into his eyes. "You have enriched me beyond all material wealth. I will love you all the days of my life also."

They stood together, their hands still linked and their bodies lightly touching. He remembered the time he had first knelt to her at court when she came to marry Henry: a slim, lithe girl, her eyes filled with fear and touching bravery. He had been a couple of years older than her, but still very much a junior member of the court. That first sight of her had struck a pang in his heart because he thought her perfection. So modest and gentle, but with an underlying strength and refined poise. To have her as his wife and give him children of her womb had been living a dream, and now he was waking up and it was bitter. This was the last time, the last touch. When he returned to Arundel, and sat by the fireside, he would be alone. He had sat thus on many occasions, but this time it would mean something different and he would have to deal with it well, for the sake of the future, and the six beautiful children Adeliza had borne to him of her grace.

In the final moment, Adeliza continued to hold his hand, even though she knew she had to let him go and release them both. In some ways it would be easier to be apart from him, because his need for her to get better on top of her illness had been so hard to bear. At Afflighem she could have peace and tranquillity. She was going to miss him desperately. His admiration for her and his need had always been balm for her soul.

Making a supreme effort, she disengaged and turned to the waiting children. They were lined up with their nurses, descending in height from oldest to youngest. Wilkin, so much like his father, tall and strong for his age with a mass of brown curls and golden-hazel eyes. Adelis, save for her fair hair was like Will too, robust and strong, and she was glad to see that trait in her eldest daughter, for it would stand her in good stead. Godfrey and Reiner, fair and slender, like her brother and father, and the youngest children, still folded in their infant pudginess. They would not remember her except through the stories of others.

She fixed them all with a long look as if she could burn them into her mind's eye and make them as indelible in her sight as they were in her heart. She had given each child something to remember her by. There were books for the oldest boys and rings to be set by until when they were men; rings that one day they might pass on to their wives or daughters if God was merciful. Her jewelled belts had gone to her daughters. She had given Adelis the gown in which she had married Will, and waiting for Agatha was a magnificent court dress crusted with pearls and rock crystals.

"Be good for your father," she said as she kissed each child in turn. Little Henry was held in his nurse's arms because

Adeliza did not have the strength to hold him herself. Agatha reached up a chubby hand to grasp Adeliza's hand. "Mama," she said. "Mama."

Adeliza closed her eyes. "Bless you," she whispered. "Bless you all the days of your life." She stooped to kiss Agatha's small fingers, curled them over the love, and turned away.

Agatha began to wail, as if knowing instinctively that her mother was not coming back, and the sound shredded Adeliza's heart. Will went to the nurse and took Agatha in his own arms. "Hush," he said, his voice breaking, "Hush. I am still here, little one; I always will be."

Adeliza's core was so tight and painful with grief that she could barely walk. Matilda had been standing well apart, waiting while Adeliza made her farewells, but now she came forward and took her arm, assisting her up the wide gangplank and on to the ship.

"Come," said Matilda when Adeliza's knees almost buckled. "We are almost there. Do not fail now."

Adeliza braced herself and made a final effort. Strong hands reached down to help her aboard the galley and assist her to an oar bench where she could still see the jetty. The last of the servants and attendants boarded and the crew slid in the gangplank and cast off the mooring ropes, severing the ship from the land.

Adeliza gazed at Will, still holding Agatha in his arms and with the rest of the children clustered around him. The boys were all waving vigorously and shouting. Adelis clutched Will's other hand, and waved, looking solemn.

"It feels like betrayal," Adeliza whispered, yet knew it could be no other way. With a great effort, she rose from the bench and held herself erect as the wind hurled into the sail and an open area of milky green water surged between jetty and ship. "Ah Jesu!" she gasped.

"Courage!" Matilda was immediately at her side, holding her up, shaking her slightly. "Do not let their last view be of you collapsed and weeping. You were my father's queen and you are still your husband's. Do not fail him. Never forget that there is still a crown on your head, do you hear me? Never!"

The words were like a slap and Adeliza drew on the last of her reserves, straightened up, and stood tall. She raised her hand in farewell and, for a fleeting moment, she felt the weight and radiance of a diadem on her brow and knew that it was no earthly crown. She wondered if they could see it on the shore and thought that they could, for Adelis pointed urgently towards her and looked up at Will, tugging his sleeve, and saying something in an animated voice.

Adeliza remained standing until they were out of sight, and then the last of her strength drained out of her, and she slumped to the deck. Her attendants hastened to take her inside the shelter, where Matilda dismissed them, saying she would tend Adeliza herself. She bathed her face with rose water, chafed her hands, then covered her up with warm furs, and thought about what they had both achieved and what they had lost in the journey from young womanhood to these middle years of supposed wisdom.

"Did I succeed?" Adeliza asked softly without opening her eyes.

"Indeed you did," Matilda said, swallowing.

Adeliza said nothing more, but tears trickled from her eye corners and seeped into the pillow.

The wind freshened as the galley made its way down the channel and out to sea. Matilda quietly left Adeliza's side and went to take a long look at the receding shoreline. She knew she was never going to return. England was her son's kingdom to fight for now. She had done what she could. She had made many mistakes, but she had always been battering at a closed door. The times she had won through were when it had accidentally been left open. Her feeling of frustration and helplessness receded and turned to relief as the land became the horizon and then slipped from view. Gone. Her eyes grew dry with staring and began to sting. Abruptly she turned back to the deck shelter and Adeliza.

❖❖❖

The warm wind whipped the daisy-starred grasses against the hem of Brian's dark Benedictine habit as he took the path from the chapel of Saint Adrian to the shores of the loch on the western side of the island. It was nesting season and the comical Lundy birds with their brightly striped beaks and ungainly short-winged flight were returning from the sea to make their burrows, lay their eggs, and raise their young. They made good eating, but Brian was not out to trap them today, and besides, that was Brother Anselm's task.

Soon, following the birds, the pilgrims would come from far and wide to worship at the chapel, give alms, and store up advantage in heaven, and the monks would tend to them between their prayers and devotions, providing food, water, and sleeping space. Some pilgrims, like himself, would come to bathe in the loch, believing it had healing properties.

Arriving at the shores of the loch, Brian shed his robe and alb, removed his shoes, and, shivering in the cool early May air, waded into the icy water. The shock of the cold was like a knife and seized his breath, but it was exhilarating too. He ducked his head and sluiced himself again and again until he grew accustomed to the cold. Then, neck-deep, he stood to pray.

Since arriving on the island, two months ago, the terrible dreams had diminished. He only woke in a cold sweat one night in four, and no longer felt the necessity of wearing the hair shirt under his robe. His daily immersion in the pure, icy waters of the loch had cured the abrasions and sores caused by the shirt, and it felt good to be cleansed. Each day when he bathed was an affirmation of his new life and a step away from the old, like a repeated baptism. At midsummer, he would take holy vows and shed Brian FitzCount, lord of Wallingford, as if casting away a threadbare cloak.

Eventually he left the water and dried himself vigorously on the rough towel he had brought with him, and then put on his clothes. As he tied his belt, he glimpsed the ink stains mapped in brown ink on forefinger and thumb. Even the water in the loch could not erase those. A faint smile curved his lips and then was gone. When he had finished his daily tasks and prayers, he would write her a letter, and he would not burn it…and when that was done, he would be completely free.

Fifty-six

Le Petit-Quevilly, Rouen, Autumn 1148

THE LEAVES HAD BEGUN TO TURN WITH THE SHORTENING OF the year, casting the world in shades of tawny, amber, and soft pale gold. The air was still, the sky a hard, clear blue, and residual summer warmth still clothed the sun. In Rouen, at the ducal retreat at Quevilly, Matilda had been sitting in conference with her husband and her eldest son, and now their business was almost finished.

Geoffrey rose from the table and stretched his limbs to ease the kinks. He had matured in the years of her absence from a young Adonis to a golden man in his prime. Soon he was returning to Anjou to deal with rebellious vassals while Henry stayed in Normandy to prepare for his return to England with men and supplies to continue the fight for his crown. Matilda was to act both as a regent for Normandy and as an administrative and diplomatic bridge for all their lands. She would rule and advise from Rouen, and continue to cultivate the Church and bring it as much as possible under their influence.

Geoffrey gestured round the room. "So you intend to settle here," he said to her.

She returned his look with an arched brow. "I certainly do not intend returning to Anjou."

He gave a wry smile. "Good, because I have no intention of asking you to do so. I meant here at Quevilly; you know I did."

"Is the answer not obvious?"

He shook his head, still smiling. "When you went to England, I missed you badly. I am no longer ashamed to confess it. No one else would stand up to me as you did. No other woman would fight me into bed and give as good as she received." His eyes gleamed at the memory. "Not once did I best you, even when I thought I had. I can look back on that time without anger now. What matters is the future."

She was a little thrown by his admission because she had been expecting him to make a barbed comment, when instead he had given her a kind of compliment, while being pragmatic about where they stood now. He needed the gravitas of their marriage to bolster his standing in the world and her confidence rose as she realised she was more vital to him than he was to her.

"I will see you generously provided for," Geoffrey said. "You need but ask."

"Would that you had said such things in years gone by," she said tartly.

He lifted her hand and kissed her wedding ring and then mouth in a hard salute that left their lips dry but tingling. "You do not disappoint me even now," he said with a smile. "Always the sting and never the sweetness." He left the room and she watched him go, and felt a brief pang of regret, but it did not last beyond his fading footfalls.

Henry had lingered to talk to a couple of household knights while she and Geoffrey had been speaking and she called to him. He left his companions, came over to her, and bowed in filial respect. "Mama," he said.

She could see he was eager to be off and about his preparations for England; that he was champing to seize the rest of his life. "Henry," she said, and her voice filled with affection and pride. "I bless you because you are my child, and I bless you because you have the impetuousness of your youth—as I once did—but you must temper it with strength and industry. There can be no more escapades like your last one in England. Your father will say the same thing."

He looked up and gave her a hard smile. "There won't be." Today, his eyes were his grandsire's diamond grey, full of knowing and virile manhood. The downy facial hair of eighteen months ago was now a fine, ruddy beard.

"You must set your stamp on the land like a royal seal. Men will look for justice and strong leadership and you have to give them that if you want them to follow you. Stephen has provided them with neither and you must prove that you can. It is not enough to say these things. You must do them."

"I know, Mama," he said with a glimmer of irritation.

"I am not just lecturing you like a scolding tutor," she said brusquely. "I know you have greatness within you and the potential to succeed." She gave him a long look. "Come, there is something I want you to have."

She led him to her chamber and took him to an iron-bound chest at the foot of her bed. Having unlocked it with a key hanging from her girdle, she lifted out an object wrapped and protected by a fringed stole of fabric woven with thread of gold. Henry's breathing quickened as Matilda slowly unwound the cloth to reveal the great crown she had brought from Germany. "This was worn by a reigning emperor," she said, "and it passes to another of the same name and future greatness. It is yours now, and you shall wear it to your coronation when you become England's king."

Henry took the crown from her hands and held it between his own, and his eyes were the same grey as the rock crystals set in the gold.

Matilda saw him swallow with emotion and tears stung her

own eyes. "Tomorrow, before your father leaves, we shall attend mass at Bec and your crown will be blessed and laid on the altar there until you are ready to send for it as England's king."

He replaced the diadem in the cloth, reverently refolding the stole around it. "It is yours too, Mother," he said softly. "It holds your spirit."

Matilda smiled at him, tears in her eyes. "Yes," she said, proudly lifting her head. "It does."

Epilogue

ADELIZA SAT IN THE GARDEN AT AFFLIGHEM, ENJOYING THE spring warmth. From her bench in a sheltered corner, she could admire the spring bulbs she had planted in the autumn. She had not known if she would live to see them as she buried them, alive but dormant under the soil; she had thought they might push into the light and bloom when her physical body was in the grave. But by God's grace she was still here to enjoy the cheerful gold of daffodils and hold a posy of violets, their delicate petals clad in spiritual purple. Her health was as fragile as this pale sunshine, but she had the peace to pray and be at one with God, and today she had a modicum of strength. The French Cistercian monk Bernard of Clairvaux claimed to have seen a vision of the Virgin Mary at Afflighem, and Adeliza found it easy to believe; she had not seen but she was certain that at times she felt the radiant presence at her side, giving her strength and light.

Raising the posy of violets to inhale their delicate scent, she looked beyond the beds and felt a sudden jolt as she saw a man walking along the path towards her. "Will?" Her heart began to pound and all the feelings she had put aside as she absorbed herself into a life of prayer and contemplation came flooding back. He had lost some of his robust vigour and looked care-worn with more grey in his hair, but his expression and bearing were calm and, as he reached her, there was even a slight curve to his lips.

He knelt on one knee in salute and bowed his head. "Adeliza," he said. "My queen, my wife, my reason." Then he rose stiffly and kissed her on either cheek, but did not seek her lips.

"Will." Her voice was hoarse with shock. "What are you doing here?"

He gave her a sidelong look, guarding against rebuff. "Is it not permitted to visit my wife?"

"I thought...I thought one set of farewells was grief enough." She had neither expected him to do so, nor prepared herself.

"I am ready to endure the heartache in order to have the joy of seeing you," he said. "If you are not, tell me, and I will go."

She made a wordless gesture indicating he should stay.

He gazed around. "The gardens are beautiful. There is no such tranquillity in England."

"I did not expect to see another spring," she said. "But God has granted me His grace to do so." She bit her lip. "How are the children?"

"They do well," he said. "They miss you, but they have their nurses and they have your letters even if they do not have you. They know this is your home for now and that you have an important task to do."

"And you, Will?"

He looked away for a moment, then back at her. "I manage, but there will always be an empty and aching place at my side. I do everything in your name and God's. Every coin I give, every charter, every act and deed of charity is for you."

She hoped he was not going to ask her to return with him because it was impossible, and she did not want to wound him further.

Something of her anxiety must have conveyed itself to him because he said, "I think I must always have known our time was borrowed from God. I came to tell you that I have built a leper house at Wymondham and that Rising is now a palace fit for a queen, even if I know she will never hold court there."

She had to swallow before she could speak. "Then fill these places with love and life, Will, in my name; do not make shrines of them. I will send you bulbs to plant in the autumn and they will flower this time next year for you and our children."

He shook his head and cuffed his eyes and for a moment they sat in silence. Then he said, "I have been talking to men from both sides of the divide, and we all agree that Henry FitzEmpress will be our next king. Stephen does not see it now, but it will happen before Wilkin is old enough to grow a beard—I know it."

"Then I must believe you," she said.

"I have always spoken the truth to you."

"Yes, you have."

The abbey bell tolled for the service of nones. Adeliza rose from the bench and so did Will. Their arms clasped, they entered beneath the decorated arch of the abbey door and walked up the nave to kneel together before the altar as the monks filed in for the service. Between the great candles and beside the cross, the crown that Adeliza had worn to her marriage with Will and upon her wedding night gleamed with soft points of reflected light. Sunshine rayed through the windows, lighting Adeliza and Will where they knelt, and her sense of tranquillity returned. She felt peace settling over Will too, as if, side by side, they had received a joint blessing from the angels that were said to spread their divine light over Afflighem.

When the service was over, Adeliza laid her bunch of violets on the altar step, and went out with Will into the quiet warmth of the afternoon sun, and neither of them spoke, because the things unsaid were already known.

Author's Note

*E*MPRESS MATILDA, AS ONE OF THE STRONGEST FEMALE PERSON-
alities of twelfth-century English history, has often been
the subject of historical fact and fiction. She is frequently
portrayed in a less than complimentary light and I was curious
to investigate her story and find out if she really was the termagant that some chroniclers and historians have made her out to
be—or was there more to her than that?

The empress, as she liked to be known, seems to have been
her own worst enemy at times. The *Gesta Stephani* reports that
after Stephen's capture, she was "headstrong in all that she did"
and that she insulted and threatened men who came to submit
to her. She did not rise to acknowledge men who bowed to
her, and she refused to listen to their advice, "rebuffing them
by an arrogant answer and refusing to hearken to their words…
she no longer relied on their advice as she should have and had
promised them, but arranged everything as she herself thought
fit and according to her own arbitrary will."

From this I read that she had a strong will and did not suffer
fools gladly, but I also think she was kicking against a society
that had rigid conceptions about the spheres of female roles
and female power. I also have a notion (that I can't prove)
that Matilda suffered from acute premenstrual tension and this

might account for some of her sharp behaviour. A fraught political situation and a certain time of the month may just have combined to create disaster for her.

Despite her prickly relations with her cousin Henry of Winchester, she was on excellent terms with the Church and a monk, Stephen of Rouen, praised her greatly, saying that she was much loved by the poor and the nobility alike. She was, according to him, "wise and pious, merciful to the poor, generous to monks, the refuge of the wretched, and a lover of peace." (It is ironic how hard she had to fight and how much misery and mayhem was created before any sort of peace came about.) Marjorie Chibnall in her biography of the empress also states that the Cistercian monks of Le Valasse remembered her as "a woman of intelligence and sense."

There has been modern speculation that Matilda and the baron Brian FitzCount were lovers, but that notion comes from a misreading of a piece in the *Gesta Stephani* about the flight from Winchester. The text says in translation: "But she and Brien gained by this a title to boundless fame, since as their affection for each other had before been unbroken, so even in adversity, great though the obstacle that danger might be, they were in no wise divided." There is no other reference to their closeness and this comment should be read in terms of a bond of service and friendship and not physical intimacy. Had there been even a hint of such, the chroniclers hostile to Matilda, including the *Gesta Stephani*, would have run with it for all it was worth. My own belief is that there was a powerful attraction between Brian and Matilda, but that it remained unspoken and was never acted upon.

No one knows for certain what happened to Brian. The most likely scenario is that he became a monk at Reading Abbey shortly after Matilda returned to Normandy. Certainly he disappears from the historical record at about this time. A suggestion that he went on crusade can be discounted as a fabrication. I have a strong feeling that Brian was not cut out for warfare and fought because he had to. Wallingford was one of the strongest fortresses on the empress's side, but Brian was travelling with Matilda's court for much of the time and the heroic defence of the place fell mostly to its castellan William Boterel. I suspect when Matilda left for Normandy, it was the last straw and Brian retired to a religious life. Since Reading Abbey had responsibility for the chapel on the Isle of May off the coast of Scotland in the twelfth century, I chose to send him there to end his days in peace.

In the matter of Matilda's troubled marriage to Geoffrey of Anjou, I was interested to find out how long it took for her to become pregnant with the future Henry II, and it's the reason I have introduced the contraceptive thread into the story. She married Geoffrey in 1128 and returned to Normandy a year later, not going back to her husband until September 1131. It was to be another nine months before Henry was conceived. She went on to have two more sons in swift succession. Was this just chance, or was there something else going on? I think it well within the bounds of possibility that there was, and perhaps she hoped for an annulment.

Matilda did indeed escape from Oxford Castle during a severe and bitter winter, crossing the frozen moat and the Thames to reach Abingdon and eventually the safety of Wallingford. The chronicles differ in her method of escape. Once source says she escaped via a postern door, another that it was via a rope from a window.

When Matilda went to Normandy in 1148, she continued to work behind the scenes to help her son win England's throne. She sought in particular to foster relations with the Church and was a respected benefactor of numerous religious houses, to which she donated a considerable treasure in her will. When she died in 1167 her son Henry was a king reigning over a vast European empire that stretched from the Scottish border to the Pyrenees. As she had wished many years earlier, she was buried at the priory of Bec-Hellouin. Sadly, her bones were disturbed during various religious and political upheavals and her remains were eventually gathered up and buried in Rouen Cathedral, burial place of the Dukes of Normandy. So in the end her father got his way!

In fiction, the empress is usually paired with Stephen's wife in the struggle for England. Matilda of Boulogne (she is called Maheut in the story to avoid confusion as it is another medieval form of the name) was Matilda's cousin and shared the same maternal bloodline and thus a link to the English royal house. She was the rod in Stephen's spine and although sometimes portrayed as a gentle sort, she had an underlying toughness and was an excellent negotiator. She also had the advantage of being able to function in a deputy's role and not be seen as a threat to the natural order by taking power of her own volition.

The above pairing has often been written about before and I wanted to take a different slant. During my research, I became very drawn to Henry I's second queen, Adeliza of Louvain, who is less well known.

Adeliza's story, which runs parallel to Matilda's, is an interesting one. Negotiations to marry Henry were already under way before the disaster of the sinking of the *White Ship* in 1121 robbed him of his only legitimate son. Adeliza was born circa 1103 and the chronicler Henry of Huntingdon praised her beauty and said that gold and jewels paled beside it. The fact that she did not bear Henry any children although they were together for fifteen years was a source of deep distress to her. She wrote to a friend, the churchman Hildebert of Lavardin, bishop of Le Mans, seeking his counsel on the matter and he told her:

...if it has not been granted to you from Heaven that you should bear a child to the King of the English, in these (the poor) you will bring forth the King of the Angels, with no damage to your modesty. Perhaps the Lord has closed up your womb so that you might adopt immortal offspring...it is more blessed to be fertile in the spirit than in the flesh.

Henry, meanwhile, continued to beget bastard offspring on other women on a regular basis.

When Henry died, Adeliza retired to the nunnery at Wilton, near to which she had founded a leper hospice. Although she didn't entirely seclude herself there (there are charters from her witnessed at Arundel and she was present at Reading Abbey on the anniversary of Henry's death to give a hundred marks), she did spend much of her time at Wilton until the autumn of 1138 when she married William D'Albini, whose family were baronial officers in the royal household. They began a family immediately and in the next ten years Adeliza produced at least six children, thus confounding all her years of barrenness.

Adeliza seems to have formed a strong bond with Matilda and they would have come to know each other well in the years when Matilda was at court before her marriage and then in the intervening years when she was estranged from Geoffrey. Certainly Adeliza welcomed Matilda to Arundel in 1139, despite Adeliza's husband being staunchly Stephen's man. Although very different women, they were close in age and had plenty in common by way of family ties, social standing, and their dedication to religion and religious benefaction.

In 1148, Adeliza entered the monastery at Afflighem in modern-day Belgium, of which her family were patrons, and died there in 1151. I suggest in the novel that she had contracted some form of wasting illness, because she retired to a religious life (but did not take vows) when her youngest children would still have been little more than babies and her eldest son only nine years old. William D'Albini did not remarry, although he outlived his wife by twenty-five years.

Adeliza has two places of burial recorded: Afflighem and Reading Abbey. I suspect one house received her heart and the other her body, but I cannot say for sure. Descendants of William D'Albini and Adeliza of Louvain own Castle Rising in Norfolk to this day, and the innovative latrine arrangements mentioned in the novel can still be seen by the interested visitor!

William D'Albini was one of the barons foremost in brokering the peace agreement between the future Henry II and King Stephen whereby Henry was to receive the throne when Stephen died. This came about in 1154, outside the scope of this novel. D'Albini was favoured by the new young king; Adeliza's determination in permitting her stepdaughter the empress to land in England in 1139 paid its dividend fifteen years later.

Readers will notice I have made frequent reference to crowns in the novel. Other than the obvious reason that the story involves the fight for a crown, I wanted to mention them because the empress set great store by hers and brought several from Germany. One was of solid gold set with gemstones and was worn by Henry II at his coronation. It was so heavy that it had to be supported by two silver rods and the front of it held a jewel of great size and worth with a gold cross superimposed on it. She also had another smaller crown of gold belonging to the emperor, and one that was decorated with gold flowers. Crowns at this time were often made in hinged sections so they could be packed flat when not in use.

Matilda also set great store by nice tents. When the emperor of Germany asked for the return of the hand of Saint James, Matilda declined to oblige, but did send him a magnificent travelling tent instead, made of rich fabrics and so large that it had to be raised mechanically. That was part of the inspiration for including the windy tent scene near the beginning of the novel, the other part being research garnered from my strand of research involving the Akashic Records, a belief that the past can be accessed by someone with the skills to tune into its imprint. Readers can find more information and links on my website.

Concerning other sundry details that interested me and might interest readers: the Latin on page 354, *"Matilidis Imperatrice, Domina Angliea, Regina Anglia. Wallig,"* translates to "Empress Matilda, Lady of the English, Queen of England. Wallingford," and is based on actual (rare) coinage minted at Wallingford.

The name of Will's warhorse Forcilez translates into English from the original Anglo-Norman as "Little Fortress." I have my Akashic Consultant Alison King to thank for coming across his name at one of our sessions.

It has been a fascinating journey, following part of the lives of these two linked but very different women and observing their struggles to survive, and be heard in a world where the odds were stacked against them. Yet each in her own way, despite setbacks, succeeded in the end and they have my deepest respect.

Select Bibliography

Bradbury, Jim, *Stephen and Matilda: The Civil War of 1139–53* (Sutton, 2005, ISBN 0 7509 3793 9).

Chibnall, Marjorie, *The Empress Matilda: Queen Consort, Queen Mother and Lady of the English* (Blackwell, 1999 edn, ISBN 0 631 19028 7).

The Chronicle of John of Worcester, vol. III, ed. and trans. by P. McGurk (Oxford Medieval Texts, Clarendon Press, 1998, ISBN 0 19 820702 6).

Crouch, David, *The Reign of King Stephen 1135–1154* (Longman, 2000, ISBN 0 582 22657 0).

Davis, Michael R., *Henry of Blois: Prince Bishop of the Twelfth Century Renaissance* (PublishAmerica, 2009, ISBN 978 1 60749 753 0).

Gesta Stephani, ed. and trans. by K. R. Potter (Oxford Medieval Texts, Clarendon Press, 1976, ISBN 0 19 822234 3).

Green, Judith A., *The Government of England under Henry I* (Cambridge University Press, 1989 edn, ISBN 0 521 37586 X).

Green, Judith A., *Henry I: King of England and Duke of Normandy* (Cambridge University Press, 2009, ISBN 978 0 521 74452 2).

Hilton, Lisa, *Queens Consort: England's Medieval Queens* (Weidenfeld & Nicolson, 2008, ISBN 978 0 297 85261 2).

The Historia Novella of William of Malmesbury, ed. by K. R. Potter (Nelson, 1955).

Hollister, C. Warren, *Henry 1* (Yale University Press, 2001, ISBN 0 300 08858 2).

Huntingdon, Henry of, *The History of the English People 1000–1154,* trans. from the Latin by Diana Greenway (Oxford University Press, 2002 edn, ISBN 0 19284075 4).

The Letters and Charters of Gilbert Foliot, ed. by Adrian Morey and C. N. L. Brooke (Cambridge University Press, 1967).

Norgate, Kate, *England under the Angevin Kings, Volume 1* (Elibron Classics, ISBN 1 4212 5984 2).

Tyerman, Christopher, *Who's Who in Early Medieval England* (Shepheard Walwyn, 1996, ISBN 0 85683 132 8).

Warren, W. L., *Henry II* (Eyre Methuen, 1977 edn, ISBN 0 413 38390 3).

Articles and Related Items

Brown, R. Allen, *Castle Rising Castle* (guide book, English Heritage, ISBN 1 85074 159 X).

King, Alison, Akashic Record Consultant.

King, Edmund, "The Memory of Brian FitzCount," *The Haskins Society Journal,* Vol. 13, 1999 (Boydell, 2002, ISBN 184383 050 7).

The Greatest Knight

WHEN WILLIAM ENTERED THE QUEEN'S CHAMBERS IN Poitiers, he was immediately struck by the familiar scents of cedar and sandalwood and by the opulent shades that Eleanor so loved: crimson and purple and gold. He drew a deep, savouring breath; he was home. Eleanor had been standing near the window talking to Guillaume de Tancarville but, on seeing William, she ceased the conversation and hastened across the chamber.

Somewhat stiffly, William knelt and bowed his head. Clara had shorn his hair close to his scalp to help rid him of the remainder of the lice and the air was cold on the back of his neck.

"William, God save you!" Eleanor stooped, took his hands and raised him to his feet, her tawny eyes full of concern. "You're as thin as a lance, and I was told that you had been grievously injured."

"A spear in the thigh; it is almost healed, madam," William replied, not wanting to dwell on his injury. "I am for ever in your debt for ransoming me."

Eleanor shook her head. "There will be no talk of debt unless it is on my part. You and your uncle sacrificed yourselves for my freedom and I can never repay that. Patrick of Salisbury was my husband's man, and did his bidding first, but he was honourable and courteous and I grieve his death. His murderers will be brought to justice, I promise you that." Behind Eleanor, de Tancarville made a sound of concurrence.

"Yes, madam," William agreed, his mouth twisting. He had sworn an oath on his sword on the matter. Until the Lusignan brothers had taught him the meaning of hatred, he had harboured strong grudges against no man. Now he had that burden and it was as if something light had been taken from him and replaced with a hot lead weight.

"You have no lord now, William." Eleanor drew him further into the room and bade him sit on a cushioned bench. He did so gratefully for his leg was paining him and he had yet to regain his stamina.

"No, madam." William glanced at Guillaume de Tancarville, who was watching him with an enigmatic smile on his lips. William had half expected the Chamberlain to invite him to rejoin his household, but the older man remained silent. "It is the tourney season, and I still have Blancart. I can make my way in the world."

De Tancarville's smile deepened. "Are you sure about that? You seem to have an unfortunate skill for losing destriers and putting yourself in jeopardy."

"I would have done the same for you, my lord, were you in my uncle's place," William replied with quiet dignity, thereby wiping the humour from de Tancarville's face.

"I'm sorry, lad. I should not have jested. Perhaps it's because I know more about your future than you do. You won't need to ride the tourney roads or accept a place in my mesnie."

"My lord?" William gave him a baffled look; Eleanor shot him an irritated one, as if de Tancarville had given too much away.

"What my lord Tancarville is saying in his clumsy fashion is that I am offering you a place among my own household guard," Eleanor said. "I will furnish you with whatever you need in the way of clothing and equipment...and horses should the need arise," she added with a twitch of her lips. "It is more than charity. I would be a fool of the greatest order not to take you into my service. My children adore you, we have missed your company, and you have proven your loyalty and valour to the edge of death."

Her compliments washed over William's head in a hot wave and he felt his face burning with pleasure and embarrassment.

"Lost for words?" she teased, her voice throaty with laughter.

William swallowed. "I have often dreamed of such a post but I never thought..." He shook his head. "It is an ill wind," he said and suddenly a sweeping feeling of loss and sadness overtook his euphoria. He put his right hand over his face, striving to hold himself together. He had managed it for four months under the most difficult of circumstances. He wouldn't break now, not in front of the Queen.

"William, I understand," Eleanor said in a gentler voice than was her wont. "Take what time you need and report to me as soon as you are ready. Speak to my steward. He will see that you are provided with anything you lack. Go to." She gave him a gentle push.

"Madam." William bowed from her presence.

Acknowledgments

$\mathcal{M}$Y THANKS TO THE MANY INDIVIDUALS AND GROUPS OF people who have worked behind the scenes to enable me to bring *Lady of the English* to fruition.

Carole Blake—my long-term agent and dear friend.

Rebecca Saunders, Joanne Dickinson, Manpreet Grewal, and Barbara Daniel at Little Brown—my enthusiastic editors and teamworkers.

Richenda Todd—also part of the editorial team and catcher of the continuity errors and surplus children. Any that remain are down to me.

Dominique Raccah, Shana Drehs, Beth Pehlke, Danielle Jackson, and Regan Fisher—my dynamic publisher and team at Sourcebooks.

The Romantic Novelists Association, where I have made many lasting friends and who offer such excellent support to their members.

The Historical Novel Society, which has done so much to promote the historical fiction genre.

The members of Historical Fiction online, who have created a forum where it's fun to talk about all sorts of historical fiction, life, the world, and everything.

The many good friends I have made on Twitter across a diversity of interests.

Thea Vincent—my Web designer at Phoenix Web Designs.

Roger, my husband—driver, companion dogsbody (or so our dogs inform me), soul mate, and champion ironer!

And last but first as well, my lovely readers!

About the Author

*E*LIZABETH CHADWICK LIVES IN Nottingham with her husband and two sons. Much of her research is carried out as a member of Regia Anglorum, an early medieval reen-actment society with the emphasis on accurately re-creating the past. She also tutors in the skill of writing historical and romantic fiction. Her first novel, *The Wild Hunt*, won a Betty Trask award. She was shortlisted for the Romantic Novelists' Award in

Charlie Hopkinson

1998 for *The Champion*, in 2001 for *Lords of the White Castle*, in 2002 for *The Winter Mantle*, and in 2003 for *The Falcons of Montabard*. Her sixteenth novel, *The Scarlet Lion*, was nominated by Richard Lee, the founder of the Historical Novel Society, as one of the top ten historical novels of the last decade, and *To Defy a King* won the Romantic Novelists' Association Historical Fiction Prize in 2011.

For more details on Elizabeth Chadwick or her books, visit www.elizabethchadwick.com.

A FORGOTTEN HERO
IN A TIME OF TURMOIL

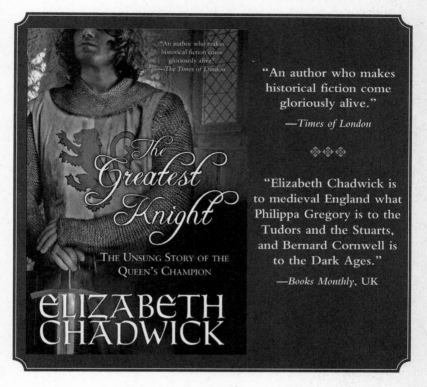

"An author who makes
historical fiction come
gloriously alive."
—*The Times of London*

The
Greatest
Knight

THE UNSUNG STORY OF THE
QUEEN'S CHAMPION

ELIZABETH
CHADWICK

"An author who makes
historical fiction come
gloriously alive."

—*Times of London*

❖ ❖ ❖

"Elizabeth Chadwick is
to medieval England what
Philippa Gregory is to the
Tudors and the Stuarts,
and Bernard Cornwell is
to the Dark Ages."

—*Books Monthly*, UK

A penniless young knight with few prospects, William Marshal blazes
into history on the strength of his sword and the depth of his honor.
Marshal's integrity sets him apart in the turbulent court of Henry II and
Eleanor of Aquitaine, bringing fame and the promise of a wealthy heiress
as well as enemies eager to plot his downfall. Elizabeth Chadwick has
crafted a spellbinding tale about a forgotten hero, an ancestor of George
Washington, an architect of the Magna Carta, and a legend of chivalry—
the greatest knight of the Middle Ages.

978-1-4022-2518-5 • $14.99 U.S.

The Legend of the Greatest Knight Lives On

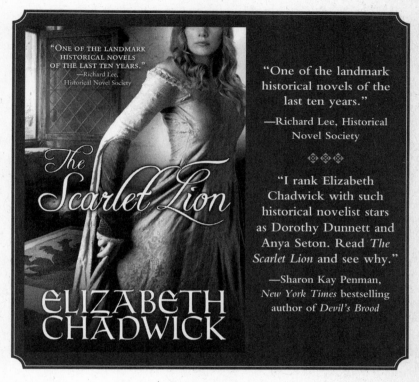

"ONE OF THE LANDMARK
HISTORICAL NOVELS
OF THE LAST TEN YEARS."
—Richard Lee,
Historical Novel Society

The
Scarlet Lion

ELIZABETH
CHADWICK

"One of the landmark
historical novels of the
last ten years."

—Richard Lee, Historical
Novel Society

❖ ❖ ❖

"I rank Elizabeth
Chadwick with such
historical novelist stars
as Dorothy Dunnett and
Anya Seton. Read *The
Scarlet Lion* and see why."

—Sharon Kay Penman,
New York Times bestselling
author of *Devil's Brood*

William Marshal's skill with a sword and loyalty to his word have earned
him the company of kings, the lands of a magnate, and the hand of
Isabelle de Clare, one of England's wealthiest heiresses. But he is thrust
back into the chaos of court when King Richard dies. Vindictive King
John clashes with William, claims the family lands for the Crown—and
takes two of the Marshal sons hostage. The conflict between obeying his
king and rebelling over the royal injustices threatens the very heart of
William and Isabelle's family. Fiercely intelligent and courageous, fearing
for the man and marriage that light her life, Isabelle plunges with her
husband down a precarious path that will lead William to more power
than he ever expected.

978-1-4022-2999-2 • $14.99 U.S.

A Bittersweet Tale of Love, Loss, and the Power of a King

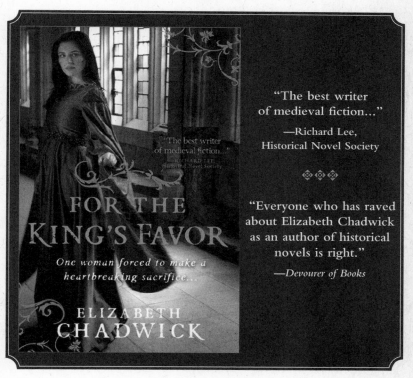

"The best writer of medieval fiction..."

—Richard Lee,
Historical Novel Society

❖ ❖ ❖

"Everyone who has raved about Elizabeth Chadwick as an author of historical novels is right."

—*Devourer of Books*

When Roger Bigod arrives at King Henry II's court to settle a bitter inheritance dispute, he becomes enchanted with Ida de Tosney, young mistress to the powerful king. A victim of Henry's seduction and the mother of his son, Ida sees in Roger a chance to begin a new life. But Ida pays an agonizing price when she leaves the king, and as Roger's importance grows and he gains an earldom, their marriage comes under increasing strain. Based on the true story of a royal mistress and the young lord she chose to marry, *For the King's Favor* is Elizabeth Chadwick at her best.

978-1-4022-4449-0 • $14.99 U.S.

SPIRITED DAUGHTER.
REBELLIOUS WIFE.
POWERFUL WOMAN.

"You don't just read a Chadwick book; you experience it."
—Shelf and Stuff

TO
DEFY A KING

*Spirited daughter. Rebellious wife.
Powerful woman.*

ELIZABETH
CHADWICK

"Chadwick's great strength lies in her attention to detail—she brings to life all the daily humdrum of the medieval age but also seduces with the romance of her characters and the raw excitement of their times. *To Defy a King* is Chadwick on top form."

—*Lancashire Evening Post*

❖ ❖ ❖

"You don't just read a Chadwick book; you experience it."

—*Shelf and Stuff*

The adored and spirited daughter of England's greatest knight, Mahelt Marshal lives a privileged life. But when her beloved father falls foul of the volatile and dangerous King John, her world is shattered. The king takes her brothers hostage and Mahelt's planned marriage to Hugh Bigod, son of the Earl of Norfolk, takes place sooner than she expected. When more harsh demands from King John threaten to tear the couple's lives apart, Mahelt finds herself facing her worst fears alone, not knowing if she—or her marriage—will survive.

978-1-4022-5089-7 • $14.99 U.S.